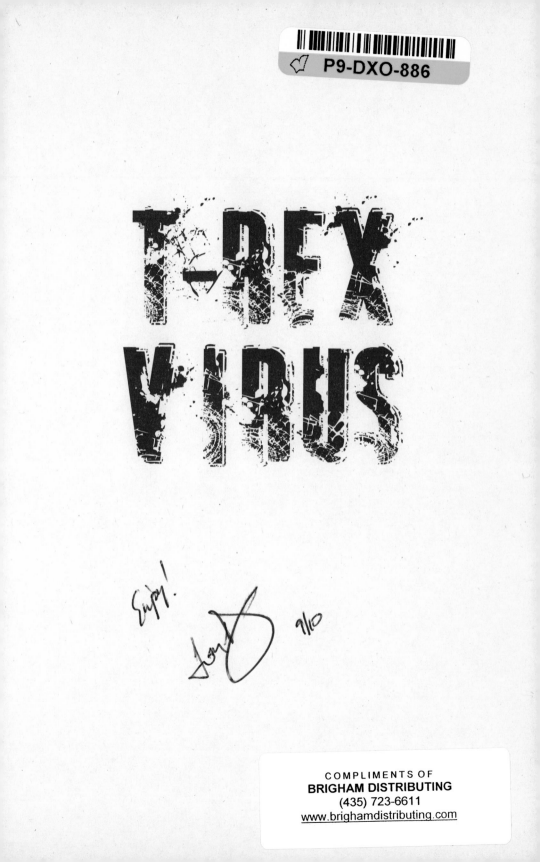

T-REX VIRUS

T-REX VIRUS

A NOVEL BY TOM FOREST

Distributed By:
Brigham Distributing
110 South 800 West
Brigham City, UT 84302
435-723-6611
www.brighamdistributing.com

13-DIGIT ISBN: 978-09664447-8-0
10-Digit ISBN: 0966444787

Typesetting by Adam Riggs

PREFACE

A small hunk of ferrous rock from an ancient asteroid which has roamed the cosmos for eons falls to earth. Discovered by a university paleontologist, a long dormant enzyme impregnated within the large galactic stone is revitalized by accident in a university laboratory. A deadly virus erupts from the small boulder, taking the lives of the laboratory team within days. Members of the U.S. Army biological warfare operations staff from Fort Detrick, Maryland seize the extraterrestrial ore. During transportation to a U.S. Government weapons research facility, the rock and its escorts disappear. Now an offshore megalomaniac pharmaceutical giant, possesses the deadly, diseased rock, and the only known antidote. Driven by the greed of billions in profit, the CEO of the pharmaceutical firm won't give up the cure until the virus becomes widespread. FBI agent Dale Fox hits the ground running in pursuit of the geode, and the medicinal remedy for the viral infection that is infecting hundreds of thousands of people. Battling an elite team of killers within the pharmaceutical company, Fox has very little time to succeed since he, too, has contracted the terminal virus!

ACKNOWLEDGEMENTS

In writing this novel I attempted to utilize as best as I could, real technology, tactics, strategy, and accuracy in-so-far as creative license would allow. Any errors are mine alone. Special thanks to my brother, Dan - who served as the working model for Special Agent Dale Fox. I need to recognize the efforts of Dr. Gordon George, a superb surgeon, who was very generous with his time in helping me with the medical background information. Any technical errors of a medical nature are strictly mine. I'd also like to express my appreciation to the firefighters of the Seattle Fire Department who run the wharf fire station, without whose help integral parts of this work could not have been done. You guys made it real. Curtis McPherson at Illusion Productions and Brandon Hill of BX Designs who provided the great graphical work that graces some of the pages of this novel. I also want to thank my publishing manager Georgia Carpenter, for accepting phone calls at all hours of the day and night on all the phones I had numbers for her. Finally, my wife and kids made the ultimate sacrifice in time with me when I was "in the zone" and on a roll. Thanks guys, I am truly blessed.

Website sponsored by Handsay, products for the deaf community. Visit them at www.handsay.com.

SPECIAL DEDICATION

I wish to personally thank Mr. George Wahlen and his lovely bride. George served as the model for the father of the two brothers in this book. The fictional father in this story is a Medal of Honor recipient. Mr. Wahlen is one of America's shrinking core of living M.O.H. recipients. He earned his Medal of Honor on Iwo Jima in World War II as a U.S. Navy Corpsman. George repeatedly placed his life in mortal danger for the sake of the lives of his downed Marines. Mr. Wahlen was kind enough to offer his time and perspective so that I could pattern a real personality for the character portrayed in the novel. There is no substitute for the real thing.

Just before the publication wheels moved forward on this story, we lost George. The funeral procession was well over a mile long and included Navy, Marine and Army flag officers.

George was the epitome of what we envision in our heroes. He personified the very essence of integrity, credibility and virtue. His willingness to lend an honest portrayal to the character in this book is truly a unique endeavor. In his passing, I was made privy to a stunning piece of information long forgotten. George was recommended for a second Medal of Honor. Among his military awards are three Navy Crosses (second only to the M.O.H.) and several Purple Hearts.

CAST OF CHARACTERS

The Good Guys

Law Enforcement Personnel

Dale Fox	FBI counterterrorism agent
Sullivan Casse	FBI counterterrorism agent and Dale's partner
Anthony "No-Knock" Petrocelli	FBI assistant special agent in charge of the Seattle FBI office
Rod O'Brien	detective, King County Sheriff's office, Washington state
Dan Covery	director of the FBI's CTU (Counterterrorism Unit)

Fire Rescue Personnel

Sean Fox	fire captain of the Lone Peak Fire District, rescue expert, paramedic and Dale's older brother
Barney Davis	lieutenant in the Seattle Fire Department, rescue diver, paramedic, and captain of the fireboat Chief Seattle
Robert "Bobby" Booker	Chief Seattle's pilot and paramedic
Terry Folsom	Chief Seattle's engineer and paramedic
Dave "Speedy Huey" Griffin	Chief Seattle's firefighter and paramedic

Other Characters

Betty Jo Case	Dale Fox's girlfriend and international research attorney
Kelly Fox	Sean's wife
Dalton Jordan	chief paleontologist from Brigham Young University, Utah
Tori Evans	Ph.D candidate and paleontologist from Brigham Young University, Utah

The Bad Guys

Douglas Odin	multibillionaire megalomaniac
Thor Odin	Douglas Odin's eldest son, oversees shipping conglomerate
Magnus Odin	one of Douglas Odin's twins
Tobias Odin	one of Douglas Odin's twins
Ingvar Wallen	captain of the Nord Island submarine

TERMINOLOGY

ADIZ: U.S. Air Defense Identification Zone, 200 miles off the U.S. coast

AGL: above ground level, altitude above the ground, but below an aircraft as measured by the onboard altimeter

ANG: Air National Guard

ASAC: assistant special agent in charge of an FBI field office, the number two person in the region representing the FBI

BC: Buoyancy compensator, a device worn by scuba divers, which they inflate or deflate to control their buoyancy, ascent, or descent while underwater

BOLO: Be on the lookout, law enforcement terminology, watch for a stolen vehicle

CDC: Centers for Disease Control, a federal medical organization

CHINO torpedo: chemical high-impact nautical ordinance torpedo

CO: commanding officer, generally associated with a military officer in charge of a vessel or organization

COB: chief of the boat – a naval term for the senior enlisted man aboard a submarine or combat vessel

CTU: the FBI's counterterrorism unit

DCI: director of the Central Intelligence Agency

EGT: exhaust gas temperature gauge on an airplane

Flying Squad: A group of federal agents assigned to follow a high-profile or high-risk investigative case, as opposed to having the case worked by local or regional agents

HAHO: High altitude, high opening, parachute jump which allows military forces to come in from a significant lateral distance, always done wearing arctic weather gear and oxygen

IC: incident commander, the person in charge of a specific emergency response event

IR: infrared vision capability

MOH: Medal of Honor – the highest military award for anyone in the U.S. Military, must be confirmed by the United States Congress and is generally presented by the President of the United States in the White House to the person receiving it

NBC: nuclear, biological, and chemical warfare

NCIS: Naval Criminal Investigative Service – Navy and Marine Corps detective agency

NCO: noncommissioned officer

NMCC: National Military Command Center

NRO: National Reconnaissance Office – federal agency

NSA: National Security Administration – federal agency

PADI: Professional Association of Diving Instructors

PD: periscope depth

Port: left side of a ship

SAC: special agent in charge of an FBI field office – the number one person in the region representing the FBI

Starboard: right side of a ship

VLF: very low frequency – designed for short distance radio communication

XO: executive officer, the number two ranking officer aboard a ship or military organization

PROLOGUE

The Sagittarius Dwarf Elliptical Galaxy
66 million years ago

The massive iron oxide asteroid, replete with jagged edges and pitted depressions across its 11 mile length, tumbled along its axis, continually rotating its leading edge. The celestial body had barreled through the endless void for the past hundred twenty million years. Its immense shape served to modify other heavenly masses it encountered in deep space, a result of sometimes violent confrontations.

The universe was immeasurable beyond any possible means of comprehension. Swirling multicolored displays of decaying gaseous refuse painted parts of some galaxies through which it ranged. The asteroid roamed through them unscathed, passing numerous sights like a silent sentinel, observing the birth and death of matter. The monster rock skirted black holes, nebulas, globular clusters, and the trailing edges of exploding supernovas. Through the eons it encountered debris fields, radiation belts, and gas clouds comprised of indescribable material in the vastness of its travels.

From out of the darkness loomed another asteroid of significant proportions. Its direction of travel and velocity placed it on a collision course with the first. In the space of a few breaths, the inevitable occurred. The rendezvous of the two long-dead planetoids caused the behemoths to merge and careen off each other at shallow angles. The mountainous rocks changed course slightly and continued on their unguided journeys. But not before a one hundred sixty ton slab of the ferrous asteroid had been calved off, sending the corpus on its own trajectory.

The Milky Way galaxy
65 million years ago

The galaxy the rock now traveled through was so immense that it would require seventy thousand light years to traverse from end to end. Yet the one hundred sixty ton boulder suffered periodic clashes with other floating rubble transiting its path, serving to further diminish its volume. The tumbling ore made its way toward a solar system comprised of eight planets orbiting elliptically around a brilliant sun that occupied its core. Passing six of the planet-sized bodies, each one unique, it was now on an intercept course with the brightly illuminated blue and white sphere looming ahead.

Simple, single-celled, amino acid life forms had appeared on the round luminous orb almost four billion years earlier. Primitive animals finally emerged and began scurrying over it six hundred thirty million years ago. Now mammals and other odd creatures roamed its surface.

The sliver of asteroid was drawn in by the round mass's strong gravitational pull. As it entered the outer shell of the planet's atmosphere, the metal chunk of rock lit up with a blazing trail of superheated phosphorous particles streaming in its wake. Its brilliance could be seen for thousands of miles from the surface of the planet. Heated to a reddish-blue glow, it penetrated the oxygenated ring surrounding the planet. The molten temperature from the friction encountered upon entering the atmosphere quickly ate away at its mass.

In the early morning stillness, herds of giants gazed upon the sudden intrusion in the sky. Reduced now to eighty pounds, the rock crashed into the solid surface of the planet at several thousand miles an hour. An incredible, explosive display of earth, water, and steam played out at the edge of an ancient marsh which formed the characteristics of a rudimentary lake shoreline. The local inhabitants, spooked by the blast, remained at a distance for several days.

The rock lay imbedded at the watery edge of the lake. In its millions of years in space, the rock had become impregnated with foreign matter of incalculable categories. Now, in the oxygenated atmosphere, a long-dormant enzyme awoke; the life-supporting elements had been stirred. As the current in the lake ebbed and flowed, a deadly virus washed out into the lagoon and spread. It was the late Cretaceous Period of earth's prehistoric past.

Periodically the ground shook as distant volcanoes thrust themselves up through the earth's crust, surfacing with panoramic displays of bright red and yellow eruptions, spewing forth molten magma. A Megalosaurus thundered slowly by, dust from its massive footprints rising above the dry earth. An airborne dinosaur named Quetzalcoatlus flew overhead, detached from the dangers its earthbound neighbors faced. Nearby, a Triceretops looked down on the lush plain below it from a precipice, eating vegetation near a favorite grazing spot.

Not far away, a large carnivorous animal stalked a ground-dwelling Anatotitan. This preoccupied, four ton, duck-billed dinosaur was oblivious to the forty foot long female Tyrannosaur moving quietly through the trees a mere hundred yards away.

The carnivore patiently advanced toward the plodding herbivore, cautiously stopping to remain hidden among the pines whenever the grazing Hadrosaur raised its head.

Now, less than one hundred fifty feet away, the hungry Tyrannosaur charged full speed from the last stand of tall trees at the edge of the forest, in pursuit of its next warm meal. The startled Anatotitan dropped its attention from its food and broke into a dead run to escape the terrifying queen of the savanna. Every animal for a mile around heard the bone-chilling roar of the giant killer lizard as it gained on the hapless Hadrosaur.

The long, wide beak of the male herbivore was whipped with froth as he tried unsuccessfully to gallop away on his hind legs, his herd now running off in another direction. The hundreds of abrasive teeth in his mouth, designed for chewing plant matter, were no match for the foot-long flesh and bone-crushing canines of his pursuer. The stocky-necked plant eater ran across soft mud at the edge of the water and onto a sandbar. The gap in the chase disappeared quickly as the longer stride of the thundering beast behind him closed in rapidly. The luckless Anototitan was outpaced.

On the edge of the lapping shoreline the carnivorous predator leapt upon the left side of the fleeing dinosaur, carving three gashing wounds into the animal's hide. A blood-curdling scream echoed across the open expanse of the lakeside feeding ground. The duck-billed dinosaur slowed momentarily from the shock of the razor-sharp claws digging into his flesh. The T-Rex took a few more instinctively measured steps and leaned forward to sink her massive jaws into the doomed prey. The herbivore rolled to his right side involuntarily, crashing to the wet ground with a considerable splash. The fierce carnivore ripped 50 pound hunks of meat from the frame of the Anatotitan. Death was excruciating; it was eaten alive.

Birds fluttered back to their tree top dwellings as the noisy chase came to an end. The cannibal-like carnage of the Tyrannosaurus's breakfast was over. With a full stomach, the huge, female T-Rex wandered a few dozen yards into the lake to drink from the crimson stained water; water now laced with the extraterrestrial virus. Other dinosaurs moved off to a safe distance and stood almost stock-still, watching the tyrant of the Cretaceous amble away with a temporarily pacified demeanor.

As the giant lizard trudged over a nearby hillside and out of view, an opportunistic Deinonychus, a swift, lightly built Theropod commonly known as a raptor, ran forward with ravenous abandon. Others eager to dispose of the fresh carcass joined him. With their sickle-shaped claws, the band of hungry marauders descended on the remains of the T-Rex's sumptuous feast. Eating as much of the scrap nourishment from the ribs of the herbivore as they could pull off, the small raptors also partook of the enzyme-laden water at the end of their meal. The incubation period for the active, alien virus had begun.

Over the next few weeks, weakness, loss of motor function, and coordination would give way to an illness from which the dinosaurs of the Late Cretaceous Period would never recover. The enzyme-based virus spread from herd to herd, from herbivore to omnivore to carnivore, as the cycle of life and death continued.

It was not the change of seasons, the coming of the Ice Age, or volcanic activity with its attendant clouds of smoke, ash, and pyroclastic lava flows that would doom the dinosaurs. Neither would the earthquakes, nor concentrated meteor showers spell the end for the majestic monarchs of the final dinosaur era. Their fateful encounter with the iron ore had created a disease from which there was no recovery. Over the next fourteen years, it would spread to blanket landscapes near and far, spelling the end of the great beasts.

In time, the moist, lush foliage of the woodsy marshland environment gave way to a warmer climate and the waters dissipated. The valley floors fell to the elements and the mountains rose. The forest gradually vanished as generations of animals evolved and migrated to other life supporting ecosystems.

As millions of years passed, the area was transformed into a dry, rock-strewn desert. The wildlife now living there bore no relationship to the earlier landlords from the millennia of time. The inhabitants were less imposing, having adapted to the changed environment. The struggle of life and death continued on a less grand scale, but continued nonetheless.

The dominant animal of the plains now was a bipedal species of an unusual sort. Small in stature compared to past inhabitants, it possessed a superior intellect. It made tools. It reasoned. It anticipated events. And it retained experiences from which it discovered new skills.

The waves of multihued, towering cliffs where it lived and hunted stretched to the horizon. Its surroundings became a marker by which the prehistoric past was slowly revealed. Over time, the two-legged creature learned to read the story in the craggy bluffs it occupied, and grew naturally curious. It wasn't long before it dug into the dusty prairie, mountainous terrain, and cliffsides inquisitively searching for answers to the mysteries it found. The intense desire to excavate for knowledge would eventually unearth a tiny, nonindigenous piece of landscape just waiting to be discovered.

And so it was that the future of the newcomer would be inextricably linked with the far distant past; a past that had devastated the original dominate species; a past about to become the future.

1

The San Juan Straits
West of Seattle, Washington
Wednesday, 1035 hours Pacific Time

The thirty-two foot-long cabin cruiser rolled with the slight swell, its stern and bow lights bobbing to the rhythm of the undulating water. The boat showed evidence of many past trips. The padding was slightly worn and the teak wood was in need of staining and polishing. A few bare spots in need of marine caulk were also evident. A free-swinging cabin light in the passageway below deck caused weak shadows to dance around the inside of the boat. The scent of fish from previous adventures lingered in the air.

The warm night air hovered at seventy-nine-degrees, with a slight breeze drifting in from the west. Several illuminated, private boats appeared to move slowly across the bay miles to the south, making progress toward their late-night destinations. Aside from the dim lights that flickered from distant island homes, the night was calm and the channel was dark. Twinkling stars dotted the clear, black sky. Yet an otherwise idyllic night on the water was laced with tension.

Three men inside the cruiser sat at the slightly worn, round tabletop below deck. Several half-empty beer bottles and a bag of chips lay strewn across the table. Two of the men were obviously apprehensive and wanted to get the interview over; their escape to safety was incomplete.

Desiring better lighting, one man reached up and flipped on the seventy-five-watt halogen lights.

Two of the men began to talk animatedly about their dangerous escape. The third man, obviously very focused on his task, wrote copious notes on a lined, yellow pad.

"We barely got out alive," the seasoned engineer explained. "I was waiting at the north end of the island jetty, adjacent to the runway, with Earl. The rocky outcropping is a great place to sit unnoticed. It was pitch black, quiet, no one around, or at least that's what we thought. Donnie navigated his sport cruiser by GPS and arrived right on time." He tapped his foot rhythmically on the fiberglass floor without realizing it.

Donnie looked up with his stained, yellow teeth, "It weren't easy gettin' there alone. I raced through some big swells. That really slowed me up some. Thank goodness the sea weren't stormy or I'd be at the bottom now. The cabin cruiser ain't really designed for open ocean travel."

The engineer continued his account. "Donnie shot us a burst with his flashlight and we started swimming. When we were almost to the boat, they started shooting from the shoreline. We crawled up the ladder, shivering and wet. Donnie gunned the engines and we fled toward the mainland. It was about 3:30 in the morning. Ten minutes or so passed and a helicopter with a high-powered spotlight started searching for us. It flew back and forth in a pattern trying to pick up our wake. Donnie turned north and we managed to get away."

<hr/>

"Bridge, sonar."

"Go ahead," the captain said.

"We're painting multiple contacts coming out of the south in the main channel," the sonar operator replied.

"Anything of consequence?"

"The biggest contact appears to be an inter-island ferry, sir. She's about forty-eight hundred yards due east of us on a heading of two-seven-five-degrees and moving at twenty-two knots. She'll pass just north of us in a few minutes. The rest of the noise sounds like small craft, sir."

"Any submerged traffic, Lars?"

"Negative, Captain. I'm not even seeing a thermal layer under us. The area looks clean."

The captain knew that U.S. submarines generally transitioned this area on the surface, but he was not a man to take unwarranted chances.

"Let me know immediately if anything appears on the passive."

"Aye, sir," the sonar man answered. He went back to the bank of digital information displayed on the panel before him. Captain Ingvar Wallen clicked his pen for a moment and walked down the passageway deep in thought.

Like his boss, Wallen was also driven by the basic instinct to prosper mightily. So long as his billionaire mentor kept the checks coming, he would do the job. Concern for the consequences was relegated to afterthoughts. He had no qualms, however, with turning the destructive power of his submarine against the island if he perceived any duplicity on the part of his employer.

The sleek, black submarine cut quietly through the water like a prowling shark. It was invisible to both sonar and magnetic anomaly detection systems, courtesy of the advanced design of the reconfigured hull. The sub had started life in the early 1960s as the last of the American, post World War II diesel boats. All that was left of the original structure now was a large portion of the hull, recently extended by twenty-four feet. A process called friction stir welding bonded the molecular composition of the individual metals together, resulting in exceptionally enhanced structural strength at the hull's joints.

Wallen was pleased. The interior of the ship's shell had been retrofitted with new, octagonal support beams that were also friction stir welded to the extended frame. The previous operational depth of the sub was six hundred sixty feet. With the new modifications, it was now almost one thousand feet. Her emergency dive depth was a little beyond that.

⚸

" . . . at dawn I seen another boat that looked to be follerin' us about ten miles back. I pushed the engine to the max and opened up a little more distance. It disappeared into the horizon and we was pretty sure at that point we'd lost him," Donnie added. He took a swig of beer from the bottle in his hand. He was visibly nervous.

"The sea was flat, thank goodness, since we was stuck pourin' gasoline from them five-gallon gas cans I brung along. We wouldna' made it without the extra juice."

The engineer looked directly into the investigator's eyes. "When we came to the coastline we turned north toward the headlands and spotted the same boat again in the distance with the binoculars. We followed the coastline around into the straits and ducked into the north end of Seiku Harbor. We waited until late in the day and finally called you on the cell phone when we thought we were safe. Before dusk we pulled out and made a run for Friday Harbor."

The investigator could feel the warm, stainless steel .40 Smith and Wesson under his left arm, sitting in its abbreviated holster. His sense of security and command came from years of experience, but the semiauto provided an added measure of confidence. Looking up from his note pad, he locked eyes with the engineer. "I'm glad you escaped. What happen to Earl?"

"He got off the boat at Seiku Harbor and made his way into Seattle. He said he'd meet us at Friday Harbor at 9:00 p.m. But his cab got caught in rush hour traffic and he missed the last ferry."

The engineer fished around in his shirt pocket and came up with a folded piece of paper. "Here's his cell phone number. His plane leaves to-morrow right after lunch. He said you could call him and arrange a meeting in the morning to talk."

"Sounds good, thanks," the investigator replied as he palmed the paper.

The engineer rubbed the dry, cracking skin on his knuckles with hand cream while staring at the bulkhead and thinking of recent events that had brought him to this moment.

The exterior of the stealthy submarine was covered with a thin but tough crossweave laminate of gas permeable, flexible, ceramic microtiles.

A gas plasma generator charged the tiles when the sub was underway. The ionized particles that flowed along the surface of the submarine's outer skin interacted with incoming sonar energy and absorbed it, rendering the sub invisible.

The black submarine was as ominous as it was deadly. The traditional recessed periscope mast was replaced by an advanced digital camera array. Its complement of six officers, thirty men, and the triple redundant computer systems operated the highly automated sub with relative ease.

"Bridge, sonar."

"What do you have, Lars?" Wallen asked.

"Sir, we're coming into the shallow area. I'm picking up lots of bottom clutter. Looks like some old sunken boats, a couple of commercial fishing nets, and miscellaneous debris. There are some natural irregularities to the contour of the bottom as well. It may get a little tricky if we stay at five hundred feet."

"Thank you, Lars. Helm, take us up slowly to three hundred feet."

"Aye captain, three hundred slow," the helmsman repeated. He pulled back on the sports car style steering wheel and the submarine's deck inclined slightly.

The boat carried eighteen powerful exothermic CHINO torpedoes. The torpedoes were housed in a one hundred twenty-five-millimeter-thick, skin-tight, Mylar capsule contained within a deck-mounted enclosure. Prowling warships with sensitive listening gear could hear the flooding noise normally associated with a nuclear sub opening its outer torpedo doors. But they couldn't hear this submarine. To further quiet the torpedoes, the sub mounted them on a soundproof, Teflon railing system.

Unlike conventional, electrically driven propeller systems, the CHINO torpedoes were powered by the sea's salt content. A miniature diffusion power chamber extracted hydrogen-sodium atoms from the surrounding seawater. The atoms were stored in a fuel cell and transferred to the torpedoes' battery when it was energized. Power was shunted to an inverter, which in turn drove a Teflon-coated radial compressor forcing the water out the rear of the casing under high pressure. As a result, the CHINO torpedoes had an almost unlimited range at approximately ninety knots.

The targeting system boasted similar upgrades. When a target was identified, information was transmitted to an onboard microchip from the sub's main computer. Then a shooting solution was confirmed and accepted. The torpedo accelerated out to the last known position and postulated the best scenario to pursue its quarry. A magnetic anomaly detector and a copy of the enemy warship's propeller sound signature were then engaged to acquire and close in on the target. Best of all, the torpedo was not fooled by thermal inversion layers in the sea.

No submarine in the world could outrun the torpedo, and by the time its propulsion system was detected by an enemy sub it would be too late to launch countermeasures; the target warship would be only seconds from a watery death. The wizardry of the sub's design engineers didn't stop there. They had numerous resources available to them through the parent manufacturer's many technical and engineering subsidiaries. Other warships crossing her path would find out about those the hard way.

⚷

The little cabin cruiser swung casually in the light breeze and occasionally tugged at its anchor. Donnie kept looking out the small, round porthole behind him into the night.

"What can you tell me about the Nord Island operations that you think will help?" the retired FBI agent turned private investigator asked the two seated men.

"I've been there for the past two years in the staff engineering department. We stay pretty busy since the island is still growing. There's plenty to occupy our time." The engineer took a drag on his beer and wiped his forehead.

"In my opinion, Mr. Odin is an egomaniacal psychopath. One late evening at the airport, I was standing in the shadows of a hangar when I saw one of his bodyguards beat a man pretty seriously. Odin simply stood by and watched. I don't know what it was about, but be assured Odin's got all the warmth of a coiled up, hungry pit viper."

The engineer described several other experiences he'd witnessed involving the brutal multibillionaire's cadre of vicious security personnel.

"What about the island itself?" the investigator asked.

The engineer rubbed his sweaty hands together, then scratched his stubbly face while thinking how best to answer the question.

"Great for visitors and guests, it's a resort destination of sorts for the rich, but behind the scenes the security is as tight as Fort Knox. There are several levels of control badges issued to employees for access to various facilities on the island. Mr. Odin has a reputation as a paranoid control freak. A few nights ago, Earl and I were in the back kitchen of the main complex cafeteria. We were finishing a test of the fire suppression system. I'd just picked up my tool belt when the back door flew open. Three tough-looking guys came strolling in with their own access key card. The card didn't look like any that I'd seen before. They wore military camouflage uniforms with enlisted rank insignias. They weren't people I recognized; we know pretty much everyone on the island. Fortunately, they didn't see us in the back."

The husky engineer shifted in his seat as he went on to describe the near encounter.

"It was pretty late, so I'm certain they thought the place was empty. They were laughing about the sinking of a big cargo ship near Burnaby Island, up north along the Canadian coastline. It sounded like a self-congratulatory accomplishment. We didn't hear much of the details of their conversation, but what we did hear was outright barbaric. To make matters worse, these guys were openly armed, but they weren't our cops. We got spooked and slipped quietly out the back door." He wiped the sweat from his forehead again. The humidity was like a blanket of mist. After taking a final swig from his beer bottle, he reached into the little refrigerator for another.

The black submarine cruised along on a modern diesel power plant, capable of pushing her out to a sustained speed of twenty-three knots on the surface and thirty-three knots when submerged. The latest Fairbanks-Morse high efficiency diesel engines, of which four had been installed, carried her smoothly along. Her patrol range was just over twelve thousand miles with a full fuel load.

In contrast, a nuclear submarine could remain submerged almost indefinitely, so long as her crew's food supply lasted. But even with the most modern computer-aided propeller design, it still made subdued noise that could be detected by other warships, above or below the water, especially at speeds over five knots.

While a conventional diesel sub had numerous drawbacks when re-charging its batteries, which was generally required every thirty hours or so, the battery-powered drive design gave it a distinct advantage in running silently below six knots.

To supplement the new diesel sub's ability to pull oxygen out of the sea-water, a series of racked, encased hydroponics trays scrubbed carbon dioxide from the sub's air system. When the metering device indicated twenty-one percent oxygen in the enclosed environment of the hydroponics lab, it was pumped into a pressurized dispersal system. From there, the sub's onboard computerized monitoring equipment would release fresh oxygen into the ship's atmosphere. Then the process would start all over again.

"Bridge, radio."

Wallen keyed his microphone. "Go ahead."

"The chase boat indicates the target is off the southwest point of Rich-ardson Township. It's less than twelve hundred yards, Captain."

"Very well, XO, put the divers in the chamber and have them stand by."

The newly installed, long-duration, polymer batteries easily exceeded the sub's original operational battery life of thirty-six hours. They allowed the submarine to remain submerged for nine to ten days before being re-quired to surface for fresh air. The new batteries also shaved the sub's weight by a hundred thousand pounds over the old lead acid battery design.

The extensive modifications were greatly appreciated by the crew. The smell of cigarette smoke, diesel, and battery acid was eliminated. Maximum operating temperatures with the new environmental controls also made life aboard the sub quite comfortable.

World War II submarine crews, on the other hand, were routinely sub-jected to one hundred-plus-degree temperatures under combat conditions, especially when the ship was submerged for extended periods of time.

" . . . and there's good reason to believe Odin's behind the sinking of those two huge container ships in the Pacific last summer, as well as the Burnaby incident."

"What does he stand to gain by doing that, and how exactly does he sink them?" the retired FBI investigator asked.

The engineer lit up another cigarette as he stubbed out his last one in the ashtray. Smoke drifted up and out the hatch into the night air.

"Do you have any idea how long it takes to build a highly specialized super container ship? Add that to the loss of transport capacity in the Pacific, and an expanding marketplace, and the shipping contracts become very lucrative for the right firm. According to a friend on the island, Odin owns about twenty-seven percent of the supertankers and container ships along the Pacific Rim through a variety of subsidiaries. He operates another twenty-two percent through leases. All he needs to do is eliminate about nine more competing vessels and he controls fifty percent of the routinely available capacity. If we assume a few ships may sink annually in bad weather, typhoons, etc., then he's already picked off three of the nine and made it look like storm related losses."

The engineer opened a small notepad and looked it over.

"He's got four of the six construction yards on the Pacific Rim capable of building a super container ship under contract already. So that avenue's pretty well tied up. Profits to his operations will bump up about one and a half billion a year in the contract bidding process, if he can pull this off. If you want a reason, that's it."

The old FBI man leaned over the table. His laptop computer had accessed the maritime incident archives. "The accident report on the ship that sunk west of Burnaby Island said it was the storm that bowed the vessel's keel and caused it to break up."

The engineer laughed, "Maybe, but I don't think so." He leaned back and closed his eyes for a moment.

Donnie got up and walked out on deck. He felt cooped up below deck, like a target in a shooting gallery.

"There's rumor of a military-style operation of some kind running out of well-hidden warehouses next to the private docks on the southwest side of the island. It's reserved for Odin and his super rich buddies. No one's allowed in the area, not even my engineering guys. The place has bodyguards and special security measures.

I'm pretty sure there's some kind of advanced warship that sank them. What does the Canadian Coast Guard report say about the depth of the seabed at that location?"

The investigator paged down the report and rummaged through a list of footnotes. "Let me see, ahh . . . looks like there's a fifteen-thousand-foot-trench that runs parallel to the coastline a few hundred miles out."

"Well, that ought to tell you something. It was probably sunk in that area to avoid a thorough investigation. There's no commercial marine system that can go that deep to video the remains of a ship. Even if you could go that far down, by the time the sunken hulk of the ship reached that depth, the surrounding water pressure would have crushed it and imploded structural components. That would make an accurate investigation nearly impossible."

⚷

The sonar operator listened intently as the screws of another ferry crossed the channel to the south. He closed his eyes tight and put his hands to his stereo headphones to concentrate. Then, with one eye slightly open he watched the superheterodyne oscilloscope. In a minute, the sound began to move away.

The sub's conventional active sonar arrangement was replaced by a trailing sonar drape. The drape was a tough, fiberoptic cable that followed the submarine and could be reeled out to fifty-five-hundred-yards astern. The operator could swim the unit up, down, left, or right to fine-tune its acoustical properties.

When the boat's skipper wanted to emit an energy pulse, the sonar shack had its pick of sea creatures to imitate. A studio quality audio CD of whales, dolphins, shrimp, and other noisy ocean dwelling inhabitants was activated and sent down the cable. An omnidirectional speaker then transmitted the false sound into the water. Any sonar return picked up by the trailing transmitter was routed back up the cable to the sonar shack. It was then displayed on a digitized computer screen in the shack and on the command deck for the captain to see.

Other warships detecting the sound of whales and dolphins would naturally assume sea life was intruding upon their sensitive detection gear, never suspecting a stealthy sub was lurking in the neighborhood. The renovated diesel sub could then attack or disappear as the mission objectives dictated.

Tonight, it would attack.

Lone Peak Wilderness Area
Northern Utah
8,644 foot altitude
Wednesday, 2205 hours Mountain Time

Sixteen miles from civilization and the nearest paved road, the dusty vehicle pulled hard to the right as the tire quickly deflated.

"I'm your guest, so you have to change the flat," Dale Fox said with mock seriousness, getting in the first of several verbal blows.

"Uh huh . . . Get out of the car and hold the jack or you can walk the rest of the way," his older brother insisted.

"Cranky fire twit," Dale grumbled with feigned sarcasm. "It's an SUV, not an Abrams Tank."

Fire Captain Sean Fox and his brother, FBI counterterrorism agent Dale Fox, walked to the back of the SUV and opened the rear door. Inside was the spare tire Sean had fixed just that morning.

Dale was an intellectually gifted, strapping, 6'4" bodybuilder with a law degree - a conundrum within a conundrum. It came in handy when intimidating suspects. He lived in a world of violent, aggressive personalities that begged for constant attitude adjustment services.

Sean, on the other hand, was an inch shorter, with a very easygoing personality that most people found charmingly disarming. He, however, dealt with more carnage, as one of the top vehicle extrication and rescue experts in the state.

Both men had served their country as U.S. Marines, Sean in combat at the end of the Vietnam War.

The brothers managed to achieve similar results in their work, although they came at it from different directions.

"That's the second blowout today. Just my luck." He moved the fishing poles, tackle box, and rappelling gear out of the way. He handed the well-worn, battery-powered spotlight to Dale.

"The off-road demons seem to have it in for you," Dale said as he turned on the spotlight. "Since I'm on vacation, you can do the heavy lifting."

"Well, pull the jack out while I undo the lug nuts, then."

Dale's free time was occupied by warm, sunny California beaches, while Sean was an outdoor enthusiast of the high, heavily forested mountains. Each man found peace and harmony within his preferred environment.

Right now, Dale was thinking he was slightly out of his comfort zone. Even though they'd both grown up on a Montana cattle ranch, it was Sean who spent the bulk of his time hunting up in the mountains, sometimes alone.

The tail and running lights of the SUV bathed the nearby trees with a soft, faint glow. The dark night sky and twinkling stars were pretty much blotted out by the tall treetops. It was truly pitch black outside.

Blinking hard a few times to adjust his vision, Dale looked around slowly, searching the night for pupils staring back. He knew all cats, including mountain lions, had a reflective covering at the back of their eyes that lit up in the dark when a light hit them. He wasn't sure if bears had the same mirrored, ocular coating.

It suddenly occurred to Dale that they were probably parked at the off-framp of the predator freeway in the woods. He was hoping it wasn't the late-night, snack-hunting hour. He touched the .40 caliber Glock firearm at the small of his back without thinking about it. His ears were on high alert for any sounds other than his brother changing the tire.

Dale glanced down at Sean, who seemed oblivious to the potentially hungry wildlife that made their home deep in these woods. Sean was probably attuned to everything around him, given his excellent hearing and the personal satisfaction he derived from his quick draw skills. Dale wasn't certain it would be enough if they were surprised by one of Mother Nature's ravenous, roaming denizens.

Sean was wearing his old, low-slung, western leather holster, which held a marbled Vaquero .357 Magnum with a semiflattened hammer on his right hip. He was an old West 1880s gunfighter reenactor on weekends. He shot noisy, smoky Hollywood blanks at other reenactors at public festivals and county fairs when he had the time. He was a self-taught quick draw artist who could shoot six rounds downrange into a target in a little over one second. It was Sean's chosen stress reliever from the highway mayhem he often dealt with. His speed didn't make him legendary by any means, but Dale had seen him shoot and he was impressively quick.

Weird, a firefighter with quick draw skills, Dale told himself, *just too weird for a firefighter.* It suddenly made Dale wonder how many shots it would take to down a fast-charging, four hundred pound, black bear.

"Yellowstone's just north of us, isn't it?" Dale said, looking out into the void. He wanted the question to sound like normal conversation.

"Yeah, it's a couple hours up north."

Seven-hundred-plus-pound grizzlies are the king of the Yellowstone woods. That and wolves. Wily, big, smart, quiet wolves . . . Wonder if there's any wolves around here?

"Got any wolves in these mountains?"

"Might be," Sean said, twisting the lug wrench with a grunt. "They've caught a few males on the range to the north of us in the past couple of months. Soon as they catch a female we'll know they're here to stay. The coyotes will have to be on their toes when that happens."

Dale let that comment pass. "What kind of ammo you carrying in that .357?"

"Hundred fifty-eight grain semi-jacketed. Why?"

"Just curious," Dale replied.

Sean pulled the flat tire off the SUV and dropped it to the ground.

Dale kept scanning the darkness. He knew all too well from personal experience that bad men could be as dangerous and deadly as some predatory animals. But at least he could reason or talk with a human being, and if not, maybe distract them into making a mistake he could capitalize on to turn the tables. Big bears, fast mountain lions, and cunning wolves operated on a different frequency. Animal instinct was deadlier than human ego and stupidity.

Dale continued searching for reflective eyes.

Four minutes and two very dirty hands later, Sean stood up next to the right rear wheel.

Dale looked at Sean and squinted, "Next time, let's stay on the paved roads."

"Coward."

Dale just shook his head, "Prudent human beings don't use their off-road vehicles as wildlife fly swatters."

"I thought you'd enjoy seeing a big moose up close. You don't have that in San Jose."

Sean cleaned his hands and face off with a couple of alcohol wipes. He reached over, grabbed two cold bottles of water out of the cooler in the back of the SUV, and handed one to Dale.

"Beautiful, isn't it?" Sean asked, slowly uncapping the water bottle.

"Beautiful? Its pitch black out here, I can't see a damn thing," Dale replied, still searching the tree line to his right.

"Close your eyes and smell the woods. Let your hearing take in the peacefulness we're surrounded by. Feel the calm, quiet atmosphere. It's incredibly refreshing."

A chorus of crickets filled the background. Dale counted silently to ten, as if acceding to his brother's Zenlike request. "Okay, I'm impressed. Let's get the hell out of here." He took a swig of his water and headed for the passenger door.

They hopped back in the SUV and Sean flipped the headlights on.

"While I appreciate the late night sightseeing detour, that bull moose didn't look the slightest bit amused," Dale said, referring to the reason for their unexpected slide into the shallow ditch. He glanced sideways and hooked his seatbelt in. "If he hadn't moved, you'd have antlers for a hood ornament."

"You need to get out more often. That was a hoot."

Sean pulled his seatbelt on and repositioned the rearview mirror. He shoved the SUV into low four-wheel drive and powered his way out of the shallow ditch.

"*Time for a hot shower*," Dale decided, as he got comfortable in the padded cloth seat.

Sean sniffed the air suspiciously. "Oh man, it's you . . . You smell like fish guts. Yuck. We may have to hose you down outside first. Let's stop by the fire station on the way home."

"I don't think so. I'll roll the window down. Just drive us home, cowboy."

The San Juan Straits
West of Seattle, Washington
Wednesday, 2207 hours Pacific Time

"Depth?"

"Two hundred ninety feet, Captain."

"Bring us around to a heading of two-two-five and level off at PD."

Captain Ingvar Wallen turned to his senior chief.

"Are the divers ready?"

"Yes, sir. They're geared up and in the chamber."

Several minutes passed silently. The submarine glided into position six-and-a-half miles south of Friday Harbor in the San Juan Straits of Washington state. The sub had been hidden on the Canadian side of the international border until an hour earlier.

"The pursuit boat was correct, Captain, she's just ahead," the sonar operator said.

"Release the shadow boat to return to Nord," Wallen ordered.

"Aye, sir."

The gray, thirty-seven foot, cigarette-racing boat had followed the cabin cruiser at a discreet distance soon after it left the island. The submarine crew scrambled to get underway after the shooting on Nord Island's rocky beach. It had been trailing the racing boat and keeping track of the escapee's progress by encrypted radio. Now in the dark of night, with the submarine on station, the shadowy racer pulled out of a cove several miles away. The powerful boat headed south for the channel to the open ocean and away from the sub's hidden position.

Douglas Odin, the elusive billionaire whose vast wealth controlled this operation, had quietly demanded the capture or death of the engineer and his friends. He didn't particularly care which one.

"Range to target?"

"Eight hundred yards, Captain."

"Helm, slow us to four knots."

"Aye, Captain, four knots."

Ingvar Wallen, a native of Sweden, stepped up to the automated control panel in front of him. The stocky, 5'10", former bare-knuckled, bar-brawling mariner had morphed into an all business submarine commander. The atypical, full, blond, Nordic beard and blond, thinning hair rounded out his appearance. He reached down and pushed the console button for the digital camera. A split second passed and the high-definition image appeared on the screen in front of him. With the microphone headset sitting firmly on his head, he spoke into the audio boom at his lips, "Pan left."

The computer-slaved camera slowly rotated left until the cabin cruiser came into clear view.

"Stop rotation." The captain rubbed his tired eyes and then took a moment to observe the view through the thermal imaging optical eyepiece. He breathed slowly and concentrated, searching for movement onboard the boat.

"Sonar, move us up to two-hundred yards, upwind of the cabin cruiser into the current, and report."

"Aye, Captain, two-hundred yards."

The submarine slid into position.

"Stand by, UV Splash light."

A few minutes later, the sonar operator sang out. "Two-hundred yards, Captain. We're nose-on to her, sir. She's just riding the swells. Her engines are off."

"Very well . . . Engine room, battery status?" the captain called out.

"We're at ninety percent, sir."

Wallen looked up to confirm it with his bulkhead mounted indicator gauge. He could ill afford an instrument error and made a habit of double-checking his situational circumstances.

"All stop. Trim us out, helmsman."

"Aye, Captain. All stopped and trimming."

Wallen detested certain aspects of the responsibilities he was forced into. When he went to work for Douglas Odin, he did not realize the breadth or depth of the billionaire's depravity. But he was stuck now. Any premature attempt to bail out would only get him killed by a team of elite thugs that Odin kept on tap for such matters as employee disloyalty.

Wallen felt that combat operations should be honorable, vessel versus vessel. The business of sending armed mariners to kill was more personal than he really desired.

"Chamber, Captain . . . we have a light rolling sea at two-and-a-half feet, no wind chop. We're out of the ferry lanes and we show no traffic in the immediate area. The current is two knots, at two-three-zero degrees. That should put you straight on to the target. We'll reposition downwind of the cabin cruiser after you depart . . . Stand by."

"Radio, bridge."

"Radio here, sir."

"Where is the chase boat right now?"

"She's thirty-five hundred yards south-southwest of us, running at thirty-six knots. Do you want me to signal her, sir?"

"Negative. Just let me know when she turns for the main channel." The captain switched to the computer-slaved camera array in front of him again.

"Magnify array by two." The selective magnification shifted its lens to provide an enlarged image twice the standard setting. "Stand by to splash UV."

The captain spoke into his boom microphone again. "Rotate right." Seconds passed.

"Stop rotation." He looked at the cabin cruiser and saw a man pacing the deck with a cigarette glowing from his lips.

"Chamber, be advised I have one man up on deck . . . You are a go," the captain said.

"Copy, we're flooding the chamber now."

Fifty-two degree seawater seeped into the aft deck diving chamber until it equalized with the outside water pressure. Three divers exited and headed for the surface just sixty-five feet up. The digital clock on the bulkhead read 2300 hours.

Wallen aimed the crosshaired reticle at the portside bow of the cabin cruiser and pushed the console button. A pulsed beam of extreme, high-energy, ultraviolet light fired from the sturdy laser camera, painting the side of the cabin cruiser with an invisible mark a microsecond later.

The UV Splash, as the crew knew it, was a unique development from a privately owned, high-tech electronics lab. The electrochemical, Plasma-Luminal Gas Laser was one of a kind. No other marine vessel in the world had anything like it. Firing a very tightly focused energy beam, it left a mark like an exploded paintball shell, roughly the size of a basketball. The apparition remained viewable for about fifteen minutes, and then only by those who looked at it through a special ultraviolet lens. Even in inky black darkness or fog, the targeted vessel stood out like a flashing, neon sign above an all-night bar in the middle of a desert wasteland.

With their UV goggles, the three armed divers spotted the splash of vivid color on the cabin cruiser's hull a couple of hundred feet away. In the dark, they drifted toward it on the current for several minutes, keeping a very close eye on the open deck of the cabin cruiser.

Off in the distance behind them were the dim lights of a cliffside home, almost five miles away near the little island town of Richardson. The divers pressed on, their attention riveted on the man sitting in a deck chair.

⚷⎯✦

" . . . I had a friend on the island, an accountant," the engineer said. "We played backgammon regularly. Last week when we sat down to play at our usual, quiet, corner table in the recreation center, he spoke to me in a whisper. He was afraid to have anyone else overhear. He's the one who told me about the fleet of ships the company controls."

The tired engineer took another pull from his beer and rubbed his eyes as he relaxed against the sticky vinyl seat back.

Donnie sat outside on the open deck, staring up at the stars and listening to his friend talk below.

"Apparently, he couldn't reconcile expenditures for diesel fuel consumption with the information he had on total storage capacity. Seems we were going through a lot of petroleum without being able to account for it all. So he started asking questions. Someone called down to accounting and told him that the matter wasn't important for him to delve into. But, being a good employee, he persisted, thinking he might be viewed as something other than diligent in his work if he didn't."

The engineer stopped to swat at an annoying fly, then continued.

"He disappeared the following day . . . went out for a walk and never came back. They found him by one of the island fishing boats a day later in the north cove. Supposedly, he slipped on a dock unnoticed, smacked his head, and fell into the water."

"Sounds plausible to me," the retired FBI agent said.

"Yeah, only one problem. He didn't swim, he was afraid of the water. There's no way he would go out there at night alone. It's windy, cold, and the docks can be slippery sometimes, from all the fish guts that get toted around at the end of the day. I haven't been able to come up with a good reason for him to be out on the north jetty alone at night. Anyway, I stopped by his room that evening before I knew he was missing. I found the place empty, as if it had never been occupied. It was strange; he would have told me if he was going to change quarters. And then he turns up dead."

The engineer scratched his right elbow and contemplated his next thought.

"As for Nord Island, forty-one other countries officially recognize it as an independent sovereign country, with more coming on board every week. Next year Nord Island will have its own ambassador at the United Nations."

The old FBI agent motioned for the engineer to wait a second until he caught up with his note taking.

"There's a governing council on the island for domestic matters," the engineer continued. "Investigative jurisdiction is the responsibility of the national police, though. Realistically, no one exercises real authority on the island aside from Odin, since it sits beyond the two hundred mile territorial limit claimed by either the U.S. or Canada."

Wrapping his sweaty palms around the brown bottle in front of him, he took another swig.

"As you probably already know, the U.S. and Canada have yet to recognize his claim to sovereignty. Most people know he went to the trouble of publicly declaring himself a subject and citizen of Nord Island in numerous published interviews. As crown prince of his new island kingdom, he enjoys diplomatic recognition and immunity privilege. Not bad, considering it was nothing but open sea fifteen years ago. Shows what a few billion dollars can do for you."

The retired FBI agent wrote quickly in his own special shorthand, subconsciously stroking his gray mustache with his left hand. The engineer waited a few moments for him to stop writing so he could go on with his story.

"It's the fourth smallest nation in the world, just ahead of the Vatican, Monaco, and some other country I can't recall. A year from now, he'll have it built out to twenty-four-square-miles. The estimated population should reach almost five thousand people if the expansion project continues uninterrupted. The U.S. can't even stop him from filtching solid ground off the Aleutian Islands chain the corporation owns. They have surface rights and more, so long as the islands remain twenty-two feet above the high tide mark."

The old FBI investigator flipped his note pad over and ran his hands through his thinning, wavy hair.

The engineer continued talking.

"He has his own bank, justice court, sixty-four-man police force, two fire stations, impressive medical facilities, a dozen doctors, four dentists, three chiropractors, and an immigration operation. Three commercial deep-sea fishing charters operate year round, providing the weather is cooperative. I'm told the sport fishing is phenomenal."

He reached in and grabbed another cold beer.

"There's a newspaper that publishes every day. They have sixty-three miles of paved road and a shoreline maintenance department. They have a six-boat Coast Guard unit, a couple of rescue choppers, and three fully stocked retail store operations. For entertainment, there's a four-screen theater, a huge multifaceted entertainment center, and a new, two hundred sixty-room, five-star hotel that opened last month. That's in addition to the old one with two hundred ten rooms that was renovated last year, plus the casino and its facilities. Oh, and he has two impressive eighteen-hole golf courses that he regrades bi-annually to change the challenge and keep avid golfers coming back."

"You mind slowing down a minute so I can get this all in?" the investigator asked.

About thirty seconds later, the man continued. "There are also a few sanctioned, illicit pastimes available as well. But you probably already know about that."

The investigator yawned and sat back. He put down his pen and listened without writing.

"Out at the airport, there's a fleet of expensive, luxury helicopters and private jets, parked out of view in numerous hangars. A great deal of money is coming into the island, and not just to the casinos."

Donnie stepped back in, opened the small refrigerator, pulled out a bottle of cold water and put it on the table. The boat continued to rock gently in the long swells. He took a seat and listened to the conversation.

"The island has two windmill farms on the northwest side that provide most of the island's electric power. The transmission lines are below ground in a tube system that has redundant power routing grids. They have cattle and sheep grazing pastures that occupy about one hundred twenty-five-acres on the east side. I think they have about two hundred fifty-head of cattle, and a couple hundred sheep. Mr. Odin possesses an almost complete, self-sustaining infrastructure with little need to make trips to the mainland for basic supplies. McDonald's, Taco Bell, KFC, Mrs. See's Candies, Pizza Hut, and a few others have franchise operations there."

The old FBI agent picked up his pad and started writing again.

"As for people, the island has about four thousand or so, including about seventeen hundred Nordian citizens at last count, complete with passports. Almost a third of them are the folks who've settled in the fishing village in the north harbor area. Like I said, the fishing is good and the folks in the village make a pretty decent living. There's a national sales tax of five percent. With such close proximity to the mainland, people are lining up to move there as the place continues to expand. And rich folks from other countries who want to shelter assets are making inquiries about Nordian citizenship."

The third diver let some air out of his buoyancy compensator so he'd float low in the water. He was about twenty-five feet from the cabin cruiser, covering for the other two with his high-powered spear gun at the ready.

"*Nu går vi* - roll up on the tailboard when the swell drops it back down in the water. I'll follow you on the next rise," one of the divers said to the other.

The two, black-suited divers gently shimmied up on the transom's teak platform, just above the water line. Quietly, they removed the small pony bottles they'd been breathing from, along with their fins. They velcroed the dive gear to the stainless steel ring on the back of the transom. One of them peeked over the back of the boat to recheck the location of the man on deck. He was nowhere in sight. From special waterproof bags came two 9mm semiauto firearms with suppressors. Their hip holsters held shiny, stainless steel, U.S. Diver fighting knives, authentic right down to the serial numbers on the base of their blades. The divers crept silently over the back of the cabin cruiser and along the aft deck.

Donnie exited a moment later from the enclosed cabin, coming up on deck for another smoke. The lead diver clamped his hand over the man's mouth like a vise, as the sharp point of the knife sank up to the serrated cuts at the top of the blade. Donnie's body twitched a second and then went limp. The diver dumped him silently onto the deck, where blood ran freely from the fatal wound. The other two occupants of the boat were not as lucky to die so easily. A vain but vicious fight for survival ensued.

The retired FBI agent put up the greatest resistance. He pulled out his pistol and fired two rounds. A bullet to his head ended his life almost immediately, but only after he got off another shot that went wild, barely missing his attacker.

The brave engineer smacked one of the divers in the head with a beer bottle, which broke over his polyurethane dive suit. Moments later, the grizzled maintenance supervisor was in the open, up on deck. The third diver, who was floating in the water close to the boat, took aim and fired.

The barbed spear shot through the engineer's right shoulder, piercing the fiberglass bulkhead behind him. The pain was excruciating; he screamed in agony. Blood poured from his upper chest as his body spasmed involuntarily. Looking down, he spotted Donnie lying dead on the deck.

The lead diver stepped out on the open deck, "I'm gonna do you a favor," he said to the impaled engineer.

He grabbed the man's arm and slashed through the brachial artery with the razor sharp dive knife. Rich, red blood shot out of the engineer's arm with every beat of his heart.

"With any luck, maybe you'll bleed to death before you drown."

Two minutes passed and the divers quietly stepped back over the deck, which was now awash with blood, to the rear transom. They donned their diving equipment and slid into the water. The small stains of blood on their Henderson dive suits dissipated into the salty ocean.

The cabin cruiser rapidly took on water from the hole punched through to the bottom of the fiberglass hull. In a few minutes, it would disappear beneath the waves and drop five hundred feet to the bottom of the bay.

The maintenance engineer, still alive and pinned to the bulkhead of the little pleasure craft, futilely tried to stem the escaping blood with his left hand. What remained of his life was measured in mere seconds.

The gurgling air escaping from the sinking sport boat was evident in the sonar operator's headset.

"She's going down, sir," he said.

"Radio, where are the divers?" the captain asked.

"The divers are on the surface, flashing us now, sir."

Once in the water, one diver keyed a tiny, waterproof, three-watt VLF radio to signal the sub that they were on their way back. Their radio emitted a weak signal that was designed for close in work.

In response, the sub flashed a faint, ultraviolet light from the extended camera mast for a half second so the three divers could obtain their bearings and swim in the direction of the submerged vessel. When they reached the black, parkerized buoy floating in the water above the sub, they dove down.

Six minutes later, the aft deck chamber drained and the three divers removed their gear.

"Chamber, report," Wallen barked into the intercom.

"The engineer and his friends are done talking to U.S. authorities. We have the notepads, laptop, and documents in waterproof bags, sir," the senior diver replied. "We'll bring them forward for you as soon as we dry off."

"Very well . . . three down, one to go. Meet me in the galley when you're dressed."

Wallen pulled out a notepad from his shirt pocket. He opened the cover and crossed off another in a series of data blocks. When the form was filled in, he and his crew would have to consider whether they wanted to continue their employment with Odin Industries.

He turned to his executive officer standing nearby. "Mr. Sjorkon, change heading to two-four-five-degrees and put us straight on to Port Angeles. When we're six-thousand yards north of that location, change course to the center of the channel. Notify me when we come abreast of Otter Point and Port Crescent. Stay sharp and keep an eye on the instruments. If a U.S. sub is in the channel, move to the Canadian side of the border and wait her out."

"Aye, Captain," the executive officer replied.

"XO, you have the bridge."

The no-nonsense submarine captain was operating in classic combat mode. Wallen's thoughts momentarily drifted to the six big transport ships he had sent to the bottom of the Pacific in the past fifteen months. In his cabin were the plans to send another half dozen to Davy Jones. It reminded him of his youth, when all he had were his wits, fists, and the exhilaration of the moment. It was also beginning to pain him somewhere deep inside. He pushed it to the back of his mind and busied himself with other tasks. He turned and disappeared down a ladder. His muted footsteps echoed across the metal deck and open grating as he made his way aft, ducking a pipe and several overhead gauges as he went.

The executive officer stepped down the ladder behind the captain to the chart table just below the sail and looked over their positioning.

The Canadian shoreline at Otter Point and the little U.S. hamlet of Port Crescent sat directly across from each other, fourteen miles apart. From there, it was thirty-six miles to Neah Bay and the headlands west of Midway to the open ocean. Running silently at six knots, they had about a forty hour trip back to their deepwater warehouse on the south side of the island nation of Nord.

Although U.S. subs periodically transited the area around Nord en route to their patrol operations, they were not aware that the tiny, manmade island harbored its own stealthy submersible warship. The captain of Nord's only combat vessel was vigilant and wary of their passage, and operated on a constant wartime footing to ensure that they never found out. He moved his ship slowly and quietly, always searching his surroundings for any sign of a U.S. or Canadian warship.

Tonight the invisible sub had struck once again, with swiftness, silence, and deadly precision. The Nordian naval assault team caught up to three of their four "enemies of the state."

A fourth person was still on the loose, but not for much longer. A Nordian ground team had infiltrated Seattle to hunt him down. And it would not be the last time the secretive security forces from the small island nation would wreak havoc on U.S. soil.

⚷

Sean spun the wheel to the left and pulled the dirty SUV into the driveway.

"You stink. You better go through the servant's quarters round back and scrub down good," he said to Dale.

"Servant's quarters . . . That would be your shower, wouldn't it?" Dale was up the steps to the two-story, four-thousand-square-foot home in a flash.

Sean had been making additions to the home since he and his wife had purchased the property fifteen years before. It was just now getting to the point where he was happy with it and its upgraded interior.

He watched his brother bound up the steps and open the front door.

Sean pushed the garage door button on the SUV's console and pulled into the three-car garage. It was almost 11:15 p.m. *I hope he leaves me some hot water.*

State Highway 92
Highland, Utah
Thursday, 0830 hours Mountain Time

Conversation in the SUV between Sean and his brother, Dale, stopped as a beeping sound from Sean's Motorola fire pager intruded. His agency was hosting their annual firefighter recruit testing day. The fire chief had asked Sean to carry a pager and stick around town in the event he might be needed during the exercises.

The fire dispatch center announced a three-car accident over the little pager's speaker. The location was just a mile ahead on the same road Sean and Dale were traveling. There were injuries, and one of the cars was overturned and on fire. Sean pressed the gas pedal down harder on the silver Jeep Grand Cherokee. The sport utility vehicle shot past two cars and picked up speed.

"I can see the smoke from here. I hope no one's trapped," Sean said to Dale. He rehearsed in his mind what he would do once they stopped at the wreck.

Fifty-two-year-old Sean Fox was a fire department officer and an instructor in, among other things, vehicle extrication and rescue. With twenty-plus years on the job, he'd seen a lifetime of vehicular misery and lives carelessly wasted by inattention, drugs, alcohol, and sheer stupidity.

"When we stop, grab the big extinguisher in the back and go after the fire. I'll pull on my turnouts and check the car to see if anyone is still inside," Sean told his brother.

⚷——

A black-over-red, Class 'A' fire engine with its dedicated rescue gear pulled away from the main fire station back lot. The driver slid the horizontal lever on the electronic control box to the right and the red and blue strobe lights on top of the fire truck cab lit up. Several cars just ahead pulled over to get out of the way.

"Rescue one-eight-one is ten-seventeen," the officer in the right seat growled into the microphone. "Copy, Rescue one-eight-one," the dispatcher replied. She could hear the siren in the background.

⚷——

The dark, acrid smoke from the fire curled high into the air. Sean braked the Jeep hard, pulling off to the side of the road. Several passersby had pitched in and were spraying small, hand-held bottle extinguishers onto the flames of the upside-down vehicle as the engine compartment blazed away.

An elderly man, seeing the fire department issued turnouts, yelled out to Sean that someone was still in the fiery wreck. Sean ran down the slight embankment to the overturned sedan and raised his yellow fire-jacketed arm to shield his face from the heat. His fire-resistant Nomex hood was draped his head. In his pocket was a steel-tipped center punch for shattering automotive safety glass. He felt for it through his gloved hand. A couple of heartbeats later, the window glass was laying on the ground.

Dale let loose with the larger fire extinguisher and the flames died down.

"Hey, kid, come here!" Sean hollered to a high school athlete standing nearby. "Grab my legs. When I yell out, pull me back. There's someone trapped inside."

The lanky, redheaded teenager nodded confidently.

Sean crawled through the broken side window. A woman's body lay sprawled across the car's interior ceiling. The pungent smoke swirling around the inside of the car obscured his vision and burned his eyes. He grabbed a handful of long, brown hair and got a grip on the woman's lightweight jacket collar. When he pulled, she moved in his direction. Then her body stopped. She was hung up on something.

Sean squirmed around her and saw that her foot was tangled in the seatbelt. The seatbelt cutter in his jacket pocket was hard to reach, given the lack of elbow space. Finally, he managed to yank the tool out and sliced away at the safety strap.

Outside the vehicle, Dale's extinguisher ran dry. He dropped it when the gasoline and oil-fed fire erupted to life again. The searing heat and flames forced him back, and the fire's intensity grew rapidly.

Flames from the vehicle leapt twenty-five feet in the air. The temperature inside the car was becoming unbearable.

The sound of the sizzling vehicle crackled in Sean's ears. Through the sweat on his face, Sean's thoughts were quickly turning to self-preservation. His lungs ached. Would he have to abandon the woman, or would his last breath of useable air hold out?

The high school athlete was hanging tough with Sean in spite of the growing car fire. Suddenly, a second set of hands gripped Sean's other foot.

The seatbelt slapped away. Sean tightened his grip on the woman's clothing and pulled for all he was worth. The two sets of hands yanked him back as a surprising shower of water played over him through the open window. With the sound of crackling flames roaring in Sean's ears, the fire truck's siren announcing their arrival had been drowned out.

Sean pulled the unconscious woman out through the window of the twisted wreckage and onto the grass. Several firefighters grabbed her and hustled her away from the blazing hunk of molten metal. The high school athlete dashed from the car. Sean scrambled up off his knees and followed, the heavy turnout gear protecting him from the flames leaping out the car window in his wake. His mustard colored fire jacket emitted steam as he bolted from the wreckage.

Moments later, Sean was sprawled across the freshly cut grass, face up under the shade of a tree, arms extended, his chest heaving with every breath he took. The turnout jacket and bunker pants he was encased in were soaked. His eyes were closed. Dale lay next to him, watching the fire and smoke.

Minutes passed and a firefighter approached Sean and Dale. "Like to work up a little sweat before breakfast, do ya, boss," the man said, directing his humor at the supervisor of rescue operations.

"Feels like I've been through the wash and rinse cycle. Maybe you could just hang me on a clothesline before you go," Sean replied as he lay motionless, his eyes still shut. The firefighter laughed and walked away. Sean finally inched his way up on his elbows. Watching as the fire crew beat down the blaze, he shook his head from side to side to throw off the excess water. White smoke curled high over the charred car.

The firefighter returned with a green-colored bottle of oxygen. Sean slipped the mask over his face and inhaled deeply. A paramedic ambulance rolled up on the accident scene and killed its siren.

Dale and Sean sat back on the grassy embankment, watching the orchestrated havoc. Sean finally worked up the energy to slip off his fire jacket, dropping it on the grass; he was exhausted. His tee shirt was soaked to the skin from sweat, his hair matted down under the Nomex hood he'd removed. He wondered if the female driver he rescued would survive the accident.

Dale looked at Sean with a worn out weariness. "I guess a nice, leisurely breakfast at the restaurant is out."

"Good guess. You look like you just escaped from the Titanic."

"You don't exactly exude GQ yourself, cowboy."

Sean lay back and closed his eyes again, the sizzling sound of metal finally gone.

Dale and Sean Fox were big men, standing 6'4" and 6'3", respectively.

Now in his early 50s, Sean was graying at the temples. His energetic personality and dedicated physical exercise regimen maintained his two-hundred-thirty-five-pound athletic frame. The old-fashioned, handlebar mustache and the cheerful, pleasant demeanor made him appealing to almost everyone he encountered. Only his wife was acquainted with the numerous physical scars that tattooed his body - from the underside of his jaw to the bullet wounds that stitched his lower, left leg.

Sean's twenty months in the South Vietnamese jungle as a Marine sniper near the end of the war had permanently hardened him. The rules of engagement in I Corps were loose, thanks to the Viet Cong and the North Vietnamese Army regulars, and their well-known atrocities.

As a Marine sniper, the NVA had a bounty on him. He was a rich target of opportunity for every NVA soldier and peasant supporter of the Communist north. The NVA hated snipers with a passion. Stories of captured Marine snipers and their spotters being skinned alive while tied to a tree were not lost on Sean. He evolved into a stalking, almost invisible, character in order to survive.

After several harrowing escapes near the Laotian border, Sean decided the existing restrictions had to go or they were going to get killed. Since he and his spotter frequently worked alone without other combat units for close support, they modified the rules of engagement to suit the risks. After that he slept better. He came home in one piece, with fewer nightmares than lots of other combat vets.

Returning home from Vietnam, the transition to an orderly civilian life filled with societal rules became a difficult process. The war experience had invaded his soul and became a permanent part of his unchecked character.

Now, years later, although the vehicular carnage and horror he encountered was still terrible to see, it had little effect on his ability to operate at the scene. Rookie firefighters, on the other hand, needed time to acclimate themselves to the shock and revulsion that was natural with the occasional automotive slaughter they encountered on the road.

With a background in swift water rescue, high-angle rescue, heavy rescue, and his certification as a rescue scuba diver, and vehicle-extrication instruction wizardry, emergency calls had taken Sean into places and conditions that would ruin most ordinary people, both mentally and physically. As tough as he may have appeared to other firefighters, he remembered exiting some rescues with his reserves spent; on the other side of that was a pine box with his name on it. He reminded himself frequently that only Superman was bulletproof.

The worst rescues involved small children, injured so badly that their little bodies shut down in shock. He said silent prayers when he reached the limits of his paramedical skills. The rest he simply shrugged off as business as usual. He couldn't do anything about it at that point, anyway.

Reliving nightmare moments involving death and dying was an unfortunate hazard common to emergency service personnel. Sean's calm confidence was very reassuring to new firefighters when they were thrown into difficult working situations. Lack of experience meant drawing on a senior firefighter's direction.

His work skills benefited from the many life-defining lessons under his belt. Blessed with rugged, good looks from his tanned and fit rancher father, he was nonetheless a reserved person. His father, a man who still rode a horse on a daily basis, was his inspiration.

Growing up on an eighty-four-thousand acre Montana cattle ranch, Sean and Dale both learned self-reliance and independence at an early age. Their mother instilled virtue and integrity into their character from the moment they were able to comprehend. Their father, a career Marine officer and Medal of Honor recipient from the Vietnam War, imparted an analytical approach to problem solving. They retained the guidance their parents had shared at every opportunity, and more. The two men also had a well-tuned sense of responsibility to family, and a long-standing obligation to contribute to the security of their nation. Sean and Dale were part of the sixth generation of Fox family members to do so.

Sean's chocolate-brown, slightly graying, full head of hair and thick mustache lent itself to a mature and credible image. The hazel-eyed fire captain would have been right at home as a range cowboy or trail boss one hundred forty years earlier.

In spite of the horrific experiences in his life, Sean displayed a soft side, serving the community as a little league baseball coach and a Boy Scout leader. He frequently took school groups on tours of the main fire station, answering questions and putting fire turnout gear on the youngsters so they could see what it was like. He was always a hit with the kids, especially when he let them run the siren and lights on a fire truck.

Then there was the other side. It was something over which he seemed to have little control. Sean could be tough, unyielding, and menacingly ferocious if his personal trigger point was squeezed hard; it was an unusual trait for a firefighting personality. His experiences as a combat veteran lay dormant just below the surface, waiting for justification to shift into action.

His brother, Dale, eight years his junior, shared many of the same characteristics, born of his experiences as a deputy sheriff and SWAT team leader.

The flames were gone, but the smoke and steam lingered in the air. Dale took in the scene around them. Inch-and-a-half attack lines from the first arriving fire truck still littered the immediate area. A tow truck operator was at the corner standing by, waiting for the word from the cops to do his job. A firefighter with a metal clipboard sat a few feet away beginning his fire report. Traffic on the street behind them was down to one lane. A cop was directing the gawkers and trying to keep it all moving along.

Sean looked at the teenager who had assisted them. "Thanks for the help, kid. You okay? You didn't get burned, did you?"

"Naw, I'm fine. Glad I could help ya . . . Captain Fox, is that lady gonna be alright?"

"Don't know . . . It'll be in the paper tonight. You can find out then. Why don't you go over to the fire engine and grab a cold soft drink. There's a cooler on the tailboard. Next time I see your dad, I'll tell him he has a son he can be very proud of. You did great, thanks."

The auburn haired teenager walked away with the satisfaction that he'd done something personally rewarding. He threw a wave to Sean and Dale and disappeared into the gathering crowd.

Just beyond him, the ambulance finally pulled away, lights flashing and siren screaming. Sean and Dale watched it race off into traffic.

The two brothers rose from the grass a minute later and headed for the silver Jeep, turnout gear and empty extinguisher in hand. Suddenly Dale started laughing out loud.

"What's the matter?" Sean asked.

"Jeep's got another flat," Dale replied as he pointed to the right front tire. "Good thing you got the tire repaired this morning."

Sean looked at the Jeep in disgust. "I'm thinking of buying a horse."

Dale laughed again, "With your luck, it'll throw a shoe."

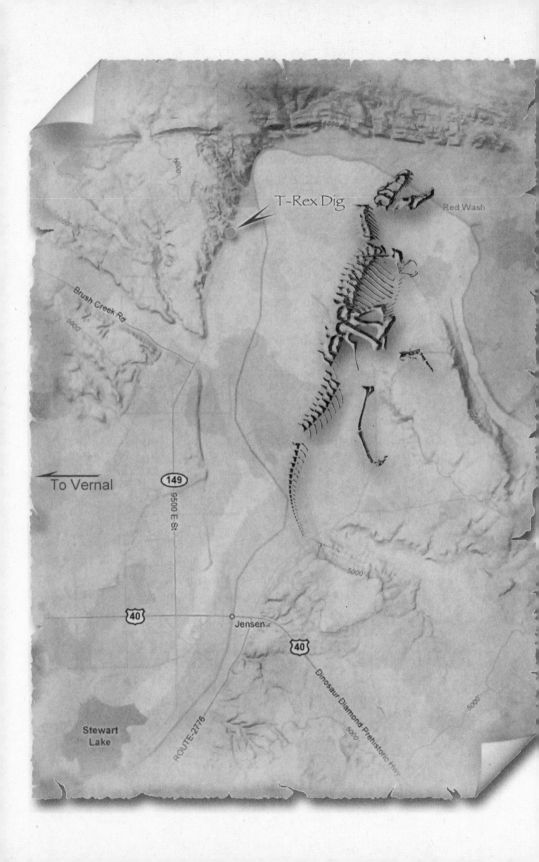

T-Rex Dig

Red Wash

Brush Creek Rd

To Vernal

(149)

9500 E St.

(40)

Jensen

(40)

Dinosaur Diamond Prehistoric Hwy

ROUTE-2776

Stewart
Lake

Utah-Colorado desert
Near Vernal, Utah
Thursday, 1030 hours Mountain Time

The old, white pickup truck rattled noisily as it bounced down the rutted dirt path. A fine, powdery dust flew in its wake. It was ninety-one degrees outside and the air-conditioner had conked out on the road six miles back. The driver occasionally cussed out the mechanic for not paying closer attention to the vehicle's maintenance and upkeep.

Dr. Dalton Jordan sat in the passenger seat looking out across the desert to the mountain. They had only a few more miles of bad road to the dig site. He unbuttoned his shirt cuffs, rolled up his sleeves, and squirmed. His butt was sore from the poorly padded seat.

"You'd think the dinosaurs could have been more cooperative and died next to the highway near a fast food place," the driver lamented, "in a shady spot wouldn't have hurt either."

Dalton laughed, "If they did that, then we wouldn't have the joy of adding camping out under the stars in the desert to our list of employment benefits."

The lean, tanned, unmarried Dalton was related to the late Harry Longbaugh, affectionately remembered as "the Sundance Kid" of old West legend. This mountainous desert area was the notorious bandit's turf, and thanks to that genetic relationship, Dalton was quite comfortable in the somewhat inhospitable environment.

The sun beat down on the rugged eastern Utah wilderness near the Colorado border. The temperature would reach a hundred before lunch. Fortunately, the remote digging location had temporary facilities erected, and a portable generator to run a computer and a few fans. The Brigham Young University associate professor in charge of the dig site had called Dalton with uncharacteristic excitement in his voice hours earlier. He wouldn't say what he'd found, not even a hint, just that "she" was beautiful and unbelievable. Only a paleontologist who saw his work as his mistress could immerse himself in such a fashion as to refer to dusty, ancient bones with the tenderness and excitement of a long-awaited, hot date. He didn't let on that they'd made the discovery days before since he'd failed to comprehend its magnitude until two days ago.

The professor had been looking for Dalton ever since, without success until this morning. Dalton and Ken Schiffler, a graduate student in paleontology, were joining the dig crew to help supervise the removal of the new find.

Ken hit the brakes and slowed the pickup to a crawl to allow a five-foot sidewinder to cross the dirt road in front of them.

"I thought they slept during the day," he said, watching the reptile slither off into the brush.

"He probably thinks you should be somewhere else as well," Jordan replied, swatting a bug from his face.

"What do you suppose they uncovered at the dig?" Ken asked.

"No way to know until we get there, something in the way of a nice surprise I suspect. The area is loaded with skeletal remains, a fair number of which have been unearthed over the past seventy years. We have about forty tons of bones crated up under the stadium at the university, which have yet to be cataloged. We've even loaned some of the boxes out to the dinosaur museum at the north end of the county for study by their paleo group. I'm wondering if they've come upon a new raptor. That would be fun."

Dalton loosened his shirt collar and yawned. His ears popped.

"They've found partial remains all along this area. Maybe they've discovered a more complete specimen. This was their stomping ground way back when. In any case, we'll be there in a few minutes.

This road ends up against the cliff, near an old river bed."

On the floor of the pickup was a new cooler with five gallons of Neapolitan ice cream. The dig team would appreciate the gesture of a cold dessert in the blistering heat.

Dalton was an exceptionally accomplished paleontologist, with a solid reputation that spanned over fifteen years. He'd been fortunate to discover a rare, full skeleton of a little-known species of dinosaur years earlier, now referred to as Utah Raptor. It was the Cretaceous Period's second-most dangerous predator. His career was further enhanced when Hollywood used his surprise discovery in a major motion picture.

With his household celluloid notoriety in the paleoentological arena secured, he joined other world-class scientists of the genre. He'd been invited to many research locations around the world as a result. Brigham Young University's Chancellor recognized his newfound fame was a boon to the school's reputation. When the job of department head opened up a few years back, Dr. Dalton Jordan was promoted and given relatively free reign.

The battered pickup truck slowed to a stop in front of a large, heavy, sunbleached tent. Dalton stepped out, looked down for a moment and watched as the dust settled on his hiking boots. He gazed up and took in the view of the research area from under the brim of a beige Stetson cowboy hat.

The dig site, not far from Vernal, Utah, was one of the richest fossil locations in the world. The eastern Utah desert town was ripe with dinosaur museums, specialty theme restaurants, and any associated retail products, such as videos and games that marketers could dream up to turn a profit.

The sun was high in the cloudless, blue morning sky. Its brightness matched the temperature that was still climbing. Two people walked over to greet Dalton from the camp's tented facility.

"Dalton, thanks for coming out so quickly," his colleague, Dr. Lawrence Hamilton said excitedly, shaking Dalton's hand. "I'd like to introduce you to Tori Evans, the grad student who made the discovery."

Dalton had seen the tall, blond woman before at the university, but had never been formally introduced to her. Every male student in the paleontology lab knew who she was. She had turned them all down for dates in her first few weeks on campus, explaining "an eagle never defecates in its own nest."

"It's a pleasure to meet you, doctor," the leggy, blonde grad student responded with a firm handshake.

"It's nice to meet you too, Tori . . . Is it alright to call you Tori?"

"Absolutely," she beamed. She knew that Dalton was a paleorockstar, and a highly credible scientist. She wanted to emulate the man's successful approach to the hard work ahead of her.

"This is Ken Schiffler. He's completing his doctoral work. I asked him to join us. Lawrence, what do you say we call a halt to the work for a few minutes and enjoy a little ice cream while it's still in an edible state?"

"Good idea. Tori, would you round up the others and meet us back in the tent, please." With that, she trotted out of view up the hill to the excavation site, her ponytail waving behind her. Tori's long, shapely, tanned legs, bracketed by tight, faded green cutoffs, held their attention for a moment.

"Come, let's step out of the sweltering sunshine, shall we," Lawrence said.

Dalton put his arm around his colleague's shoulder as they walked. "Lawrence, I've known you to get excited on very few occasions. What have you found?"

"I'll show it to you after we eat. Meanwhile, I think I'll let Tori enjoy the privilege of sharing her discovery with you."

A group of college students, twelve in number, walked in line down the narrow hillside path toward the tent. Once inside, they wiped the sweat off their faces, popped open folding chairs, and sat down.

"I'd like to introduce you all to Dr. Dalton Jordan, head of the bone department at the university." Hand shakes and greetings followed the introduction. Then everyone grabbed a bowl and spoon, and helped themselves to the ice cream.

"Tori, would you tell the good doctor about your find, without telling him exactly what it is yet? I want to see the look on his face when we climb up to the pit," Lawrence said. His intentional slyness was not lost on Dalton.

Tori finished the last spoonful of chocolate ice cream in her bowl, took a drink of water from her canteen, and began.

"Seven days ago, I was taking a little break and eating a sandwich up on the plateau just above us. I was enjoying the view from the hillside, sitting in the shade of the only rock outcropping above the camp. In between bites, I took my hammer and rapped the shale to my right, and a few pieces of rock fell away. When the shale broke apart, it exposed something that looked like a smooth surface. I put my sandwich down and tapped again. More rock crumbled, and the surface took on a curved outline. I ate the last few bites of my lunch and started to look closer."

Tori cleared her throat . . . the excitement rising in her voice. "I brushed away some more rock over the next few minutes and discovered what appeared to be a jaw. I kept working it and the jaw got bigger, and then a tooth appeared. I came back down to camp, got my brushes, tool belt, and a chair, and went back. When I walked back up, Kyle, over there, was sitting about thirty feet away in the shade," she pointed, " . . . so I asked him to take a look. When he got up, more shale crumbled away behind him. I noticed a slight protrusion that turned out to be bone." Tori went on for several more minutes describing the intricate details of the find with enthusiasm, but without revealing the specifics of the animal they'd discovered.

Dalton's interest was peaked. They certainly wouldn't have run him out here without good cause.

"Okay, I think we've said enough. Let's go take a look at our new acquisition," Lawrence interjected.

Dalton noted that every student in the tent was sporting one of those ear-to-ear Cheshire cat grins.

"Let's walk up to the plateau, shall we," Lawrence offered, gaining his feet.

A few minutes later, now high up on the hillside, Dr. Dalton Jordan saw a well-organized activity, with squared string sections detailing a few of the individual excavation spots. To the side were several growing mounds of dirt and rock, sifting screens, and other miscellaneous equipment. He stopped and scanned the balance of the site. The find was mostly covered over with tarps.

"We're about twenty-six inches down across the entire skeleton," Lawrence explained. "It's almost ready for extrication and casting."

Dalton absorbed the character of the dig for a moment and then turned to the group. "All right, who's doing the honors?"

With that, several students began carefully pulling back the tarps to reveal their prize.

Dalton couldn't contain his surprise. His jaw dropped and he stopped breathing for a moment at the first glimpse of the truly remarkable specimen.

"My God, Lawrence, you've kept a lid on this for the past seven days!" he said in stunned disbelief.

"We wanted you to be the first to see it," Lawrence said, with a measure of obvious pride. They stared at the perfectly intact remains of a full-sized adult Tyrannosaurus Rex.

"I think it's a female, from the dimensions of the pelvis and the overall size," Lawrence continued. "We'll know more when we get it back to the lab."

Ken Schiffler walked the length of the skeleton. "It's massive, what's the measurement?"

"We have it at 13.9 meters from skull to tail," Tori replied.

"That's uh . . . over forty-six feet." Schiffler exclaimed.

"That's right. It's bigger than South Dakota Sue. And this one is complete; every bone is accounted for."

Ken whistled in amazement behind his mirrored sunglasses, unable to take his eyes off the huge dinosaur. "She must have been really impressive in life."

The hot sun bore down on the assembled crowd. Tori adjusted the worn, tan pith helmet over her blonde ponytail as she pondered her next statement. Several of the male grad students commented quietly among themselves that her shapely legs had somehow managed to avoid the scratches and scrapes suffered by the others. A drop of sweat trickled down her abundant cleavage.

"We have some preliminary figures on her dimensions. She's 4.4 meters at the hip. Aside from her tail and the fact that she's hollow-boned like a bird, we estimate her live weight in the neighborhood of four-and-a-half tons. So far, we've counted fifty-eight teeth, and her forelimbs are completely intact. All of the ribs and vertebra are also accounted for and in excellent condition. Several front teeth are just over a foot long. They're bigger than railroad spikes."

"Over a foot," Dalton responded with surprise. He strode around the skeleton slowly, making notes on his PDA. He looked closely at the animal's features and overall frame, walking all the way around to where he'd started. Pulling out a small measuring tape from his pocket, he leaned down next to the skull. A few seconds later, he stood erect. "This one is thirteen-plus inches. That's incredible."

The group could tell he was clearly pleased. Turning to the blonde student, he began to speak. "Well, Tori, she's your discovery," he said, still somewhat shocked by the apparition before him. "I think it would be appropriate to grace her with a name. What would you like to call her?"

She stood silently, twirling her long, blonde ponytail while contemplating the unexpected question. One of the other grad students, with a slightly demented, sophomoric sense of humor, spoke up quickly. "Let's name her Tori the T-Rex." With a forlorn look, Tori Evans grimaced and shook her ponytailed tresses *no*, but it was too late. She'd been tagged with a nickname that would follow her from here on out, thanks to the brainless outburst of a youthful colleague. She made a mental note to try and discover some insignificant, innocuous, little, prehistoric rodent that she could name after him just to get even.

The largest ever Tyrannosaurus Rex skeleton, Mother Nature's most feared creation, was lying there before the happy group of paleontologists and university grad students. The magnificence of the discovery would put them all on the front page of every newspaper and trade journal around the world.

Dalton swore them all to secrecy until he was able to arrange a press conference for the next day. Brigham Young University would be the benefactor of one of the most important dinosaur finds in decades.

But that wouldn't end up being the only surprise.

An undiscovered, thirty-six pound remnant of ferrous metal was still to be unearthed from beneath the remains of the skeleton. About sixty five-million years ago, it had decimated the earth's largest wildlife population. The bone dry rock was devoid of the necessary elements to reawaken the dormant enzyme that lay within. Inquisitive university researchers would soon rectify that small detail.

The students and the paleontologists had no idea how much international panic awaited them. The real, earth-shaking event, however, was yet to unfold. The mysterious virus that caused the mass extinction of the dinosaurs millions of years ago was an historic mystery that would soon haunt their very futures.

Dr. Dalton Jordan, FBI counterterrorism agent Dale Fox, Fire Captain Sean Fox, and a reclusive billionaire would be hurtling headlong into a clash of disparate opposing interests when news of the find would finally be presented to the press.

It would also be a busy week for the local coroner.

Highway One
Seattle, Washington
Friday, 0815 hours Pacific Time

The King County Sheriff's helicopter raced along at a hundred twenty-five miles an hour trying to catch up to the northbound pursuit on Interstate 5. The cops spotted the vehicle almost immediately and gave chase. It began in downtown Seattle near the Space Needle. Ten minutes after the call came out they were racing down the freeway with the highway patrol and sheriff's units joining in.

Along the way, several police cars suddenly and mysteriously developed mechanical difficulties, causing them to drop out of the pursuit. Other law enforcement agencies that joined in to assist were experiencing the same problem. Just when they'd get close en masse, the police cruisers conked out and slowed to a stop on the freeway, creating a traffic jam and effectively blocking other chase cars trailing behind them.

The dark-blue sedan they were trying desperately to stop was roaring along well in excess of one hundred miles an hour. Inside were three men. The male driver had a ski mask over his face to conceal his identity and wore black driving gloves.

A middle-aged, white male in the front passenger seat was slumped over unconscious, while a hooded man in the back seat was intently watching the police cars chasing them. Every so often, he pointed and pulled the trigger on the odd, riflelike device at the trailing cars. The highly focused, invisible energy beam was calibrated to disrupt the frequency wavelength of the computer driven controls in the police vehicles' ignition systems. Once the firing sequence of the engines' pistons and the fuel injection systems failed, the cars' engines would quit.

The chase was far from over, though, as other police agencies took up the call and were preparing to spike the highway if they could clear away sufficient traffic to roll out the portable road hazard.

The helicopter pressed on through the intermittently foggy sky, slowly closing the distance. As it came into view of the chase, the pilot notified ground units that he was now on the scene to coordinate their efforts.

Freeway offramps in the semirural area were miles apart in this stretch of the north coast. The pilot maneuvered his chopper a quarter mile behind and five hundred feet above the fleeing suspects. The chase continued with three police cars still in the running.

As the sheriff's pilot and his observer focused on the escaping vehicle, an ominous, dark shadow slowly crossed over his helicopter from the right. The pilot instinctively reacted by gripping the collective harder while his senses responded to a change in his peripheral light. He snapped his head to the right and was startled to see a much bigger, camouflage-painted combat helicopter pacing him.

"Where the hell did that guy come from?" he complained angrily to his partner.

Enraged by the surprise intrusion into his airborne chase, he switched to a common safety frequency on his second radio and depressed the voice button on his headset.

"Black Hawk chopper, this is King County Sheriff's Department, Guardian One. We are involved in a law enforcement pursuit and have airspace priority. Take up a new heading to the east and depart immediately."

The nasty tenor of the police pilot's voice was meant to convey to the errant chopper pilot next to him that he would not tolerate anything other than immediate compliance. Satisfied with himself, he paused to watch the big attack helicopter comply and retreat.

The reflective face shield of the Black Hawk chopper pilot's helmet looked over at the much smaller sheriff's helicopter. The mystery pilot keyed his microphone, "This is no longer a local criminal issue; it is now a federal matter and will be dealt with accordingly. You are hereby ordered to cease your activity and clear the area."

With that, the combat helo surged forward on its immensely more powerful twin jet engines and dropped in front of the sheriff's aircraft, aggressively cutting it off.

"Who the hell does he think he is?" the pilot of Guardian One fumed to his partner. He wasn't about to go along with the military pilot's order. He stayed the course and kept a safe distance from the bigger combat aircraft's rotors.

The Black Hawk dropped out of the sky as the chase entered a long, straight section of remote freeway. Even the three police cruisers were now aware of the sinister looking military attack chopper.

The copilot of the Black Hawk switched radio frequencies and keyed his radio microphone, "Dragnet, this is Flyswatter. We're descending ahead of you. Stand by for show time."

The driver of the dark-blue sedan speeding down the freeway depressed the side button on his walkie-talkie, "Copy, Flyswatter. We're ready."

The combat copter pulled in front of the fleeing sedan with the three men inside. Dropping to within forty feet of the highway and below the towering, forested tree line boarding the interstate, the big chopper slowed to thirty miles an hour and spun backwards to face the car. The pilot continued to slow down until both he and the escaping vehicle were almost stopped. He lowered the helo to the ground.

The three police cruisers halted a hundred-plus feet behind the escaping suspect sedan. The officers exited their emergency vehicles and drew their weapons as they took up safe positions behind their cars.

From both sides of the attack chopper, sliding doors popped open and four camouflaged, M-16 wielding soldiers raced out and took up positions in front of and next to the stopped sedan. Ignoring the police, they took aim through the windshield and side windows.

The three police officers were stunned to see the combat clad soldiers take control of their fleeing suspects. They radioed their dispatcher and waited to see what would happen. Their pistols and shotguns were no match should a gunfight break out with the suspects and the full auto machineguns of the soldiers started throwing lead around.

Meanwhile, the sheriff's helicopter took up a landing spot one hundred fifty feet to the rear of the Black Hawk and settled on the freeway. Up ahead, the big blades of the Black Hawk continued to spin furiously. The sheriff's pilot and his observer were intent on arresting everyone aboard the military chopper for interfering with official police business.

As the blades of the sheriff's helicopter shifted into neutral and the pilot powered down the small, single-turbine engine, a military officer stepped out the right door of the Black Hawk chopper and onto the almost deserted freeway. He walked briskly up to the stationary car and yanked open the driver's door. The soldier opposite him did the same on the passenger side.

The soldiers hustled the two suspects into their helicopter at gunpoint, along with the unconscious man they dragged from the front seat.

The two deputies from the helicopter started forward and called for the three officers on the other side of the halted sedan to join them at the military aircraft. As the five cops strode toward the attack helicopter, it suddenly powered up, its big blades spinning faster. Within seconds it lifted off the freeway and rose a hundred feet straight up into the morning mist. The big attack copter swung around and headed northwest into the fog, accelerating away quickly from the scene.

The angry pilot of the sheriff's helicopter and his observer turned and ran for their aircraft. The pilot started the engine, spinning up the blades as soon as sufficient power was online. Guardian One lifted off in hot pursuit. Thirty-seven seconds had passed since the larger combat chopper had departed the highway.

Turning to follow the combat aircraft, they spotted the Black Hawk in the patchy fog almost two miles away. They adjusted their heading and the pilot added power to give chase. Within a minute it became quite clear that the more powerful combat helicopter was opening the distance with a dramatic advantage in speed. To make matters worse, the thick fog was closing in as well.

The two deputies finally lost sight of the big military chopper. The pilot reluctantly slowed his aircraft and turned back for the freeway to rejoin his fellow officers at the scene of the hijacked suspects. He was mad as hell and he wasn't going to let the incident just go away until someone with a gold badge that said "police deity" made him back off. His white-knuckled grip on the collective eased.

The unmarked military helicopter disappeared from view as it flew further into the heavily wooded mountains that periodically gave way to remote pasturelands and wilderness.

"What's our altitude?" the pilot asked, busy looking out the windshield into the patchy fog.

"We're running at seven hundred feet AGL," the copilot replied.

"It's pretty sparse from here to the coast. Engage the terrain computer. We'll crank up the antiradar tiles and drop down to avoid the radar sweeps. How's our errant employee doing back there?"

"He's out cold, sir. I'll administer the drug to reverse his stupor after we land. What does our ETA look like?" the corpsman asked.

"We'll turn west in about five minutes and dash for the barn on the coast. It should be about twenty minutes to touchdown."

"The radar isn't painting us anymore," the copilot said. "We're down to one hundred twenty feet."

"Okay, turn to a heading of two-two-zero and backtrack a few miles before we head due west." The copilot hauled the big combat chopper around to the left in a tight turn and lost another thirty feet in altitude. Their last known direction of travel would be recorded on radar as northbound. Forty-four miles northwest through the mountains and valleys, and they would be done flying for the day. The rural setting of the old farmhouse and barn were miles from any inhabited dwellings, deep in the Pacific Northwest forest.

"Key the barn's strobe," the pilot ordered.

A beacon on the barn was set up to a UHF frequency that could be remotely operated by turning one of the helo's onboard radios to a matching wavelength and keying the microphone. The quarter-second strobe light would pinpoint the old structure in the forested mountain wilderness. At this time of the morning, shadows still dominated anything below the towering tree line.

Several minutes later, the turbine engines wound down, and the semiconscious kidnap victim was carried into the barn. The helicopter was refueled from an underground fuel bladder. Hours before dawn they would depart the Washington coast, flying low over the waves toward Nord Island.

The San Juan Straits
West of Seattle, Washington
Friday, 0822 hours Pacific Time

"There's a body floating in the water just off Richardson's Point," the dispatcher said over the radio.

The deputy sheriff in the patrol boat looked at his partner and pointed toward the south. The drone of the engine picked up as the rescue patrol craft cut into the water and changed direction. He made a quick note on the dashboard pad.

"Tell 'em not to touch it, our ETA is about fifteen minutes. We'll notify you when we get there."

The deputy hung up the microphone and turned to his partner. "Richardson's Point . . . some folks on a yacht just found a body in the water. Nice way to start the day, huh. Just glad I didn't have scrambled eggs and sausage for breakfast. I hate yankin' someone else's overripe pork out of the drink."

Fifteen minutes later, the two King County deputies spotted a white, fifty-nine foot Carver yacht. The people on the bridge waved a large, red scarf to catch the attention of the deputies in the Boston Whaler. The rescue boat's red and blue emergency lights reflected off the larger pleasure craft's pristine, ivory hull.

A man on the bow pointed to an object bobbing in the water about fifty yards away.

"Sit tight for a bit while we retrieve the body," one of the deputies said over the patrol boat's PA speaker. "We'll need to get a statement from you for our report."

Forty minutes later, with the body secured in a rubberized body bag and a statement in hand from the people in the yacht, the deputies headed for a Seattle pier.

Home of Fire Captain Sean Fox
Alpine, Utah
Saturday, 0948 Mountain Time

After showering, Sean opened the dining room closet door and pulled out a favorite board game. Meanwhile, in the basement bedroom, Dale was sitting on the edge of the bed putting on fresh socks and listening to the weather report on the AM radio.

A few minutes later, the two men were seated at the cloth-covered table in the formal dining room, engaged in mortal tabletop combat. The competitive game was the best way to pass time while waiting for their respective women to return from an early morning shopping trip.

An hour passed and the women finally drove into the garage with an armful of grocery bags.

Dale slid his final soldier tentatively across the colorful playing board in the best defensive posture he could muster. He'd been trying to outmaneuver Sean for the past few minutes without success; he was cornered. Sean had four playing pieces still standing. The two men had been challenging each other's prowess at the game of Stratego since elementary school.

Sean had won more games in the ensuing decades than his younger brother. It was the only place in life where the two close-knit siblings threw out their brotherly love in favor of a take-no-prisoners combat mentality. Even the annual Super Bowl party, hosted on Sean's big screen, provoked less aggression.

"You're blocked, sport. Wanna concede, or would you prefer to die a glorious but vain death in battle?" Sean sneered with mock malice from the other side of the sizeable, mahogany table. He leaned back and folded his arms across his chest in an attempt to intimidate Dale.

"There's no way for you to win, hotshot. I have your entire contingent of miners and my flag is still well-protected by a minefield," Dale fired back, twisting his heavy mustache in Snidely Whiplash fashion.

Sean moved in and trapped the lone playing piece still controlled by Dale. In three moves, he managed to jump the last opposing soldier and clear the field of opponents.

"As is the proper order of the universe, I win once again in a dazzling display of tactical brilliance and strategy. You, sir, are out of men," Sean declared.

"You haven't won, you dunce. It's a draw," his brother shot back.

"Oh, I'm so sorry. Forgive me. It must still be your turn then, little brother. Go ahead and move."

"You don't win until you capture the flag, hoss," Dale replied heatedly. "And as we can all see, you've clearly failed in that endeavor."

In the kitchen, Sean's wife, Kelly, and Dale's girlfriend, Betty Jo, rolled their eyes at the testosterone cloud that enveloped the dining room. The conversation that wafted out of the adjacent room for the past couple of minutes was hard to ignore.

"I've never seen Dale like that. Does this happen often?" she asked Kelly.

"It gets like that when they play that stupid board game. They've been like this ever since I met Sean over twenty years ago. I asked my mother-in-law about it once and she said they've been doing this since grade school. When they sit down together, the idiot game demons take over. There are times that you'd think their brains were leaking out the bottom of their shoes. But I suppose it's a good stress reliever. Lord knows they both need it."

"No one in your kingdom cares about the silly flag anymore. They've joined the new world order and been disposed of," Sean growled over the table. "And besides, little brother, your inability to lose gracefully is just downright sinful. You should learn from my example. I win without an overt display of excess pride," Sean added comically.

"Alright, I'll let you declare yourself the winner next time it happens. But for now, it's still a draw."

"Gentleman, and I use the word with trepidation, we're hungry. How about taking us out to lunch?"

Kelly asked.

Looking directly at the two women, Dale smiled impishly. "You've been saved by your wife once again, fire twit. Let us withdraw until we meet again on the battlefield."

"You know what FBI stands for, little brother? Faulty Battle Instincts," Sean said. "And you got 'em."

The two men pushed back from the table and stood side by side to face their ladies. Each man threw an arm over the other's shoulder - an outward demonstration of obvious brotherly love - as they stared back at the girls. The two women shook their heads in feigned disbelief at the rekindled spirit of unity between the two former tabletop combatants.

"Are we really in love with them, or just too stupid to know any better?" Kelly grimaced as she turned with Betty Jo to walk toward the garage door. Dale and Sean just grinned.

"I love doing that to them," Dale said with a laugh.

"Yeah, me too. But you still lost the game sport . . . Let's go eat."

A few minutes later, the car moved down the hill.

"What would you two lovely creatures like to consume?" Sean asked.

"There's a new Mexican restaurant just down the road, how about that?" Kelly said.

"Sounds good. You up for south of the border, Sean," Dale asked.

"So long as I don't have to eat refried beans, we don't get along well."

Dale Fox was one of the FBI's star counterterrorism agents. His responsibilities took him all over the country, and to U.S. territories and possessions. His was a life with a schedule dictated by the misdeeds of others. Despite his federal law enforcement status, the people he pursued seemed stunned to run into his aggressive, merciless approach.

Jail cell bellyaches from his incarcerated guests ranged from *"he didn't act like a cop"* to *"where the hell did that guy come from?"* He scared some and angered others.

Dale was a forty-three-year-old body builder with twenty-one inch biceps and a matching intellect. He was also a skilled private pilot who'd flown over a dozen different types of aircraft, thanks mostly to his father's encouragement and the available aircraft at the ranch.

He and Sean shared similar personality traits derived from their sibling upbringing.

Dale was the more studious of the two, having earned a law degree in his spare time while still a deputy sheriff in Santa Clara County, California. His analytical and deductive reasoning had served his career well. And it didn't take long before the powers-that-be discovered his size wasn't his only asset.

The handlebar mustache was a little out of regulation but tolerated by his boss, the director of the FBI's CTU unit. His steel-blue eyes reflected the sapphire color of his shirt. The poker face expression made him seem both pensive and reflective at the same time.

His ability to absorb and process a great amount of information on the fly added to the sixth sense that had saved his life on more than one occasion. Sharp instincts and the ability to calculate risk on the run led others to believe he was an exceptionally courageous man. He wasn't.

Divorced years ago, he was now on the edge of a formal engagement to Betty Jo Case, the love of his life.

Dale's beautiful, long-legged, auburn haired girlfriend was the managing research lawyer with a major, international law firm headquartered in San Jose, California. Dale had utilized her special resources on a few occasions to gather information that was not found in official databases.

Somewhere along the way, they discovered a deep attraction for each other.

They shared a small mountaintop home in Saratoga, California, overlooking the Santa Clara Valley. The comfortable retreat possessed a commanding vista from the edge of a redwood forest. At night, the lights from the cities below and across the valley added a holiday-like atmosphere to their elevated view.

"Dale and I are going to watch a game on the big screen. Are you two off to shop?" Sean asked his wife.

"Yes, we'll be back in a few hours. Enjoy yourselves, and try to stay out of trouble. And don't eat the lunch meat in the fridge; it's for tomorrow's picnic."

The car engine started up, followed by the sound of the electric garage door closing. The girls were gone.

Sean and Dale settled into the comfortable sectional sofa and turned on the seventy-three inch TV.

A pro baseball game was just beginning.

Dale found himself annoyed by a lone fly that kept buzzing near has face as he ate chips from a bag. Walking over to the bar counter, he reached down to a lower shelf and retrieved a fly swatter. He walked back to the couch and sat down. A minute later, the fly landed near the bag of chips. Sean watched while Dale swung the swatter and squashed the bug. "Your flight has been cancelled," Dale whispered triumphantly.

A few minutes into the sporting event, the fire engine phone on the wet bar rang out with a mini air horn sound. Sean muted the TV, stepped over to the counter, and picked up the receiver.

"Hello . . . Yes, hang on a second."

"It's for you, your office in San Jose," he said as he turned to face Dale.

Dale pulled himself out of the soft couch and ambled over to the counter, taking the phone from Sean.

"Hello, this is Agent Fox . . . Yeah, just a minute."

"Sean, do you have a pen and some paper?"

"In the drawer on the other side of the counter."

Dale opened the drawer, pulled out the paper, and sat back down on the bar stool. "Okay, go ahead." Dale listened to the person on the other end of the phone and began taking notes.

"When? Yeah, Okay . . . why me? You're kidding. Is it confirmed? Do they have a positive ID?" He grimaced at the details.

"I knew him well. He was an instructor at the counterterrorism school. We stopped an armed robbery together in a convenience store a couple of years back during a lunch break." He turned and looked at Sean with a sad face.

"What else?" Dale continued writing.

"Any idea how he got there or what he might have been working on? Yeah . . . Uh huh . . . Yeah. Who's on the case right now? Sure, the name rings a bell, but I don't know him. Is he aware that I'm coming out to join the investigation? No, huh . . . Well, someone better give him a heads up so I don't surprise him. You will? Thanks I appreciate that. I won't be able to get back before late this evening. Book me a flight from San Jose first thing in the morning. Tell the ASAC he still owes me four days on my vacation, and I'm charging interest."

Dale replaced the handset in the little fire truck bed receiver.

"Vacation's over, I have to catch a plane back to San Jose, pronto."

"What's up?"

"One of my old academy co-instructors in the counterterrorism group was just fished out of the water in Seattle, shot in the head. We worked on several cases together. He retired less than a year ago from the Seattle office and joined a big PI firm as an investigator. They don't know yet for certain what he was working on, but a partner in his company seems to think it was a terrorism-related matter. For those two reasons, they want me on it." Dale picked up the note he'd made, folded it, and put it in his pocket.

"Give me a few minutes to pack and let's head for the airport," he said.

While Dale got ready to go, Sean called Kelly on her cell phone and explained the situation. Betty Jo decided to remain behind and enjoy the balance of her time off. The two women had bonded like sisters, enjoying each other's company. Betty Jo felt there was no point in wasting a perfectly good summer day.

Dale walked back in with his rolling suitcase in tow. "Hey, aren't you headed for Seattle in a few days, too?" he asked.

"I'm going out Thursday," Sean answered. "I'm on loan as one of the Homeland Security dive evaluators for the new gas dive training system. Seattle and some surrounding agencies are getting advanced certification as part of the new Homeland Security shoreline response requirement. I'll be there for two weeks. Let me know if you need a diver. I plan to get in a little recreational scuba time on some local wrecks while I'm there. If you're still around, let's see if we can hook up for a seafood dinner."

"Sounds good. Call my cell phone when you get into town. I'm not sure which hotel I'll be in, but they usually do okay by us when we're on the road. If it's not good, I'll do the usual upgrade. I may be there for a few days or a couple of weeks, no way of knowing."

The two brothers chatted about family and hobbies on the way to the airport. An hour and a half after leaving the house, Dale's plane lifted off for San Jose, California.

Nord Island
Pacific Ocean
Sunday morning

The artificial island was situated at forty-seven-degrees latitude and one hundred twenty degrees longitude. Its perimeter was surrounded by numerous high-tech self-defense mechanisms stretching from the shores of its coastline out to sea.

Sonar, radar, magnetic anomaly detectors, temperature variation equipment, water flow directional analyzers, thermal and infrared imagers, and other passive gear surrounded the area. A Japanese firm specializing in military grade surveillance and detection gear had been contracted to do the work.

The hilly, wooded area just a few miles inland from the Washington coastline was still dark.

"Start the checklist," the pilot said. It was 0433 hours. The power to the Nordian Black Hawk helicopter came online. Nearby, a slumbering, white tail deer jumped to its feet and sprinted off into the forest when the whine of the turbines pierced the silence.

"What's the status of our guest?" the pilot asked the corpsman, leaning into the open door of the chopper.

"We'll be up and ready in a few minutes, sir."

"Let's plan to lift off in five, then. Have the team leader shut down everything and shovel off our tracks prior to boarding," he ordered.

"Yes, sir, I'll pass it on."

The isolated island was the inspired creation of its somewhat mysterious owner. Douglas Odin was one of the wealthiest and reclusive men in the world, and the self-proclaimed monarch of his own kingdom. Only a handful of personal assistants knew he was an insidious cutthroat who discarded untrustworthy employees and anyone else who got in his way, like trash in a dumpster. They were very well paid to be the gatekeepers.

Odin hadn't begun life with a malicious nature.

He'd been a good son, with parents who openly expressed pride and love in their offspring. As an only child, he grew up in a privileged household with servants, nannies, gardeners, caretakers, and security people. By the time he was sixteen years old, he spoke fluent English, Japanese, and Spanish. His default language was Swedish. He had an appreciation for the arts, the ballet, classical music, fine horses, and antique artifacts.

His parents vacationed at the best resorts throughout the world. Odin was worldly and savvy long before he was old enough to obtain his driver's license. His acumen in business showed a remarkable maturity that came from years of observing his mother and father in action.

A well-educated man by the time he was in his early 20s, Douglas had an MBA and a Master's in accounting. He was eloquent, articulate, and impeccably well-dressed.

Upon completion of management school, he found himself in the firing line of serious decision making on behalf of the family business. He had the advantage of underestimated youth and a sharklike approach honed at his father's knee, a skill which frequently caught business competitors off guard. Odin played hardball; it was the only game he knew.

His Swedish-American, shipping tycoon father also owned the largest closely-held multinational pharmaceutical firm in the world, along with numerous high-tech companies that held government contracts with the U.S.

military and NASA. His tough but loving Japanese-Swedish born mother was reared in Stockholm. A brilliant lawyer and celebrated corporate raider, she ran the legal affairs of the family enterprises. The legacy didn't end there.

———

"Hurry up, we're losing darkness," the pilot yelled over the spinning rotor wash.

Seven of the eight men from the barn ran for the helicopter and climbed in. The runaway assistant engineer they'd liberated from the police chase the day before was dropped on the floor of the helo, bound but fully conscious.

The eighth man raked over the chopper's tire tracks that led from the old barn. He placed the rake inside the barn door and closed it behind him. A few seconds later, they were lifting into the predawn sky.

"IR on?"

"Check," the copilot replied.

"You have the aircraft. Take a heading of two-six-five and stay low," the pilot said. With his infrared headset on, he looked around outside the cockpit at the surrounding woods. He saw nothing moving and picked up no unexpected heat signatures as they climbed into the sky.

———

Douglas Odin learned to instill fear in competing vendors by emulating his mother's carefully constructed, tactical maneuvers. By the time he was twenty-six, he was quickly dispatching them like a toreador executing a bull in the ring. The ancient Chinese general and philosopher, Sun Szu, would have been proud of Douglas. His vast fortune was inherited from his parents shortly after his thirtieth birthday. Their deaths in an aircraft accident near the mountain retreat of Vail, Colorado, was devastating enough. His wife's sudden passing from a cerebral aneurysm shortly thereafter was the catalyst that finally unhinged him. Six weeks in a hospital that specialized in grief, depression, and psychological counseling put him back on his feet and returned him to life.

In the world of opulent wealth, the difference between an emotionally unstable, demented human being and an eccentric philanthropist was the size of one's bank account and the power and influence it wielded. Odin was functional, but he was irrevocably changed, and not for the better.

The ever confident, heavyset, 5'7", sandy-haired, pencil-thin mustached Odin now measured his personal success on a much grander scale. A workaholic mentality had supplanted the remnants of his tattered family life. The loss of stability in his existence had forever altered the man and his demeanor. He progressed from the satisfaction of winning in business to the bizarre joy of inflicting emotional and sometimes physical pain on those who stood to block his path.

He calculated his movement through life now instead of enjoying its vibrancy. The chase to the finish line and crushing competitors along the way was the only real thrill worth savoring. He'd grown cold and withdrawn to all but his three boys.

Odin invested and collected those things that he could take personal pleasure in. He owned two thoroughbred training facilities in Tennessee and Kentucky. His collection of art was one of the finest in the world, outside of the Louvre and the Hermitage. Only his sons knew of the "other" paintings and sculptures in a separate room off the main display museum on the island. When the opportunity presented itself, he would often go to the room, sit, and think of the masters upon whose works he gazed. It offered him solace and inspiration to consider the tortured lives of some of the great artists whose brushstrokes he could admire. He felt parallels to his own existence.

Odin also possessed an unhealthy thirst to surpass the accumulated wealth of another well-known billionaire living in the Seattle area. His personal goal in life was to be the first human to amass a fortune in excess of one hundred-billion dollars. It was how the superrich played the game of numbers.

"I can see lights moving south on Highway 1, off to the left," the copilot said. They'd been airborne for several minutes.

"I have the aircraft," the pilot announced as he seized the collective. "Take us to damper mode."

The copilot adjusted the angle of attack on the rotor blades and engaged the rotor shielding.

"The chart shows a set of hundred-foot tall electrical transmission towers just ahead," the copilot advised.

The aircraft commander gauged his over flight of Highway 1 between the car headlights he saw moving across the north-south ribbon of road. The chopper rose quickly to clear the power lines.

The helo was dark; the warning strobe beacons were off. On the instrument panel, the airspeed indicator pushed past one hundred five knots as the helicopter dropped over the cliff edge to the sea three hundred feet below.

"Set the flight computer for fifty feet. The surface is pretty calm, and we may be able to drop lower in a bit. I almost wish there was a storm that we could hide in on the way back," the pilot said.

"Power up the ceramic tiles. Let's change our radar footprint to a dump chicken." A "dump chicken" was a reference to seagulls.

The camouflaged helicopter enjoyed the same thin, gas permeable, flexible ceramic tile exterior that was installed on the lone Nordian submarine. Radar would have a tough time picking up the real return indicating to a radar operator that a big metal object was hurtling through the sky.

⚷

Douglas Odin and his destiny were entwined in the island that he'd begun to build fifteen years earlier. He was on a quest to continue its impressive expansion.

Many years ago, while apprenticing for his father on the company's largest container ship, an unusual event occurred. Several hundred miles offshore from their Seattle base, the ship's captain suddenly changed course as a gathering storm from the arctic north began to bear down on them.

A half hour passed and again the captain ordered a new heading further to the south.

"Why the second course correction, Captain?" Odin asked.

The ship's seasoned master motioned Odin to a table a few feet away and spread out a laminated navigational chart.

"Have a look, Mr. Odin. What do you see in this area?" the captain asked.

Odin studied the map a moment before he hit on the anomaly.

"There's a spot here on the chart where the seafloor rises close to the surface. I imagine it plays havoc with the ship's automated guidance systems. I suspect there are shallow twisting currents that cross over it. It looks to be about eight miles long and five and a half miles wide, with an elongated conical shape. The highest, flattest area seems to cover about thirty-two square miles," he offered.

The captain suddenly interjected as he walked to the opposite side of the table, "You are correct, Mr. Odin. Years ago, there was a series of warning beacons located around the edge of the Velisnokov Rise at regular intervals. But with newer satellite navigational systems the beacons were abandoned, and over time, they disappeared as storms destroyed them. We'll go around it and resume a new heading to put us on track with our original course after we pass the storm cell."

Odin never forgot the location of the odd, elevated seabed.

Years later, he purchased Howard Hughes' old mothballed Glomar Explorer from the reserve fleet in San Francisco Bay, and had the ship retrofitted to drive massive steel pilings into the ocean floor. Thus prepared, he contracted a group of foreign marine engineers to begin laying the support foundations for a literal nation building project.

A year later, millions of tons of on-site cement castings and pyramid shaped slabs of concrete were firmly secured on the shallow seamount area.

The concrete foundation was chemically treated, after which boulders and a rock bed were added as filler material. An industrial, superadhesive surface coating of thick, rubberized, bidirectional fabric was applied. It added a secure measure of cohesiveness. Several months passed, and one square mile of new land was finally above water.

8—🔑

"Do we have anything airborne in the vicinity?" the pilot asked.

"Negative. Wait, stand by," the copilot said. "Looks like a commercial jetliner at zero-niner-zero degrees from us, on a heading south-southeast about thirty miles out. It's going away from us at about two-hundred-seventy knots, probably toward SEATAC. We're clear to the east, north, and west."

"Anything on the surface?" the pilot asked.

"Switch modes . . . I've got a return from a tanker about twenty miles southwest. A second return at about thirty-three miles looks to be another ship directly south of us. Nothing else definitive is showing up. We're being painted with radar from the south in a routine sweep, but I seriously doubt that we're showing. Our interior emissions capture gear indicates a negligible signature to the radar sweep."

"Alright, take us out of damper mode and keep an eye on the EGT."

8—🔑

Odin tasked four of his fleet's largest container ships, now retrofitted, to haul raw earth from a family-owned archipelago in the far west reaches of the Aleutian chain, just south of the Rat Islands. The container ships delivered massive volumes of rich, brown dirt to row after row of dump trucks that lined the half-mile-long pier on the rapidly growing island.

A continuous stream of heavy construction equipment operated twenty-four hours a day grooming and adding to the project. A fleet of bulldozers molded the unorganized matter into a recognizable landscape as the island of rubber, rock, and cement disappeared beneath the ever-expanding imported soil. Engineers checked, double-checked and rechecked all of the various land parcels to ensure permanence and adherence to the master building plan.

Following in their wake was an army of nurserymen planting grasses, trees, bushes, and various groundcovers. The emerging atoll was a little over three hundred ninety-four miles from downtown Seattle, Washington.

Within a few weeks, the first permanent structure was erected. Now, fifteen years later, the Island of Nord, as its owner had christened it, boasted almost twenty-four-and-a-half square miles of land, with an average above sea level altitude of almost eighteen feet. The kidney shaped islet even had a small mountain on the southwest side that rose five hundred fifteen feet. A two hundred forty foot hill occupied the opposite end of the island. It was festooned with antennas, microwave dishes, and weather radar. Mapmakers around the world added the new ocean-based creation to their charts, maps, and computer based software.

8—✶

"Let's boost the power to the tiles. We're coming up on the ADIZ," the pilot ordered.

"Copy . . . power is coming up to a hundred percent."

"Slow us another ten knots so we don't overheat the turbines with that generator all the way up."

The younger copilot pondered a thought, "I wonder if the Klingons had the same limitations when they engaged their ship's cloaking device?"

The husky, weathered pilot looked across at his copilot and shook his head in amazement, "Just keep an eye on the EGT, will ya!"

8—✶

Small rolling hills, trees, hardy shrubbery, and ground cover were everywhere across the island. Sea birds found the sanctuary and made homes wherever they could find suitable refuge from the winds. Seals and sea lions came to occupy the tiny bay on the north end of the settlement. Killer whales frequented the area during their seasonal migration. Several artificial reefs were created to the north and west of the island to minimize rogue wave impact.

One hundred ninety-three buildings dotted the tiny landmass in the North Pacific. An eighty-nine hundred foot runway occupied a portion of the west side of the retreat. The latest navigational aids made it as advanced as any major international airport in the world.

By virtue of its positioning in the mid-north Pacific region, winds were a constant companion. A substantial windmill farm on the northeast end of the island offered an almost limitless supply of power to two generating stations. Source-seeking solar energy panels lined the south side of the airport and the shopping facilities buildings as a supplemental energy source.

And best of all, as far as Odin was concerned, the island was outside of the internationally recognized territorial claim of both the U.S. and Canada.

"Okay, we've crossed the ADIZ," the copilot called out on the intercom.

"What is our speed and altitude, Commander?" the sergeant in the back asked.

"One hundred sixty knots at ninety feet . . . we'll be home in thirty minutes."

"Permission to open the starboard door?"

"*Det är docks, gör det* - granted, get it over with," the pilot said. His distain with this aspect of his job still aggravated him.

Two of the big Nordian military team members hooked up their safety harnesses to the overhead stainless steel bars running the width and length of the helicopter's interior bay. Their fairly straightforward job, tasked by higher "island command," was to resolve the loose ends that had plagued the privacy of the tiny Nordian nation's ruler. The mantra drilled into their obligatory political training was "protect the island."

The door slid open and a blast of cold, moist ocean air invaded the cabin of the combat helicopter. The two big soldiers grabbed the engineer they'd liberated from the Seattle Police the day before and gave him a good shove.

The man's screams were drowned out by the sound of the rotor blades spinning above. He reached out in sudden panic for the side of the open doorway, but missed. His hands flailed as he dropped forward into the black void. The younger of the two special operations men seemed to be enjoying the moment, waving goodbye while the hostage fell from the helicopter.

The concrete-hard, ice cold waves absorbed the man's body a few seconds later. The nasty splash that accompanied his demise went unseen. Before long, sharks and other hungry creatures of the deep would remove all traces of the Nordian hostage.

The two soldiers unhooked themselves, sat back down, and rested peacefully for the balance of the ride home. They viewed the engineer as a traitor to their new country. The last potential threat had been dealt with. Sharing secret Nordian information with another country, in this case, was punishable by death.

8—⚷

With a dedicated island workforce of seven hundred-forty people, Odin ran his empire with a benevolent iron fist. He was indeed king . . . although technically, he was the Crown Prince of Nord. His three sons were the island nation's princes. The eldest, twenty-eight, and the twins, age twenty-six, occupied the only trusted positions of power within the family dynasty.

Thor, the oldest of the brothers, had a personality that personified his mythical god's namesake. A dedicated bodybuilder, he oversaw the shipping business. Tobias, a master of six languages, looked after his father's interests in the high-tech field of electronics, Magnus, the smartest of the three, commanded the pharmaceutical operations.

Thor was the muscle in the family, controlling a Seattle dockworker's union behind the scenes. When a problem arose, he had special talent to deal with it. Thor also had temperament issues and was prone to occasional fits of violence when things didn't go his way. His steroid use was barely within tolerable limits. Single, rich, young, and standing 5'11", he had an unlimited stable of beautiful women vying for his attention. They included playboy bunnies, models, actresses, college professors, flight attendants, nurses, school teachers, and a few sizzling hot housewives. His father had a cadre of personal assistants keeping an eye on the energetic Thor to keep his recreational appetite in check.

Ultimately it was Tobias, with U.S. government research and development funds, who managed to develop the secret technology now employed on the high-tech, stealthy diesel submarine. The U.S. government wasn't aware of the latest technological breakthroughs that the electronics company had achieved.

The Nordian sub was constructed at the Portsmouth Naval shipyard in Virginia. Her original keel was laid in 1960 and finally stricken from the U.S. fleet in 1980. A foreign transfer saw her sold to the Swedish Navy shortly thereafter. Her original Scandinavian master was none other than Ingvar Wallen.

In 1998, after sitting dockside for two years, she was sold to a marine research firm in Chile. At least that's what the Swedes thought. The research firm was controlled by one of Odin's shipping conglomerates.

⚷

The time was 6:15 a.m. The sky to the west was beginning to lighten to the new day's sun still well to the east.

"We're coming up on the island," the aircraft commander announced over the intercom.

The Black Hawk flew well to the north and then west of the island before turning back to the east for a landing behind the island's small mountain.

"Cinch up and prepare for landing," the copilot ordered.

⚷

Douglas Odin recruited the expatriate Swedish submarine crew with the same detail he applied to all of his special endeavors. Several of the original Swedish crewmen, including the retired and recently widowed captain, were enticed to come aboard and reunite with their old warship.

In the process, the Swedish skipper, Ingvar Wallen, became the highest paid submarine captain in any navy, along with the rest of the well-compensated crew. Their loyalty was purchased at a high price.

Odin was satisfied to sign the checks that ensured its continuation.

Odin Industrial, their employer, listed them as various technical and engineering professionals with classified security based jobs. Twice a year they enjoyed three-week vacations, supplemented by company credit cards and cash bonuses. Odin purposely spoiled them as part of their retainer.

To hide the submarine's existence and erase her from the rolls of maritime shipping records, she was purposely sailed out into the Pacific just off the Chilean coast during a storm. The sub was then reported to have floundered and sunk in deep water. In time, no one would be concerned with her since she was officially recorded as lost at sea.

It didn't take long to sail her to Nord in the shadow of a company cargo vessel. She underwent extensive modifications and was dramatically transformed.

Sea trials and drills occupied the crew's activities for the first sixty days, until all of the operational system's bugs were worked out.

A shakedown cruise north of the Hawaiian Islands gave the crew its first encounter with a U.S. hunter-killer submarine. The U.S. sub passed to 'the east of them just fourteen thousand yards away, but it never took any action, indicating they were unaware of her presence.

Captain Wallen took pride in reporting to Odin on his periodic encounters with the U.S. submarine fleet. He always praised the crew for their efficiency and dedication in evading detection, and protecting one of Odin's most prized possessions.

Weeks later, sufficiently satisfied that their new stealth submarine was seaworthy, they attacked and sunk their first supercontainer ship in deep water, four hundred miles west of the British Columbia coast.

The official Canadian Coast Guard investigation concluded that the ship went down in heavy, storm-tossed seas, the result of poorly loaded cargo whose weight distribution had doomed it. They surmised that the cargo shifted in the hold as the towering waves repeatedly smashed the hull of the old ship. Twenty-two sailors and one dog perished in the unfortunate sinking. The Canadian government considered the regrettable event a closed case.

The stealthy diesel submarine and her opportunistic crew were far from conducting their last atrocity at sea. The true cost of shipping goods across the Pacific would soon inch its way up. The little island's "royal" family was hard at work, actively strengthening their hold on Pacific Rim shipping through their conglomerates and subsidiaries. Soon, however, their focus and the kingdom's financial opportunities would change. Their special operations team would be deployed once again, adding to its list of victims.

⚬━➤

The Black Hawk flared to a landing on the reinforced, recessed concrete landing pad. The landing space was adjacent to the hidden submarine pen situated between two small hillocks. A camouflaged bunker was rolled forward on a set of tracks. Within a minute, it concealed the chopper from both aerial and ground observation, storing it away next to several others.

"Secure the cabin and stand by the tie-downs," the pilot ordered.

One hundred fifty yards away, Odin watched as the rotor blades of the aircraft slowed.

The commando team leader exited the helicopter and walked to the top of the bunker. He looked up at the huge bay window of the second floor of the mansion. There across the manicured lawns, Odin stood with his arms folded across his chest. The commando raised his right hand with the thumbs up salute.

Odin smiled with mute satisfaction, exhaled, and turned away to attend to other business.

Utah-Colorado Desert
Near Vernal, Utah
Monday Morning

Dalton Jordan turned to Dr. Lawrence Hamilton. "Let's take a short break, shall we? The kids can keep going with Schiffler at the helm. There's a cameraman and a reporter for *PaleoWorld* magazine who wants to talk to us."

They dusted off, put on their hats, and proceeded down the hill to the erected tent site that was home to the university crew. The summer sun was not quite at the crest of the mountaintop, where it would shine directly down on the dig site. The cooler night air that had lingered in the shade was finally giving way to the coming heat of the day. A small lizard scurried by, running from rock to rock.

Every student on the hillside was in full swing, readying the dinosaur for the journey to her new home. Plaster material was being used by the excavation students to cover the various bones and skeletal segments in preparation for their move to a transport vehicle. "Tori the T-Rex" was in disassembly. By the end of the day, the entire remains of the massive carnivore would be out of the ground and on her way to a lab at Brigham Young University.

The press conference held earlier that morning had gone well. A dozen reporters, nine cameramen, a *National Geographic* film team, and some people from the Science cable TV Channel showed up at a hotel in Vernal for the event. An hour after it began, they all filed out to a pair of local transit buses for the ride to the excavation site.

Seventy minutes into a slow, bumpy trip, they halted at the large canvas tent that was home to the dig crew. After introductions to the students and advisors, the next two-and-a-half hours were spent filming, interviewing, and developing the background material on the activities that led to the unique discovery. In the camp and on the hillside, cameras and photographers recorded the ceaseless movement of the dinosaur bones for posterity. A movie crew was hard at work filming the activity for a documentary special.

A single-engine, Vietnam-era Huey helicopter sat nearby. Its pilot and observer were cooling themselves in front of a bank of rotating fans in the main tent, waiting for the imported visitors to depart.

They'd been contracted by the university to shuttle the heavy bones, now encased in dried plaster, to a pickup area near the Vernal City fire station. It would take two days to complete the delicate air transfers. And it would be midway through the morning of the second day before the T-Rex's pelvis would be ready for loading under the helicopter.

Tori Evans combed out her long ponytail while sitting on a folding chair in the tent. Her mentor sat nearby, making notes on a clipboard. She admired his accomplishments.

"I never bothered to ask, but how long do you think it will take to do the initial cleanup, given her enormous size?" she inquired.

Dalton Jordan thought about it for a minute, pushed back his hat, and looked up at Tori.

"You and four other doctoral students will be spending the balance of the last semester erasing millions of years from the Rex's skeleton. Dr. Hamilton's grad students will be assisting you. You'll have ample time to finish your thesis, and from the looks of it, you shouldn't have any problem before the committee when you're ready for your Ph.D. interview." He wiped the sweat from his brow.

"I have a permanent field researcher position coming up in the department next year when Shenae Sousa takes her new position at North Dakota State. Are you interested?"

"Are you kidding? You bet I'm interested."

Jordan was happy to hear it. Not only was Tori an exceptionally dedicated paleontologist, but Dalton had to admit as he looked at her, she was a nice addendum in a male-dominated working environment.

"Good. Get that Ph.D. and the position is yours. Now, shall we get back to business? . . . Pass me the strap and let's walk back up the hill and hook her into the harness."

A few minutes later, the helicopter hovered over the last major bone as Jordan secured the cable to the sling. The Huey slowly rose, circled the camp once, and finally headed south toward Vernal, clearing a nearby rise by less than fifty feet.

A first-year student walked up the pathway to where Dr. Jordan and Tori were sitting.

"We're ready to start breaking down the camp, sir. It'll take a few hours. Is there anything you want done before we begin?"

"No, I think the rest of the site cleanup is pretty much finished. Leave the tent up until last so we have some shade from the sun. It must be in the high 90s."

"Actually, it's one-hundred-three, but hot is hot," the twenty-one year old said as he wiped his sweaty forehead with a rag.

Tori sat down in the dust and wiped the sweat from her neck. She pushed back the mass of blonde hair and repositioned her tan pith helmet. With a gloved hand, she swept away the pebbles from under her to smooth out the flat spot she was sitting on. Jordan let out a sigh and sat next to her with a big yawn. He hadn't had much sleep in the last two days.

"It occurs to me that this may be the biggest find of a career that hasn't really begun yet," Tori said.

"The way to look at it is that this is the best opportunity to start a long, successful career. You're a famous paleontologist now. Without question, it's the nicest way to develop a professional reputation. Things will go well for you when your credibility precedes you." Jordan took a drink from his canteen, tipped his cowboy hat back, and continued. "You've begun to pay your dues to the business in a big way. It won't be as uphill for you as for some of the others here. You should thank that kid who blurted out 'Tori the T-Rex.' It'll make you famous. Your name will be synonymous with good field research and hard work," he said.

"I know you're right, but I'd still like to part his hair with a heavy two-by-four."

Jordan laughed and pulled out a small rag from his pocket. He soaked up the sweat rolling down the sides of his face. "Shall we go?"

He stood up and reached back for Tori's hand to help her up. As she got to her feet, a small notebook fell out of her back pocket. Leaning over to retrieve it, she noticed that the rock she'd been sitting on was different from the others around it. Staring for a moment, it finally registered that it was a gray-black porous material, not at all like the dusty, brown colored rocks surrounding it.

"Hang on a second. There's something odd about this piece of ground." Tori pulled a small paint brush out of her shirt pocket and brushed away the collected dust and sand. More dark-gray lump emerged.

"What is it?" Jordan asked.

"Looks like a nonindigenous rock."

Tori carefully brushed it for a few more seconds. "It's a hunk of metal, ferrous iron, if I'm correct. It's certainly not native to this desert landscape." She continued brushing away at the edges of the rock, revealing more of it as she went.

Jordan pulled up his socks, sunk to his knees with a small whisk brush, and began clearing away dirt. Ten minutes later they had the rock pretty much free from the surrounding earth. They sat back in curiosity and stared.

"It's a meteorite," she said.

"Two great discoveries in one place. That's terrific, I should take you to Vegas," Jordan said.

"I wonder how much it weighs. How long has it been here? Where did it come from, and . . ."

"Whoa there, girl . . . Let's get it out of the ground first and tote it down to the tent. The geologist hounds at the university rock shop will appreciate it."

Ten minutes slipped by. They walked back up the path with a canvas sack and a six-foot-long pole. Announcement of a second discovery brought two cameramen and several students. The meteorite was the last item off the hill. Sixty five million years of dormant rest would soon change.

The granddaddy of all grim reapers was back.

Above Seattle, Washington
Monday, 0758 hours Pacific Time

Breaking out of high, thin clouds, the view off to the right side of the plane was magnificent. "It's a deep emerald-green, like Ireland. Looks like an outdoorsmen's paradise. I can even see Mount Rainier," Casse said.

Lakes stained with a light-aqua color dotted the ground, and a crystalline-blue sky opened the way to a rare, sunny, Pacific Northwest day.

"Ladies and gentlemen, this is your captain speaking. We will be landing in Seattle in about eight minutes. The temperature is eighty-one degrees. The wind is out of the northwest at about three miles an hour. Looks like a pretty nice day. On behalf of the entire flight crew, I want to thank you for flying with us."

Dale leaned past his partner, Sullivan Casse, and looked out the window.

"The King County detective will be waiting for us at the gate. He told me on the phone that not everything on this investigation is in the reports. I'm eager to see what else he has," Dale said. "Turns out his twin sister is an agent of ours in Charlotte, North Carolina."

"So he's Fed-friendly?" Sullivan asked.

"The best we can hope for is open-minded. He's the lead homicide investigator on an associated case Perry was working on. My sixth sense tells me that Perry's murder stretches well beyond the initial homicide report. I think we should assume for the moment that there's more going on then the record indicates. Either way, we'll know soon enough. He's driving us to the hotel out on the wharf."

"What about 'No-Knock'?" Sullivan asked.

Anthony "No-Knock" Petrocelli was the Seattle FBI ASAC.

"The Seattle ASAC will meet us after we check in at the hotel. He's coming over with the files."

"Does he know about the detective yet?"

"I haven't mentioned it to him. It's our investigation. Probably best to keep it low profile for now. We don't know who the players are yet, or for that matter, who may be motivated by political gain. Besides, our flying squad approach is going to aggravate some people. By the way, that was a fast trip you made from Florida to San Jose. Sorry I couldn't give you more details on the phone beforehand, but we'll have about ninety minutes to play catch-up at the hotel before No-Knock shows."

Sullivan looked out the window again as the plane descended.

Sullivan Casse was a native of Traverse City, Michigan. His mother was a dentist and his father the branch manager of the largest banking outlet in town. He was the oldest of three kids, all boys.

Sullivan had a wicked sense of humor that got him into as much trouble as it got him out of. As a thin, wiry, happy-go-lucky kid, he frequently found himself beset by school bullies who were the victims of his rapid-fire, caustic rebuttal to their taunts. He lost more fights than he won, but he always managed to get a piece of whoever was throwing punches at him.

In the summer, he enjoyed kayaking the river through downtown Traverse City and out to the Lake Michigan bay with friends. In the winter, he skied and hunted. His pastimes included any contact sport or activity that found girls wearing bikinis on the beach.

Sullivan's favorite hangout was the Cherry Pit, a restaurant a few miles away, where guys with hot cars and even hotter girlfriends could be found. He figured that you never knew where your luck with girls might manifest itself. Besides that, he liked the muscle cars almost as much as the girls.

One late summer night while returning from the Cherry Pit, a buddy dropped Sullivan off near the state mental hospital on the outskirts of town. He had to hike about three quarters of a mile through the thick woods to emerge into his own neighborhood on the other side. It was that or a long walk around.

Halfway across the dark, wooded area lit only by a partial moon, he noticed a flashing red light reflecting off the trees. Following it, he came upon a police car on a narrow, overgrown path. There on the ground was a man in uniform. Sullivan looked around quickly and stepped cautiously forward. The man was a police officer.

Somewhere between instinct and exposure to TV cop shows, Sullivan figured out the right thing to do to deal with the shock of encountering a downed police officer. He reached in for the radio to call for help, but found the microphone ripped from its mount. The officer had clearly been surprised and attacked by someone.

Sullivan, all of sixteen years of age and one hundred forty pounds sopping wet, managed to pull the much bigger, unconscious officer into the back seat of the patrol car. Jumping behind the wheel, he turned the car around and quickly drove straight to the hospital emergency room a few miles away. He ran inside and yelled for help.

The next day, the Traverse City newspaper, along with local radio and TV, heralded him as a hero for saving the police officer's life. The mayor and other important city notables made sure he was recognized and rewarded for his quick thinking. He got a new car from a local dealership, a full college scholarship to Michigan State, and an introduction to the local ROTC. Through it all, he discovered that the feeling of having saved a life was its own reward. His path was set.

The wheels of the jet squealed as they finally kissed the runway. Fifteen minutes later, Dale and Sullivan grabbed their luggage from the baggage turnstile. The two FBI agents and the Seattle detective headed for a side door in the terminal. An unmarked sheriff's sedan was sitting just outside.

"I understand you're a former deputy," Detective Rod O'Brien said. Dale let the question hang in the air for a moment before answering.

"I spent a year and a half in the jail and ten on the street. I worked patrol, accident reconstruction, and held a SWAT team slot while I was there."

"You got a law degree in your spare time, too, I hear."

"A little variety goes a long way," Dale said.

"I heard you salvaged one of their guys in a courtroom shootout," the detective commented, referring to an FBI supervisor Dale saved.

"After an unfortunate incident in one of our Superior Courts, I was invited to join the FBI. How about you? How did you come to be in the dick bureau?" Dale asked.

The forty-eight year old detective took a minute to offer his own background. He was a solid investigator with an impressive history and a few high-profile homicide cases under his belt. Dale and Sullivan were sufficiently satisfied that the man was capable.

"I have a little less than three years to retirement. Oddly enough, I have a standing offer from the head of Shyreve Investigations for an interview as soon as my retirement papers go in. Shyreve is the private investigative firm whose ranks are filled by retired federal guys and some local detectives. Their reputation is impeccable. You already know that Perry was working for them when he was murdered." O'Brien scanned the traffic, looking for an opening to pull out.

"About two weeks ago, another Shyreve investigator was killed while on a lone stakeout. He was retired DEA. He was sitting in his car, parked between two banks in an alleyway, around one in the morning. He was there to meet someone regarding a robbery yet to occur. The notes in his file say simply that someone was planning an unconventional bank robbery."

"Unconventional, what's that mean?"

Sullivan made a note on his PDA and let Dale do the talking.

"Something other than the average, over-the-counter, gun wielding photo op. We gave it some thought and looked over his prior bank robbery notes with the FBI. If he meant embezzlement, he would have used those words. So this use of 'robbery' meant just that, but how and what kind we just don't know. We have a couple of banks here locally that keep substantial funds on tap, and a few with oversized, climate-controlled, velvet-lined vault drawers. The only thing we could come up with is that someone wants to pick off irreplaceable artwork, bullion, or something along those lines. The question is, what kind of robbery is it if it's not embezzlement or a stickup?"

Sullivan tapped away furiously with his personal shorthand, trying to keep up.

"He took a single .22 to the left side of the head, through the ear canal, while he was sitting in the car. The driver's side window was all the way down. The lead bullet fragmented and we never found a shell casing. No fibers, no fingerprints, no witnesses, no usable physical evidence. By the time the first patrol unit happened upon the scene, it was wet. Rained about fifteen minutes after the shooting based on the coroner's investigation. The hit was up close and personal. He had powder stains and burn marks in his hair and at the entry wound. Best guess from the angle was that the shooter was about six-foot-one and slightly behind him. It's a wide-open case. So far, we've exhausted all the leads that have come over the horizon, but we're still hoping for a break to pick up the chase," the detective said.

"What about his case file and activity log?" Dale asked.

"Dry hole."

Provo Canyon
Orem, Utah
Monday, 0822 hours Mountain Time

The tractor-trailer rig with the T-Rex bones exited Provo Canyon followed by the air-conditioned bus with the crew from the dig site. Another five miles and they'd be at the lab on the campus of BYU. The legacy of Tori the T-Rex was just beginning.

After a long anticipated hot shower and a decent lunch, they would reassemble and begin the task of offloading the ancient animal artifacts. Several athlete-students from the adjacent rugby field offered to help lift the heavier bones onto lab transport carts. Reporters showed up at the facility parking lot to watch the event. The media feeding frenzy was on again.

Around 3:40 p.m., the final set of bones rolled through the side door of the building to the last open space on the long, white work counter. The final item to be unloaded was the unusual rock.

"The geologists are no doubt eager to explore their new gift," Tori said. "Please place it carefully on the tabletop. We don't want the old chunk of rock to break up sixty five million years after it entered the atmosphere."

Tori's humor was lost on the two muscle-bound rugby players. They smiled politely at the slightly nerdy but gorgeous woman.

At half past four, the last two people left in the building were a Ph.D. candidate paleontologist and a third-year student. The Ph.D. student walked passed the meteorite on his way to the soft drink machine at the end of the room. He reached for some change from his pants pocket and pushed a button that dispensed a bottle of cold water from the machine. He turned and placed it on the end of the counter behind him, next to the forty-pound, deep space specimen.

Sitting down on the stool in front of the rock, his curiosity peaked. He pulled back the canvas cover from the pitted and pockmarked geode, casually looking over the hunk of iron ore. He wondered what sights the object had seen in the millions of years and miles it spent traversing the galaxy.

Scanning it slowly, he looked for metallurgical abnormalities and irregularities. Like all dinosaur hunters, he had a basic understanding of geological formations. He slowly reached out for his water bottle and took a healthy swig. Preoccupied, he absentmindedly placed it back on the table. As he leaned forward, he tipped it over, inadvertently splashing the rock. Jumping up from the stool, he surveyed the spill and righted the plastic bottle. A paper towel dispenser was in the restroom, so he walked off to retrieve some to sop up the mess.

In the dark crevices of the ancient asteroid, dormant ingredients absorbed the moisture and began blossoming with activity. A cascade of the deadly, extraterrestrial compounds joined within the droplets and slowly leached out to adjacent areas of the spilled water that occupied the surface of the rock. By the time the student returned, the base components of the long dormant enzyme were reacquiring the building blocks of life.

He proceeded to wipe down the counter top. Then, running his fingers over the irregular surface of the rock, he tried to erase any evidence of the accidental spill. As he did, the prehistoric virus clung to his dry fingers and was absorbed into the pores of his skin.

"It's nice and smooth from the heated re-entry millions of years ago," he said to the third-year student.

Now it was the third-year student who examined the rock more closely. He, too, ran his hands over it for a few seconds.

Soon, both young men would replicate the enzyme a million times over. They would become the breeding ground for a flash disease of horrible proportion. Unsuspectingly, they would pass it on to others with whom they came in physical contact.

At long last, the virus, far more deadly than any African Ebola, made contact with a new Alpha host. Its last victim was a sixty five million year old, fossilized Tyrannosaurus Rex . . . a denizen who'd died an agonizingly slow death.

The parasitic, autotrophing phagocyte had found a new home.

Fisherman's wharf
Seattle, Washington
Monday, 0911 hours Pacific Time

"Here's my card. I'll see you tomorrow," Detective O'Brien said with an outstretched hand.

Sullivan turned and looked at the revolving glass door to the hotel entrance. Pacing himself, he timed his entrance to pull the rolling suitcase in behind him. Dale shook his head in amusement and walked to the electric sliding door, trotting on through to the lobby. They reached the front check-in desk at the same time.

Less than an hour later, there was a knock at Dale's door.

"Hey, Sullivan, Tony's here," he hollered through the open, adjoining hotel room door.

The FBI ASAC walked into Dale's suite and introduced himself. Dale had talked to him several times over the phone from San Jose. After popping the tops off a couple of soft drinks, they settled down to business.

"Nice room. I didn't know the agency paid for upgrades."

Dale looked him in the eye. "They don't. It's on my credit card. Might as well have a good view of the bay rather then some faded-out building wall facing my hotel window. So what do we know about what happened to Perry?" he asked, changing the subject.

"Perry was a very good agent. Extremely thorough, didn't miss many details. He had a high conviction rate. I'd really like to know what he was doing in his last minutes. He took two 9mm slugs to the left temple and died almost instantly, according to the coroner. He was working a carryover case that started in our office. His former partner didn't have a good rapport with the man who came to us at the start of the investigation, so we contracted it to Perry at Shyreve. We were in the loop on a regular basis with report updates. The man who started all of this is a maintenance engineer out on Nord Island."

Dale glanced at Sullivan and frowned.

"We still aren't sure what it's all about. Perry was just beginning to connect the dots. The engineer was scared. Now we can't find Perry's notes and the engineer is missing. We contacted Nord authorities, but they don't have anything on the engineer, other than he disappeared." A sour look crossed No-Knock's face. "No one seems to know what was going on, except Perry."

"How far away is Nord?" Sullivan asked.

"It's about four hundred miles due west of this window. Do you know the story on the island?" the ASAC asked.

"Yeah, I'm up to speed on it. Fascinating what a few billion dollars can do for you."

"Isn't it, though. Here's a copy of the file," he said, opening his brief-case. "I'll have an agent pick you up at 7:00 a.m. and bring you over to the office. I have a room and a terminal set up for your use. We'll get you a car from the motor pool in the morning. The vehicles have plug-in GPS units. I assume you'll be going over the reports the rest of the day?"

"That's the idea," Dale said. "We're going to have to play catch-up, and quickly. Anybody else at the agency read into this case?"

"No, it's practically virgin territory. Start from scratch, and then let's talk about a game plan. The coroner will meet you at 10:15 to review the autopsy report. You both have encrypted cell phones for your laptops. Remember, traffic here can be miserable."

The sour look appeared again.

"Just one final question, if you don't mind. Out of curiosity, why are two counterterrorism guys working on a local homicide? Why the flying squad approach? The J. Edgar Hoover operations people have been unusually silent to our inquiries . . . they won't fill in any blanks."

Dale stared at Sullivan a second, as if to say "I told you so."

"It's a CTU case. This particular item is also of interest to other agencies. Since Nord Island is essentially a foreign nation, the State Department is a little sensitive. Headquarters and Homeland Security have decided to let us lead. I knew Perry from the counterterrorism school at Quantico, and some field work," Dale said. "I understood the man and his methods."

No-Knock looked pensively at the two agents. "Some of the senior guys don't like the idea of reconstituting the old 'Flying Squad' operations. They see it as insulting to their capabilities. Just be aware that there's an undercurrent in the office among a few people."

"These guys wouldn't be the same folks who refer to the J. Edgar Hoover building as 'hindquarters,' would they?" Sullivan said over his shoulder as he made a note on a pad of paper.

"One in the same, I'm afraid."

"Good, I like rabble rousers. Are you one of them?" he inquired, turning to look No-Knock in the eye.

"You've got my full cooperation," No-Knock replied, not offering any indication as to his personal opinion.

"What did headquarters say in the e-mail they sent out?" Dale asked.

"They were very specific . . . It's your show."

"You gotta love electronic manure," Dale replied with relish. "Tony, we'll be happy to push the credit in your direction. We want to keep a very low profile. You can do the TV interviews, if it gets that far."

"Fair enough, I appreciate it. I'll see you guys in the morning. Let me know if there's anything else you need." Anthony "No-Knock" Petrocelli pulled the door closed behind him and walked on down the hall.

Sullivan looked at Dale. "His butt's in a sling. He gave up control of the case and now the lead investigator's dead. He definitely needs our help to get the stink off his finely tailored suit."

"Yup, that was the sound of a stalled career. We just made our first politically motivated contact. He's gonna need all the good PR he can muster to get it moving again. What did you think of him and his rapport building skills?" Dale asked.

"He wasn't all that eager to open up about his impressions was he? Talking to him was akin to reading a sanitized case report," Sullivan answered.

10

Fox and Casse's hotel room
Seattle, Washington
Monday, 1410 hours Pacific Time

Dale and Sullivan ordered room service for a late lunch. The reports, notes, call logs, and timesheets from the FBI's side of the investigation were not proving terribly helpful. The table and bed were strewn with documents and photocopies of documents from various financial institutions, credit card companies, and other organizations.

The afternoon passed, it was pushing 5:00 p.m. The private hotel room balcony overlooked the expansive bay. Dale gazed up from his report binder and waved back to a couple passing by in a large cabin cruiser. The sun was blazing away in the cloudless sky to the southwest.

The large, log-paneled, fourth floor room, with a fireplace along the wall, had an outdoor comfort to it. Dale could afford the small luxury since his family was independently wealthy.

His parents' Montana cattle ranch employed well over a hundred people. He, along with his brother and sister, owned the bulk of the stock in the operation. It paid handsome quarterly dividends. And their share continued to grow with each passing year.

Rather than occupy a modest, per-diem hotel room downtown, he and Sullivan decided to splurge a bit. It wasn't the first time in his FBI career that he'd used his station in life to up the quality of accommodations on an assignment. It wouldn't be the last. The scenery was worth every penny.

From the Edgewater Inn, you could see the Cascade mountain range and Bainbridge Island several miles across the water. The Port of Seattle was off to the left, about a mile and a half away. The commercial shipping area crawled with orange colored cranes, tall derricks, and numerous rigging operations. Several long container ships plowed slowly through the water in the distance, heading for the port facility. A big cruise ship was docked a few piers off to the north.

Large ferries, pleasure craft, and tour boats plied the waters back and forth. Just below the balcony, a small sailboat with two beautiful, scantily clad women in their mid-twenties came drifting slowly by on the calm water. They smiled and waved up at Dale, purposely bending forward to show ample cleavage to the handsome man on the fourth floor. Dale noted that their assets were surrounded by sun-bleached blonde hair.

"Very impressive," Sullivan blurted out from behind Dale, "We could commandeer a power boat, give chase, and detain them for questioning."

"I didn't see any elements of criminal activity that we could detain them for," Dale retorted.

"Are you kidding, it was in plain view. I don't think those things were legal, they're way over the limit for catch and release," he said, fixated on the boat's occupants.

Dale looked down at the boat again. "They could be original equipment, in which case seizure would be illegal."

"I'm willing to risk it," Sullivan said with a smile, his eyes still glued to the boat. He watched as it drifted off. A minute passed in silence. He could barely see the two blondes now. "I'm thinking of torturing myself by having lunch at Hooter's for the next week."

Dale sighed audibly. "Yeah, I'm bored, too. Aside from them, it's been, what's the word I'm looking for . . . sluggish." They both watched as the two women sailed out of sight past the hotel's restaurant dock. Dale reached around and plugged his laptop into the T-1 dedicated phone line at the desk.

A knock at the door interrupted them. "Room service."

Sullivan let in the hotel staffer from the kitchen and had the food set on the table, just inside the sliding glass door to the outside patio. He signed the check, closed the door again, and walked back to the balcony.

Outside, several hundred feet above the hotel, an orange and white Coast Guard helicopter roared noisily by. A half mile away, the city fireboat, *Chief Seattle*, raced off in the same direction.

Dale turned to Sullivan, "We need to reconstruct Perry's last forty-eight hours and see if we can turn up some anomaly that hasn't seen light yet."

"Any thoughts in particular?" Sullivan asked.

"Let's divide this stuff up and pour over every line in the reports. There has to be something that hasn't jumped out at us yet. I just have a feeling there's a clue staring at us that we haven't picked up on. Perry was pretty diligent. It's in here somewhere. We just have to find it. I'll take the cell phone printout and start running down the call list. Why don't you take the credit card receipts and log book," Dale suggested.

"Do you have the computerized Shyreve activity log he was keeping?"

"Let's see . . . I think this folder has it." Dale handed Sullivan the yellow file.

Sullivan rummaged through a stack of papers. Over the next forty-five minutes, they silently immersed themselves while periodically consuming fruit off the platter on the table behind them.

Both men stopped at intervals to make notes and watch the occasional seagull float by on the warm breeze.

"This is interesting. I wonder why no one mentioned it," Dale said.

"What have you got?"

Dale underlined a call, "Perry's cell phone shows an incoming missed call from an international phone number. It's the Nord Island area code. It was last Saturday at 7:22 a.m. The local cell tower is located at the Space Needle. I have a supplemental report that a man was kidnapped within minutes from the same location. Seattle PD and the King County Sheriff ended up chasing the suspect car up I-5. It looks like the King County Sheriff's pilot was pretty hot about losing the chase to a U.S. military chopper. Says here that the military made off with the kidnappers and the victim. The Black Hawk chopper disappeared. The FAA says they don't have anything on their radar showing where the copter went. The military and other government agencies with Black Hawk choppers say it isn't one of their birds, according to the report."

Sullivan scratched his nose and looked over the bill. "Really, I haven't seen anything on the evening news about that. You'd think something like that would be all over the place."

"According to the news reports, the cops arrested and OR'd a suspect for failure to yield on a traffic stop. Not much of a cover story, if you ask me," Dale said suspiciously.

"Kinda makes you wonder, doesn't it," Sullivan replied, equally disbelieving.

Dale leaned back in his chair, thinking out loud, "Okay, so we have a call to a dead man's cell phone, a possible kidnapping from the same place the call originates, a helo no one can account for, local cops who don't know what's really going on, and all of Perry's personal notes are missing, along with an engineer from Nord Island. Hmmm . . . We need to find that King County S.O. pilot and have a chat with him after we see the coroner. We probably oughta talk to the on-duty FAA radar supervisor as well. This stuff feels like information from the twilight zone . . ." Dale stood silent in thought for a moment. "Let's keep digging."

The two men sat for several minutes contemplating the information. Outside, the cruise ship inched away from the dock, lights blazing, people on deck reveling. After the side bow thrusters moved her off, the ship slowly headed toward the main channel.

Sullivan walked out to the balcony and bit into an apple while he watched her slip out, dwarfing the private yachts on the water that were now drifting out of her way.

Dale stood next to Sullivan at the balcony railing. "Maybe we should divvy up the chores tomorrow and then compare notes. I'll call No-Knock in the morning and see if we can get a second car. What I don't want is another field agent looking over our shoulders as we work. Why don't you take the FAA center and run down the radar tapes. I'll set up the interview with the pilot and we can meet for lunch."

"Okay, "Sullivan said. "I'll talk to the secretary in the office in the morning and see what she can pull together on Nord Island."

"Hmmm . . . I think a call to Betty might be in order. She may be able to scrape something together from other sources," Dale thought out loud. Sullivan walked downstairs for a quick snack.

Betty Jo Case had a U.S. government secret clearance from two years earlier. She had been instrumental as the top negotiator for a private firm that made aircraft radar components, ensuring that "certain" technical personnel were kept out of the support package when the highly lucrative contract was signed. She was effectively working for the U.S. Ambassador in the host country seeking the contract. Dale had tapped her unique background on several occasions.

After watching the 9:00 o'clock news, Dale stepped out on the balcony again for fresh air. He ran his hand along the smooth, stainless steel railing while watching several lit up yachts cruise by.

Sullivan looked in on Dale to confirm their schedules for the morning.

"Anything good on the news?" he asked.

Dale turned as Sullivan entered the room, "The most accurate thing on the news these days is the weather forecast."

Sullivan concurred with a humorous grunt.

Straight out of college, Sullivan Casse had begun his working career as an insurance agent with a financial background. Within three years, he was making good money but was bored. He joined the Army, became a second lieutenant, and gravitated to the intelligence field and on to the FBI.

His passion was motorcycles - street, touring, dirt bike, it didn't matter, as long as it ran on two wheels. Like his partner, Dale, he had earned a fixed wing, private pilot's license.

In the last seven years, Sullivan had been engaged to three different women. They saw him as a decent guy flawed by commitment issues. He simply decided that they didn't quite measure up over time.

"I've been thinking that we might want to call our friend in security at the State Department and see if he knows something about that island that the computers don't," Dale said. "Oh, and there's one other place we should stop by. We should visit the submarine base out at the Point, talk to someone about the surface and subsurface tidal action, and currents in the straights. Maybe we can back track Perry's path in the water."

"Isn't the King County detective running that down?" Sullivan asked.

"Yeah, from another source . . . it may be helpful to have a second opinion to see how close two independent sources can come. We might get a better starting point. Besides that, this isn't the only case O'Brien is working and we need to move faster. I don't want him slowing us down."

"Sounds good," Sullivan said as he walked off the balcony. "Now that

that's out of the way, I'm gonna turn off the TV and hit the sack. See you in the morning."

Dale closed the sliding glass door to the balcony and pulled the curtains together. A jumble of pieces kept floating around in his mind as he lay in bed. After twenty minutes of restlessness, he hit on a thought: Does someone on Nord Island have a Black Hawk *helicopter*?

11

The doctoral candidate from the museum lab couldn't describe the symptoms beyond the feeling that he was starting to come down with the flu. As the day progressed, his muscles cramped and a mild nausea and achiness crept into his body. By late afternoon, he was suffering from a general malaise and loss of energy. He left the museum early and stopped by the local pharmacy to pick up some aspirin and honey flavored throat lozenges.

His sweaty hands left the live virus on the pharmacy counter. He headed back to his apartment, and bed. He was miserable.

At the end of the day, his girlfriend stopped by to check on him and find out how he was feeling. After seeing his condition, she decided to stay and watch over him. Along the way, she managed to kiss his warm forehead and cheek in nurturing sympathy with his pains.

Another victim was immediately born.

The deadly virus was hard at work consuming the man's basic cell structure from the inside out. His immune system was the first thing to go. Blood platelets and amino acids were dissolved. Mucous membranes and cartilage were being destroyed at the molecular level.

Slowly his vision blurred. He chalked it up to the headache that had come on in the past half hour.

His joints ached when he moved them. His toes were tingling as if pricked by a pin. His back muscles around his kidneys hurt like someone had punched him hard.

Replication of the virus was in full-blown overdrive. His was a weariness from which there would be no hope of recovery. By sundown, irreversible physical damage would be well on its way, and new victims were already doing their part to turn the enzyme into a major epidemic.

Before the dawn, his ability to swallow would be severely impaired. The water he drank with medicine would find its way into his lungs instead of his stomach. Pneumonia would quickly set in.

Three miles away in a studio apartment, the third-year student was experiencing the same symptoms. He, however, lived alone. His dead body wouldn't be discovered for several days.

Inside Dale's car on Columbia Street
Seattle, Washington
Tuesday, 1008 hours Pacific Time

The phone vibrated and the sound of "La Bamba" toned over the small cell phone speaker. "Fox."

"Dale, I'm done with the FAA. We have a hit on a tape. It's somewhat intermittent, but solid on what we can see. What about that pilot, any news?"

"I've got him set up to interview at 1345 hours at his operations building." Dale passed the address to Sullivan and continued, "What did you find out at your end?"

"An inbound Alaskan National Guard AWACS heading for Boeing Field painted a spotty return for about thirty seconds, a hundred miles north of Seattle. The airport at Victoria also picked up a weak return on three sweeps of their radar dish. Both radar units pinpointed the location right at the coastline." Sullivan flipped through his notepad.

"They have a hit and miss along one remote transmitter site on the coast. Initially, they wrote it off as a weather cell disturbance. I checked the local Doppler with a U.S. Weather Service meteorologist after I left. He indicates that there was no weather cell present in that area during the time frame in question. Could be something, might be nothing. When I asked the Coast Guard office if a big helicopter could hide in the wave top clutter over the water, they said it wasn't possible. The seas were calm and flat at the time. They have sophisticated coastal coverage that would make even the smallest aircraft stand out like a pregnant woman in a convent."

"Not quite conclusive, is it," Dale said.

"Yeah. How'd you make out with the coroner?" Sullivan asked.

"Perry was dead before he went into the bay, no salt water in his lungs. The coroner did a salinity test on Perry's tissue to try and figure out a possible lividity factor. The time of death looks to be around midnight last Wednesday. Oh, one other thing. Perry had traces of paraffin on his right hand and wrist."

"He fired a gun."

"Looks like it."

"I wonder if he hit someone. How much paraffin?"

"Coroner says it's impossible to tell, given the corrosive properties of the salt water. But he felt comfortable saying it was more than one round. Time enough to recognize a threat and respond to it," Dale replied.

"Yeah, however, we don't have any other bodies floating in the bay. But now that we have the time of death pretty well pegged, I'm eager to get that info on the tides."

"The local coroner is also an officer in the Coast Guard Reserve. I called the guy and gave him the information we already have. He's going to work on it. He thinks that the tidal action, surface winds, and currents won't be too tough to sift through with his software program. He phoned an oceanographer buddy of his at the Anacortes C.G. Station. As soon as we're done with the chopper pilot, let's head over there and see him."

"Let's hope he can help us pinpoint Perry's last known location."

At 3:30 p.m., the Coast Guard station at Anacortes came into view through the windshield of the FBI sedan. Sullivan had left his car behind at the hotel and drove out with Dale. An hour later, they had what they'd come for.

Dale looked at Sullivan at the first stoplight they came to. "Okay, so we know he was out in a small cluster of islands, probably on the leeward side.

Let's go down to the port ferry terminal in the morning and start looking over their security tapes. We might get lucky and spot him in the crowd boarding an inter-island boat. His yellow and green parka should make him easy to identify from the surveillance cameras."

The two men headed back to Seattle and their bayside hotel. The flashing phone light in his room alerted Dale to a message. He walked down to the desk clerk and introduced himself. Back in his room, he knocked on the adjacent door. Sullivan opened it. Dale ripped into a manila envelope. He slid out a stapled set of handwritten notes on the desk.

"Our King County detective came through for us. It's the balance of info on Perry's activities," he said.

"Why don't you start reading. I'll go down to the restaurant and make us a reservation," Sullivan suggested. " . . . Be back in ten minutes."

Fifteen minutes passed when Dale noticed an oddity and brought it to Sullivan's attention.

"The coroner's report stated Perry's time of death was about midnight last Wednesday," Dale said.

"Yeah, why?"

"Perry's bank sent over the printout on his debit card. It ends on the Monday prior to his death."

"Call them back on the twenty-four hour line and see if you can find out why."

Dale already had the phone in hand before Sullivan finished his sentence. He was connected to the evening manager at the bank processing center a few moments later. Shortly after he hung up, the fax on the encoded laptop computer received a single page from the debit card center.

"It looks like they originally sent us the 'end of period' printout rather than the whole activity report." Dale reviewed the page from the point where the previous statement ended.

"Hey, looks like the detective gods are smiling on us. You got O'Brien's pager number?"

Sullivan fished it out of his shirt pocket and started dialing. "What do we need?"

"We gotta get out to Friday Island. See if he can rustle us up a boat or maybe the chopper."

Thirty minutes later, the King County Sheriff's patrol boat pulled up to the hotel's restaurant dock.

The two FBI agents were now in pit bull mode.

Friday Island had a small harbor. The businesses in the immediate vicinity might have seen something useful. Perry had been there for certain; dinner for three was on his debit card.

The boat roared away from the restaurant dock on its twin engines, the sound echoing off the surrounding buildings.

Student housing apartment on BYU campus
Provo, Utah
Tuesday, 1544 hours Mountain Time

The twenty-four year old doctoral candidate crawled painfully from his bed and trudged to the bathroom. His girlfriend was asleep on the couch with a movie still running on the DVD player. He bounced off the doorway, injuring his shoulder, yet the muscle cramping in his stomach overshadowed the pain. He was bent over so far he appeared to be bowing from the waist.

He went straight to the white porcelain toilet and wretched his guts. It was difficult to catch a breath between convulsions; he was physically drained. His face was a splotchy red color and his cheeks appeared sunken. Opening his eyes a minute later, in between involuntary spasms, he was able to make out blood in the water bowl. He leaned in further in an attempt to identify the source, not comprehending what little his vision could recognize.

Panic-stricken, he called out weakly to his girlfriend for help. Startled awake, she rushed into the bathroom to be by his side. He couldn't see the horrified look on her face because his eyesight was too blurred. The ceramic commode held a substantial amount of blood. But more telling were the mucous membrane particles and tissue floating on the top of the water. Something was terribly wrong.

She ran out of the room for the phone in the kitchen. Four minutes later, a Provo city ambulance rolled up to the apartment complex address. When the two paramedics knocked on the apartment door, a female voice screamed from inside. They pushed the door open and stuck their heads in.

From the doorway, they could see an unconscious man sprawled across the floor tiles of his bathroom. A pool of blood surrounded his head. The woman standing over him was yelling incomprehensibly. The paramedics thought they were looking at a fresh homicide. They backed out and called the police on their hand-held radio.

Less than a minute passed and a black and white Provo police car, with its snow capped mountain logo on the side door, pulled up. It was followed seconds later by two others. The police officers entered the apartment with guns drawn. The woman inside was kneeling over her unresponsive boyfriend, oblivious to the men coming at her.

Not long thereafter, the ambulance with the body that barely registered signs of life slipped out of the apartment parking lot to the hospital trauma center a few miles away.

Emergency room physicians began flowing one hundred percent oxygen and drew blood for a lab analysis. The high saturation oxygen momentarily stabilized the patient's condition. Meanwhile, the lab on the second floor was told to rush the blood tests.

Both the red and white blood cell counts were dramatically off. His lipid count was a long way from normal. All of the test results indicated the patient was gravely ill.

The physicians were facing a daunting problem. They observed symptoms that fit several serious illnesses but had no clear catalyst to work from. By trial and error, they began a regimen of pharmacology. The physician's creed of "first do no harm" became a difficult slogan to adhere to.

Around 8:30 p.m. a local police detective stopped by the hospital to follow up on the patient's condition. What he encountered was a medical staff trying to interview him instead for information that might help them treat their patient.

The detective began with a staff nurse who'd helped when the patient was first admitted.

"What can you tell me about how he became ill?" he asked.

"Nothing yet . . . I guess we're both trying to find out what happened. At first, we ran a 'tox' screen because we thought he'd been poisoned. But that doesn't look like the source of the problem."

The detective cleared his throat, "I'm going to need to talk to the attending physician to see what he knows about the cause of the man's condition. We're holding his girlfriend on suspicion of aggravated assault. Who should I speak to?"

"Dr. Miller is on the phone with the lab right now. I'll tell him you're waiting." She turned and hurried away.

Fifteen minutes passed. A tall, older gentleman wearing wire-rimmed glasses, a white coat, and a stethoscope wrapped around his neck approached the detective.

"I'm Dr. Miller. I understand you want to talk to me about the college student we admitted."

"Yeah ... thanks. I see you're having a busy night. I'm PJ Turner. I'm the detective working the case. I came down here to get some information on his condition. Was he poisoned?"

"We're still running tests. The lab he works in at the university has formaldehyde, silver iodine, and some kind of acidic etching chemical. But so far, the problems we're seeing don't coincide with the initial toxicology screening."

The detective made a note in his PDA and continued, "So the chemicals you mentioned aren't the source of his medical problem. Any idea what is?"

"Not yet. Right now we have no idea what induced his medical condition, and we're at a loss on an effective treatment. His situation is not improving. Our lab has a highly qualified microbiologist and molecular pathologist working on it right now. If you'll sit tight for a few minutes, you can walk up with me and we'll talk to them. Maybe they'll have something ... Excuse me a moment will you."

The doctor stood up and walked off. A few minutes later, Dr. Miller came back down the hall and motioned for Detective Turner to follow him to the elevator. A woman crossing the room accidentally bumped into the detective and headed for the stairwell.

"Anything new on his condition?"

"No ... Let's see what the experts in the lab have to say."

The elevator door opened to the second floor. The two men stepped out and walked down a long, empty hallway lit only by every other ceiling light fixture. The hospital was on an energy saving program. The light reflected off bleached white walls that echoed the sterile, utilitarian function of the second floor.

As they approached the end of the hall, the open double doors to the lab came into view. Voices from inside could be heard. " . . . and the specificity of this particular substrate is unique . . . like nothing I've ever seen before. It's incredibly smaller than the enzyme itself," the molecular pathologist stated.

The lab manager, a microbiologist, thought about that for a moment and responded, "That's typically the case, though."

"No . . . not this small. Look for yourself."

The bench held a stereo electron microscope and an atomic force microscope capable of producing three-dimensional images of the surface of a molecule. The electron microscope could identify subatomic particles. He looked in the eyepieces and focused carefully.

The molecular pathologist, Dr. Sandy Keller, narrated as his boss concentrated on the slide.

"It's catalyzing a number of different reactions based on temperature, and the glucose phosphate keeps morphing. Trying to optimize the pH doesn't help either. I can't find a saturation point."

"What have you done to the samples to defeat its production?"

"It's a non-typical, complex, acellular structure. I can only describe it as explosively reproductive. Watch it for a moment . . . the replication is almost violent."

The two men observed the slide.

"I tried denaturation to destroy its solubility, but it won't coagulate . . . It retains its original properties. One other thing, I found the acidic concentration needed to kill it also kills the surrounding patient tissue."

Dr. Miller and the detective stood idly at the doorway, listening intently to the ongoing conversation. The two scientists conversed, unaware of the police detective and emergency room physician.

"What about ultraviolet radiation?"

"It doesn't have any effect at survivable levels, same thing with the lead, cyanide, arsenic, and mercury tests. I applied sulfanilamides and the enzyme just shrugged it off. I did positive and negative stain tests with the same results."

Dr. Keller cocked his head, choosing his words carefully, "Walt . . . I think it's time to call the CDC."

Dr. Walter Hunack sat down on the stool behind him. He put his head in his hands and rubbed his five o'clock shadow.

"I trust your judgment. Are you absolutely certain we're not being premature?"

"This enzyme is like no other. You saw it for yourself. It has no nucleic acid base. I checked it five times, thinking the analytical composition was improperly computed. It wasn't. The spectral analysis, light wave analysis, and the gas chronometer all draw a blank."

Dr. Keller rapped the metal table with his fingertips while his shoes tapped the chrome rung of the polished stool he was sitting on. Although he was famished his clinical curiosity had overtaken his hungry stomach.

"There are no atoms, hydrogen or otherwise, bonding it. In fact, the atomic composition doesn't possess any known adherence properties that I can match it to. Whatever it is, it's not on the periodic table of elements. There's no informational link in any research database that might suggest what we're seeing here. Take a look at the petri dish in the isolation container. That cadaver sample is an hour old."

Dr. Hunack peeked into a second electron microscope that held the cadaver sample. Ashen-faced, he looked up in disbelief.

"That's not medically possible! A mistake must have occurred somewhere in the process."

"Here's the data," Keller said as he glanced at his watch. "I introduced the enzyme exactly fifty-eight minutes ago. What do you see?"

Walt took a moment to look again, "I see something that's scientifically unexplainable."

"Exactly my point. I took the liberty of sending the lab data over to a close friend at the Fort Detrick NBC warfare research facility in Maryland. He's a molecular microbiologist. He called me a few minutes ago, thinking that I'd been put up to a practical joke by his colleagues. When I told him it was no joke, his tone of voice changed. He asked me where I got the chemical composition. I gave him the background on it. That's when the analytical researcher in him took over. He said the elements of the unknown composition were 'brilliant.' "

"Did he have anything useful to offer besides that?"

"He did. He said contain it and secure it. He's catching a plane and flying out immediately."

"He's coming here?"

"Yes . . . said he'd never seen anything this spooky before. He went clinical on me."

Hunack paused to let the idea sink in.

"I've been doing this for twenty-seven years. This virus is going to make Ebola look like a summer cold. If this thing spins out into the general population, bodies will be dropping faster than coins from a slot machine payoff."

The lab manager let out a long breath. "We won't be able to keep the lid on this for long. Where's the phone number for CDC."

Walt Hunack strolled over to his desk and pulled a scotch taped note off the wall next to his phone.

"Once we do this, the proverbial worms are out of the can," he said as he handed the note over. "Go ahead and make the call. I'll notify the boss and the hospital board."

Detective Turner's jaw dropped. His eyes went wide as he looked at Dr. Miller. He turned and rushed on down the corridor. Miller stood immobilized, contemplating what he'd just heard.

12

Utah Valley Medical Center
Provo, Utah
Tuesday, 1753 hours Mountain Time

In the room adjacent to the lab, twenty-five feet away, was Bettina Jessup. Bettina was a stunningly beautiful, hard-driving pharmaceutical sales rep for a major firm. Her aggressive approach to everything in life suggested she was driven as much by testosterone as she was by estrogen. She worked for Odin Pharmaceuticals.

The single, twenty-eight year old had her degree in pharmacology and had once worked as a pharmacist for a regional grocery store chain. She quit when she realized that the people selling wholesale drugs to the pharmacy were making far more than she was. Financially, all she wanted out of life was a little more than she'd ever get. Even sleeping with an occasional purchasing manager from a potential client company was not above her. She was in it strictly for the money, the more, the better.

Bettina was sitting close by in the emergency room when she overheard the detective and ER doc talking. She slipped quietly up the stairway as they stepped into the elevator five minutes before. Now, hidden in the adjoining room, she had listened in on the entire conversation.

She walked silently out the door she'd entered minutes before. Hurrying back downstairs, she went straight for the exit. *There's something deadly at the BYU paleontology lab. They have a virus they don't know how to treat.*

There's opportunity here, Bettina. She reached the hospital parking lot and drove over to the BYU campus.

It was dark outside the BYU paleo lab. In her car, she kicked off her high heels and tied the laces of her athletic shoes. A few minutes later, she found an unlocked door on the side of the building. Aside from a janitor who didn't see her, no one else was there. Bettina snooped around silently for a few minutes until she came across a small, scientific laboratory set off in a corner of the facility. Several ongoing projects were covering the examination tables. *Is one of these the culprit?* she wondered.

Each table had a binder with handwritten notes corresponding to the fossilized bones laid out on the counter. On one table was a chunk of rock. *Odd, why a rock in a paleontology lab? It should be over at the geology department.*

A door opened somewhere down the hall. Numerous loud voices drowned out any more thought. People were coming her way. Bettina looked around for a way out. Another door led off to the women's restroom. She rushed through, closing the door behind her. Seconds later, BYU and Provo Police, led by a department paleontologist, stopped at the door to the lab.

"That's it right there, on the small work desk against the back wall," the paleontologist pointed out through the lab door window.

Bettina was straining to hear the conversation. Background chatter could be heard from the police radios outside the room.

"Lock the lab doors," Turner ordered. "Sergeant, tape the building off. No one in, it's a crime scene now. I want officers posted on both lab entry doors."

"Doctor," Turner said, addressing himself to the paleontologist, "I want a list of all the people who've had access to this laboratory since that rock showed up."

The doctor pursed his lips tightly and frowned. "I'll have to get ahold of Dr. Dalton Jordan. It may take an hour or so. When will the state lab people be here?"

"They're on the way now, maybe thirty minutes. A highway patrol vehicle is escorting them. The FAA is diverting the small military jet from Fort Detrick to the Provo airport, and that molecular pathologist at the hospital is in one of our cars on the way over."

Outside the building, the deputy chief of detectives arrived in an unmarked police car. Turner met him in the building foyer. After bringing him up to speed on the investigation, the chief asked Turner, "What about the woman in custody?"

"She, along with three of our officers, one technician, and the two paramedics are being rounded up for testing and possibly isolation. Our people all wore latex gloves in handling her . . . but it's no guarantee."

Turner looked down at his gloved hands. "No telling where the virus may have been deposited around here. We've called the CDC. Several of their medical experts in viral and bacterial events are on the way. Meanwhile, it looks like the state is taking over the alpha patient. The hospital is moving him to an isolated corner of their facility and a media blackout's in place. When the Feds get here they'll decide what to do with him."

"What about the rock in the lab?"

"It was beneath the skeleton of a T-Rex dinosaur they unearthed. It came out of the ground four days ago. The alpha patient's girlfriend filled us in based on what he told her. He spilled water on it the first hour it was in the lab. A chemical or biological agent may have been activated by the water. That's all we know so far. The pathologist from the hospital will be here in a few minutes. Maybe we can find out more then."

Inside the women's restroom, Bettina waited . . . and worried. She hadn't planned on being trapped in the same room with something life-threatening. *Glad I didn't touch the thing.*

Bettina pulled out her cell phone and dialed a number. Her mentor, Donald, the director of corporate sales, might be in his office in Seattle. It was time to pass on the info she acquired.

"Odin Pharmaceuticals, how may I help you?"

"Donald Hagler's office, please. This is Bettina Jessup." The music on hold was laced with fifteen second commercial vignettes for Odin Pharmaceuticals. The narcissistic pharmaceutical rep waited impatiently.

Bettina mulled over the possibilities. A difficult-to-deal-with virus could become widespread if it was aggressive enough. This new virus, whatever it was, was certainly scaring enough people. Pockets of the virus that were located in different cultures, with a variety of different strains and incubation periods, could prove very profitable. The company that could provide a patented medicine to deal with it had a once-in-a-lifetime opportunity.

Promotion, raise, bonus, prestige, and recognition thoughts ran through her head. It simply needed to be well managed.

"Donald Hagler."

"Don, this is Bettina from the Salt Lake City office. Hope I'm not interrupting a meeting."

In fact, Hagler was about to have a late-night conference in the adjoining suite with several corporate officers and the company CEO, Magnus Odin himself. Bettina took a few minutes to give Hagler the rundown on what she knew.

While she was busy talking, Provo Police were cordoning off the lab building with yellow crime scene tape. Federal officials had arrived on the premises and were donning level three hazmat suits.

"You say it's in a lab on the campus?"

"Yes. The cops are here. The CDC is on the way. The military may be coming to check it out."

Hagler took it all in for a moment. "Here's what I want you to do . . ." He gave her instructions to stay out of sight, and if they moved it, to find out where it was going. "Call me back with any new information, and keep your cell phone on so I can call you back. Make sure to set it on vibrate only so the ringer won't give you away."

He cancelled the meeting and went straight into Magnus Odin's office without knocking. Ten minutes later, Magnus was on the phone to his father. Sensing an incredible opportunity, Douglas Odin started issuing instructions of his own.

On the southwest side of the island, the Nordian military team was once again moving. In an hour the submarine and the helicopter would be on their way. Other resources in Seattle and Utah were being mustered into place, including a top research scientist from Odin Pharmaceuticals.

Douglas Odin and Bettina Jessup were on the same wavelength. Bettina would eventually be rewarded . . . but not until she fulfilled her final obligation to the company.

Salt Lake City Airport
Salt Lake City, Utah
Wednesday, 0736 hours Mountain Time

The silver Durango pulled up to the curb and stopped. Sean Fox popped out of the passenger door and walked to the rear of the vehicle. The back hatch opened with a snap. His wife, Kelly, had also gotten out of the SUV to give Sean a proper sendoff. She stood there while he retrieved his luggage.

Kelly couldn't help but look at Sean and admire his handsome face, with its faded scars across his chin and below his right ear. She briefly recalled the plane crash on her father-in-law's ranch years ago in Montana, when they were waiting for Sean to land on a grass runway. As they watched him touch down, a strong gust of wind caught the right wing and flipped over the small Cessna. Dale, his father, and two ranch hands pulled Sean free of the burning wreckage before it was too late.

His voice suddenly broke through her memory. "I'll see you in two weeks," he said. "I love you."

He wrapped his arms around her and gave her a big kiss. She made sure she got two.

"I love you, too. Be safe," she replied.

Snowflake, their golden lab, was standing on the back seat of the SUV with his head out the window, as if to say "me, too." Sean stopped to scratch his ears and then headed into the terminal. In an hour and a half he'd be in Seattle.

Dale's hotel room
Fisherman's Wharf, Seattle, Washington
Wednesday, 0645 hours Pacific Time

Dale awoke to the sound of a ship's air horn blasting the sleep from his subconscious mind. Light streamed through the long blinds and played vertical shadows across a wood carving of a bear on the opposite side of the bedroom. He heard seagulls carping in the background. Then a knock came from the door of the adjoining room.

"Dale, you up?"

Dale could hear running water from a sink. *Sullivan, why can't you sleep all night like everyone else?* he thought.

"I am now," his groggy voice replied. "What time is it?"

"It's a quarter of seven. We gotta pick up your brother at the airport in an hour," Sullivan said.

Twenty minutes later, both men exited the hotel and headed toward the agency car in the parking lot. Dale paused at the vehicle door to admire the sound of a clanging trolley car across the street. He enjoyed the character it added to the waterfront.

Fire captain Sean Fox walked off the ramp from the passenger jet and down the escalator. Once in the terminal it was a quick trip to the passenger luggage carousel and out to the street. Looking skyward, he saw the unique shape of a U.S. Navy E2-C Hawkeye aircraft flying by in the distance, a reminder of the Navy's presence in the area. He'd have some of their divers in his class the day after tomorrow. An unmarked FBI sedan pulled up to the curb. "Throw it in the back," the driver yelled out the window. The trunk popped open. Five minutes later they were on the freeway back to Seattle.

Heber Airport,
Heber, Utah

At the same time, twenty miles east of Provo, Utah a corporate jet came in for a landing at a private air strip. Inside were five passengers: a geologist, a Nordian pilot, two Nordian Special Forces NCOs, and a fifth man.

14

"How many people have been exposed so far?"

"Two dead and ten more admitted," the ER doctor said to the CDC physician.

"Aside from the deceased alpha patient and his girlfriend, we have two police officers, two paramedics, a pharmacist at the local grocery store next to the campus, three pharmacy clients, a nurse, and a lab janitor. By no means is it a full accounting. We expect more patients, especially after our conversations regarding the lab's assessment. The pattern from the alpha patient is repeating itself with each new patient. We're administering one hundred percent oxygen, but so far we have nothing on the disease or a treatment," the ER doctor explained.

The CDC physician flipped the page on his yellow pad and continued, "Dr. Hunack, what do you have so far?"

The hospital's molecular pathologist had been sitting silently at the end of the conference table. Dr. Walter Hunack cleared his throat and spoke up.

"We've written a detailed report for you . . ." He passed it across the table " . . . that summarizes our findings so far. We expect to have tissue samples within the hour from the autopsy on the alpha. Aside from the information it contains, I have to say, this is a fast-acting virus. Cellular decomposition, organ degradation, and immune system failure are its key manifestations. Aside from one-hundred

107

percent oxygen slowing it down, it appears to be a terminally destructive infection of some sort. We haven't been able to determine type; it defies definition from the conventional sense. We're hoping you can help, which leads me to a question." He cleared his throat, looked around the room, and gauged the impact of his next few words, "Is this a military or government lab creation?"

The CDC physician leaned over to the military scientist from Fort Detrick and whispered in his ear. The scientist shook his head.

"No, it's not ours. Doctor, why don't you elaborate?"

The Fort Detrick NBC warfare scientist scratched his nose. He'd been flying half the night and was tired.

"This isn't one of our projects. The cellular data that Walt sent me yesterday surprised us, too. Our lab has been running the composition through our computer database. I've been given government approval to share this much with you, but it has to stay in this room. So far, we've been unable to analyze it . . . it has elements that cannot be classified. We have a team working to break it down, but without some understanding of the base structure of its cellular design, we're as much in the dark at this moment as you. We're open to ideas. We've contacted Tooele Army Depot. They have level four hazmat equipment on the way over. They're about an hour from here."

"Why don't we just have them incinerate the damn thing!" someone blurted out.

"We can't do that until we know its composition. We may need it to develop a vaccine. We can't manage a potential epidemic without a means of addressing it," the CDC physician replied.

"We have limited quarantine facilities at the hospital, any thoughts on that?" Dr. Hunack asked.

The scientist looked toward the end of the table, "The U.S. has five biosafety level four facilities. We want to bring out some of that gear and a working group from one of the labs. Mr. Montock, can we count on the hospital to work with us on putting together the space resources we'll need?"

Nils Montock was the hospital administrator. "Of course, just tell us what you need and we'll see to it."

"Great, let's chat further when we're done here."

"Let's talk about quarantine, then," Dr. Hunack said. "One of our ER nurses has the bug. She may not have followed our safety protocol in treating the alpha patient. Do we isolate the staff on duty at the time the alpha patient was admitted?"

"Pull them off rotation for forty-eight hours and let's see if anything develops," the CDC physician replied.

The molecular pathologist looked over at the hospital administrator with a pernicious glance. Glaring across the table top, he slowly emphasized his few words, "Just one more thing then . . . We're going to need a second working group."

"For what?" the CDC physician asked.

"Epidemic control!" Hunack got up from the table, slammed his briefing book closed, glared at the CDC scientist and walked back to his lab.

"Everything's ready, let's go." The five men buckled up as their SUV pulled out of the hangar door and headed for the small airstrip exit. The Nordian commando sergeant leaned over the seatback and pulled the blanket all the way up. Their gear bags were covered.

"Do we know where it is?" the sergeant asked.

"Yeah, last report from that female pharmaceutical rep said it was being held temporarily at the hospital lab under local guard. The Feds landed at the Provo airport last night, along with some CDC people. They'll move it out to a secure facility later today, probably to a government lab somewhere," his partner said.

"Doesn't give us much time to recon the grab and run."

"They'll be flying it out of the city airport," the fifth man said. "The switch should go off well if all the pieces fall into place. Team two will be waiting for us in the park at noon. We'll go over it with them so they can cover us, no matter what happens. We have plan B if the primary attempt isn't successful. We'll know soon enough. Either way, we'll be out of the area quickly."

"The sergeant punched a telephone number into his encrypted satellite phone. It took a moment to shake hands with the satellite. The phone rang three times and a woman answered. "Bettina Jessup."

"Bettina, this is Mr. Gariepy from the pharmaceutical company. I'm told that you can help us with the administration of a new prescription drug."

The "new prescription" was the code words she'd been told to wait for. From her bathroom hideout, she overheard the CDC people talk about moving the rock to the hospital for safekeeping. That was last night. Early yesterday morning, with her pharmaceutical ID, she'd managed to bluff her way into the back of the hospital where she discovered the security team that had been set up to keep out anyone not connected to the investigation.

"Yes. You may pick it up on the third floor in room 325. And there's a clear Lexan box about twelve-by-twenty inches that appears to be the sealed container in which it's being kept. There are two caretakers outside the room."

"Thank you very much. We'll see you at the home office next week." He pushed the "end" button on the phone.

"Give the info to Team Two's leader so they can handle our recon," the senior sergeant advised. "Make sure they run film inside and out of the hospital, and let's get a diagram of the stairs, elevators, and windows. Find out what's adjacent to three twenty-five on either side as well, and find out where the pull-down fire alarms are located. Do the same thing at the local airport. Find the hangar their plane is in, and where the bathrooms are. See what other kinds of aircraft are sitting at the airport; I don't want anyone giving chase from the adjacent runway. Get me a local map and mark it with the nearest police station, sheriff's office, and National Guard unit. I want it all. You know what to do."

The sergeant made the second call and hung up a minute later. He checked his watch and adjusted for local time.

The fifth man, Thor Odin, looked over the seat at him. "We have the element of surprise on our side. It'll be dark, and they won't know what, let alone who, hit them. Whether we do it in the hospital or the airport matters little to me, kill them all. I want no witnesses. Above all, don't damage that rock casing. The specimen is invaluable and deadly. Break the casing and we all die."

The Nordian commandos nodded their understanding. Thor Odin might have been wearing an expensive three-piece suit and a Rolex watch, but he was as vicious and merciless as a rabid dog when he was angry. Getting on his bad side wasn't a healthy thing to do.

Fisherman's Wharf fire station
Seattle, Washington
Wednesday, 0922 hours Pacific Time

Dale pulled into the fire station driveway on the Seattle wharf front.

"If all goes well, we'll see you at the hotel for dinner, "he told Sean. "I'll drop your bags off there. You have the room next to us."

Sean grabbed his briefcase and waved goodbye to Dale and Sullivan. The FBI car disappeared into traffic.

He walked up to the fire station and rang the buzzer on the wall next to the door. A few moments later, a Seattle firefighter let him in.

"Can I help you?"

"I'm Captain Sean Fox, with the dive training team. Is Lieutenant Davis available?"

"Yeah, come on in. Follow me. He's in the kitchen."

"Lieutenant, you got company," the firefighter announced.

"Ahh, you must be Captain Sean Fox."

"That I am. Nice to finally meet you after all the calls and e-mails," Sean replied.

"You hungry?" Davis asked with a smile.

"Not yet. What time you guys eat lunch?"

"Sometime in between the morning and the afternoon calls. See all the tourists out there on the sidewalk? They don't limit themselves to getting in trouble on land. Yesterday a wheelchair-bound vet did a full gainer into the drink just up the street, scared the hell out of the sea lions under the dock. We were right in the middle of lunch."

"Hey, LT, the Homeland Security boat is pulling up out back," a firefighter said.

"Oh, yeah. Hey, Sean, come on out and meet some of the folks we get to abuse for the next two weeks," Davis laughed.

The two fire bosses walked out the back door of the station and down the steps to the dock.

Dale's phone vibrated in his shirt pocket. "Fox."

"Dale . . . it's Tony." Anthony "No-Knock" Petrocelli, the FBI ASAC, had news.

"Your hunch was right. After you were able to establish that Perry had been to Friday Harbor for dinner, we found an ATM camera shows him, along with two other men, getting into a cabin cruiser. As it pulled away from the dock, we got the name and ID of the boat. We've checked the registration number with the state. It belongs to a carpenter who lives out on Farrow's Inlet. He has a brother who's been employed as an engineer on Nord Island. The boat owner and his brother haven't been heard from since last Thursday. And Perry is wearing the same yellow and green windbreaker from the ferry terminal film."

"Got any idea where the boat and the other two men are?" Dale asked.

"Negative. We've run their credit cards, debit cards, bank accounts, and were checking with the neighbors and co-workers right now. So far, it looks like they dropped off the radar as well."

"How about the film, does it clearly show the other two men? Can we make an ID?"

"It's a bit shadowy, though there is some detail. I'll have it run over to the local lab to be digitized for clarity."

"Hang on a second, Tony," Dale said as he turned to Sullivan.

"Hey, Sullivan, they got film of Perry and the two guys he was with. Let's head downtown to the PD. I'm willing to bet that the dash cams from the local cops may have picked up some detail worth reviewing."

Sullivan took a left at the next corner and headed toward downtown Seattle.

"Tony, get the film punched up if you can. We're going over to Seattle PD and track down their dashboard camera film from the chase on Saturday. Call me back as soon as you get to the lab, okay."

"I'll talk to you shortly," Tony said. The phone went silent.

Ten minutes later they drove into the underground parking lot at the Seattle PD. A day shift sergeant from the patrol division met them. He had retrieved the tapes from all four patrol cars involved in the chase from the previous weekend.

"TV's up, let me turn on the tape," the patrol sergeant said. The video-disc ran for about sixty seconds.

"Right there, back it up just a bit. There . . . as they turned right at the intersection, the passenger in the front seat is clearly visible. He's awake. He's looking out the window trying to see the officers following. I thought you guys said the passenger was unconscious," Sullivan said to the sergeant.

"When the Black Hawk took the passenger from the freeway, he was either unconscious or drugged," the patrol sergeant replied.

"Interesting," Dale said. "Can you print us up a hi-res photo of that frame? I need the picture."

"Yeah, give the tech a minute."

Sullivan turner to his partner, "We need to find the contractors who provided aircraft for Nord Island, or Douglas Odin and company. How tough do you think it will be to reverse trace a Black Hawk helo from the manufacturer's records?"

"If we can get cooperation, a research support staff, and access, which we may not get at this stage, I'd say it's a fifty-fifty proposition," Dale concluded. "Then there's the secondary sales market. We'll need a whole bottle of aspirin to follow anything there. We could try to track replacement parts and see who's doing the buying. We'd need to know every corporation that Mr. Odin owns, controls, or exerts influence over. It would be better to set a trap and see if anyone bites. Problem is, we need something big enough for it to work. We don't have enough information on their hot buttons. Let's see if we can get into the satellite surveillance side. Navy and NRO probably have over flight photos."

A Seattle Police Department technician came into the room with a picture and handed it to Sullivan.

"Thanks," Sullivan responded, taking the photo from him.

"Looks good," Dale said, handing the print back to Sullivan. "I got a friend from Foggy Bottom in Los Angeles. Let's see if we can interest him in a new terrorist group."

"Think he'll bite?"

"Don't know; we can give it a try."

"Let's head over to the Navy base. We'll need a secure line away from the FBI's office to call on. Besides, I introduced the spook to his wife a few years ago. He owes me."

Sullivan adjusted his sunglasses as he picked up his briefcase, and with a slightly sarcastic grin said, "I hope they're still happily married."

Fox raised an eyebrow and headed for the exit.

Pacific Ocean
200 miles west of Washington
Wednesday, 1337 hours Pacific Time

Captain Ingvar Wallen stopped and looked up at the red digital indicator mounted on the bulkhead over the passageway. It displayed the speed, depth, battery status, and location of the submarine. He walked on toward the command console, the sound of his shoes echoing off the steel decking.

"Captain on the bridge," the sonar man called out.

"Report," he replied.

"We just entered the American ADIZ. We have three cargo haulers north of us all headed toward Alaska, and a Canadian oiler just over the horizon to the east. No other surface or subsurface contacts, sir."

"What's the speed on the oiler?"

"She's doing sixteen knots on a course of zero-two-seven, sir."

"Any aircraft that fit the hunter profile?"

"Negative, sir. No air assets of any kind in the past . . ." He looked up at the bulkhead clock, " . . . hour and forty-one minutes.

"*Jätte bra* - helm, come right ten degrees. The oiler will fall behind faster. I don't want any mistakes on our way in."

Captain Wallen undid the center button of his khaki shirt, reached in, and pulled out a dark-blue envelope. In front of the crew, he ripped the end off and tapped out the contents. A single piece of tan paper slipped into his hand. He turned the edge up and opened it. Scanning its contents for a moment, his face devoid of any emotion, he read it to himself. Finally, he looked up at the crewmembers in the command center."

"XO, call the Special-Ops team leader to the bridge."

Wallen wiped his hand over his face and yawned. Otherwise he stood immobile at the map table for the twenty-one seconds it took the ranking NCO to reach the command center. He handed the paper to him and waited as he read it. When the NCO was done, he handed it back to Wallen.

"If you'll excuse me, Captain, I have to get my men and equipment ready." The commando turned and departed the bridge.

Wallen looked at his crew and read the message aloud. The crew listened quietly and then went about their tasks without questions being raised. This submarine crew, as was the case with all sub crews, appreciated knowing the mission and associated risks. Wallen reminded himself that these were his personal, handpicked men. Every one of them had earned their place, and his respect. He returned the paper to his uniform shirt and rebuttoned it.

"Helm, at half past the hour, slow us to seven knots, then take us down to eight-hundred-fifty feet, and set our course at zero-three-five degrees. XO, have the chief engineer meet me in my quarters immediately. You have the bridge."

The helmsman repeated the order but the captain had already walked down the passageway. In the galley, he stopped long enough to grab four kabobs and headed off to his quarters. When the chief engineer reached the captain's quarters, the door clicked shut behind him. The submarine continued quietly northeast at eleven knots. The smell of lunch wafted through the passageway to the command center.

"Sonar, run the tether out to three thousand yards aft, and queue the porpoise tape. Let's clear the area around us and make sure we're clean. Gentlemen," he said to the bridge crew, " . . . time to earn those hefty paychecks you've been cashing."

He turned to the burly, 5'10" Norwegian, the only non-Swedish crew-member, "COB, get down to engineering and see to it that they have every tool, implement, and all test gear secured. We'll be coming up on the commercial sea lanes in less than an hour."

"Aye, sir."

The COB swallowed the last of his coffee and headed aft.

Orem, Utah
Thursday, 0744 hours Mountain Time

At their breakfast table just two blocks from the local hospital, a husband and wife both displayed early symptoms of the unnamed virus. A coughing fit came upon the wife. She wiped her hands over her eight-year-old son's face a few minutes later. He finished his cereal and was out the door for the school bus. Another victim was born.

16

The NSA had run an eavesdropping program known as "Echelon" for over a decade. It was designed to intercept key words and phrases, programmed into its software searching for terrorist and major crime related communications. These came in the form of satellite, cellular, microwave, fax, e-mail, voice and data link, both encrypted and burst communications, across a broad spectrum of frequency wavelengths. Its shortfall was its language recognition limitation. English, Spanish, and a handful of Middle Eastern languages, along with a few select dialects, were all it could understand. In many cases, a specific communiqué had to be backstopped by human ear after the fact. It could be a slow process, when what was needed was a greater real time approach.

After 9/11, an expanded budget was quick in coming. Unlike other federal agencies that had a wish list of unfunded projects, NSA wasn't one of them. They wanted a major upgrade and they got it.

"Eagle's Claw," their new program, had Chinese, German, French and fourteen other languages programmed in, with twenty-two specific dialects associated with its new capabilities. In addition, it had a root language matrix to recognize language type. Unfortunately, the Germanic root recognition option didn't work well with Swedish. Even if it had, the highly encrypted algorithm would require dedicated computer time to break it down.

117

The encrypted satellite phone was on its fourth beep when it was answered.

"*Hejsan* . . . Hello," Thor Odin said.

"I have a change of plans for you," his father, Douglas Odin, replied. He was sitting in his gold flake decorated study on Nord Island, looking out the massive picture window at the blue sky and sunshine. He was as calm today as the waters of the Pacific Ocean that washed against the sandy beach a half-mile away.

"I want you to split the teams up. Have one hit the hospital lab after it closes and get a sample of the alpha patient's tissue from the autopsy. I don't want them drawing attention to themselves. Bring it back here to me. Have the other team go to the airport and seize the aircraft and geode. I'm sending you GPS coordinates for the pilot for an airfield in Washington." Douglas continued on with a few other details.

"*Slå en signal när det är färdigt och på vag* "Call me when everything is completed and on the way."

Douglas Odin waited a moment and hung up.

Thor, the oldest and most vicious of the three sons, leaned forward in the SUV as it traveled down Highway 15 from Salt Lake City toward Provo. "We have a change in the schedule." He related the details to the NCOs leading the two teams.

"When?" the senior leader asked.

"Right after dusk, I want both teams to go in simultaneously. The lab will be closed and locked by then. It must be done covertly. We can't afford to draw attention to ourselves. The plane's schedule is unknown, but we believe it hasn't been flight prepped yet. Our man at the airport is watching them closely. Barring any unforeseen complications, take the plane down at 2200 hours. Keep the bodies onboard so we don't have a mess to clean up here."

"That's only seven hours from now," the second NCO team leader replied.

"Yes. Get into place at dark, and do it as we discussed."

"We have everything we need," the CDC scientist said. "Let's load up, recover our people, and get ready to go back to Fort Detrick. I have another crew coming out tomorrow morning to take over here. We need to be in place for any expansion of this illness."

"I talked to the chief of the ER a few minutes ago," his fellow scientist said. "He says they've seen twenty-seven cases so far. With the exception of a young Caucasian kid, the rest are worsening. Three other hospitals are reporting symptoms along the Wasatch Front, and there may be one in Boise, Idaho. We have a comprehensive review process in place to look for any commonalities among the patients."

"How about the little kid?"

"Both sets of parents are on one hundred percent oxygen. We haven't much information, but the kid's condition is stable. We don't know why yet." The tired, bleary-eyed scientist tapped his foot nervously under the table, his thoughts all over the place.

"Why don't you stay behind, follow his case, and see what you can come up with. I'm going to go have dinner with the state emergency management folks before I head to the airport. We're going to discuss what we can do for them under the FEMA emergency response protocol. Do you want to come along?"

"No. This thing is heading for epidemic status, so I need to stay here. What are we going to do about the media? This story is going to break before morning. We can't keep a lid on it much longer by calling it a bad flu outbreak."

"The hospital administrator, state medical examiner, and our public information officer will deal with it when it's time," the CDC scientist replied. "I need to get a little sleep before dinner. I'm heading back to the hotel. You look like you could use some rest as well."

"I need something more than rest. I need to know this isn't the beginning of a nightmare."

U.S. naval base
Everett, Washington
Thursday, 0915 hours Pacific Time

The authoritative voice of the admiral boomed off the walls of his office, "Your father is a longtime friend, a man I admire and respect. He tells me you've hit a technical problem. How can I help?"

The crisp, white uniform and the two gold stars on his shoulder boards contrasted with the wormwood paneling of the well-appointed room. Dale's call to his father for an introduction to the admiral, whom he hadn't seen in three years, had opened the door for Dale.

Dale and Sullivan glanced at each other. Sullivan spoke first.

"We lost a retired agent who was on a private investigation in the field. We think he was interviewing a couple of guys on a small cabin cruiser somewhere east or south of Friday Harbor. His body was found floating in the bay last week. We think there's a sunken boat out there somewhere. It's an educated guess on our part. No other bodies have surfaced as of yet. But we'd like your assistance in using more powerful sonar than we have available to us to search for the boat on the bottom. Any chance we could get the navy to help us out, sir?" Sullivan inquired respectfully.

The admiral asked a few more questions to further clarify the situation he was being asked to consider. He leaned back in his chair and looked up at the ceiling for a moment.

"Hmmm . . . I see your problem."

The admiral leaned forward again and hit the intercom button on his phone. A grizzled master chief appeared in the doorway soon after as if Houdini himself had performed a magic trick. "MC, get me the incoming ship list for overhauls and upgrades."

"Aye, aye, sir." The master chief spun around and was gone.

"How's your dad doing with the ranch these days? We didn't get a chance to talk too long. Are you still feeding the MarSOC operators at the camp?"

The admiral was referring to the Marine Corps Special Operations Teams. They did some of their best clandestine training away from the prying eyes of certain elected officials who were more supportive of the wrong elements than their own troops. Training on private property kept those eyes at bay.

The Marine Corps' association with its war heroes was a source of personal pride for the Corps. The ranch had been supplying contract beef to the U.S. military for years.

Dale measured his words carefully since the training area, known as "the Tulip Farm" was a secret that even Congress didn't know about. It acquired its name from the hoards of tulips planted behind the patio by Dale and Sean's mom.

By virtue of the fact that the admiral knew, Dale's father had obviously taken him into his confidence somewhere along the way. Dale responded to the Admiral's question after first looking over to make certain that the door was closed.

"Uh, well yes, sir." Dale lowered his voice almost to a whisper. "No one is supposed to know about the covert combat training program since Detachment One was disbanded. The black budget folks out of Pendleton still run a couple hundred guys a year through the mountain and river combat course. Dad says it works well since the MarSOC Marines are able to hide some of their training schedule from the southern command group. They run training ops that the congressional oversight committee would never allow. And of course, all the guys who make it through the 'Punch and Pulverize' program get to meet Dad and see the medal."

"Yeah, I can imagine the opportunity to visit with a real, live Marine hero is a unique privilege.

That and he always show's up with the juiciest, corn-fed, eighteen-ounce New York steaks they ever ate," the admiral replied. "Any man with three Purple Hearts, two Navy Crosses, and the Medal of Honor is one we want to take very good care of, especially since there's only twenty or so Marine MOHs left alive. There is one question I never got an answer to, though."

"What's that, sir?" Dale inquired.

"I've always wondered who a 'Medal of Honor' recipient looks up to. Your dad and I were talking about past military leaders and the frustrations they faced in battle. I asked him if he had any heroes and never got an answer. We were fishing on the lake and the conversation moved to Alaskan salmon."

"Yes, sir, he does. Dad, Sean, and I all have the same hero as it were."

"Really, who is it?"

"Any guy carrying a medical bag and a .45 into combat when everyone else has an automatic weapon, grenades, and heavy artillery deserves a great deal of respect. Those Navy corpsmen are worth their weight in gold."

Dale's father had started his military career as an enlisted man in the Navy in the mid-1950s. As a corpsman, he'd been detailed with "his" Marines to a few hotspots overseas and he had distinguished himself on several occasions. When his Navy enlistment was up, he found he so admired the fighting spirit of the Marines that he joined them. He was awarded the Medal of Honor as a Marine major in Vietnam, turning the tide of battle against superior forces and saving the lives of his men in the process.

The admiral thought about what Dale had said, a moment, nodded his head, and eyed Dale. "Your brother was a sniper in Vietnam, wasn't he?"

"Yes, sir. I guess it's been awhile since you've seen Sean."

"Actually, he went fishing with me and your dad last spring. He also served the Marines well . . . kid's got the same sense of hard charging bravado as his dad."

"Yes, sir, it kinda runs in the family."

And indeed it did. Dale's heritage was a mixed bag of risk takers and inventive personalities. His grandmother, Theonne Cook-Bell, was born at the turn of the twentieth century in Birmingham, England. She immigrated to the United States with her family before WWI. Theonne took a job as a secretary at a company in New Jersey owned by Alexander Graham Bell. She fell in love with Bell's nephew, Geoffrey, himself a graduate electrical engineer from Harvard. They were married in the midst of the Great War. The younger Bell was credited with several inventions, including the foundation for modern telephone switching apparatus. After Alexander sold out to a conglomerate, he and his nephew went into the power plant business. They eventually bought a substantial stake in the Ohio Valley Dam system and controlling interest in the early, privately-owned, Tennessee Valley Authority. Alexander wanted to go the route of direct electrical current service, while Geoffrey felt that alternating current was cheaper and easier to build. Geoffrey eventually won the argument, but he and his uncle had a serious falling out.

Geoffrey sold his interest in the power companies shortly thereafter, which made him a very wealthy man. He and Theonne took off for a long vacation to see America.

While visiting Yellowstone a year later, they fell in love with the area. Geoffrey and Theonne bought twenty-two thousand acres in Montana, just thirty minutes from the park's entrance. They built a fifty-five-hundred-square-foot, fourteen-room log cabin with every possible modern amenity available. Over the next decade, they acquired more land and went into ranching, providing beef to the U.S. military for WWII and beyond.

In 1933, Theonne gave birth to their only child, Anna.

In 1949, Anna met George Fox. Fox's family ties went back almost a century in Canada, where his father and uncles had all been Royal Canadian Mounted Police officers. His dad and an uncle had been instrumental in tracking and capturing German saboteurs and agents of Hitler's Third Reich. Several joint U.S. - Canadian operations headed up by George's father paved the way for him to immigrate to the United States. He became a naturalized citizen, and his talent and skills eventually led him to become an FBI agent for J. Edgar Hoover.

George married Anna and they had two sons and a daughter. Dale was the youngest of the three. Dale knew that the admiral, a former Navy SEAL team commander, was acquainted with the ranch from fishing trips to the lake on the property. The admiral and his father had known each other for decades.

Just then, the master chief petty officer knocked on the outer door.

"Enter," the admiral barked.

The master chief had returned with a clipboard, which he handed to the admiral. The flag officer looked over the list and grunted. "MC, send a message to the captain of the *Jonathan Cooke* to contact me tomorrow morning at 0630 local. Write me up an op order for a training exercise in the San Juan Straits for tomorrow. Let's say 0700 to 1600 hours."

"Aye, aye, sir. Anything further?"

"Negative, MC. Just that."

The senior enlisted man excused himself, walked to the door, and stopped. "Sir, you have an appointment with General Stritikus at the officers' mess in fifteen minutes."

"Have McManus bring the car around the back in a half hour. Close the door, MC."

"Aye, sir."

The admiral lit his pipe and leaned back in the overstuffed, chocolate colored executive chair, "We have an inbound destroyer that should be hitting the San Juans sometime before noon tomorrow. I'll task them to the area in question. Do you want to go out to the ship?"

Dale and Sullivan were caught by surprise with the question and looked at each other for a moment. Dale mulled over their appointments in his head.

"We'd appreciate it, sir," Dale replied, looking over at Sullivan.

"Alright, be back here at 0630 and I'll ferry you out to the ship on a chopper. See you in the morning, then."

The admiral stood and shook the two agents' hands. "Tell your dad I'm ready to go fishing or horseback riding again whenever he has the time."

"I will, sir. Thanks for your help." The master chief appeared again to escort Dale and Sullivan out. Once outside, the morning sky forced them to don their sunglasses.

Sullivan hopped into the driver's seat. A few minutes passed as he drove, then he finally aimed a question at Dale. "What do you think?"

Dale was deep in thought. They were getting closer to a major part of the puzzle, maybe. Finding the cabin cruiser might answer some questions and move the investigation along, but it would certainly raise new ones.

Whoever killed Perry was still out there, looking to cover up whatever they were into. How wide a net had they cast? Who else might be in danger? And the big issue, why?

He looked over at his partner with a blank stare, his mind still engaged in thought. Dale reached into his pocket for a pack of cinnamon gum. "Want a piece?"

"Sure. What are you thinking?"

Dale paused and didn't answer immediately. Sullivan knew from the look that he was mulling something over.

"Money, power, or sex? Which one is it?" Dale said out loud as his thought process began to work. "Those are the three main reasons for almost all the major crimes we've ever seen. It's probably not sex . . . too much at stake. So it has to be money or power. People with power don't always have really big bucks. But people with really big bucks can wield power with it. Money becomes a tool. My bet is that we're up against someone with really big bucks. Kidnapping, murder, and who knows what else that we have yet to discover. Someone with a huge checkbook and a helicopter that looks like a U.S. military bird. Complex, expensive resources are in play by someone who feels insulated or isolated from the activities they're directing. How insulated are you? I wonder. All we need is one small break to push forward."

"What about the boat on the bottom of the straits?" Sullivan interjected.

"If they locate it, it's still up to us to get answers. I wonder if Sean's available for a dive." Dale pulled out his cell phone and dialed his brother. The phone rang in his ear.

"Hey, it's me. Why don't you meet us at the hotel restaurant in twenty minutes . . .Yeah . . . Okay, twenty-five then. See ya."

"Sullivan, did the Sentinel's criminal index files have anything even slightly interesting when you ran them?" Sentinel was the FBIs main information database.

"Nothing I saw," his partner replied.

"Did you get a chance to go through the CTU query system yet?" The CTU system was the highly restricted, red case file database.

"We'll need to get to an agency office to access the database at HQ. Do you want to go over to the local office though? The SAC and No-Knock will know."

"Kay Show is riding out her last month in the San Jose office before retiring. Let's see if she has some time to do a search of the CTU system and LexisNexis."

"What are we looking for?"

"The master chief passed this fax to me as we were leaving the admiral's office." Dale unfolded the sheet of paper and passed it to Sullivan. He pulled over to the side of the road and opened it. Reading the contents quickly, with his foot on the brake, he thought for a second about the information.

"Show should be in. Let's get her on it," Sullivan said, moving his foot back to the gas pedal. He handed the page back to Dale.

"Sullivan, how would you feel about running some classified info by Betty Jo?"

Sullivan thought about it a minute. "Risky. How do you feel about betting your career?"

"Let's face it, she has resources outside the U.S. and access to foreign databases," Dale said, staring out the windshield.

"Do it verbally then," Sullivan suggested.

Betty Jo Case, Dale's girlfriend, was a well-placed, high-powered international business attorney. She was owed more favors by more people than a dirty politician on the take. The woman had the uncanny ability to find sensitive information quicker than the CIA or Interpol, when they could find it at all.

Provo Airport
Provo, Utah
Thursday, 2158 hours Mountain Time

The Doxy watch on the man's wrist moved up to 2158 hours. He let out a deep breath and nodded to his companions.

The motor on the fuel truck started right up. The old, vinyl seats were faded and cracked, with gray duct tape strips arranged randomly to hold it together. A light-gray puff of smoke blew out of the exhaust pipe. The gasoline engine needed new piston rings. Pushing down on the clutch, the driver slid the floor shifter into first gear. The truck moved forward with a lurch.

"After we take the plane, repark the truck and head back to the rendezvous point. The two of us will be out of here immediately," the pilot said to the driver.

The three Nordian NCOs rolled closer to the back of the hangar. The pilot and the other commando jumped off the sideboard and edged closer to the back wall of the building, hugging the shadows as they went.

The driver could hear the brakes squeak as the truck ground to a halt near the hangar's rear door.

⚷——

In an SUV situated in the crowded back parking lot of the hospital, Thor Odin sat patiently waiting for the sweep second hand of his watch to hit the twelve mark. It was 2159 hours. The two Nordian NCOs at the hospital were in a locked linen closet across from the lab on the second floor. They'd confirmed that the lab had no alarm system and the lock was a simple affair to breech.

Thor leaned back, closed his eyes, and stretched his thick neck to the right, then back to the left, and finally in a circle. He reached out with his left hand, eyes still shut, and slowly brought the encrypted radio to his lips. A manicured, battle-scarred fist wrapped around the plastic radio casing. The finger with the diamond-encrusted ring arranged to resemble the family crest tightened up. The push-to-talk button slid back into its recessed space . . . "Go."

Thor's watch hit the 2200 hour mark. The fuel truck driver turned the dirty handle on the back hangar door and pushed it open with a creak. The small military transport jet from the Fort Detrick weapons research facility glistened under the overhead lights.

At the sound of the opening door, two seasoned Army Rangers stationed inside turned their attention from the plane to the intrusion. A man in oil-stained tan overalls, who looked like a typical grease monkey mechanic, entered their field of view. They separated and moved swiftly to intercept the unauthorized stranger at the back door.

"Howdy, ya'll," the fuel truck driver said. He ignored their obvious intentions and went about his intended task. Behind him in the large double doorway sat the old fuel truck, apparent for everyone inside the hangar to see.

"Been fixin' to come over and top off yer tanks. We're closin' up in a bit, and heard ya' all were probably gittin' ready to depart soon." The fuel truck driving commando could feel the cool metal of the 9mm pistol in his large left overall pocket. He found it hard to talk like a backwoods apple farmer . . . but he was ready.

As the Rangers closed in on him, he purposely turned his back to them. Kneeling down, he opened the scissor door to access the fuel hose and ground line from the fuel truck he'd laid out. As the armed Rangers got closer, a muffled shot spit out from the corner of the hangar door. The Ranger closest to the shooter fell backwards and onto the floor with a hole in his right temple.

Another silenced bullet found its mark a second later, just as the remaining Ranger comprehended that there was something wrong. He fell forward onto his face, also dead.

The two hidden commandos at the edge of the doorway rolled inside the hangar. Grabbing the dead Rangers by their boots, they pulled the inert bodies to the wall behind a paint locker. The fuel truck driver silently pushed the scissor door back down.

Inside the building adjacent to the hangar, the Army copilot walked down the hallway toward the jet.

The pilot was in the back of the aircraft, sitting with the scientist from the CDC and an Army lieutenant colonel. The lieutenant colonel was a biological weapons expert on loan from Fort Detrick. They were securing their deadly geode passenger for immediate transport to the military research facility.

Outside the plane, the Nord Island pilot and his partner, an imposing hulk, rushed to the bottom steps of the jet. The tall fuel truck commando raced for the door to the hangar office suite. The lookout, who had been watching the hangar from across the way in an old utility van, radioed him through his earpiece that the copilot was still inside. Their orders were to ensure that all six targets would be on the jet when they flew out. They had only a few minutes to seize the plane and get away.

A roving security detail comprised of local sheriff's deputies patrolled the area looking for anything out of the ordinary. Fortunately for the commandos, the military wasn't keeping the sheriff's department apprised of their activity schedule.

The tall commando's rubber heeled boots squeaked slightly on the polished hangar floor. At the hangar door to the hallway, he stopped and listened carefully for movement. Hearing nothing, he cracked it open and peeked inside. Given the late hour, there was no staff in the office, only the copilot. Soon after, he slipped through and disappeared from the hangar.

Moving silently down the hall, he passed three doors. He watched the end of the hallway for sudden shadows. His senses were energized as he stepped forward. Nearing the end of the hallway, the sound of a flushing toilet drifted through the wall behind him.

Instinctive reactions took over as the bathroom door suddenly opened.

Stepping into the bathroom doorway with a wet hand towel was the copilot.

The commando whirled to his left and fired once down the hallway. The bullet clipped the copilot's jacket and lodged in the alabaster drywall.

Surprised, the copilot's adrenaline went through the roof. He retreated into the bathroom, where he drew his 9mm pistol from his hip holster.

Rushing the door, the commando kicked it open in a bid to eliminate the time the copilot needed to defend himself. As the door flung open, a shot slapped the tiled wall inches to his left. *Shit!*

He dropped down to one knee and spotted the copilot in the wall mirror with gun in hand. Putting two hasty shots into the edge of the tile near the corner of the wall he watched numerous small ceramic pieces blow off and spray the area. Launching himself across the floor, the tall commando rolled to his right and fired three more times. The second shot connected.

The copilot's shoulder went limp and he grunted loudly. His gun bounced on the linoleum floor at his feet. Leaning over to retrieve it with his other hand, two more shots caught him in the chest. He fell backward, hitting his head on the sink, and slumped to the ground on his back. The commando trained his gun on the man as he moved forward. The copilot was dead.

With their silenced 9mm pistols in hand, the two remaining Nord Island commandos stepped quietly up the jet's stairway.

"Hang on, I think I have a couple of bungee cords up front," the pilot said over his left shoulder as he moved past the open doorway toward the cockpit.

The two commandos ducked as he walked by the cabin hatch.

"Do you want to sit back here during take-off to keep an eye on it?" The CDC scientist asked the Fort Detrick Army officer.

"A couple more tie lines and it should be secure for take-off, landing, and turbulence. It'll be okay as long as the analog gauge reads four percent humidity. I think we'll get it to the lab without any difficulties."

Switching subjects, he straightened up in the cloth-covered seat. "You know, that police detective was none too happy about being silenced by his chief," the Army biological weapons expert said.

"He was plenty angry. But when I told him that making this public could worsen matters, the police chief couldn't have been more cooperative. Now that two of their own people are sick with it, I think the lid is on, at least for the time being. Both men reflected on the meeting.

The conversation from the two scientists carried out to the jet's stairway.

"You go right and take the pilot; I'll take the two in back," the big commando whispered. His partner, the pilot-commando, nodded and a second later they were up and moving. The first commando charged right as quietly as one hundred seventy pounds could. It was twenty-six feet to the cockpit.

The two scientists were startled to see a rush of black colored clothing flash by eight feet in front of them. It was the next man who ratcheted up their surprise to terror.

"What the . . ." It was the last word out of his mouth as the second Nordian commando double pumped the semiauto at point blank range. The CDC scientist's head blew open and snapped back violently as the one hundred fifty-five grain, semi-jacketed hollow point blasted past bone. His body involuntarily carted backward with the second bullet, as it too, hit home.

The Army lieutenant colonel was already on his feet charging the intruder. He reached out and grabbed the gun as the third shot sped down the four-and-a-half inch pistol barrel. In a nanosecond, the bullet reached the exit point of the gun and plowed through the center of his right hand. Blood spattered onto his pants as his face registered the impact on his nervous system.

The back blast at the muzzle of the pistol prevented the explosive gases from completely discharging. Contained energy inside the stainless steel barrel forced the gun's top slide back over its stop. The 9mm pistol blew apart in the direction of the big Nordian commando. Metal shrapnel sprayed him, seriously injuring his shooting hand. He reeled from the pain and shock but managed to recover before the Army lieutenant colonel.

Spinning all the way around in reaction to the pain, he pulled the fighting knife from his combat vest with his other hand. Turning back to face the scientist, he slashed sideways across the aisle, reallocating the man in the process.

The sharp leading edge of the black chrome-moly steel met flesh and carved through it. The lieutenant colonel barely felt the cold blade slide through him. In an instant, bright-red blood erupted from his left carotid artery. Blood immediately soaked his collar and sleeve. He swung his left fist at the black-clad commando and missed.

The knife arced down and forward with tremendous force, connecting with the Army scientist's midsection. The commando pulled up and twisted in one swift motion. The serrated edge sliced into the officer's lower ribs. The Army scientist slumped to the ground and collapsed into a heap, dead. *No corpsman up for you,* the commando said silently.

Up in the cockpit, the Army pilot heard heavy feet pounding toward him. He was bent over behind the right seat, picking out several bungee cords from a canvas sack. He rose quickly when he heard the muted sound from the silenced firearm. Swiveling right, he started to rise from his crouched position between the two cockpit seats.

The Nordian commando-pilot brought both hands together on his gun and fired. His shot went slightly left and ripped through his target's leather flight jacket, hitting cowhide and a muscled right arm. Recoil from the 9mm gun raised the muzzle up and to the left as the empty shell case flew out in the opposite direction. The copper colored casing bounced off the cabin wall with a ping.

Too close, the commando told himself. Time seemed to slow as he tucked the gun into his side and charged ahead.

As the Army pilot stood up, the commando jumped at him feet first. Both men crashed full force into the console.

The commando recovered quickly and regained his feet. The Army pilot lashed out with his leg and connected with his attacker, knocking him rearward and onto the aisle floor.

Rolling onto his back, the commando raised his pistol up and pulled the trigger.

Windshield! Windshield! . . . he screamed to himself. He adjusted his aim point when he suddenly realized that he might miss his target and hit the aircraft's multilaminated window.

The shot rang out.

Stunned, the Army pilot abruptly stumbled back in his tracks as if suspended in time. Looking down, he saw where the bullet had connected with the metal belt buckle at his waist. His stomach contracted, the impact knocking the wind out of him. He fell forward to his knees, feebly putting his hands out to break his fall. As he looked up from the floor a second later, another bullet rocketed out of the commando's pistol. The round smacked into his right shoulder, breaking it cleanly. A third bullet hit him squarely in the chest, snapping a rib and shattering his left aorta. Death was almost instantaneous.

The third commando from the office suite reentered the hangar with the dead copilot slung over his shoulder. He cut the switches to all of the high intensity overhead lights, leaving only four fluorescent lamps on the maintenance desk. Running across the hangar, he bolted up the stairway and half dumped, half threw the body into the plane. A man's shoe, with blood on it, stuck out in the aisle. He repeated the exercise with the two dead Rangers who were in the corner of the hangar.

In the rear of the plane, the big commando who had taken out the two scientists stumbled over the bodies to the open plane door. He yanked on the interior handle, and closed it. "We're buttoned up. Let's get the hell out of here," he yelled forward, his face and hands bloody.

From outside the hangar, the third commando, backed the fuel truck in and attached a tow hook to the top of the front wheel strut of the jet. He pulled the jet from the hangar to the blacktop just outside. Hurrying back to the front of the aircraft, he pulled off the hook, grabbed the handle for the nearby power cart, and pulled it up to the nose of the military plane. He had to step carefully over several oil spots so as not to leave a footprint.

Attaching the power cable, he backed away and gave the pilot the thumbs up through the cockpit window. The pilot pushed switches and a minute later the left engine came alive.

The commando moved the fuel truck back to its parked location and trotted over to close the rear scissor doors. He got busy cleaning up any trace of blood left behind by the dead Rangers, stuffing paper towels into a black plastic bag as he worked.

Outside, the pilot lit off the right engine and immediately made for the taxiway. The airport had no nighttime air traffic control tower. The place was quiet, with the exception of a small Cessna that had flown off a few minutes earlier.

The third commando doused the remaining hangar light, closed the walk-through door behind him, and with garbage bag in hand, he headed for the surveillance van. Eight minutes had passed in well-rehearsed, almost total silence. It was over. They had the rock; now they just needed to make their escape. By the time the jet passed the end of the runway, the overcast night had swallowed it up, like a hungry cannibal wolfing down a meal.

⚷

"We're clear," the voice over the radio reported. The SUV engine started and the vehicle drove out of the parking lot down the block. The two-man team at the hospital, now safely in the shadows of the warm summer night, exited from the second floor engineering inspection catwalk. In another minute, they too would drive off.

The phone rang in the recessed alcove where Douglas Odin was watching the closed circuit action in the casino on the opposite side of the island. A well-known, male Hollywood celebrity, now slightly inebriated, was finding success with a well-built, green-eyed blonde close by his side. As his winnings climbed, the blonde's considerable cleavage spilled further from her twelve-ounce dress. Her makeup, hair, long legs, beautiful smile, and other assets were impeccable. Soon the famous playboy would find the distraction impossible to ignore and would leave the table. Odin compensated her, and several others like her, well for their services.

Recognizing the toned call, he picked up the handset. *"Godkväll* – Yes, Thor . . . Very good, I'll see you tomorrow."

He replaced the phone and went back to the TV monitor. Odin watched as the well-groomed movie star couldn't resist the lady's charm any longer. He threw the dice with his right hand for the last time. All eyes at the table watched the two red cubes bounce across the green felt. With his left hand, he surreptitiously gave her firm double D's a soft squeeze. His successful run at the craps table was over.

Provo Airport
Provo, Utah
Thursday, 2213 hours Mountain Time

The jet aircraft lifted off the runway and cleared the trees at the end by a hundred feet. Seagulls scattered in various directions, illuminated by the runway departure lights. Several small sport fishing boats dotted the dark-blue lake below, their wakes highlighting their movement across the water toward the harbor. The pilot's only friend at the moment was the lack of a headwind.

The Nordian pilot peeled off to the right and headed for the mouth of the canyon, according to the filed flight plan. Never having flown in the area before, he was justifiably concerned with the thirteen thousand foot mountain peaks scattered along his flight path. He twisted around in the chair in an attempt to get the seatbelt harness around his body. In his rush to get off the ground, he'd neglected to do several things. Now he was distracted and in the dark, which made things worse. He trimmed out the aircraft to climb and looked over the instruments. *Full fuel, EGT is okay, altimeter set, rate of climb is good. Why do the controls feel sluggish?*

Oxygen . . . Where's the backup bottle? He looked around the cabin and found the emergency O_2 set up behind his seat with the face mask attached. *Pressurization, where is it, where is it?* The pilot turned back around again, looked at the controls, and reached over to pressurize the aircraft to eight-thousand feet. A sudden rush of air in the vents adjusted to the setting. He looked at his hands; they were sticky from the blood. It felt uncomfortable. Ignoring it for the moment, he yelled over his shoulder.

"Sergeant, you buckled in okay?" A few seconds went by without an answer. "Sergeant!!"

"Yeah, I'm fine except for the blood," the voice trailed off.

"What, you're hit!"

"It's a little cold back here. You got any heat?"

"Uh, gimme a second to find it." The pilot scanned the controls until he came upon a dial that said "cabin heat" and cranked it up to seventy-two-degrees. He turned the aircraft further to the right and gained altitude, watching the altimeter rise.

"I got the heater on. It'll warm up pretty quick. Where are you hit?"

"The hands and face . . . I'll be okay . . . Just fly us outta here."

"We'll be clear of the area in a few minutes. Go back to the rear and see if there's a first aid kit near the head and clean up. When you're done, get the IDs off the bodies and then come up here and sit in the copilot's seat. I may need your help with the plane."

There was silence from the cabin.

"Sergeant, are you with me?"

There was no answer.

The pilot unbuckled himself and turned to catch a quick glimpse of the cabin. The commando in the front row seat was dead, his head hung limply to the side. The pilot spun around and buckled back up. *Damn.*

After a few seconds, he refocused his view out the windshield. The mountain peaks that formed the edges of the canyon loomed into view. *Jeez, what else is gonna to go wrong? Now I gotta carry the whole load myself.*

Then he noticed what he assumed was a sloppy hydraulic response from the ailerons and steering. *Why are the controls so sluggish? Crap, I hope this bucket will get over the canyon rim without any trouble. Please tell me they didn't shoot any holes in the fuselage . . . still a few miles to go.* He trimmed out the ailerons again.

His thought process shifted to the bodies piled up in back. *Damn. All that dead weight is throwing the center of gravity off for sure. No wonder it's a mess.*

He couldn't do anything about it at the moment, not until he was higher. The carnage they'd wrought was returning and his stress level rose noticeably. His habit of blaming other people for his problems was falling squarely on his own shoulders now, and he didn't like it.

The canyon edge passed by just below him a minute or so later, as the altimeter registered fifteen thousand feet. *I'm slipping around all over the place. The air is gonna get thinner and stability will get worse.*

Peering out the windshield, he glanced across the sky in front of his aircraft, searching for other planes. Not seeing any, he set the autopilot, unbuckled himself, and trotted into the cabin. Taking the commando's hand, he felt for a pulse. There was none. He grabbed the arms of the first body he came to on the floor, pulled it forward and in between the seats. A second one went on the opposite side of the aisle. He turned and hustled back into the cockpit for another look out the window. *Okay, I'm still looking good.*

Once again in the cabin, he grabbed two more bodies and repeated the process of pulling them forward in an attempt to balance out the aircraft's center of gravity. The trails of blood across the carpet caught his attention. He swore at the bodies, "Amateurs, you deserve what you got." He wiped the blood off his hands and onto his pant leg. "Jeez, I hope none of you losers had AIDS," his stress level was evident in the outburst.

He turned, stepped to the back, and looked over the double encased Lexan box with the virus-laden rock. The container appeared to be in good condition. The analog gauge glued to the outside of the case indicated four percent humidity inside. Satisfied, he left the last body sprawled across the floor at the rear of the cabin. He turned, walked back to the small cockpit and settled in.

He adjusted the aircraft's trim one more time and felt the jet respond immediately. Twenty-two minutes passed in silence when the radio crackled to life.

"Army two-seven-niner, Salt Lake Center."

"Now what?" The agitated commando pushed the talk button on the yolk and spoke into the boom microphone on his headset.

"Salt Lake Center, Army two-seven-niner at flight level two-two-zero, on a heading of zero-niner-four."

"Army two-seven-four, you are clear to climb to two-six-zero. You have traffic at twenty-five-thousand westbound at nine miles. We're going to hand you off to Denver Center. Contact them on one-two-six-point-five." The commando reconfirmed the information he'd been given and killed the mike.

He leaned back in the seat and relaxed a moment; he'd pulled it off. A big grin crossed his face and the moisture on his forehead dissipated. Suddenly he felt a lot cooler. *This is just too easy . . . if they only knew.*

Looking at his hands, he reached over, hit the autopilot again, unbuckled himself, and went back to the head to wash off. Returning to the cockpit, he flipped off the autopilot and rubbed his forehead with the wet hand towel. He scanned the instruments, found everything in the green, and rehearsed the next radio call in his mind.

"Denver Center, Army two-seven-niner." A few seconds passed.

"Good evening, sir. Please squawk five-one-one-three and ident."

The commando pushed the buttons to line up the numbers and hit the detent on the side of the transponder. The FAA center radar recorded his aircraft on their color monitor.

"Thank you, Army two-seven-niner. We have you at flight level two-three-zero, on a heading of zero-eight-six. Altimeter is three-zero-point-one. We have a northbound jumbo heavy to the south of you about eleven miles. You should be clear of his track; he's at twenty-nine thousand and climbing. No other traffic in your immediate area, sir."

"Thank you, Denver. I'm showing a minor hydraulic problem, not an emergency. We're going to divert to Vernal and check it out. Let's close out the flight plan for now. We'll recontact you after we've had a chance to look it over. Do I have anything below me on that heading?"

"Army two-seven-niner stand by, you look clear to descend on a gradual heading. There's no traffic between you and Vernal. Can we be of any further assistance, sir?"

"Thank you, no. I think we'll be fine from here. Army two-seven-niner out."

The pilot pressed on the right rudder and banked the small jet around, losing altitude, and coming to a northerly heading. Vernal airport didn't have a manned control tower after dark. No one would be able to check up on him anytime soon, which didn't matter anyway since he wasn't going there.

Dale's hotel room
Fisherman's Wharf, Seattle, Washington
Thursday, 2215 hours Pacific Time

Sean Fox looked over the equipment list, checking the hydrostatic test date on the group of oxygen tanks they would be using for the dive class. He was a stickler for safety details. Checking the O-rings one tank at a time, he found two that needed to be replaced. The rest were in good condition.

"Have we confirmed all the students for the class yet?" he asked Barney. The two men had spent the day together and hit it off from the moment they met.

"We have a couple of dropouts from NAS San Diego. Their spots have been picked up by two Homeland Security guys from the San Francisco office. I called on the other instructors as well. They'll be in town by lunch tomorrow," Barney replied.

"How's the wreck diving around here?" Sean asked. "I heard a couple of places just north of us might be good for recreational diving."

"Yeah, the Navy lost an F-14 Tomcat just across the bay a few years ago - that's a good dive. A hundred fifty-five foot fishing trawler lies just a couple dozen yards away. You wanna get in some wreck diving?"

"I was thinking about it. My brother is here on an assignment and we talked about getting in the water if we had time."

"What's he doing here?"

"He's an FBI agent running down some info on a case. It's rare to be together on business in the same town. We thought we'd enjoy some diving and seafood if we can get some time together."

"I'd be happy to set up a dive if you want some company."

"Hey, that would be great. I'll check with him and see how his schedule is going."

Sean continued down the equipment list.

A ship's air horn blast reverberated off the dockside metal storage shed as he check marked another item with his ballpoint pen. He looked across the end of the dock and watched as a well-lit, oceangoing freighter passed by. The squawk of sea lions somewhere under the dock reminded him of the open ocean diving that he enjoyed so much.

Marine Corps Command and Control Center
Camp Williams, Utah
Thursday, 2246 hours Mountain Time

"Sir, the county sheriff is on the line," Master Sergeant Ernie Holden said.

"Put him through to my desk, Ernie," the Marine colonel replied.

The closest full-time military installation with the capability to directly monitor the Provo virus situation was on a Utah State National Guard base twenty-two miles north of the Provo airport. It was a fully operational, well equipped training facility capable of running real time operations. By virtue of a top secret presidential finding signed two days before, the Marines were now monitoring the military transportation of the isolated rock with the foreign virus. A Marine Corps MarSOC team and their helo were on standby in the event that something required their special talent.

The Army jet that was to fly the encased rock to the Fort Detrick, Maryland, biological warfare lab was supposed to be sitting in an enclosed hangar in Provo, waiting for clearance from the Pentagon to depart.

"This is One-J-One. I'm looking for Colonel McKay," the sheriff said.

The sheriff frequently used his radio call sign to let folks at the other end of the receiver know that the top law enforcement officer in the county was speaking. It had a tendency to get quick results out of whoever was listening. The military call sheet he was holding had an immediate response contact party in the event it was needed.

"This is Colonel McKay. How can I help you, Sheriff?" the Marine officer responded.

"Colonel, I've just been informed that the jet is gone. I was expecting a call from the Pentagon so I could release my roving patrols. It never came."

The digital call interceptor on the desk in front of the Marine master sergeant showed a bank of horizontal, red LED lights indicating that the phone call was being recorded.

"I have a detective at the airport who informs me that he and his partner have discovered an empty hangar and blood spatters in the bathroom." The Marine officer's hearing perked up. "They've just sprayed Luminol on the hangar floor and found several pools of blood and bloody drag marks that were cleaned up. Do you have contact with your aircraft, Colonel?"

"Stand by one . . . Ernie, what's the status of the Army aircraft in Provo?"

The senior enlisted Marine looked at the high-definition, flat screen panel on the wall to his left, "Sir, we show it in the hangar."

"It's not there anymore, Ernie. Call Pentagon D-217 on the secure line and confirm status with their op center, now!"

Pentagon D-217 was the special operation command center office set up by presidential decree for overseeing the virus emergency.

"Sheriff, you say the jet is gone. Are there any military people still in the building?"

"Negative, Colonel. The place is unoccupied, according to my detectives. We've cordoned off the area as a crime scene. I have additional units pulling up now. They're taking a look around."

"All right, sir, I'm dispatching my security team by helicopter immediately. They'll be there in ten minutes or so. Please secure the area; no one in, no one out. Your people know the drill. I want to interview your detectives and see what they have."

The master sergeant was listening to the one side of the conversation he was privy to in anticipation of his next move. He pushed his glasses up his nose a bit and hit the hold button on his phone, "Colonel, D-217 shows the same status we do."

"Ernie, activate the MarSOC unit to the hangar. Get their bird moving now," he ordered. "Call the local ATC and clear their airspace for them."

The master sergeant jumped into action and kept D-217 holding the line. He turned to face his assistant, a staff sergeant.

"Get the FAA and NRO on the secure line. We're going to need to open a track on that Army jet."

The staff sergeant was already pushing buttons on the STU phone before the final word left the master sergeant's lips.

"Sheriff, can you hold for a minute?" the colonel asked. "I need to talk to my counterpart in the Pentagon."

"Go ahead, Colonel."

About two minutes passed when the Marine officer finally hung up the blue colored phone.

"Ernie, get Salt Lake radar on the phone and talk to their supervisor. I want to know what traffic departed Provo since 2130 hours and where it went. That was the last time the sheriff's roving patrol saw the jet in the hangar. Find that plane!"

"Sheriff, you still there . . .?"

Eastern Utah desert
Near Vernal, Utah
Thursday, 2252 hours Mountain Time

The digital clock on the aircraft instrument panel was coming up to the top of the hour. In a few minutes the pilot-commando would be below the mountain pass and out of radar coverage. It was dark outside except for the stars. His map indicated a private airstrip about thirty miles ahead. The information plate said it was exclusively for sport parachuting. It also showed the altitude and direction of the runway.

Definitely not designed for a jet. This is gonna be tight; hard braking, no thrust reversers. Better overfly it first and have a look. I wonder what's at the end of the runway.

Eight minutes went by. He was down to two hundred fifty feet above ground and flying slow. The airport was closed; no lights were evident.

Landing lights on, flaps down, one hundred fifty knots. No wind sock I can

148 — T-REX VIRUS

see. Wonder when was the last time a plane landed or took off from this dump? Yeah, looks to have all the charm of an old, abandoned cemetery, he thought.

The end of the runway flashed by in the landing lights. The gray cement color was instantly replaced by harsh brown tones. *Hmmm, nothing but dirt, rocks, and raw prairie running off in the distance. If I overshoot this, it'll be a long walk out.*

At two hundred feet over the ground, he pushed on the throttle, gained altitude, and turned around for another pass. The small military jet flew back down the taxiway at one hundred feet.

No planes on the tarmac, three hangars all closed up. Looks like the taxiway is longer than the runway. Decisions, decisions, and a half ton of dead weight in the cabin. He licked his lips and grimaced. *The stiffs have to go.*

He applied power again and pulled up to eight hundred feet. A few winking celestial lights broke the monotony of the black night sky. The sleek jet banked around and lined up again.

With a death grip on the wheel, he watched the ground race up at him. *Landing gear down, flaps down, tighten up the seat belt harness, no grazing animals . . . sphincter check.* He looked for the desert floor as the aircraft dropped out of the sky.

One hundred thirty knots - where's that damn taxiway?

Big rocks came into clear focus in the landing lights. He was almost down.

There.

He chopped the power and the wheels settled to the ground. He pushed the top of the pedals hard forward. The brakes grabbed. He pushed harder until he felt the aircraft begin to skid.

One hundred twenty, one hundred ten, one hundred. He blew past the first hangar, then the second, and finally the last one . . . . *eighty . . . seventy.* Flying desert bugs went splat against the windshield.

An old, 60s Ford fuel truck sat off to the side of the taxiway. Weeds sprouted up in the tarmac here and there.

. . . forty . . . thirty . . . twenty . . .

The tarmac ran out and the plane bounced off onto the hard packed desert floor. The three-inch drop from the solid taxi area didn't hurt the aircraft. The jet was finally down to walking speed. The pilot turned the aircraft around slowly, goosed the throttle, and climbed back up on the blacktop. A plume of dust and loose debris blasted across the bone-dry desert from the exhaust of the twin jet engines. The aircraft rolled across the asphalt, back on the cement, and slowed in front of the last hangar. There was a lit up soft drink machine off to the side of the hangar's vertical scissor door. His racing heartbeat was finally slowing.

Landing lights off, shut down left engine, idle the right, and another impressive landing for me.

The gauges pulled back to their stops, the pilot unbuckled himself, wiped the sweat off his forehead with his sleeve, and stood up. His runaway heartbeat returned to normal.

Damn, I'm good.

He walked to the back of the aircraft and stepped over a bloody body. Ignoring it, he opened the cabin door.

Ahhh, fresh air.

As he walked down the steps, he felt a slight cold wind from the north.

Dale's hotel room
Fisherman's Wharf, Seattle, Washington
Thursday, 2256 hours Pacific Time

Sean Fox reached the last item on the checklist and marked it off.

"I'm done. How are you coming with the refills?" he asked, referring to the gas mixture for the dive tanks.

Barney Davis twisted a clean cap cover over the valve of the bottle in front of him, "That's it, I'm finished. They're all at three thousand pounds. You hungry, Sean?"

"Actually, yeah, I am. We forgot to eat dinner, didn't we?"

"Yup. Let's go down the block to Ivar's and get some chow. They have great clam chowder and crab."

Sean nodded and laid the clipboard down on the air compressor. They walked out of the shed and flipped the light switch off. Barney locked the door handle from the inside and closed it tight.

⚷—⚡

The Nordian pilot walked over to the soft drink machine and dropped in some quarters. He pushed a button and a can dropped down into the swinging drawer. The cold, caramel liquid tasted good. It erased a metallic feeling in his mouth that had been there since the shootout back in Provo.

His eyesight adjusted to the darkness. It was eerily quiet. He could hear his own breathing, which reminded him that he was the only one left on the jet who was.

Time to get the dead weight off so I can get on with the scenic portion of the flight.

Looking around, he spotted a battered dumpster next to the hangar. He walked over, opened the top, and looked inside. It was half filled with boxes and trash. Putting both hands on it, he pushed the grimy, blue container in the direction of the idling jet. Finally, he stopped next to the fuselage door and went up the steps. Back in the cabin, he grabbed a body and dragged it to the doorway. He unceremoniously heaved the first one into the dumpster and returned for the rest, except for the dead commando still seatbelted into the aircraft.

You stiffs have outlived your usefulness, he laughed, *reinforcing the fact that my skills are infinitely superior to yours.*

He threw a mock salute at the dumpster and pushed it back against the hangar wall. Looking at his illuminated watch, he checked the time.

So much for that, ten minutes down.

Walking back to the jet he noticed a glistening spot under the wing.

What the . . . It's fuel . . . Oh, hell.

Darting anxiously up the cabin steps and into the front of the aircraft, he looked at the fuel gauge. Somehow during the fight in the cockpit, the fuel dump valve had been cracked partway open; he'd been losing fuel the entire time.

"Shit!" he cussed as he slammed it shut. Looking around, he grabbed a handheld flight computer off the seat while letting loose a barrage of four letter words.

What the, I'm down to forty-four percent. How far is that gonna get me? Where's that sectional chart of Washington and western Idaho?

Rummaging around on the copilot's seat, he fished for the map. Finding it, he flipped it over, looked at the route distance, and punched numbers into the flight computer. He waited impatiently for the digital window display to appear and started thinking out loud, *Lets see, if there's no head wind, I might make it. I wonder if the fuel truck has any jet fuel. No, probably not, it's avgas for prop planes.*

Gotta get the hell out of here. He ran his right hand through his hair for a moment before moving,

Why me?

With the idling engine still pitching a low whine, he hustled back to close the fuselage door. The blood stains underfoot scarred the tan carpet. He lifted one shoe and looked at the mess with disgust. Climbing back into the left front seat, he buckled up and brought the other engine back online. The jet taxied to the very end of the hold short area and turned toward the runway. He took a deep breath and noticed for the first time that his black flight suit smelled of sweat. He blinked a couple of times, pushed down hard on the brakes, and shoved the throttles forward.

Hold on, baby, we'll go in a minute. Landing lights on. The jet started shaking and bucking. *I hope like hell this piece of American tin can get off the ground.*

Releasing the brakes, the jet leapt forward, quickly gaining speed. A few agonizingly slow seconds passed.

Seventy ... eighty ... ninety ... come oonnnn.

He pulled back gently on the yoke and the nose of the jet slowly rose. *One hundred ... hundred ten ... hundred twenty.*

Just ahead, the Portland cement color of the runway ceased in the lights and the desert appeared. The sound of the jet engines straining to accelerate filled the cockpit. The airspeed indicator rushed past one hundred thirty-five. He pulled harder on the wheel.

He talked the aircraft into the air. *Come on, you hunk of junk, fly!*

The vibrating jet clawed its way into the cool desert air, the end of the runway disappearing under the wheels. Inside the cockpit, the stall warning horn blared as the undercarriage cleared the rocks by only a few feet. He was finally airborne and accelerating out to two hundred fifty knots.

Gear up, flaps up, lights off. That was an expensive soft drink.

He gained altitude and looked outside the cockpit for any other aircraft. Seeing none, he started to think of his next move. The cabin was in disarray, with paperwork and equipment strewn about the cockpit. He leaned over and tidied up as best he could.

Alright, now to call Salt Lake Center. I hope like hell this works. I'd hate to fly out of here at three hundred knots for nothing.

"Salt Lake . . . Beech Craft six-one-three-one-Juliet."

He waited a moment, searching the sky for any lights.

"Beech Craft six-one-three-one-Juliet. Squawk two-five-five-three and ident."

The pilot repeated the instructions and pushed the button on the transponder. The radar center painted the aircraft on a twenty-eight inch color screen. The air traffic controller saw the transponder box blink.

"Beech Craft six-one-three-one-Juliet, we have you in the Vernal area on a heading of two-niner-niner and sixty-seven-hundred feet."

"Affirmative, Salt Lake. Climbing out of Ripple Valley en route to Boseman, any traffic in the immediate vicinity?"

"Negative, Beech Craft. Are you VFR or IFR?"

"I'll be flying VFR."

"Very well, you're clear to climb to flight level two-one-zero. Wind out of the northwest at fourteen knots and altimeter at three-zero-point-two. We have a C-130 climbing from eighteen thousand feet, about nineteen miles straight ahead of you on a heading of one-eight-zero."

"Copy, Salt Lake, I'm looking. Thank you and good evening."

"Have a safe flight, sir."

He accelerated out to three hundred twenty knots, typical flying speed for the aircraft he claimed to be.

Wouldn't be good to get busted flying way too fast for a twin engine Beech, he told himself. Looking down at the fuel gauge, he cussed angrily. He needed more altitude to get the best fuel consumption and that wasn't going to happen. He worried about the rock in back as well. His problems seemed to be compounding themselves. Peering at his chart, he could see several purple spots marked

MOA. He'd have to skirt them and stay out of the military training areas.

Digging out the note from his pocket, he checked the GPS coordinates and instructions. *Next stop is an airstrip somewhere in north central Washington . . . hopefully.*

He cussed at the fuel gauge again.

U.S. Marine Corps Command and Control Center
Camp Williams, Utah
Thursday, 2312 hours Mountain Time

"Colonel, they lost it in traffic in the mountains after the pilot declared a non-emergency hydraulic leak. The jet disappeared off radar near Vernal, Utah. The pilot said he was setting down there to check it out. Local cops are on the way to the airport to have a look," the senior enlisted Marine said.

The Marine MarSOC team leader, a first lieutenant, pushed the button on his encrypted radio inside the specially equipped Black Hawk chopper.

The blades of the Marine Special Forces helo were still spinning slowly. "Bulldog, this is Line Handler. We got a problem . . ."

" . . . and Ernie, wake up the local commander for the Utah ANG. Get a crew out to their facility at the Vernal airport. I want one of their birds in the air ASAP. Give them the radar track for the jet and start a search. Put them on the satellite so I can talk to the pilot, and one more thing, Ernie, no discussion regarding this homicidal hunk of stone."

9370 feet AGL
Somewhere over north central Idaho
Thursday, 2333 hours Pacific Time

Aircraft at ten o'clock, low and slow. Small, private plane going south, the Nordian commando said to himself. He flew well north of the Boise area and began a descent into the mountains.

It's time to say goodbye to American radar coverage and vanish. So much wilderness in this country; no wonder they can't keep the illegals out.

He adjusted his setting for the flaps and noted the fuel gauge. By his estimate, he had less than an hour's flying time left in the tanks; it was going to be close. The massive wilderness area was no place to go down and get lost.

Dale's hotel room
Fisherman's wharf, Seattle, Washington
Thursday, 2334 hours Pacific Time

Dale and Sullivan were chewing on breadsticks when Sean walked into the hotel's all-night restaurant. He looked around and saw Sullivan raise his hand. The previous year, the three of them had been river rafting for a week on the Snake River in Idaho. Sullivan was a riot, with a sense of humor that poked fun at politicians, teenagers, anyone above his pay grade at the bureau, and just about everything else. But Sean also found out that Sullivan was a good guy. When Dale got thrown into the river on a nasty Class 4 rapid, before Sean could go over the side to snag his brother, Sullivan grabbed the rope in the rubber raft with one hand and Dale with the other. Together they pulled him back in before he could drown.

"You hungry at all?" Dale asked.

"Naw, I ate at a seafood place down the street a while ago. But I'll have dessert . . . It's a little late for a big dinner, isn't it?" Sean queried.

"Been a real long day for us. We saw an old friend of Dad's while looking for some help. We're running down our best lead on that homicide I told you about back at your house."

"Dad has more friends than acreage on the ranch. Which friend?"

"The admiral over at the Navy base just north of here. We're gonna go look for a sunken boat out by the islands in the morning. What do you have going on tomorrow?"

"Well, training doesn't start until day after tomorrow. I just have some familiarization with a couple of instructors, safety protocols, and that's about it. We got the equipment check done a little while ago, so I'll be free soon. Why, what's up?"

"The Navy is being helpful, but we might need a non-government diver, if you know what I mean."

Sullivan raised his eyebrows and lowered his head. "We don't need their ROV poking around and recording everything. Sailors talk too much, especially on shore leave when they've been drinking. We want them to find the wreck if they can. We'll use another vessel to recover whatever is possible if we can reach it. Otherwise, we'll have to call headquarters and bring in more muscle to do the job."

"Who's the local head honcho?" Sean asked, referring to the local FBI supervisor in charge in the area. "Can't he help?"

"The ASAC's name is Anthony Petrocelli. We call him "No-Knock," after a particularly lucky raid. He caught four nasty, well-armed bank robbers with only his partner as backup. More balls than brains. We're going to bypass him." Dale took another bite of the breadstick and looked at his brother.

"Someone you can trust who's not in official channels, okay, I got it," Sean said. "I'll need another diver."

"Got anyone in mind?" Dale asked.

"Yeah, I'll take care of it. Where and when?"

The three of them talked a bit longer and finally headed back to their rooms. Sunlight would be streaming through their curtains soon enough.

3680 feet AGL
Central Washington
Thursday, 2350 hours Pacific Time

The Nordian pilot tapped the fuel gauge nervously, trying to will the needle arm to rise from its stop. He was out of fuel; the starving engines would die in a few more minutes.

Where the hell is that airstrip? the Nordian commando asked himself nervously.

He hadn't seen a light on the ground for the past twenty minutes. Now he was down to thirty-five-hundred feet, trying to stretch out the fuel as he slowly descended toward his GPS target. *Damn trees everywhere, no open space in sight. Where the hell can I put down? Come on, you beast, we're almost on top of it.*

The GPS said he was just a few miles east of the coordinates he'd been given to land. It was dark outside with the exception of a sliver of moon that splashed pale illumination behind him. All he could see were the tops of trees as far as his sight could make out. The right engine began to sputter, and then a few moments later, the left.

"No, no, no, no, nooo!"

He pounded his fist on the console in anger and fired off a fountain of four-letter words.

Best angle of glide, he recited, adjusting his descent.

Stay clean until the last second. Where's that landing strip?

His eyes went wide searching for an opening in the forest, anything that hinted at an open space to set down in.

Off to his left, he spotted an area that looked like Paul Bunyon might have cut a swath. Then he saw a light flickering on and off through the trees. He was down to eleven hundred feet.

There, to the left about a mile, he said to himself.

He banked the plane over slowly, dropping further toward the woods. It was going to be a huge stroke of luck not to crash and burn. He turned slowly toward the runway, ignoring the slight tailwind. He didn't have the luxury of lining up into the headwind. It was straight in or nothing.

Five hundred feet, don't sink below the treetops, you tub. Keep the runway in sight. A little left aileron, straighten up. Sweat trickled down his forehead.

The jet slid to the side just a bit and was finally dead on to the asphalt runway. The trees were climbing in the windshield.

This is going to be a little close, one forty-five . . . one forty . . .

His unobstructed view of the runway was closing in quickly. A treetop started rising in the center of the cockpit window.

Only a few hundred feet to go. Stay up, you ugly, old cow.

The stall warning horn chirped in his left ear.

One hundred thirty, come on, come on.

The left engine nacelle clipped the tree and sheared off three feet of greenery. A shudder slammed the small aircraft. He was over the clearing and dropping. Jamming the gear lever down a moment later, he saw the three green lights come on, indicating the wheels were down and locked. The stall warning horn was screaming at him. The jet was out of momentum. The aircraft settled rapidly and bounced on the runway, blowing out the right tire. He leaned on the brakes hard; the runway was for small, single-engine aircraft.

He ate up one thousand feet in no time. The end of the asphalt was rushing at him in the windshield. Aiming for an opening slightly to the left of the center of the runway, he saw a spot where the trees parted. The jet bounded off the pavement and onto the forest floor at forty knots. Tree limbs and branches lashed the sleek gray jet as it careened out of control, digging a shallow trench with the nose wheel.

Dust from the forest floor rose up as the jet sped by. Seconds passed as it bled off forward momentum. The nose of the fuselage softly kissed a tall pine and stopped. The three-point harness holding him in place restrained his body, but his head snapped forward.

Loose pine needles fluttered down onto the cockpit windshield.

The Nordian commando leaned back in his seat and breathed a sigh of relief. *Unbelievable, I'm still alive.* He sat there collecting his thoughts while he ran his hands over his face and rubbed his eyes. Then it hit him.

Oh crap, did the ELT go off? He turned on the radio again and tuned it to the ELT frequency. No beeping noise, he was home free. Relief washed over him and he sat back again.

Looking around the disheveled cockpit, he finally vented the last of his frustration. "What a mess ... I need to get the hell out of here. Damn ... the rock!"

Unbuckling himself, he went warily but quickly to the rear of the cabin. The meteorite and its casing were still intact.

"Guess I won't be dying today after all," he said with smug satisfaction.

Walking aft, he popped the fuselage door open, took a deep breath, and inhaled the piney woods. He wiped the sweat off his forehead again. Stepping down the stairway, he looked around. It was dark, but there was a light on outside a building a couple hundred feet away. He went back into the cockpit, found a flashlight, and walked out of the aircraft to check his surroundings. He peered at his watch and saw it was just after midnight. He hefted the pistol into his right hand and headed off.

The place was unoccupied; it looked like a private airstrip. He returned to the jet in a hotwired Chevy pickup truck ten minutes later, this time with a full tank of gas. As he drove off the paved runway, it was difficult at first to figure out where the plane went. That was good. It would be hard to spot from the ground and air.

The commando found the groove in the dirt and followed it into the trees. Fifteen minutes had passed.

He managed to move the sealed, Lexan container with the suspended rock into a nondescript, black backpack with an aluminum frame that would sit comfortably on his hips and back. He tested it to see how even the weight distribution was. If he had to carry it, it would be acceptable. He took it off and placed it on the seat next to him. Turning around, he stood occupied in thought. Scratching his face, he walked forward.

"Well, partner, you're a little heavy, but we need do something about you. Sorry to see you go, pal," he said, reaching into the dead man's pockets and taking his money and watch. "Between you and the dead Americans,

I'm up about six hundred dollars, though. It was a lousy flight, but a marginally profitable one."

He shoved the green cash into his pants.

Reaching down, he snapped the seat belt off the body and took hold of the dead man's right arm. Slowly, and with some difficulty, he got the body in a fireman's carry and staggered to the back of the aircraft. After some grunting and groaning, he managed to dump the big Nordian sergeant's body into the back of the pickup truck bed.

"Man, you're heavier than you look."

A deep growl came from behind and the commando-pilot froze in place.

"Shit!"

He launched himself into the bed of the truck, grabbed his pistol, and saw a set of jaws snap behind him. The dog's head cleared the side wall of the truck. Sticking the muzzle of the 9mm out, he pulled the trigger. Hopping back down from the pickup a few seconds later, he took in the bloody mess.

"Where the hell did you come from?" he wondered, making sure the dog was indeed dead.

He looked down at the German shepherd. "Doesn't pay to sneak up on more dangerous prey, does it, pooch."

A few minutes later he drove out of the woods, back down the runway, and off the property. Seattle was still two hundred forty miles away, most of it by way of back roads. He needed to get some rest; he'd been up for almost twenty strenuous hours.

Marine Corps Command and Control Center
Camp Williams, Utah
Thursday, 2354 hours Mountain Time

"Colonel, NSA and NRO indicate no ELT signal anywhere in the area. The ANG pilot is running a grid pattern between Vernal and the next nearest airstrip about eighteen miles to the west. They have a second bird in the air now, working with them. So far, nothing," the Marine master sergeant reported.

"Ernie, how many other airports, airstrips, private runways, and deactivated military facilities are out there, say, within one hundred miles or so?"

"I'm putting it up on the screen now, Colonel."

Colonel McKay, a Marine major, and the three enlisted Marines in the center all stopped to look at the flat screen wall monitor.

"Looks like nine places to set down within a one hundred twenty mile radius," the major reported.

"Sir," the master sergeant interjected as he pointed with a red laser pen, " . . . these two . . . here and here, have runways too short to accommodate our jet."

Colonel McKay studied the colored map on the wall for a minute, "Alright, split the choppers up and have them head for these places and check them out. That includes the two places you pointed out as well, they can hit them last."

"Ernie, can the CO of the ANG unit get another helo in the air?"

"I'll check, sir."

The staff sergeant hit the hold button on his phone. "Sir, NSA has the voice tape of the jet's pilot notifying the Denver Center of his hydraulic leak. They're going to wash it against a tape of our missing Army pilot and see if it's the same person. They'll have something for us in a few minutes."

"Okay. Ask them if they can . . ."

Wasatch mountain range
Above Provo, Utah
Friday, 0623 hours Mountain Time

The sun crossed the valley and hit the mountain peaks to the distant west.

The colors yellow and gold sprinkled the heavily forested mountaintops. On the western slope of the mountain range to the east, one look from the second-floor bedroom window said it was cool outside in the mountain canyon. Birds were chirping, and somewhere a noisy woodpecker was pounding away for insects in the bark of a tree.

Dalton Jordan had fallen asleep in the padded wicker chair on his elevated back deck in the woods, listening to coyotes further up the mountainside. He woke up in the middle of the night and made his way sleepily to the bedroom. Once there, he dropped into the thick, multilayered comforter adorning his king-sized, dark-oak paneled bed. And there he lay until the projection alarm clock lit up the ceiling and finally crowed with the sound of a rooster.

Dalton rolled over and looked up. The time was 6:23 a.m. He had a plane to catch, or more accurately, a helicopter. The Feds had called the night before wanting to go to the exact location where his team of paleo-discoverers had found the long-hidden rock from the cosmos. He'd beeped Tori right after the call. It took three tries to rouse her from her girlfriends and their party. In the name of science, she'd excused herself and headed home to get some sleep for the early morning hop to the desert.

He yawned and picked up the phone to dial her number. On the second ring she answered.

"Hi there, I'm up and rolling. How about you?" she said after looking at the caller ID. Dalton found her perkiness refreshing, if not somewhat annoying this early in the morning.

"Yeah, I'll be out of here in ten minutes," Dalton said, "I'll see you at the parking lot at 7:15."

He hung up the phone and stared out the window at the tall, dark-green pines and aspens. A redheaded woodpecker flitted back and forth in the foliage. It was beautiful when he had an opportunity to enjoy it, which was getting more infrequent with all the notoriety.

Grabbing an empty Mason jar from the pantry, he dumped corn flakes in and poured milk over the cereal. He shook the whole thing with the lid on and trotted down the steps of the six-room cabin to his car.

The engine on the old Volvo turned over with the first twist of the key. He let it idle a minute, as his dad had taught him, to warm up the engine and circulate the oil. Dalton then spun the lid off the Mason jar and pro-ceeded to drink his breakfast.

Four minutes later, he was off the hard-packed gravel road and onto pavement. He headed for the parking lot across from the BYU stadium where the Fed's helicopter was waiting. On the way down the mountain, he felt a stiff ache creep into his bones. He stretched his legs and arms out as he drove, hoping the day and the sun would warm him up.

Tori struggled to button her blouse as her VW Bug - a present from her parents at her master's graduation - exited the apartment complex where she lived. Shifting into third, she beat out the yellow light at the end of the block. She had an ice-cold quart of chocolate milk, a luxury she never had in the desert on a dig site, on the seat beside her.

Two miles later, she wheeled into the large, open BYU parking lot to the west of the football stadium. The empty milk carton rolled around on the floor of the passenger side. The military helicopter was waiting.

Getting out of the car, she inwardly acknowledged to herself that she felt sluggish and achy. She would feel much worse before the last vestige of sunlight dropped beyond the mountain at the end of the day.

"Yes, General. The bodies of our team have been discovered at an airstrip used by a parachute club, about thirty-eight miles north of the local city airport. The FBI is on the scene and NCIS will be there shortly," Marine Colonel Mark McKay replied. "It's in a remote area in the desert, sir . . . Yes, sir, I know. I will, sir."

The two-star general in the Pentagon D-217 office was in the hot seat with the chairman of the Joint Chiefs. A full court press was on to find the missing Army jet from Fort Detrick, and its deadly cargo. The chairman, likewise, was about to talk to the president, who would not be happy when informed that the viral killer was on the loose.

"Yes, sir, they're pouring over the radar tapes right now, trying to identify anything that we can track. I have three of my officers there now." He listened as the general issued expanded instructions.

"Yes, sir, I'll update you every thirty minutes or sooner if we have something solid."

The general's phone went silent.

McKay hadn't slept for almost twenty-two hours. His feet hurt from the new shoes and the tiled floor he'd been walking on most of the night. At this point, even thirty minutes of sleep would put him back in a better analytical frame of mind.

"Ernie, it's 0635 hours, I'm going to hit the rack upstairs. Wake me in forty-five minutes, sooner if something breaks."

"Yes, sir."

McKay was partway up the stairs when he suddenly stopped and raised his head as if he smelled something in the air. He turned to the seven men in the operations center with a loud voice.

"Master Sergeant, does the FBI have a list of the belongings found on the bodies at the airstrip?" he asked with renewed intensity. "Find out if they all had cell phones on them."

"Give me a second to find out, sir." McKay bounded back down the steps and across the room.

"Master Sergeant Holden at Marine C&C. Put the lead investigator on, it's urgent."

Twenty seconds passed as the master sergeant waited impatiently. He repeated his request when the man at the other end of the phone answered.

"Everybody had a cell phone with the exception of the pilot. Oh, and his watch was missing, too."

"Okay, wait one FBI." He put his hand over the receiver. "Colonel, all the guys had cell phones that we can account for, except the pilot."

"Tell him 'thanks' and hang up."

"Where's the cell phone list for the crew, major?" McKay asked.

"Got it . . . Want me to call it, colonel?"

"Negative, major. Do we have the registration number for the pilot's cell phone?"

"Yes, sir."

"Give it to Ernie. Ernie, let's get the NSA on the secure line, give it to them, and tell them we're going to call it and we need a trace. Tie them into the call." Less than two minutes later, the master sergeant said NSA was ready.

"Dial the pilot's cell phone now, major, and let's see what happens. Put it on the speaker."

A few seconds passed and a ringing tone could be heard on the overhead speaker. The command center was dead silent, everyone anticipating the next couple of moments.

After four rings, an automated female voice answered with the standard "take a message" recording.

"Colonel McKay here," he said as he snatched the nearest phone handset off the hook. "Do you have a cell tower on it?"

The NSA officer on the other end of the phone passed over the information on the cell phone's location - north central Washington state. The signal strength on the call indicated the cell phone was less than a mile from the transmission tower.

"Major, get D-217 on the line. We have the location of the cell phone, and hopefully our missing aircraft."

In the woods
North central Washington
Friday, 0550 hours Pacific Time

The soft tone of the alarm on the commando's watch went off and he awoke. The pickup truck he was hunkered down in was parked a mile off the beaten path in the woods, fifty-two miles from the private airstrip. It was uncomfortable and cramped, and his rest was anything but relaxing. In the dark of night, he'd dug a hole in the forest floor and unceremoniously dumped his dead companion in. Then he lay down and went fast to sleep.

Not the most peaceful rest I've ever had. I wonder what's on the radio. He started the engine and tuned to the only station he could bring in clearly.

Eleven minutes to the top of the hour, and local news, he thought to himself.

Opening the door, he exited the truck, stretched, then walked a few feet away and relieved himself. When he was done, he yawned and got his cramped muscles warmed up. After listening to the local news, he started the engine and drove off toward the little, scenic highway in the mountains. The two-lane road would take him toward Seattle, slowly, at forty miles an hour for now. No clues had been discovered regarding the disappearance of the government jet he'd hijacked. At least nothing that made the news.

North central Washington
Friday, 0556 hours Pacific Time

"There, in the trees, see it. A straight edge at a forty-five degree angle tucked in at the far end. Take us down," a voice in the headset ordered. The night vision goggles lit up the area in a green hue. Daylight would be breaking pretty soon and the need for them would end.

The Marine Super Cobra helicopter dropped out of the sky like a roller coaster ride heading for the bottom of a long, fast run. It flared a few seconds later and touched down just short of one hundred yards away. Dust and pine needles swirled around the combat chopper. Behind it, a Washington Army National Guard Kiowa helo followed suit. The men in the Kiowa were out quickly and headed for the military transport jet that was mostly hidden in the woods off the runway, their loaded M-16 rifles at the ready.

"Bloodhound Two, C&C Authority says to be very careful what you shoot, there's some kind of biotoxin impregnated rock on board," the disembodied voice on the Apache reminded the Kiowa pilots. "It's in a clear Lexan container and isn't dangerous unless it's out of the case; should be mounted at the back of the aircraft." The rotors of the Apache continued to spin at full speed, ready to climb and defend the two men on the ground, if necessary.

"Stand by Bloodhound One, we're entering the aircraft."

Moving carefully and methodically, taking in their surroundings, the two National Guard pilots slowly walked up the open stairwell. One headed for the cockpit, the other surveyed the empty shell casings and blood that saturated the tan carpet. Less than a minute later, the pilot of the Kiowa was out in the woods again.

"Bloodhound One, it looks like an Arnold Schwarzenneger movie set inside - blood everywhere, bullet holes in a few places in the cabin seats and partitions, spent 9mm shell casings. Looks like frangible rounds were fired, and there's plenty of physical damage in the cockpit. Someone put up a hell of a fight. There's no Lexan casing with a rock, though. Whoever grabbed the jet made off with it. I'm outside now. The engine nacelle is stone cold. I'm going to call the cell number they gave us. Wait one."

He punched in the Army pilot's cell phone number from his own cell and waited for it to connect.

Inside the fuselage, the Kiowa copilot heard a ring. It took a few seconds to find the cell phone in the cockpit.

"I got it!" echoed out the fuselage door.

Unbeknownst to the Nordian commando, during the struggle on the jet the Army pilot's cell phone had fallen out of his pocket and rolled onto the canvas sack under the copilot's seat. It lodged itself in the folds of the khaki bag, and there it remained.

A few moments later, both men were out and hustling back to their chopper. From the other end of the runway, red and blue lights flashed onto the scene.

"Bloodhound One, give me a minute with the locals," the Kiowa pilot said.

"Copy that."

Five minutes passed as the county sheriff made contact by phone with the family that owned the private airstrip. They discovered that the pickup truck that should have been parked on the side of the cabin was gone. A couple of minutes later, the local police had a BOLO (be on the lookout) issued across the state for the license number, make, and model of the pickup truck.

The Apache pilot pulled back on the collective and twisted the throttle, "Bloodhound Two, we'll be in the air."

"Copy that."

The Marine attack chopper rose quickly to several hundred feet and flew a circular pattern around the private airstrip.

"Bulldog, this is Bloodhound One."

Colonel Mark McKay hit the button on the radio at his desk, "This is Bulldog . . . report."

"Aircraft identity confirmed, plane empty, package missing, interior of jet shows obvious signs of CQB, lots of blood. Local law will guard until the forensic team from Navy arrives, should be about twenty minutes out at this point."

"Confirm, package not onboard, Bloodhound!"

"Affirmative, Bulldog, package not onboard."

McKay was turning the wheels in his head, thinking of his next move. Master Sergeant Ernie Holden was standing by McKay's desk, waiting to see if he was needed. He'd never been involved with anything that had presidential authority before.

"Have the Kiowa pilots stand by until the forensics team arrives. They have been granted federal law enforcement authority per a presidential directive. Do not release the scene to the locals. Maintain federal custody of the aircraft and inform the pilots of their new status. There's an FBI agent onboard the forensics chopper who will take over when he arrives. We'll contact the local sheriff and inform them as well. Keep everyone away from the plane. Then start checking the back roads from the air – find that pickup truck, copy?"

"Affirmative, Bulldog."

The Marine officer flying the Super Cobra repeated the instructions back and then headed down to the airstrip.

"Bloodhound Two, switch to two-eight-eight-point-seven."

The Kiowa pilot dialed up the new frequency and keyed his radio. "Bloodhound Two on tactical, go ahead."

Ninety seconds later the Super Cobra lifted off and went on the hunt for a battered blue pickup truck.

In the upper seat in the Apache, the weapons officer keyed his intercom, "Jack, if you were a bioterrorist, would you try to hide in the woods?"

"Hell no, too easy to get caught. Everyone probably knows everyone else who should be around the area. If it were me, I'd steal another vehicle if I could and head for the big city, much easier to get lost there."

The Super Cobra climbed to a thousand feet while the two men inside started scanning the roads.

Utah Valley Medical Center
Provo, Utah
Friday, 0745 hours Mountain Time

The two lab physicians stood at the empty water cooler on the second floor mezzanine, waiting for a third doctor, a radiologist, to finish putting in a new bottle. The open-air view of the floor below included a local TV reporter, a couple of uniformed cops, and the hospital's public information officer, among the staff. So far, the story of the nasty influenza outbreak was holding. The radiologist finished his task and walked away.

"If the rest of the employees and the public knew about this disease, there would be cameras and outsiders crawling all over the place," the tall molecular pathologist said.

"I suspect it'll happen soon enough," his friend with the unruly mustache begging to be trimmed replied.

"You see the morning tally yet?"

"Yeah, four more dead and nine more admitted here, two further up the valley. They're being transferred here today. That's probably why we have so much activity so early."

"Three of our own people are infected. Too bad about that swing shift ER nurse; I understand she wasn't wearing gloves when she started working with the alpha patient."

"Actually, she was. I have her stethoscope; it's got the bug on it. It's in a white bin on one of my lab tables. The virus has been active for four days now, and I'm still getting a reaction to it with the acid test. The stethoscope picked it up from the alpha, she got it on her skin somehow, and it was absorbed from there."

"Four days, that's nasty," his friend replied.

"It certainly appears to be unforgiving." The molecular pathologist stopped talking while a nurse walked by. He leaned forward with a whisper, "I wish I could offer these people more than prayers. This infection is voracious. The CDC guys and their mobile lab don't appear to be any closer to a treatment solution."

Not good, his friend thought. *Life is too precious and too short to be emotionally burdened by a killer I can't defend against, or see coming.*

"I need to get back to my lab. See you at the lunch meeting." He disappeared down the hall, absentmindedly rubbing his long mustache as he walked.

In the large foyer below, three men in suits entered the hospital and stopped to look around. One of them pointed to the left. They proceeded down the hallway in unison, their hard-soled black shoes tapping out a staccato rhythm.

The tall one was a full bird Army colonel, while the other two were biological warfare experts from the Tooele Army Depot, the nation's top chemical warfare incineration center. All three men wore dour looks on their faces. They had trained for it, but never expected this kind of nightmare to appear in their own backyard.

25

U.S. Naval Base
Everett, Washington
Friday, 0652 hours Pacific Time

Fire Captain Sean Fox and his brother stood about fifty yards from the well-worn dock where a Navy tugboat was tied up. Seattle Fire Department Lieutenant Barney Davis was walking their way. Barney had spent six years in the Navy, almost all of it as a firefighter at an airfield not too far from San Diego.

Two weathered five-foot-long boxes with dive gear sat alongside the men on the tarmac. Off in the distance, a lone U.S. Navy Sikorsky helicopter beat the sky with its rotors, the noise just becoming audible.

"Where's Sullivan?" Sean asked his brother.

"Got a call about forty-five minutes ago at the hotel. We tossed a coin and he lost. A Navy chopper took him off to central Washington about fifteen minutes ago with a forensics team to check out an Army executive jet that was hijacked last night. He's going to call me when he has something. We don't really need him for this hop."

Sean knew that whatever Dale revealed to him was strictly confidential. The two close-knit brothers had long ago worked out an occasional "need to share" system in spite of the fact that there was no real need to know. Dale found Sean was a good sounding board, and sometimes it was constructive to see if he had thoughts on a subject that Dale might not have entertained.

As Barney Davis walked up, Sean stuck his hand out. "Ready to get wet, maybe?"

Barney grinned and took in the cool, fresh, ocean air as he shook Sean's hand. "It's a great day to get in a boat, drink some cold beer, chew on some fresh grilled hot dogs, and just do a little fishing." Sean chuckled, "If only that was an option . . . Lieutenant Barney Davis, my brother, Dale Fox."

"Nice to meet you," Dale said with a hearty handshake and a friendly smile.

"Likewise. So, what kind of trouble are we looking to get into?" Davis asked, his enthusiasm evident in his response.

Dale filled in the blanks for Lieutenant Davis and ended with a cautionary warning to keep it to himself. If there was any glory for the work, he would eventually be recognized by the FBI . . . if and when he could do it. "On a personal basis, let me say thanks. I really do appreciate your willingness to help."

Suddenly Dale's cell phone vibrated in his pocket. Retrieving it, he recognized the incoming number on his digital display.

It's No-Knock. Wonder what he wants.

"Excuse me a moment, guys." Dale walked off a few yards.

Sean and Barney continued an animated conversation about diving and what they might encounter on this "off-the-books" trip.

On the third ring, Dale pushed the talk button. "Fox."

"Dale, it's Tony. Got some good news for you, can you talk?"

Dale frowned, "Yeah, go ahead."

"Word's out that you and Casse have been bumped to supervisory status. Same job, better paycheck. It just came over the computer." There was a pause. "Congratulations. What's going on?"

Dale's boss, Dan Covery at the CTU, had told him it would probably happen in advance of the "flying-squad" being expanded. Dale and Sullivan were the prototype pioneers for the new program. He had commented to Covery, a longtime friend, at the conclusion of the initial kickoff meeting that he felt more like a wandering, clueless, guinea pig. The powers that be decided after he left that Dale and Sullivan were definitely the right guys for the job. The GS-15 pay scale would follow in a check or two.

The last thing Dale wanted No-Knock to hear was that the program was about to grow more feet. Success in the bureau could breed contempt amongst some field agents in spite of the common sense outcome intended.

"I honestly don't know. I'll have to call headquarters and see what's up. Anything new on your end?"

"Yeah, the inventory of the latest version of the Black Hawk choppers within flight and refueling range was completed and it confirms no U.S. or Canadian aircraft were involved in our highway kidnapping. There was some holdup on the info due to a black-ops unit somewhere that has a couple of them. Headquarters just got back to me this morning on it. It definitely wasn't ours." No-Knock paused for effect. "Got any idea who it might be, Dale?"

His question dripped with the obvious probing slant to it.

Yeah, I got an idea, but I'm not telling you, pal.

"A pack of pygmy gypsies, angry clowns, cloistered nuns, I don't know who it could have been, Tony. That's what we're searching for."

The sound of the Sikorsky chopper was growing louder as it descended. "I gotta go, Tony. My ride is here. I'll call you later."

He pocketed the phone and walked back to Sean and Barney.

The helicopter hovered and dropped slowly to a spot just a couple dozen yards away. The helmeted crew chief hopped out and trotted up to the three men.

"You guy's the FBI agents?" he yelled over the loud rotor wash.

"Yeah . . . FBI and fire. We need to put those boxes onboard," Dale said.

"Fire?" the crew chief asked somewhat puzzled.

"I'll explain onboard, petty officer. Let's go."

A minute later the rotor wash increased and the helicopter lifted off for a half-hour ride out to the destroyer *U.S.S. Jonathan Cooke.*

Pacific Ocean
Due west of Seattle, Washington
Friday, 0724 hours Pacific Time

Seventy-four miles away, a silent stealth submarine, not of friendly origin, entered the outer San Juan Straits of Washington state.

"Bridge, sonar."

"Go ahead."

"Sir, we have a significant surface contact. Looks like an Arleigh Burke class destroyer, and possibly a smaller combat vessel, type unknown."

The lines in his face creased a little as the information routed its way through the game plan burned into his memory. Captain Ingvar Wallen pushed the intercom button, a slight frown on his brow. "Where are they, Lars?"

"Which one is ours, petty officer?" Sean asked. The cool air and winds aloft produced some chop, causing the helicopter to bounce around.

"The *Cooke* is the one out front, sir. I suggest you tighten it up. We'll be touching down real quick, it might be a jolt." Sean tugged on the shoulder harness and pulled his legs in closer. He could see the white, foamy wake trailing behind the destroyer from his mesh net seat.

Thirty seconds passed, in which Wallen had to make a dicey choice: wait out the two American combat ships or press on with a critical mission. He had little room to adjust the timing of the planned pickup of his agent with the encased sliver of diseased asteroid.

Wallen leaned on the comm button again, "Helm, come right to zero-nine-six, slow us to four knots, and boost the tiles to ninety-five percent."

"Aye, aye, sir."

"XO, take us to red light condition." The executive officer flipped a lit toggle switch on the command console next to him. It bathed all of the spaces aboard the submarine in a dim-red glow.

"Weapons . . . bridge."

"Weapons . . . Go ahead, sir."

"The contingency I planned for has arrived. Charge numbers one, two, three, and four CHINOs, give me a firing solution, and maintain the track."

"Aye, aye, sir."

Wallen moved to the left side of the console and grabbed a calculator.

"Sonar, bridge."

"Sonar," the young man with the stereo headset replied.

"Stay on those two ships and let me know of any change in their course or speed."

"Aye, sir."

"Weapons . . . bridge."

"Weapons, sir."

"Stand by to engage, COB . . . Make the boat ready," Wallen ordered. "Radio, bridge . . ."

Wallen pushed back from the plotting table and took a moment to consider the deaths he had a hand in over the past two years. He let out a slow breath and sighed to himself.

There were some things he regretted. Demons were starting to haunt his sleep.

North central Washington
Friday, 0752 hours Pacific Time

The Nordian commando pulled into the rundown, 1950s-style fuel stop in the woods. The faded, blue sign at the corner of the property read, "Red's Gas and Repair Shop." A few green weeds swayed back and forth against the bottom of the sign in the light breeze.

The gas station attendant moved slowly, like a lizard waiting for the warmth of sunshine to speed up his metabolism. The lone gas station employee, his dirty blond hair hanging over his eyes, shuffled out as the commando pulled the gas nozzle off the pump and started fueling the truck.

"Need any aul or anythin'?" he asked. The attendant had brake dust on his hands.

"Got it covered, thanks." The commando flipped him two twenty dollar bills. "Where's your bathroom?"

"Uh, it's jus' round side of the building. That all ya need?"

"Yah."

The man's native Swedish accent, with the tendency to noticeably inhale the word "yeah," was something that he was trying hard to avoid. He didn't need anyone recalling anything specific about him, other than he was a nondescript person passing through. He'd made the mistake in a momentarily lapse in judgment while trying to concentrate on listening. The gas station attendant's slow drawl made him difficult to understand.

The commando drove the old truck around the corner of the building a minute later. He ducked inside and counted to ten, hoping it would be enough time for the sluggish mechanic to go back inside the shop and resume his work. Looking around, he wrinkled his nose; the bathroom was disgustingly filthy.

His target was a closer peek at the back lot. When he drove up, he spotted a line of cars sitting behind the building, waiting for tune-ups, brake jobs, and miscellaneous repairs. It was time to replace the truck. The minute someone discovered the downed jet at the private airstrip, the truck would be too hot to be driving around. Peering into the cars that he could see up close, he discovered that the keys were in the ignitions.

Stupid Americans, no wonder you have so much crime, he thought.

He hopped back into the truck and drove off the lot to the deserted, narrow side road that wound its way up into the thick woods. What he needed was a diversion so he could check out a few cars. As he drove off, his luck was rewarded by a green family van pulling in. When it stopped, the side door opened, and four rambunctious kids and a golden retriever popped out. The dog ran off to the ditch on the far side of the gas station with the kids in hot pursuit.

The commando pulled the pickup off the road about a third of a mile up the hill, just out of sight of the service station. He tucked the backpack behind the seat and trotted across the blacktop and into the undergrowth.

The kids were making noise, still trying to round up their pet. The gas station attendant was out front checking the tire pressure on the van as the gas pump filled the fuel tank.

Sticking to the heavy foliage to remain concealed, the commando slid down the embankment next to a couple of overgrown trees. The fourth vehicle he looked into started right up and had almost a full tank of gas. He slipped out the back lot while the attendant was occupied with checking the van's oil.

A minute later he was back at the first stolen pickup. Switching vehicles, he drove the first one further into the woods, over a sloping ravine, and out of sight. It took him two minutes to run back to the new pickup with the backpack, where he promptly drove off in the direction of the coast.

No one will miss this thing for a day or two, he thought.

Three marked police cars sat idly in front of the weathered log cabin next to the private airstrip. The officers were talking and smoking, patiently waiting for someone to tell them why they were needed. Sixty yards away, the Washington ANG Kiowa chopper occupied the center of the runway near the edge of the forest. A Black Hawk helicopter roared into view overhead. It circled around once and headed for the asphalt tarmac below. Dust, leaves, and pine needles flew as the aircraft thundered to the ground.

The first person off was Sullivan Casse, wearing a bright-yellow windbreaker with bold, black FBI lettering stenciled across the back. He shoved the manila envelope he was carrying into his shirt and took a quick look around.

Earlier that morning, when the Navy Black Hawk prepared to lift off back at the naval base, an intelligence officer had run out to the chopper with an oversized envelope at the last second. The "secret" stamp and the contents were bad news, but they explained a lot. Their investigation had just taken a new turn. Dale would be happy to know his hunch was probably right on the money.

The sweet scent of pine trees permeated the fresh air. Sunshine was just beginning to paint the tops of the trees. The local cops, seeing Sullivan, started walking toward him, hoping for some explanation as to what was up.

Sullivan pulled out his cell phone and dialed his partner. Dale's phone rang to his take-a-message recording. *Maybe the helo's radio can contact the destroyer,* he thought. He stepped back to the open door of the chopper. The blades were spinning slowly overhead.

"Lieutenant, can you get ahold of the *Jonathan Cooke*. My partner's on it out in the San Juan Straits somewhere."

"If I can get a satellite relay, we can," he replied.

"Alright, see what you can do. Holler if you get them. When I'm done with the cops, I'll be over at the Army jet."

"Yes, sir."

⚷

"Pull the boxes off and find a place to store them out of the weather, if you would, please," Sean requested of a young petty officer.

The Sikorsky unloaded quickly and took off for its base a few minutes later.

Dale was greeted by a plump-faced young ensign, who ushered them forward to the ship's superstructure.

"If you'll follow me, sir, the captain is waiting on the bridge."

"Hang on just a second if you would . . . Sean, Barney." Dale waved them over. Out of earshot of the young officer, he whispered, "Keep the gear handy for transport. Detective O'Brien with the Seattle PD is over at Friday Harbor waiting for our call. They have a dive boat ready to go if we find something. Let's keep it to ourselves, okay."

The morning breeze over the bow picked up. A cool, misty salt spray fanned their faces. Sean and Barney nodded and went back to their equipment containers. Before following the junior officer into the ship, Dale briefly looked up at the angled superstructure.

⚷

Sullivan turned toward the police officers as the FBI forensics team passed by with their testing and lab equipment cart. The technicians headed toward the Army jet that was still firmly tucked in among the trees.

"I'm Sergeant Bell. Nobody's told us what's going on, other than there's some special deal from the National Military Command Center on this crashed jet."

"It didn't crash; it ran out of fuel and glided in, to a less than ideal landing, I'd say. The runway's short, and he overshot; he had no place else to go."

"So where's the pilot, and why are we babysitting the airstrip?" His tone of voice was demanding more than inquiring.

"Classified and classified. That's the best I can do. When the techs are done, maybe an hour or so, it'll be refueled and a crew will probably fly it out. Uncle Sam appreciates your help in securing the area. I'd like to tell you more, but the folks a couple of pay grades ahead of me set the rules here."

Out of the corner of his eye, Sullivan spotted the Kiowa pilots walking his way.

"I need to chat with the ANG guys. I'll talk to you again in a bit, but for now, I think we can get by with just two of you."

"Thanks," the old sergeant said. The deputies shook their heads and walked off to their patrol cars, discussing the various reasons why cops in general didn't like the FBI.

A few minutes of conversation passed with the Kiowa pilots before Sullivan finally excused himself as the senior FBI lab technician waved him over.

"You need to see the inside of this thing, but only if you have a strong stomach," the short, balding tech said.

"What do you have?" Sullivan asked.

"The chemical analyzer is showing blood, human sweat, lightweight oil traces, wood glue, hair mousse, and carpet cleaning chemicals, along with a few other innocuous items. The sniffer is still reeling out results. We'll be printing and dusting awhile. The nose gear looks good and that little ding on the front of the fuselage probably won't keep the plane from airworthiness if they intend to fly it out. Worst-case scenario, we unscrew the nose cone over the small radar dish and pop out the dent."

The FBI technician checked his clipboard for handwritten notes before going on. "Better check with one of your pilots to confirm the balance of its flight controls though."

He pulled a plastic container off the lab cart behind him. "We have a number of things bagged so far, and we just found this wedged between a seat and the bulkhead." He held up an evidence bag with a well-worn Doxy dive watch inside.

Sullivan took the bag and looked carefully at the expensive timepiece.

Hmmm, I wonder . . .

Sullivan had the same watch at home in his dresser drawer. It was a gift from his parents for his thirtieth birthday. It showed the time as 9:06 a.m., Mountain Time, an hour ahead of the local time. He pushed the side button and a second time appeared on the watch face. It showed 7:06 a.m.

Hmmm.

"Agent Casse," the Navy lieutenant yelled, "We're on the net with the *Jonathan Cooke*. They're going to get your partner."

Sullivan gave the evidence bag back to the technician and walked over to the helicopter. "This is agent Fox. Who's this?"

"Dale, its Sullivan. I got an envelope marked top secret from the naval intelligence center at the base just as I was leaving. It's from HQ. The note says that the Seattle office got a general copy, but what I'm holding is very specific. There's an outbreak of a major flu virus reported in Utah that's spreading out of control. CDC has been called in apparently."

"Interesting, but what's that got to do with us?"

"Dale, are you secure?"

"Hang on a second."

Dale looked at the three men in the *Jonathan Cooke's* communications room. "Fellas, Uncle Sam needs a little privacy here. Do you mind?" The lieutenant and the two petty officers stepped out of the room and closed the hatch.

"Okay, I'm alone. What do you have?"

"It's not the flu. That's a cover story that may not hold up much longer. A university paleontologist unearthed some dinosaur bones in the Utah desert a few days ago. When they dug it out of the ground, they found a nonindigenous chunk of rock underneath it. So they dug it up, too, and took it back to their lab. Someone spilled water on it at BYU and a full blast viral epidemic was borne. They have no idea what it is or how to treat it."

Sullivan paused a moment to turn to page two of the report.

"A federal hazmat crew finally encased it in an airtight Lexan container. It has an analog gauge on the front that shows the moisture content inside. CDC scientists advise that if it reaches twenty-five percent it could sweat and go active."

Dale jumped in and interrupted Sullivan, "How many people are sick so far?"

"According to this, about fifty, but they have seventeen dead on top of that. A small boy is holding his own, but again, they don't know why as of yet."

"Holy . . . How's that tie into us?"

"This Army jet was stolen from Provo, Utah last night with what they believe is the viral infected rock. They found the bodies of a couple of Army Rangers, several scientists, and the pilots in a dumpster at a remote skydiving airport in northeast Utah. Whoever is behind this is redefining ruthlessness. I'm at the Army jet now. It ran out of fuel and was ditched at a private airstrip sometime before dawn. The rock is gone. The CDC folks are saying this thing is walking death."

Sullivan put the report down on the tech cart.

"I just had one of our forensics guys hand me a watch he found on the plane. It's a Doxy, like mine. It has two time zones, one for Mountain Time and one for an hour west of Pacific Time. That means Alaska . . ."

". . . or Nord Island," Dale interjected.

"I got one more item of interest here. Odin Pharmaceuticals may be moving supplies, test equipment, and Ph.D.s out to the island. It could be a scheduled move as the island continues its expansion program, but it seems almost too convenient."

"How do you think it ties into Perry's death?"

"Nord Island and Odin Pharmaceuticals keeps coming to the forefront. Grab the rock and develop a vaccine to line your pockets. A little too coincidental if you ask me."

"Yeah, but you'd need to spread the disease in order to really profit from it. No big bucks without an epidemic to fix."

"You're thinking along the same lines I am."

"Except that Perry died before the rock became an issue."

"Perry may have been ahead of the curve, that's the missing piece. Eventually it'll come together, and damn soon I hope."

Sullivan was racing to beat the clock, trying to pull together the loose ends in an effort to unravel the unknown elements. Time was working against them and he knew it. People were dying and he was the guy in the middle. It was an uncomfortable, self-imposed pressure. He couldn't shake the feeling that things were about to get much worse.

"An unchecked virus could kill a lot of people, especially if it spreads before a vaccine is developed," Sullivan said.

"I was just thinking the same thing, but what if there is no quick cure available?"

Both men became silent. The obvious answer was not something either of them wanted to contemplate. Dale believed the two of them, together, could eventually unwind the mystery, even though it seemed to grow bigger at a faster pace then they could keep up with. The multitude of angles and elements to the case was like dealing with a variety of zoo animals. Problem was, there was no zookeeper yet, and the animals were all out of their cages.

"We've got a shooter and a pilot running loose with a killer rock," Sullivan said. "If it's Nord Island, then they're heading for the coast somewhere. We need to get the locals, Homeland Security, and a few others up to speed without tipping off the bad guys through radio or TV reports. And we're gonna have to suppress the deadly nature of that rock, too. I'm heading back to the naval base soon. I have a couple of local agents coming to relieve me here. I need to get a report out to HQ as soon as I return. We'll need to 'lid' the information, need-to-know only, regarding the virus-without-a-cure aspect."

"Alright, call me back when you're done. Maybe we'll get lucky and find the cabin cruiser and see if that will answer some more questions. While we're at it, we need to think of a plausible way to keep the good guys from getting exposed to the rock if one of them finds it."

The words hung in the air at Sullivan's end of the phone.

"Sullivan, are you still there?"

"Yeah, let's keep it off the radio frequencies, other than encrypted communications."

"That sounds good. I'll take care of it."

"I'll see you later." The cell phone connection ended.

"Sir, we have a firing solution," the submarine's weapons control officer said.

"Very well, XO, take us down to four hundred feet, and keep us on a parallel track with the destroyer. Weapons, safety the CHINOs. XO, stand by the UV Splash."

"Aye, sir, UV Splash is powering up."

Wallen rubbed his brow with the back of his left hand. Deep inside, he hoped that no more lethal action would be necessary. He was starting to wonder if he had trapped himself in a no-win situation with Odin, who was clearly emerging as a homicidal maniac.

"*Nämen fan*," Wallen cussed under his breath.

Aboard the *U.S.S. Jonathan Cooke*
San Juan Straits
Friday, 0814 hours Pacific Time

"Lieutenant, I've got a weak transient that's shown up twice in the last five sweeps," the sonar operator aboard the *Jonathan Cooke* said.

"Does it look like our missing boat?"

"No sir, it's way outside the search area. This is about seven thousand yards to the south of us."

The tall, twenty-five year old naval officer walked over to the flat, digitized screen and squinted at the image. "What's the depth?"

"It's about three hundred twenty feet down, sir."

"Stationary or moving?"

"Don't know sir, it was too weak."

"Well, it's not a sub. It could be an old Coast Guard beacon that sunk in a storm, or bottom clutter, from the angle of attack we're painting. How deep is the bottom out here?" he asked, pointing at the screen.

"It varies, but it looks to be about five hundred or so, with a sloping contour to the west."

"Any signals emanating from it?"

"No, sir, nothing."

"All right, note it and move on. Let's see if we can find this sunken cabin cruiser."

Captain Ingvar Wallen watched the return in front of him. The warship was directing its sonar energy closer in to his ship. He took a deep breath and let it out slowly.

"Bridge, sonar. The ship nearest us has gone active. They're pinging the seafloor. It looks directional, captain; they're hunting for something specific.

"Push up the tiles to one hundred percent and slow us. Belay that, all stop. Put us on the bottom gently," Wallen ordered.

He walked slowly between the chart table and his laptop computer, which was mounted to the small, fold down wall desk. He began mulling over the defensive actions that would be precipitated by an attack inside U.S. waters.

A multitude of possible responses marched through his head. How necessary was the attack to conceal his existence? Taking down two ships would trigger a massive search and retaliation if he was discovered. Then there was the need to retrieve the errant rock and messenger. Weighing the risks and odds of survival left him reconsidering his options. He looked over the underwater chart for the south channel.

Time to distance? What kinds of listening devices might they have heading out to the open sea in close to the coast? Are there other naval assets inbound? How fast can they put a subhunter on station?

Sitting once again at the chart table, he absentmindedly spun a sharpened pencil between the fingers of his right hand while pushing up his light, thin, wire rim reading glasses with his left hand. *They'll hear it coming and get off a message . . . What kind of response will they mount? They're limited on resources. How much time can I buy to get the rock if we change the location of the pickup?*

He stood up again and took a sip of coffee. Several minutes passed while he thought about the situation.

"Captain, comm. We just received a message from island command."

"Go ahead and read it, Gustav."

"HQ," the communications officer began, "says retrieval of the package is the paramount objective and orders that that alone dictate your actions." He paused. "That's it, sir."

Wallen leaned over and pushed the intercom button, "Very well, Gustav. Pull in the antenna."

Douglas Odin was sitting in front of the flat screen monitor in his study with a real time geosynchronous observation satellite at his fingertips. He could see the U.S. Navy ships in the same area his submarine was operating in. He decided to clarify his interests for Captain Wallen in the event it was warranted. His drive to obtain the rock was consuming his every energy. Other business interests had taken a distant back seat. He leaned back and took another sip from his platinum coffee cup.

Wallen looked down at the clear, plastic cover that lay atop the torpedo firing button. Running his left hand through his dark-blond hair, he turned toward the helmsman. "XO, stand us down from action . . . Secure the CHINOs and UV Splash. Take us up to six knots and steer for the west. We'll detour out of the main channel past the island here . . ." he pointed to the color console, " . . . and turn to the south. Let's continue on to our rendezvous. Keep us within one hundred feet of the bottom."

"Aye, aye, sir."

"Sonar, bridge. Keep your ears open for any changes in the nearest warship's profile."

"Yes, sir."

Wallen's rubber-soled deck shoes issued a faint squeak on the coated metal grating as he went aft toward the galley. He hadn't eaten anything in the past twelve hours.

The digital depth gauge on the bulkhead read four hundred forty feet and zero-nine-nine-degrees heading.

Eastern Utah desert
Near Vernal, Utah
Friday, 0757 hours Mountain Time

Small whirlwinds of dust spun wildly across the morning desert floor. The sun was straight ahead in the helicopter windshield. His sunglasses alone weren't quite up to the task of blocking out the glare of the sun, so the pilot peeled the smoke colored, plastic glare shield off the side window and put it between him and the bright light. The blinding intensity subsided.

"There it is, off to the left," Dalton Jordan said into the headset microphone. "Those low hills near the cliff side," he pointed with an outstretched hand.

The chopper leaned over to the left and began to descend. Two minutes later the helicopter flared to a soft, dusty landing where the dig site's main tent had once stood. They waited until the sand and dust settled back to the ground before opening the side door.

Tori, Jordan, and two FBI agents exited the military helo, the two paleontologists carrying shovels. One of the FBI agents hopped out with a couple of white buckets in hand and looked around, taking in the view.

"This way," Tori said, "up the hill toward the bluff over there."

Dalton and the two FBI agents followed in tow. The second FBI agent carried latex gloves, plastic sheeting, and small, personal respirators in an equipment bag.

At the top of the hill, they poked around trying to gauge wind direction. Tori stuck her shovel into the ground and dug in around the hole from which they had extracted the small sliver of asteroid a week earlier.

"There don't appear to be any chips or remnants here," Dalton said a few minutes later.

"Let's dig out the dirt and box it up," the tall, tanned FBI agent said. "We'll get it analyzed back at the lab."

Twenty minutes passed and the pilot of the chopper hit the start button to bring the jet engines online. The carbon fiber blades spun up. Soon after, they were leisurely flying along at one hundred twenty miles an hour. Tori's usual bubbly personality had succumbed to a weary malaise.

Dalton noticed the young woman's silence. "You okay?"

"Yeah, I'm just tired," she replied, sitting motionless in her seat, her head flopped back against the seatback. Looking at her more closely, he could see she wasn't feeling well. Her eyes were unfocused, almost glassy.

Dalton decided to change the subject. "I have to go to Seattle tomorrow night for a dedication ceremony. Dr. Baker is in Cleveland, so I was planning on leaving you in charge," he said.

"Oh, uh thanks. When will you be back?"

Her response lacked the expected enthusiasm he was accustomed to.

"Sunday evening, unless the wharf and sun look good." Jordan smiled inwardly, remembering his last visit when it rained incessantly for two days.

Tori heard his words, but she was preoccupied with the stiffness in her joints.

San Juan Straits
Near Friday Harbor
Friday, 0800 hours Pacific Time

The *Jonathan Cooke* turned twenty-four-degrees to port at the top of the hour. Dale could feel the deck tilt slightly as the ship turned to make another pass. He stood up to go find Sean and make a private phone call. Eighteen hundred yards into the new heading the sonar operator suddenly became animated.

"I think I've got something here. Check the digital monitor, sir. Looks like an upright, small pleasure craft. I make it about one hundred feet down on a narrow shelf," he called out. "It's sitting on this drift line just a few hundred yards from shore." He marked the screen with an erasable grease pencil and froze the image.

Dale put down his notepad, stepped over to the color chart, and watched the sonar record a bottom graph. A couple of seconds passed and the image of a man-made bow and squat cabin housing appeared on the glossy graph paper. The lieutenant and the petty officer were intently occupied with their drill. Dale sat back down and watched. This was where patience was a maddening pastime.

There was a high probability that the sunken cabin cruiser was somewhere in the immediate vicinity. He'd had a long conversation with the Coast Guard oceanographer a few days before. The man had painstakingly plotted out the tides, wave action, currents, temperature, and weather at the estimated time of the disappearance. There were other factors that would also affect the zone of interest.

The Navy and the Coast Guard both had acoustical data recordings that could possibly help in locating the area in which the boat had gone down. But that was a time-consuming, laborious process requiring an experienced ear to search the tapes for suspicious activity. It was a long shot at best, given all of the marine activity above and below the water.

"Is it ours?" Dale asked, obviously reserving judgment.

"Bear with me, sir. I need to bring up our records for this area. We cruise this sea lane a lot and have computer tapes on just about everything sitting on the bottom. Petty Officer Jon Gardner punched in several keys and waited patiently. He compared the frozen image, depth, latitude and longitude with the graphic overlays and waited for the computer to analyze them. The screen refreshed and a three dimensional moving image spit out the answer.

"This is new since the last update to the computer. The most recent recording on the system was . . . let's see . . . umm, looks like eleven weeks ago. It's a high probability search target. Hold on . . . we have a positive hit."

There just wasn't time for an intense analytical review. This was old-fashioned, seat-of-the-pants guesswork. Something Dale was very good at.

Cougar Stadium parking lot, BYU
Provo, Utah
Friday, 1154 hours Mountain Time

From the parking lot of the football stadium at BYU, a speck cresting the top of the mountain peak to the east could just be made out. A police officer saw the aircraft first and pointed to a spot in the noonday sky. Behind him, electronic red and blue ambulance lights were flashing silently. Two paramedics were standing by with a gurney to pick up a patient. The chopper pilot had called in the medical emergency ten minutes before. Several military officers and a doctor were milling around, waiting for the helicopter's arrival.

Four minutes passed. The military chopper flared to a landing and rolled a few feet forward to a stop. The side door slid open and out came several people. Pale and weak, Tori was offloaded and wrapped in a yellow blanket. She was close to vomiting but still holding her own, complaining that it was just the flu.

The ambulance roared off shortly thereafter with a police escort, heading for the trauma room of the local hospital. Behind them in an FBI vehicle were the soil samples from the dig site.

Dalton Jordan stood immobilized in the parking lot with a sad look on his face. He would have to call her parents. There was something very personal in his feelings for the outgoing, exuberant blonde. He watched as the ambulance turned the corner and out of sight.

Suddenly, he came to the realization that Tori Evans meant more to him than the casual student passing through the university.

Pacific Coast Highway
Near Seattle, Washington
Friday, 1327 hours Pacific Time

From a hilly rise on a back road, he could see the city of Seattle far off in the distance, still an hour and a half away. He'd made good time and saw only two police cars as he drove along, both going in the opposite direction. His map had two separate points of extraction. All he had to do now was get to the city. Tonight, under cover of darkness, he would be pulled out, along with his inert thirty-five pound companion. He wished it was later in the day.

Summer saw the sun up until 9:30 in the evening. Close in to shore, though, it was somewhat overcast and a gray pall hung over the downtown skyscrapers. He could see fog rolling in off the bay headed for the beach. *The darker the better,* he thought.

It was time to place a call for his ride.

" . . . lose yourself in the woods outside of town until 5:00 o'clock. The cops will be occupied with rush hour traffic jams and accidents. So long as that truck you acquired isn't reported as missing or stolen, it should be easy to slip into the city, dump it, and make your way to the wharf. Don't do anything to draw attention to yourself. Be courteous, drive within the speed limit, and keep a low profile. Stay sharp. You know the drill." Ingvar Wallen was not a nervous man by nature. But the commando on the other end of the line was an untested entity operating without the support of his team.

The well-organized action plan had unraveled over the past twelve hours. The commando's capture could endanger his submarine and men if he were caught and aggressively interrogated. Wallen wanted to put some of his men ashore earlier in the day when news of the changes had been passed on to him.

Douglas Odin, however, had refused that request.

Wallen had a timetable and little else to fall back on. It made him uneasy.

" . . . and don't forget that that rock is the most sought after trinket in the world. They'll stop at nothing, including the inconvenience of their legal system, to get it back. Your backup plan is the bank. Do you remember the details on that?" Wallen asked patiently but firmly.

"Yeah, I know where it is. I have to pass that way to get to the wharf. I'm all set," the commando said.

"When you get to the harbor, just key the radio frequency and let it run for fifteen seconds every ten minutes. The team will be in a high-speed rigid inflatable. They'll pull under the wharf at dusk, be ready."

Wallen signed off and hoped that everything from here on would go well. He didn't want to get into a shooting match he couldn't win.

"XO, once we recover our agent and the rock, I want to get out of here as quickly and quietly as possible. Revisit our egress plan . . . Update the weather and surface activity. I want you to start running a track on all marine vessels in the immediate area. Plot any suspected military and law enforcement craft. Have radio add another operator to start eavesdropping on the military frequencies. Give me any other options you can think of, got it?"

"Yes, sir." The XO stepped away from the captain and back to the small combat operations room.

"He's a good man, Ingvar," the chief engineer said a moment later. The two men sat across the table from each other.

"Yes, I know. I just wish we could simplify things. So many unknown variables that we can't control," Wallen replied. *Too damn many variables,* he thought silently.

U.S.S. Jonathan Cooke
Nine miles southwest of Friday Harbor, Washington
Friday, 1355 hours Pacific Time

"Winch the second one over and let's get going," Sean said to the crane operator. A minute later the heavy crate slapped loudly onto the deck of the vessel bobbing alongside the destroyer. Water spray washed off the hull of the warship and into the sheriff's boat every few seconds. The driver of the smaller craft was occupied with trying not to bang up against the bigger combat vessel or let the crate smash into the boat's cabin area. Saltwater spray in the wind splashed across the canopy, making the job just that much more difficult.

"Please convey our thanks for the help and hospitality to the captain," Dale said as the lieutenant J.G. handed over a file with the target acquisition printouts enclosed. "I'll relay my respect and appreciation to the admiral for the CO's assistance as well."

"Glad we could help you out, sir. Have a safe hunt."

Two minutes later Sean, Dale, and Barney Davis jumped, one at a time, from the gangway on the port side of the destroyer into the high performance, thirty-four foot sheriff's rescue boat.

"Permission to come aboard, Captain?" Dale asked as he shifted his weight to retain his balance in the rolling swells.

"Permission granted," King County Detective Rod O'Brien said. "Let's tie down those crates and get moving." O'Brien was dressed in a windbreaker and swim trunks, with the sheriff's green logo on the back of the lightweight jacket. O'Brien was an experienced recreational diver, but the second deputy was a certified rescue diver. Both deputies greeted the three men as they came aboard.

The second deputy was at the wheel of the gleaming, white boat.

"We ready?" he asked.

Barney and Dale pulled ropes out from under a seat, pushed the two wooden containers together, and got busy securing them. The patrol boat quickly angled away from the five hundred plus foot destroyer and gained speed in the direction of Friday Harbor.

"As you requested, we have ten air bottles and the gas system. Bob will act as the safety diver for you," O'Brien said. Bob was the second deputy.

Sean and Bob went below and laid out the long graphs in order to plot the dive on the missing pleasure craft. Not long after Dale, Rod O'Brien, and Barney Davis slid into the seats at the table. O'Brien put a couple of ice-cold water bottles on the table. Dale paused and then attacked the plastic cap on his to drown the salty taste in his mouth.

"It's right here on this shelf at one hundred five feet. I think it would be best to dive on gas. I believe there's a remote setup on the camera, isn't there, Barney?" Sean asked.

"Yeah, that's right. We'll cable your recorder up to the relay antenna and you should see everything we see," he replied.

"I have the latitude and longitude here," Dale said. He handed it over to O'Brien, who went topside. O'Brien sat down in the captain's chair, advanced the engine throttles, and turned the wheel to head northwest.

"We'll be over the target in just a few minutes," Bob explained, pointing at the nautical map. "It's the leeward side of the island, so the water should be relatively calm. King Neptune is being kind to us, so let's see how quickly we can do this before the surface winds pick up."

Dale drummed his fingers on the tabletop for a few minutes until he became restless. "I'm hoping that the missing men are on board. Closure is a good thing, especially if it moves the investigation forward." He got up from the table, grabbed the water bottle, and went topside.

The sun bore down on the white rescue boat. Off in the distance, he could see the *Cooke* making its way toward Seattle. He wouldn't be diving on the sunken cuddy, but he would be glued to the television set once his brother and Barney went over the side. He stood at the rail looking in the direction the boat was heading, his mind engaged but his eyes oblivious to the amazingly deep turquoise color of the water.

Dale was thinking of a call he got when he was a deputy sheriff in Santa Clara County. The passing of friends and small children was different from all the other fatalities he'd responded to over the years. They had a tendency to stick somewhere in the reserves of his mind, only to surface when a similar event triggered the memory. It was a late Friday night, just about the time the really good stuff started hopping. His dispatcher said a car had crashed through a hillside barrier at Steven Creek Reservoir. He rounded the curves with the lights flashing and siren wailing until he came upon a small crowd of people gathered in the roadway. It only took a quick conversation to discover that a woman with two small kids had sailed out over the trees and into deep water.

Dale dumped his duty belt in the back seat of his patrol car, and with a witness took off down the steep ravine through the brush. A distant siren from a fire truck could be heard winding its way up the canyon. Behind it somewhere, several more patrol cars were en route.

The station wagon's broken windshield was lying on the shore, part in, part out of the water. He handed his flashlight to the male bystander who'd hustled down the hillside and through the undergrowth with him. Then Dale carefully waded into the water until it was over his head. A few feet further and he felt air bubbles rushing up past him. The bystander aimed the light beam and Dale spotted the escaping air. He dove down feet first and bounced off the metal hood of the vehicle seconds later.

Breaking the surface of the water again, he yelled at the bystander to tell the firefighters to aim their searchlights at him. He grabbed a lungful of air and this time dove headfirst. Feeling his way in the dark, he found the missing windshield space and pulled himself through. There was someone inside still alive, trying to breathe air trapped at the roof liner. It was the female driver. She was in shock. Dale told her to take a breath and that the surface was just fifteen to eighteen feet up. Seconds later, she was in the spotlight from the first arriving fire engine. He tried to get her to talk, but she was incoherent. The bystander was in the water now and took the woman in tow.

Seconds later, Dale dove down again. This time he entered the car, feeling his way as he went. Just when he thought he was about to run out of air, the small body of a child came into view. With a quick snatch he had her and swam for the surface. The entire area was now lit up from several high intensity fire truck lights about seventy-five yards away. There were two blue T-shirted firefighters on the shore just about to enter the water. Dale pushed the child's body toward them. They hauled the child out of the water and started CPR. He asked if the woman had told them how many people were in the vehicle. "Two kids," they yelled back.

A third firefighter scrambled along the edge of the water and waded in next to Dale. "One more to go; you got the energy to do it again?"

Dale was tired but nodded yes. The firefighter looked at him, trying to judge Dale's stamina.

They both dropped beneath the water. Dale found the car again and swam inside. There was still a small amount of air trapped above his head. Undaunted, he rose up, turned his head sideways, and took another quick breath. The firefighter was right behind him. *Where are you little guy? Come on . . . where are you?* Dale pleaded.

On the rear floor of the car he felt clothing. He rummaged through it until he discovered a small hand. Almost immediately he exploded out of the car for the surface and past the firefighter. He gulped for air, gasping from the adrenaline. The firefighter surfaced behind him seconds later and took the child. He swam toward the muddy bank.

Breathing heavily, Dale rolled onto his back in the water. His watch, a diver's model with a luminous glow, showed the time as 11:37 p.m. It occurred to him that he was in his socks. He didn't remember kicking his shoes off on the reservoir's bank before going in.

He floated on the surface for a minute and then slowly paddled back. The bystander stepped in and helped pull him up the now slippery, muddy embankment. He noticed three deputies, all beat partners from the canyon area. Two were helping the paramedic firefighters. The third, an old academy buddy, handed him his shoes, "You're gonna need these to climb back up. Firefighters got ropes out. When the next fire unit arrives, they'll haul us up."

Dale was exhausted. He sat down on a log and looked around. Someone threw him a towel. He dried his hair and face.

Soon a third fire vehicle, a heavy-duty pickup, arrived overhead and threw more light down the hillside. A minute or so later, a rescue roped firefighter with a Stokes litter basket came through the trees. Over the next seven minutes, they hauled everyone up to the roadside. An ambulance sped away with the first child, who was now breathing but unconscious. The mother followed in a second ambulance.

Dale had a wool blanket draped over him, liberated from the trunk of one of the patrol cars. He stood at the back door of the third ambulance dripping water and watching as the paramedics defibrillated the three-year-old boy.

He was so small and helpless.

An hour later at the Saratoga substation, Dale got a call. The little guy didn't make it. This time when the captain asked him if he wanted to clock out early, he took him up on the offer. Little kids were hard.

Salt spray hit him in the face again. He wondered if someone would be mourning the two dead men they were hoping to locate. His thought process was interrupted as the cell phone in his pocket chimed.

"Fox . . . Oh, hi, honey." He listened to the soft voice of Betty Jo Case, his fiancée. "We're offshore, so I don't know how long this cell connection will last. We better talk fast before I lose you," he said.

His expression changed quickly as she relayed what she'd discovered from a private firm. A photo mission for a major, nongovernmental contractor using a *Konos* satellite produced two high-resolution digital pictures of a helicopter in flight. Under the lens of a photo interpreter's magnification, it was clear that a Black Hawk chopper was over the ocean, heading out to sea from somewhere north of Seattle and south of the Canadian border, maybe to a ship offshore. She kept up her narrative of the details she'd discovered as Dale listened intently.

At 1:54 in the afternoon, Detective O'Brien threw out the fore and aft anchors. The rescue boat rolled slightly with the occasional swells. The sun was warm on their faces, and the sky, with its deep-blue canopy, seemed better suited for a lazy fishing trip than a body recovery operation.

"Okay, the GPS says we're right on top of it," Deputy Bob said. "The sonar is warmed up. I want to see what kind of fish we have in the area first. Killer whales swim through here periodically, so I want a peek at what's under the hood."

Sean and Barney finished checking their dive gear. Deputy Cole rechecked the dive equipment a second time. A few minutes later, all three men went over the side and into the relatively clear water.

"Can you hear me?" Sean said into the underwater microphone in his face mask.

"Got you loud and clear," Rod responded. "The shelf is about thirty feet out from the boat and straight down. We're painting you and the bottom protrusion. We'll guide you in. I have you at about twenty feet and descending."

"Yeah, that's what my gauge says."

"How's the clarity in the water?" Rod asked.

"Surprisingly good, we can see about forty-five, maybe fifty feet, got a few fish looking us over."

"Anything bigger than a Cadillac?" Dale asked.

"Not yet, and hopefully not at all. We'll send up a marker buoy when we find the boat. Send down the bag after we tie off the line. Oh . . . you will let us know if something really big swims by, won't you?"

"Sure, soon as we get the fishing poles out. Bait's already in the water," Dale laughed.

Nord Island
Pacific Ocean
Friday, 1418 hours Alaska Time

Douglas Odin strolled casually from the large rose garden at the side of his twenty seven thousand square foot colonial mansion with a handful of dethorned roses. He handed the roses to his waiting housekeeper, who promptly disappeared into the ornate, covered entryway in search of an appropriate vase. He leaned in and took a whiff of the lavender colored Sterling Silver roses next to him. They had been his wife's favorite.

Strolling along, his mind moved on to other thoughts.

An assistant emerged from the sliding glass door at the corner of the mansion. He walked up to Odin, and without a word, handed him an envelope, then promptly turned and walked away.

Douglas Odin looked at his engraved, gold watch. It was twenty-three minutes before the latest incarnation of the U.S. Keyhole satellite would pass overhead. He would be out of sight when it went by.

The ocean breeze blew across the porch, riffling the green parasol behind him. He sat down under it and looked across the sloping, manicured, seven-acre lawn.

The warehouse and docking facility for Douglas's submarine could not be seen due to the hilly rise obscuring his view. Only the top of the mast on his smaller one hundred twenty-two foot yacht was visible. The larger, three hundred ten foot yacht sat in the harbor on the other side of the island. Near the wide, decorative, gravel path leading to his car collection museum stood a four foot tall berm festooned with thousands of animated wildflowers swaying in the light wind.

Odin opened the envelope and perused the contents. He typed a message into his PDC. A minute later he hit the send key, and the encrypted data burst to a private satellite twenty two thousand miles above the earth, to a satellite owned by Odin Telecommunications.

Eleven minutes passed and it was picked up by the trailing antenna in the submarine captained by Ingvar Wallen.

Odin stood up and walked past a row of tea roses in the direction of his yacht. His personal assistant trailed behind him at a discrete distance, ready to serve her employer's needs without intruding. Less than one hundred feet away, four burly security men also attended to Odin's safety and privacy. Ever vigilant, they scanned the open expanse around him, looking for anything out of place.

⊶—⊁

"Captain, comm . . . We have an incoming message from HQ," the communications operator said.

"I'll be right there," Wallen replied. He opened the door to his cabin and hurried down the passageway to the communications room.

"Let's have it," he said unceremoniously.

Wallen unfolded the paper and read it to himself in the doorway. *Cooke dropped three passengers onto a King County Sheriff's rescue boat that is now on station southeast of Friday Harbor. Suspect they may have found site of sunken cabin cruiser. Odin.*

Wallen folded the note and headed forward to the command center.

Aboard the sheriff's patrol boat
Five miles from Friday Harbor, Washington
Friday, 1425 hours Pacific Time

"Sean, Barney, if you sweep left twenty degrees, the boat should be about sixty feet away. What's the visibility down there?" Dale asked.

"We can see about fifteen feet with the lights. Hang on a minute, we're swimming against the current." Ninety seconds passed in silence. "Okay, we see it. It's sitting upright, hang on."

Sean and Barney kicked up and over the bow of the small cabin cruiser. The first sight stopped them both in the water. They hung there in stunned disbelief. The body of a man pinned to the bulkhead floated just a few yards away. Fish had obviously been eating away at the partially denuded corpse. Barney turned away momentarily, removed his regulator, and vomited into the passing current.

"You alright?" Sean asked Barney over the intercom.

"Yeah, just a little surprised by the suddenness of it."

"What's up?" rang in their ears. It was Detective O'Brien this time.

"We found it. Hang on while I bring the camera up closer," Sean said.

A murky, grainy picture slowly came into view. A bloated object centered up in the camera's lens. It took a few seconds for the three men onboard the rescue boat to digest what they were seeing. A grouper swam into the camera's field of vision and out again.

"Holy . . ." O'Brien remarked, " . . . it's a body. Sean, we'll need more video on this. It's a crime scene now."

⚷

A late model, green convertible pulled into the rear lot of the gas station and wheeled into the first open space. A little dust came off the tires and settled onto the gravel. With a cheerful disposition and a grin on his face, the driver hoped over the door. He whistled his way into the back of the open work bay.

The sandy-blond haired mechanic was preoccupied putting a new radiator hose in an old Toyota pickup. He looked up for a moment and saw his younger brother trot by.

"Y'all went out with that stacked redhead last night. How'd it go?" he asked.

"She's got a set of lips and a burnin' desire to use 'em," his brother replied. "We're goin' out again when I close up later."

"That good, huh. I seen her up close, bro. Yer in over yer head. She's a shark in a short skirt."

"She's sizzlin' man, hotter than a three-alarm fire. By the way, where's yer truck. I didn't see it when I pulled in."

"It's back there."

"No man, I looked. It ain't."

The older brother set the box wrench down on the air cleaner and straightened up. He walked across the oil-stained cement floor and looked at the back lot, squinting into the bright sunlight.

"It took a few seconds to register on his face. "Son of a . . ."

"Did ya move it to work on?" his brother asked, walking up.

"Hell, no. Walk round front and see if someone moved it on me. I wouldn't put it past Pauly to yank a prank and sneak in here while I's busy."

Four minutes later he was on the phone to the sheriff. "Sumbud stole my wheels, Morris. Git down here and do sumthin 'bout it." His face was red and his anger was boiling over.

"I told ya, ya shoulda put the LoJack in after you fixed it up," his brother said, not thinking about the impact of his words.

A wrench went flying past his right ear and banged off the door to the office.

At 5:09 p.m., the local sheriff's office issued a BOLO across the state. Police officers, sheriff's deputies, highway patrol officers, border patrol agents, and others would be notified within the next fifteen minutes that another truck had joined the hit list of missing motor vehicles.

31

Aboard the sheriff's patrol boat
Nine miles from Friday Harbor, Washington
Friday, 1612 hours Pacific Time

The cell phone in his pocket vibrated. "Fox," he responded.

"Dale, its Sullivan. I just got word that a truck was stolen from a back lot at a gas station forty-seven miles from our downed jet. Timeframe fits right into our departing hijacker. The locals are dusting the bathroom and fuel pumps for prints, but it's a real long shot. It means that the guy who hijacked the aircraft is likely headed for the coast, like we thought. The gas station is close to a small highway that feeds into the interstate heading toward Seattle. Whoever he is, instinct says he's heading for the big city."

"You got a chopper there?"

"Yeah."

"Get on it and get out here. We found the cabin cruiser and a piece of letterhead from Odin Aviation."

"What's on the letterhead?"

"A manifest sheet, we also found a couple of bodies. By the way, Dan Covery called me a few minutes ago."

Covery was the Director of the CTU and Dale and Sullivan's boss.

"The death toll from the virus is skyrocketing and the CDC folks are leaning on us to find that rock pronto. Sullivan, I gotta go. Call you back in a bit."

Dale hung up and grabbed Sean's canvas bag as he crawled up on the transom of the sheriff's rescue boat. A minute later, Barney surfaced with two bodies in tow. Twenty yards behind him bobbed four bright-orange balls. The round floats were attached to dynamic rescue lines that they'd fed over the side earlier. The ropes, in turn, were attached to the cleats on the sunken cabin cruiser sitting on the bottom.

"Get this BOLO out right now to all agencies on all channels. Code it under the operational name. Inform any unit that spots this vehicle not to approach; advise only. We'll have to orchestrate a takedown under controlled conditions. Contact each sheriff's office between here and Seattle to gear up and be read. You got all that?" Sullivan said into his encrypted cell phone. "Alright, I'm on my way out to the coast. I'll call you when I land. You can contact me through the Navy on three-three-six-point-seven."

Sullivan spun his right pointer finger at the pilot, indicating that it was time to go. The helicopter's blades started to move. Twenty seconds later, the helo lifted off, hurrying toward Seattle.

The King County sheriff's service boat loomed into view about three miles away. Rounding the nearby island, its international orange and white coloring stood out as intended. The seventy-four foot vessel had compressors, lift bags, dive equipment, a big aft deck, and a host of other maritime equipment aboard. The Coast Guard had helped outfit the boat as part of its Homeland Security mutual aid agreement.

The six divers from the sheriff's search and rescue team were assigned the job of diving onto the cabin cruiser with air bags in an attempt to refloat the sunken craft.

Dale, Sean, and Barney along with Detective O'Brien and Deputy Bob, would stick around to see if it could be done before the sun dropped below the horizon. Sean and Barney had made two dives and were unable to continue diving due to the buildup of nitrogen gas in their blood; they would need the next ten hours to allow it to dissipate. Their second dive yielded additional evidence of the savage homicide that had taken place less than a week before.

A tired Sean pushed the body bag forward and then pulled himself up the ladder and onto the back of the patrol boat with a dull thud. He peeled the hood off his dive suit, put his head down a moment, and watched the water pool at his feet. The air tank slid down off his shoulder and onto the deck of the rescue boat.

Dale and Rod grabbed the black bag that Barney was now holding in front of them.

"Easy, don't rip the plastic," he said. "It's kinda ugly."

"Pull it up on the transom. Sean, can you give us a hand here?" Dale asked, leaning out to grab the bag.

Sean unzipped his wetsuit. "Yeah."

He stepped to the back of the rescue boat and the three of them together lifted the body bag onto the deck. Then they turned back and repeated the process to retrieve the second man's remains.

Barney and Deputy Bob climbed aboard with Dale's help. Fingerprints would eventually identify the two bodies as that of the Nord Island engineer and his brother-in-law, the carpenter.

Sean and Barney were beat. Diving, working underwater, decompression ascension, and the stress of watching their surroundings to ensure that they didn't become lunch for a much bigger marine denizen were physically and mentally taxing.

"I've got a lifting dry dock being detoured from south of Friday Harbor for the cabin cruiser," the deputy said. "It should be here in about twenty minutes. We can hook the ropes under the floats and winch it up without too much trouble."

"I hope they hurry up. Take a look at the sky to the north of us," Rod said.

The five men stood and gazed off in the distance. The blue expanse had taken on a cloudy-white tinge in that past half hour. To the west and the northeast of them, towering clouds were building over the horizon. The bay water was still relatively calm, but that was going to end long before dusk.

"I hope they get here soon, too. This water is going to become a cauldron if that storm drives down on us. What's your radar show?" Barney asked Bob.

The deputy sat down at the console and turned on the weather radar. The color monitor was backlit by the southern sun, so he stepped into the boat well and came up with a piece of cardboard. Placing it next to the scope, the colors suddenly sprang to life.

"Looks to be green and yellow storm cells at the extreme edge; it's about sixty miles out. I don't see any red color, but I'm guessing that's only a matter of time." He raised his head and stared out to the north again, "Wind is coming in off the ocean from the northwest. We'll be feeling it pick up well ahead of the storm." Silence fell over the boat.

Dale looked across to his brother, still drying off with a towel. Standing on the bench seat with the binoculars in hand, Dale focused in on Friday Harbor off to the edge of the horizon. "Got a boat headed directly at us," he offered to no one in particular.

A few seconds passed. "I do believe that's our tow truck. You're gonna need to get back in the water again, older brother," Dale said with a humorous snicker. "Why in the world did you even bother to dry off? I just don't understand you fire guys, preparing to do half a job," he needled Sean. "Never happen in the FBI."

Sean dropped the towel to the deck and frowned at Dale. He sat down to breathe in the fresh, salt air. Off in the distance, a ferry blew its horn. He took note of the fact that Dale's encrypted cell phone was sitting on the table. Then he stood up again.

"Hey Dale?" he remarked.

"Yeah."

"Know what FBI stands for . . ."

Dale's eyes fell away from the binoculars and he sighed. Hearing acronyms for the agency's initials for years was always entertaining, and sometimes a little embarrassing. Barney, Detective O'Brien, and Deputy Bob were all listening. Sean stepped over to Dale, took the binoculars from his sibling, and gave him a good shove. A split second later, a splash of water cascaded off the gunwale.

The four men looked over the transom at Dale floating behind the rescue boat, his head spinning from side to side throwing off water. Sean leaned over and yelled, "Full Body Immersion."

The others couldn't contain their laughter any longer.

∘⊷

The Navy chopper with FBI Agent Sullivan Casse set down gently on the runway and taxied over to the base operations building. Sullivan was out and running for the door to the facility when a King County deputy sheriff stepped through the exit and onto the flight line.

Sullivan recognized the focused stare as a sign of recognition and stopped just a few feet from him.

"You Casse?" the deputy asked.

"Yeah, what's up?"

"We got a hit on your stolen truck. Navy "Rockeye" is shadowing him at the edge of the county, about fifty miles from here. Rockeye is a Homeland Security helo. An undercover car is moving in to identify the driver. He'll drive by and shoot some high-speed video from a camera hidden in the back seat of his vehicle. We have several other plain, brown wrappers moving into position to be directed by the chopper."

"What's the probability that it's our target?"

"Very high confidence."

Sullivan rubbed his face deep in thought. He pulled out his cell phone and hit autodial "two". A few rings later, it was answered.

The soaking wet man holding the thick towel hit the "send" button. "Fox."

"Dale, we may have found our missing vehicle."

∘⊷

"She's coming up level, go easy," the diver said into his mask.

The surface was in sight now, the light from the sky above growing more intense every time he looked up. The color on the floating dry dock winch line changed to red, indicating to the winch operator they had fifty feet to go.

"Open the sea cocks and give me another sixteen inches," he said to his partner. Seawater flooded the ballast, and the floating dry dock settled further into the water. A few more minutes and the sunken cabin cruiser would be visible. They would gently guide the waterlogged boat to the floating dock's aft deck, secure it, and get underway to the harbor. One look at the darkening sky was all the crane operator needed to see. The bay was in for some rough weather, and soon. He'd seen the normally placid, beautiful, inter-island waters turn deadly on several occasions over the years. He had no intention of being out there any longer than needed to finish and depart.

Dale closed the phone and rubbed his face. Sullivan's information boosted his overall understanding of what they were dealing with.

He sipped the last of a Coors offered to him by the boat crew. Technically, he was still on duty, but it had been a long day and the salty taste in his mouth was more than he could stand. His cell phone rang again. He looked at the incoming call, "Hi there, how are you? Two calls in one afternoon. I am truly a blessed man," he said with a huge smile.

"I love you, too. How is the dive going?" Betty asked. She was sitting in her office in San Jose, California, feet up on her desk, high heels strewn across the deep pile, pale-blue carpeting.

"We found a couple of things. Unfortunately, I can't share it with you." The sadness caused his voice to trail off momentarily. "We're out on the bay right now. The sheriff's service boat just arrived. I'm leaving in a bit on a Navy chopper."

He decided to change the subject since the reminder of Perry's death was a depressing thought. Dale found a seat on the back of the rescue boat and sat down under the canvas awning, out of the sun. The winds had tapered off and the temperature had risen a few degrees; it was just enough to be a little uncomfortable.

Sean plopped down next to him a few seconds later with an ice-cold lemonade bottle in hand. He raised an eyebrow in curiosity. Dale covered the phone speaker and said "Betty." Sean leaned back and watched the service boat and divers get set up to hoist the cabin cruiser.

"Any luck with the background search on Nord Island?"

"I have some of the material you wanted; we got real lucky in one respect. Our Taiwan office has some information that we didn't know existed. They interviewed the head of one of the security consulting firms that Odin Industries hired to set up their redundant electronic monitoring systems. Seems Odin Industries reneged on part of their service and maintenance contract with this firm. Millions of dollars are involved. The president of the company was more than a little miffed by Odin's attitude. They have a full copy of the island's master security schematics - everything from the service conduits to power systems, even the amount and specific type of fiber optics used."

"Wow, that's great. Can I get a set of copies sent up by courier?"

"For you, anything, but it will cost you. When this is over, how about a couple of those aborted vacation days out on Catalina Island? I have a friend with a beach house right at the edge of town."

Dale conjured up images of the waves lapping over his feet while sitting on the white sands, Betty strolling out in a string bikini.

"Well . . ." she interrupted his daydream, " . . . you still there?"

"Oh, yeah, just had a thought. You're on."

"Okay, I'll send what I have to you first thing in the morning. You want it at the FBI office or the hotel?"

"The hotel would be best."

"Alright, you've got it. Now how about that long weekend, or I could come up there this weekend? I'm half tempted to fly out," she said with a pixyish response.

"I'd like that, but given the current situation, I can't guarantee I'll even be around."

A few minutes later, the call ended. Dale thought about how nice it might be to come back with Betty to the Seattle area and do a little island hopping. Staying at hotels along the way and seeing the sights would be a welcomed change.

At this point, Dale got up to put on some dry clothes on. He grabbed his gear, and was ready for the chopper to airlift him when it arrived. O'Brien could continue the investigation, without him, he was needed elsewhere.

It was looking more and more like the Odin Organization was involved. As he stood on the aft deck, Dale's thoughts jelled. *Bringing down an elusive, offshore billionaire is going to be practically impossible. He has diplomatic im-*

munity, an army of lawyers, and more protection than the president. How did I get into this mess? I suppose I could always go to work with Dad on the ranch if this collapses in my lap. I wonder if Sullivan can ride a horse?

32

Downtown Seattle, Washington
Friday, 1618 hours Pacific Time

American traffic jams, the commando thought to himself. *Better take the coast road.*

He pulled off the highway at the next ramp and headed southwest through a rural area. In the distance, he could make out the tops of a few skyscrapers rising above the tree line at the far end of an open field. His apprehension increased as the drive time grew shorter. The sun was staring him in the face through the windshield as a flock of seagulls took to flight from the side of the sparsely traveled roadway.

Glancing down at the backpack on the passenger side floor, he realized that he would be grateful to be relieved of the rock; its potential for unyielding death was making him nervous. *Was the seal still intact?* He checked the analog humidity gauge and saw that it was still in the green. With a sigh of relief, he looked in the rearview mirror again and back at the fuel gauge; the truck was beginning to feel cramped.

The cell phone in his shirt pocket rang.

Finally, it took you long enough. He hit the send button. "What's the plan?" he questioned sarcastically.

The calm voice at the other end asked him where he was and gave him directions to a downtown street that would lead him to the rendezvous location.

"Dump the truck in the underground parking lot and head for the departure point we discussed earlier."

The commando ran through the scenario in his head. "I'll be there in about twenty-five minutes, providing the traffic keeps moving."

"See you soon," the voice replied. The call ended as abruptly as it had started.

He was surprised to be traveling at fifty miles an hour. So far, the late Friday afternoon traffic was light, and it was heading out for the weekend while he was inbound. He put the cell phone down in the cup holder next to him and looked into his rearview mirror for the umpteenth time.

"Coffee, I could use some coffee," he said, blinking his eyes and letting out a yawn.

Not seeing anyone behind him, he changed lanes and headed for the gas station he spotted up ahead. Out to the west, large, white thunderheads were building up. *That looks like a lot more than a simple afternoon shower,* he thought as he scanned the horizon.

I wonder if the Americans have found the jet. No matter, their politically correct mentality will not allow their police to do their jobs efficiently anyway.

Twenty-nine hundred feet above and half a mile back, a gray Bell Long Ranger helicopter crammed with electronics gear was focused on the terrorist's stolen pickup truck. A wiry, crew-cut naval officer put down his binoculars, and maintaining his observation of the terrorist, keyed his microphone.

"Top Hat, this is Rockeye. Target is stopping at a convenience store. Pull off to the right a few hundred yards ahead. There's a park and ride lot tucked into the trees."

"Copy, Rockeye," a disembodied voice replied. "Top Hat" was the senior officer in the unmarked car below him.

A team of four unmarked federal vehicles belonging to a special SWAT team slowed and turned off the two-lane road and waited.

Everything necessary to maintain control over the terrorist was in place. With people in Utah dropping like flies in the summer heat, the matter had come to the personal attention of the president. Behind the scenes, he had his nose under the tent and was receiving updates at regular intervals. His conversation with the director of the FBI's CTU several hours before had the effect of snapping heads and moving assets to deal with the threat the stolen virus-laden rock posed. The director wanted the terrorist and his accomplices for obvious reasons. His point men were CTU Supervisory Special Agent Dale Fox and his partner Sullivan Casse.

At the moment, both counterterrorism agents were rushing to the scene from different locations. Until they arrived, the local Seattle SAC was calling the shots on the ground.

When the theft of the truck was discovered, a local police officer, who fortunately was on top of his game, asked the owner if he had either a GPS or satellite radio system in the truck. The owner acknowledged that he had installed an aftermarket satellite radio. Within ten minutes, the officer had a GPS coordinate from the service provider's six satellites now locked on to the stolen pickup. That frequency was now being tracked by the FBI, which was high overhead keeping an eye on the suspect.

"Top Hat. Target is en route to Alaska Highway via Fifth Avenue. Target will pass by the federal building on Columbia Street to dump the stolen vehicle, probably at the black tower building underground parking lot. He'll rendezvous with a second suspect there. Be advised that Columbia is one-way westbound. Target is meeting his contact in that vicinity. We'll set up the takedown at that location. Other units are moving into the area now. Rockeye will advise further. Stand by. Target is on the move again."

His accomplice was at the wharf waiting for him. Between his current location and the wharf he would have to ratchet up his own surveillance. He just couldn't shake the feeling that the closer he got the greater the chance of discovery.

He had run the backup plan in his head again, trying to ensure for his own piece of mind that he hadn't forgotten some important detail. Any number of things could go wrong. He drove on, his eyes scanning the mirrors. He was getting tired from all the mental activity. The stolen aircraft had been a serious energy drain. The shootout, fuel loss, dead men, crash landing, and finally, the stolen vehicles had all taxed his reserves. He needed sleep. His adrenaline rush would carry him only so far.

I'm not being paid enough for this work, he thought.

He was almost home. Now if only he weren't driving into the sunlight.

A tractor-trailer rig took up the better part of the single lane ahead of him. Steering to the left, he looked past the truck into the oncoming lane. He squinted and wished he had sunglasses. He pounded the pedal to the floor and accelerated around the slower moving truck.

Fifteen uneventful, stress-filled minutes passed. The green light shifted colors and he suddenly realized where he was.

In a split second, he debated running the yellow or stopping for the red. He hit the brake. Downtown Seattle was dead ahead. So was the Friday night rush hour traffic he dreaded he'd run into. He moved along from light to light, never once letting his guard down. Glancing sideways, he looked at faces, studying them for overt interest in his vehicle. The clock on the truck dashboard said 5:21 p.m. Another ten minutes and he'd dump the truck, grab the backpack, walk out of the parking lot to the wharf, and be on his way home.

He stretched his arms and twisted his neck to work out the kinks, shifting his gaze once again to his mirrors.

In headsets on the tactical net a voice was heard: "The target is getting tired." A couple of radio clicks followed.

Utah Valley Medical Center
Provo, Utah
Friday, 1655 hours Mountain Time

A U.S. Navy registered nurse was less than twenty feet away, on the other side of the containment area on the third floor of the hospital. The secured, quarantined unit was home to two people: one, a young boy; the other, a female paleontologist from BYU. So far, they were the only people to survive the deadly virus, though they were in a comatose state.

With her back turned, and preoccupied with keeping detailed, copious notes, she couldn't see the patients. Her special unit was assigned to monitor their conditions, the outcome of their circumstances still a mystery. She would need to go in again after the boy's next intravenous feeding to roll him so the bed sores that constantly threatened didn't get a chance to develop. She checked her chart and made another notation, then slid her chair away to use the computer. At the monitoring station, the little boy's respiration count suddenly shot up.

The fluorescent lights seemed to flicker and sting his sight. He slowly pried open one eye. A tear formed in the lower corner, rolling off his cheek and onto the pillow. His sight was fuzzy, blurred as if looking through an opaque piece of glass. The little six-year-old wasn't able to connect his surroundings to any specific thoughts. His other eye wouldn't cooperate and open. The salty tears that welled up in his open eye clouded his sight even further. The ceiling was white, and only the hum of the special ventilation system was apparent. He moved his left index finger under his blanket.

The desk phone rang off to the side. The nurse slid past the monitoring station without looking at the green LED display, unaware that the numbers on the pulse and respiration monitor were climbing.

The discomfort of the tears caused the boy to involuntary close his eyes tight. He took one big breath, his energy expended, and lapsed back into unconsciousness.

The short, brown haired nurse finally slid back over on the rolling secretarial chair to have another look at her monitors. She scanned the readouts and made note of the fact that there was no change to her patients and continued on with her paperwork.

33

Buildings rose on each side of the truck like steep canyon walls. Picture windows of retails shops, delis, restaurants, and brick facades stared at him. Up ahead, hotels and high-rises reached even higher. Darkness from a heavy, gray sky was closing in. Boulevard street lamps armed with automatic light sensors were popping on. Illumination from store interiors spilled out onto the pedestrian sidewalk. The intermittent shafts of quickly fading sunlight reflecting off the buildings were almost gone.

He was still a good mile from the tallest skyscraper in downtown Seattle. The massive black glass landmark was somewhere up ahead.

Fifteen hundred feet above and behind him, Rockeye was watching.

"In three, two, one . . ."

A red camera light flicked on. The local Fox news station was about to interrupt its regular late afternoon programming. The floor director pointed a finger at the well-dressed man behind the news anchor desk.

"Good afternoon, I'm Ben Saven. We're just getting word from our Utah County bureau chief that there may be an epidemic brewing at the Provo Regional Medical Center. For that story, let's go live to Mara Banda. Mara, what have you learned?"

The picture on the newsroom monitors changed to a statuesque, thirty-something blonde reporter swathed in a blue wraparound, safari style jacket. "Ben, we've just been informed that the reported influenza problem, which we heard about last week, is actually something else altogether. It's believed that this medical emergency is, in fact, a highly contagious, very aggressive bacterial infection. The bodies of sixteen people, including two Provo police officers, have been quarantined and will not be released to the families anytime soon. We've been advised that the Centers for Disease Control are now in charge of the investigation."

The camera panned to the front of the medical center, with the name of the hospital prominent in the picture.

"They've just concluded a brief meeting with local authorities, and from what we've been able to learn, at least three other regional hospitals have also quarantined patients with similar symptoms. At this point, there are an estimated sixty-two people infected."

Conference room
Utah Valley Medical Center
Provo, Utah
Friday, 1705 hours Mountain Time

"Okay, turn it off," the tanned, balding man in the expensive three-piece suit demanded.

The other five men in the room turned back to face the man at the head of the mahogany conference table.

"Doctor, how long do you think the bacteria story will hold up?" the suit asked.

"A few days, maybe less. There will be tremendous public pressure to provide updates now that the media is crawling all over it. The flak we're getting from the families will become more demanding, and no doubt, very public."

The physician opened his briefing booklet.

"We have thirty-plus dead, somewhere near eighty infected and in medical facilities, and who knows how many more yet to be admitted and diagnosed. All of the local ones are being transported to us. The only bright spot, if you want to call it that, is the kid and the university paleontologist seem to be holding their own. We still don't have anything close to a commonality that we can hang our hat on. We're burning up the phone lines with CDC HQ, Fort Detrick, and the other labs. We're no closer to treating it beyond one hundred percent oxygen upon admittance to the quarantine unit. Once it reaches epidemic status in the press, things will get out of control. It will affect every aspect of daily living, from the service sector to transportation and finance. The financial implications can't be estimated, since the last time this kind of medical problem existed, it was the typhoid epidemic of the early twentieth century. One thing's for certain, the medical community will be overwhelmed in the short run. The only good news is that the infected parties aren't contagious for the first twelve hours after it sets in and organ damage actually starts. That will help us a little as medical providers."

The suit sat motionless for a moment, seemingly focused on the grain in the mahogany conference table. He opened and closed his right fist several times. The room was silent for about fifteen seconds, until he leaned forward on his elbows.

"Okay, let's reconvene here tomorrow morning at 0730 hours. I'll have a game plan for you then. Any questions?"

No one replied.

"Thank you, gentlemen. Colonel, would you and the doctor remain behind a moment?"

The other three men stood up and walked out of the room.

"Last night our jet, its personnel, and the rock disappeared from the airport around 2130 hours. That information is classified at this time. The jet was found in the woods of central Washington state this morning at a private airstrip. Our personnel were found shot to death at a small airport in northern Utah a few hours ago. We're pumping manpower into Washington in pursuit of the perpetrators. CDC tells me that without the rock, this virus is going to be a lot more difficult to deal with. The tissue samples are of limited value since they cannot be easily reverse engineered due to their degradation."

He paused and reached down into his briefcase.

"Colonel, you are being federalized, immediately." He slid a manila envelope across the table in the direction of the full-time National Guard officer.

The officer reached over and snatched up the folder.

"The police will shut down the back parking lot area and the streets to the east and south sides of the hospital. We're moving in a full portable lab from Fort Detrick to address this thing. You will provide onsite security and a QRF. We're taking no chances with civilian unrest. Your new XO will be here in the morning. He's been serving as provost marshal at the warfare training center down south. There are also risks from within. We'll have new security measures for access to restricted areas of this hospital. It's all in the envelope."

The colonel slipped the envelope into his briefcase.

On the other side of the conference table, the senior hospital physician sat stunned by the news of the murders and the loss of their only real tool to the beat the viral epidemic. He knew full well that it was already out of control. His face was an ashen mask, only his eyes blinked. It meant that there was a strong possibility that even more friends and coworkers would be dying.

Suddenly, expletives dropped from his mouth like bombs from a B-52.

"How in hell are we going to stop this virus without that geode sample?" His anger ratcheted up with each word and he was losing control, "You can't take over my hospital like this!"

"We can and we are, doctor. This hospital accepts federal monies. If you'll calm down a moment, I'll explain. You do not have the resources to deal with this emergency. I have a large resource pool of biohazard physicians, microvirologists, and biologists on the way. They will work with your lab team. This hospital will be ground zero, as a means of arresting the spread of this virus. The two hospitals to the north of you in Orem will be beefed up to deal with your reduced elective retail services. We have new equipment en route to them and military doctors being detailed to their facilities to supplement their staff. We'll be installing site trailers to provide increased capacity until this is over. Your hospital will be compensated by the federal government for revenue shortfall. Your emergency room and some of your routine functions will not be disturbed. We'll try to keep the disruptions minimal. Is that understood?"

The suit reached down again into his briefcase and pulled out another envelope.

"This will give you a structural overview of the changes. One other thing, doctor, my records indicate that you are a recently retired Navy commander. I'm federalizing you too. You're working for me now. The board chairman of the hospital has already been notified. You will not discuss any confidential aspects of this briefing with anyone, including your wife, Annette. If you do, your retirement check will come to a grinding halt and your freedom will be jeopardized. Got it? I'll see you in the morning as well, commander."

The major general with the American flag pin in his lapel and the stenciled caduceus on his briefcase rose from the table and walked out. His two-man security team fell in with him as he strode toward the elevator at the end of the hallway. He hadn't intended on the get tough approach, but felt the circumstances that unfolded in the room warranted it.

The number of infected victims could double every sixty-eight hours? I sure as hell hope that that statistical mathematician at Fort Detrick is wrong.

The elevator door opened and swallowed the three men.

34

The terrorist passed an old church, a bank, and then turned right on Columbia Street. At Third Avenue, he turned again. He was forced to a halt at a light on the corner.

People poured out of downtown business offices like bees from a hive. Pedestrians clogged the sidewalks while a cooling afternoon breeze blew gently through the high-rise canyon of office buildings and hotels.

A group of office workers walked past the truck in the crosswalk. "Sheep," he said to himself, "Enjoy your decadence. You'll be dead soon. Too bad I can't be here to empty your pockets, too."

Twenty two hundred feet overhead, the helicopter moved slowly and quietly, the sound of its rotors blending in with the noises from the city streets below. Helicopters above Seattle were not an uncommon sight; no one on the crowded, rush hour streets below seemed to take notice. Plain clothes deputies and police officers were positioned along the terrorist's downtown route in the event he spooked and decided to bail while stuck in traffic.

The sky above was beginning to fall. Streaks of gray and a hard wind were moving in like a sniffle before a nasty sneeze. The chopper pilot eased the collective over to compensate for a sudden gust.

"This is Rockeye. Target is coming up on Fifth Avenue and Columbia.

Be advised, Columbia is one-way westbound. All units stand by. Rockeye is passing control to Blue One."

Blue One was the Seattle FBI special agent in charge. Standing next to him, with a pair of binoculars in hand, was his number two, No-Knock Petrocelli.

A momentary pause and the new voice came up on the predesignated radio frequency.

"This is Blue One to all units. Target is in the brown Chevy pickup in lane two, coming up on the corner light. Blue One will change the traffic light when the target approaches the next corner. We'll take him in the intersection. Let's not spray the area with gunfire, folks. We've got pedestrians all over the place."

On the opposing street corners at the intersection, both storefronts bristled with federal agents who were just pulling down their jacket flaps that said FBI in big, bold, black letters. The secondary team was comprised of Seattle police officers. Patrons in both corner stores had been hustled out the back on the guise of a minor gas leak.

The color weather radar printout he'd grabbed off the printer fifteen minutes before showed progressively worsening cells headed straight for them. The large, dark-red splotch on the storm graph went all the way to the edge of the paper. Sean and Detective Rod O'Brien looked at the sky to the north.

"How fast can that dry dock get to Friday Harbor?" Sean asked.

"Shouldn't take more than forty-five minutes, I'd guess," Rod replied. "We should be there in about fifteen, plenty of time to get set up ahead of the squall. I've got other deputies taping off part of the dock. We'll slide the boat into the dockside warehouse and get started."

Their patrol boat was now riding across increasing swells that were growing by the minute. Small whitecaps were starting to brush by the hull.

Dale and Sullivan zipped up their windbreakers as the gusts picked up outside the Navy chopper. At the edge of the horizon, the pilot could just make out the first details of an urban skyline. In back, Dale listened to the FBI command channel on his headset as the teams prepared for the ambush at the business district site. He absentmindedly stuck his left hand in his jacket pocket and touched the micro tag transmitter he was carrying around, still in its tiny crushproof packaging. They would touch down in Seattle in a few minutes.

"This is sure cutting it close," said one special agent as he charged a round into this M-4 assault rifle. Looking out on the street, he hoped the boulevard filled with pedestrians wouldn't create a problem with the arrest. The radio headset under his baseball cap crackled to life again.

"Rockeye, Blue One. Notify the FAA to shut down all small craft over-flights of the downtown corridor."

"Copy, Blue One."

"All units, this is Blue One. Stand by to engage, target is stopped at the light one block north."

Both teams in the corner stores lined up one man behind the other, ready to charge out the door for the intersection and the terrorist's truck.

On the corner, a Seattle police officer in city utility department overalls stood near a city truck and orange pylons. To casual onlookers, he appeared to be involved in wiring a mechanical set of switches. In reality, he had a manual control box that operated the intersection lights. At the precise moment, he would render all four directions of travel red, freezing the inter-section so the SWAT team could make the takedown.

A block behind the terrorist, the helicopter that had maintained the ongoing surveillance saw a fast-moving Navy chopper drop below a high-rise to a park just two blocks to the west. "I'm guessing that would be the hotshot FBI guys," the copilot said.

"Yeah, looks like they're late for their own party," the pilot remarked.

"Rockeye to all units, the light is green. Target is advancing up the block. Stand by to engage."

Cars started rolling up the street. Four vehicles back, the commando pushed down on the gas pedal of the stolen, brown pickup truck. The well-muscled Nordian terrorist caught the reflection of a shadow on the mirror-like glass wall of the high-rise office building up ahead. A break in the overcast allowed a sliver of light to penetrate through, illuminating the chopper's movement. He slouched down on the bench seat, tipped up the rearview mirror, and saw the dark colored helicopter with the words "police" tattooed on the side of the fuselage.

"Shi…!" His eyes darted around searching for the trouble he suspected was only moments away.

A truck blocking the intersection and uniformed people on the sidewalk. Who's watching me? Air and ground units, where are they?

In one swift motion, he reached down and grabbed the backpack, hoisting it up on the seat next to him. *My only real defense is the rock. It's a Mexican standoff at best. I can use the truck as a battering ram. Where can I roll out to safety?* His head filled with options. *Just a half block to the bank building.*

Three blocks away, Dale and Sullivan touched down in the park. Rush hour traffic and pedestrians were surprised by the sudden appearance of a U.S. Navy helo where it shouldn't be. The two FBI agents charged out the side door as the chopper blades continued to spin furiously. The door of an unmarked police car popped open and they ran for the vehicle. Moments later, it pulled away from the curb, lights flashing but its siren silent.

"Where is he?" Dale demanded rather bluntly of the driver. He quickly realized that the rough chopper ride had taken away the more pleasant aspects of his character. He felt bad about steamrolling the young agent behind the wheel.

"Two blocks, coming up on the intersection, sir. They're about to pull the trigger," the man replied.

"Where's the containment unit?" Sullivan asked.

"It's in the parking garage on the first level of the black tower, all ready with four of our men inside. All they need is the okay to respond."

Friday night traffic was slow to yield to the white undercover sedan, since only its red and blue lights requested right of way. The driver leaned on the horn as he broke through an intersection against a red light and swerved around a city bus. An elderly man, annoyed by the car's lack of respect for proper traffic etiquette, flipped the driver a one-fingered salute out of ag-gravation.

Out of frustration, his senses stood on end, and his mind was in over-drive. He had one objective; get to the bank on the corner. The commando checked the rearview mirror again, looking for anything out of place. *There, two sedans a few cars back. That means they'll try to stop me up ahead and block me in.*

He shoved the gas pedal to the floor and swerved around the car ahead, gaining ground on the upcoming intersection. Automatic survival responses had taken over.

"Switch the light now!" the voice on the radio net commanded. The undercover cop on the corner pushed the button, but it was a second and a half too late.

The brown pickup banged off a new BMW and shot though the cross street. Cars ahead on the next block jammed the roadway. The stolen vehicle aimed for the bank building, hitting the corner street sign as it rammed its way across the intersection. A heavy garbage can sitting on the sidewalk in front of the skyscraper was launched across the road. The steel can bounced away, violently hitting two SWAT team members that had emerged mo-ments before from the business on the corner. Sixteen black clad SWAT officers turned and ran after the pickup, now a couple hundred feet away and still careening toward the high-rise front entrance.

Inside the smoke-colored glass building, a young, armed security officer sitting behind an oak desk saw the truck quickly climb the shallow stair steps toward the front door. He slowly rose from his wheeled secretarial chair, still gauging the level of activity on the other side of the massive windows. Thanks to the decorative foliage outside, he couldn't yet see the heavily armed SWAT team coming his way.

The commando finally reached the top step as the truck slammed to a grinding stop against two multiton rock planters with ponderosa pines growing in them. Kicking the driver's door open, he swung the backpack over his shoulders and charged up the travertine lined walkway. He looked back over the hood of the wrecked truck and fired a burst from his MAC-11 submachine pistol at his pursuers.

Office workers emerging from the business tower ran for cover, women screaming as they raced to get away. Some people collapsed to the ground when they heard the gunshots and covered their heads. A SWAT team member went down, a bullet hole drilling a superficial clean wound through his left calf muscle.

"Don't shoot, don't shoot!! He has the rock in the case. Don't shoot, we got civilians all over the place!" someone shouted out over the radio net.

Both SWAT teams were now out and maneuvering through the high-rise office complex access area. Several voices on the closed-circuit radio system were issuing commands and warnings as momentary confusion kicked in.

The reenergized commando bulldozed his way past two men exiting the dual sliding glass doors of the huge office complex. He shoved his way through the inner doors, knocking a bicycle delivery rider to the ground.

Sixty feet away, the stationary security officer pulled his semiautomatic pistol and screamed at the fleeing man to stop. The commando, seeing the lone guard, slid to the floor and squeezed the trigger of his firearm in the man's direction. Copper rounds sprayed indiscriminately inside the large, open-air foyer, hitting three people, including the security officer. A thirty-five-foot tall glazed mirror on a back wall shattered, sending thousands of shards of sharp glass flying across the interior walkway and crashing to the floor. Dozens of people were seriously injured by the jagged projectiles. More screaming filled the air of the foyer as people ducked for cover.

The commando regained his feet and ran for the door of the bank. In a few seconds, he was inside, where he promptly loaded a new magazine into the just emptied submachine pistol. Aiming high, he pulled the trigger to get everyone's attention. Bits and pieces of ceiling plaster fell to the floor.

The bank's branch manager, a pregnant, petite, blonde woman in her early 30s, was strolling across the bank lobby to the commercial loan department.

The commando ran right by her.

"This is a robbery! Everyone hit the deck!" he screamed as he came to a halt.

His hand tightened around the pistol grip, waiting to see if anyone was stupid enough to challenge his demand. The look of abject determination on his face and the small automatic machine gun in his hand were all the bank patrons needed to know to convince them he was serious.

The bank manger slunk down to the polished marble floor. Two window tellers wasted no time hitting the knee buttons under the counter. A robbery alarm was sounded immediately at the monitoring station.

Newlyweds in the computer booth nearby crawled under the desk and pressed themselves up against the wall. A female teller looked up from her customer to discover the backpack laden bank robber. She'd been robbed once before, several summers ago, by a man claiming to have a bomb. The backpack brought back an immediate flood of horrifying memories. Several other tellers prepared to hand over dye pack bundles of cash upon request. There was no question in their minds that the suspect's propensity for shooting people was well established.

At the bank's security monitoring firm a few miles away, the security room supervisor watched the bank monitors and observed a man with a gun taking hostages. "Holy . . . We've got an in-progress armed robbery at . . ." He looked at the screen ID " . . . location forty-seven."

Seconds later, he punched the button on the blue phone to the police dispatch center to report the holdup. Two other security officers in the center focused their attention on the nine cameras in the bank. They watched for possible accomplices, unsure as yet of the scope of the activity unfolding before them.

Back at the bank, several people managed to scurry out the front door, and charged right into the SWAT officers entering the building. They reported the bank robbery as they fled to safety.

Having identified the boss, the commando ordered the female bank manager to the teller gate in front of the stairwell. "Who's your assistant manager?" he asked, shoving the gun in her ribs.

"She's over there," the manager responded, pointing reluctantly to a woman whose desk was covered with paperwork.

The commando motioned the woman over with a wave of his hand. With a great deal of trepidation, she pushed back her rolling chair and walked over, fearful for her safety.

The commando pulled her close, then reached into his backpack, pulled out a plastic bag, and proceeded to rip the top off. He extracted a long, white, plastic tie wrap and slipped it over her wrists. He repeated the process with the bank manager and then linked the two women together with a third one.

He peered out the front glass window and spotted a sea of black clad people running his way. The clock on the wall ticked past 5:25 p.m. He refocused his attention on the people sprawled on the floor, looking for anyone who might appear brave.

Black Tower Building
Wells Fargo Bank
Downtown Seattle, Washington
Friday, 1726 hours Pacific Time

"He has hostages. We had a couple of people running for cover that told us he announced his intentions to rob the bank," the SWAT team leader said into the boom mike that hugged his face. "Are we sure the guy is a terrorist?"

"Secure the floor. Status, do you have a visual on the suspect?" Blue One asked.

The senior officer pulled out a small pair of tactical binoculars and focused in on the man at the rear of the bank.

"My men have taken up defensive positions and are evacuating office workers out of the immediate vicinity," the SWAT team leader said. "Team two is moving to secure the rest of the main floor. Team three is securing the perimeter. Suspect is holding three women, one of them very pregnant, in the right corner of the teller area near the basement stairs. This guy is cagey . . . he's not standing in one place for more than a few moments."

"Alright, first priority is the backpack. No one takes a shot without my authorization. If that container is broken or shattered, we'll be unleashing a fast-acting, deadly virus. The CDC doc in the command center says it'll be like killing all of the hostages ourselves. The bank security folks are patching us into their video feed. I have the city planning department bringing the schematics and building plans over right now. Stand by for further, contain the suspect, and notify me of any changes."

The SWAT team leader acknowledged Blue One and went back to his surveillance.

Blue One ordered in more officers and deputies to cordon off the skyscraper and surround the building. Like chess pieces on a playing board, he and his adjunct began moving teams of men into place to secure the entire area. He started by shutting down all of the adjacent streets. He then sent officers throughout the high-rise to escort building employees out side exits. He had the local phone company security people shut down the phone exchange in the building. And finally he had the ventilation system turned off.

Everything was going according to their training and preplanned response scenarios. Everything except the terrorist's plans, which accounted for the response from the police outside. The terrorist, however, hadn't planned on Dale or his partner, Sullivan, slipping through a side door of the bank and ahead of the SWAT team.

In the bank security monitoring facility, one of the security officers saw the door ease open and two men crawl in down low. "Who are those guys?" he asked his partner, hoping he might know. They watched as the two unidentified men pulled out guns from beneath their jackets.

"I think they're cops, but we better tell somebody. They don't have the live feed up yet to the incident command center."

Dale and Sullivan had no communication headset, just a cell phone apiece. Inside the bank, about forty people lay on the floor, murmuring and making small noises.

"Call No-Knock's cell and tell him what's up. I'll crawl to the front of the teller wall opposite the bad guy. Oh yeah, cover me, will ya? He's got a full auto tinker toy from the sound of it." *And me with no bulletproof vest, again. Smart Fox, real smart.*

Dale crawled off as Sullivan side slipped behind a pillar and hit the autodial for No-Knock.

The phone in his shirt pocket vibrated. He looked at the number, didn't recognize it, and went on conversing with the man next to him at the command center. Anthony Petrocelli was debating whether he should remain at the command center or depart for the bank. He rubbed a coin in his pocket unable to decide.

"Come on, pal, answer the call."

The voice message picked up a few seconds later. Sullivan closed his phone and concentrated on Dale moving slowly across the floor. So far, he only had a view of the terrorist from the knees down, on the other side of the row of teller windows.

Dale rolled up against the dark, wood-paneled teller wall. Several people lying on the floor glanced at him as he inched his way over. He slid around the corner and out of sight, hoping the terrorist hadn't seen the look on the faces of those who watched him. He could be in real trouble otherwise. Now he was out of Sullivan's view as well. He crouched behind a propped up calendar on the teller window. Peeking around the corner, he saw the terrorist talking to the trussed-up bank manager. She was crying and obviously in distress. This was not going well.

That's just great. He's got a baby factory for a hostage.

Dale dropped back down against the counter, leaned back as far as he could to catch Sullivan's eye, and motioned him over.

The terrorist grabbed two more women from behind the tellers' counter. He repeated the earlier process of linking the group of five together with tie wraps. He was surrounded by trembling, terrified women. He fished around the side pocket of the backpack and pulled out another object. With his head swiveling around like an owl seeking a mouse, he took in every moving person in the bank.

"We have two armed guys inside the bank opposite the bank robber. I don't know who they are, but, they could be ours," No-Knock reported to Blue One "They're moving like cops."

No-Knock watched as the live feed came up on the incident command center's video monitor.

"Anybody recognize them?" Blue One asked no one in particular.

"What the . . . they're supposed to be on a Navy ship somewhere out in the islands."

The FBI special agent in charge looked at his number two. "Are those the two counterterrorism guys who blew into town a few days ago?"

No-Knock had been tasked by his boss to keep tabs on the two out-of-area counterterrorism agents.

"Yes, sir, that's them. Last time I heard from them, they were split up, one in eastern Washington and the other on a sheriff's patrol vessel looking for a sunken boat a hundred miles from here."

Blue One was not happy, and made a point of insuring that No-Knock was aware of it.

"They're crawling closer to the terrorist and his hostages," No-Knock offered as he watched the color monitor. "Maybe we should give them a diversion to redirect the terrorist's attention." No-Knock was trying to redeem himself as quickly as he could. Blue One watched the monitor as a blue canister was thrown out in the bank lobby. Smoke poured out of the canister and began to fill the lobby area.

"He's moving the hostages. He killed the lights. See if someone at the monitoring center can boost the camera's resolution; I can't see a thing in there. And let the team leaders know that we have those two counterterrorism cowboys loose in the bank."

"Dale, he went around the corner," Sullivan whispered. No sooner did the words leave his mouth than a metal can bounced into the lobby and exploded. Smoke rapidly cascaded out from the round, metallic container and filled the room. It was too much for some of the prone customers whose fear of death finally overrode their primal safety instincts. They rushed for the exit doors and poured out of the bank.

Dale focused in on the canister, hoping it wasn't tear gas.

"Sullivan, can you see him?"

Sullivan poked his head past the edge of the wall and saw movement as the last woman disappeared. "He pulled back away from the end of the teller row. I think he may have gone downstairs with his hostages," Sullivan replied. "I don't see him anymore."

With the noise in the bank escalating - women screaming, men shouting, and many feet taking flight - Dale risked the moment and jumped over the counter, gun in hand. The Springfield XD .45 was a nonstandard FBI issue firearm, with a fourteen-round magazine capacity. He and Sullivan carried the same weapon, which made big holes in whatever they hit. His choice of firearm was a privilege of position as a counterterrorism agent. The weapon was sometimes hard to keep concealed from someone intensely scrutinizing them, but Dale preferred the heavy firepower. In reality, he had carte blanche to carry pretty much anything he felt the circumstances warranted.

Wish I had a couple of flash bangs, he thought.

Sullivan vaulted the counter a few seconds behind Dale, and both men moved up carefully. Moments later, a second canister whistled by Sullivan's head from the hallway and exploded in the lobby. More smoke poured out to supplement the first grenade.

Outside, the FBI SWAT team leader motioned for two men to enter the bank door. The black clad men crawled down low, looking for feet on the polished floor as they went. The bank lobby was now filled with smoke and visibility was impossible.

"I can't see a damn thing. What the hell is going on in there?" Blue One demanded. "Have we got the place surrounded yet? Can we get the agent in the basement in the containment vehicle to watch the doors on the basement level?"

No-Knock was on his tactical radio getting answers and moving people, while his boss stayed glued to the bank monitor, waiting for the smoke to dissipate. Blue One walked to the window. The command post was a block away, and he could see the chopper circling the tower complex down the street. Two Seattle police officers were visible on the roof of an adjacent building.

This thing is going in the crapper fast, he lamented to himself.

"Team One leader, status!" he barked into his radio.

The FBI SWAT team leader keyed his microphone. "Sir, I have two men inside and two more on the way in."

Dale knelt down low and peeked around the corner. Sullivan tiptoed across the open hallway to the opposite wall. They could barely see each other through the smoke. Listening for a second, they heard only the sounds of people running from the bank. Dale looked at Sullivan and opened his hands in a wide spread as if to say he couldn't hear anything from the stairs below.

Sullivan responded by whispering, "You're braver than I am, you go first."

Dale frowned and raised the big .45 up. "Stay off the walls, they're metal lined," he whispered back. Both men cautiously moved down the stairs, listening for voices as they went.

"Keep moving," he yelled. The group of five reached the end of the passageway, turned right, and walked another thirty feet, prodded on from behind. They came to a stop in front of a grated, stainless steel door.

"Open the gate," he demanded of the manager. With a shaky hand, she pulled the outer gate key from the strap around her neck. Inserting it, she twisted it to the right and a metal clank echoed off the wall. The bank robber shoved all five of them forward, took the key, and relocked the grated door from the inside.

To their left was another short hallway with a long, waist-high antique table. Just around the corner to the right was a one-ton vault door with a triple handle and round locking mechanism adorned with a magnetic card reader.

"Open it," he ordered, glaring at the pregnant woman.

Gathering her courage, she looked up at him, her arms linked to a woman on either side.

"I can't do it like this, and besides, I don't have the full combination. It takes another bank officer to complete it."

Turning to the assistant manager, he pointed the submachine gun at her. "If you don't have it, you're dead."

The woman shook and wet herself. "I-I-I-I have it, yes."

The bank robber cut the manager from the others and then re-linked them after they opened the vault. He pulled the heavy door open as the women backed away. Slipping around the edge of the door, he finished pushing it open until it was sufficiently wide to walk in.

Dale stopped abruptly in mid stride and turned to Sullivan. In a quiet voice he said, "We better slide our badges on the back of our belts. We don't want to run into the SWAT team upstairs and get blown away from behind." Sullivan nodded his head in agreement. A few seconds later, they advanced down the hall.

"Lie down on the floor face down. Don't move, I'll be back in a minute," the homicidal robber ordered. With that, he stepped out of sight and into the vault.

The women complied, still unsure if they would live through the ordeal. The police were upstairs, they were locked in, and the robber had the grate door key; they were trapped.

The five women listened as his footsteps inside the carpeted vault faded away.

The frightened bank manager looked at her employees. "Quietly, no noise, let's get up. We're going to shove the door closed and lock him in. We all need to push hard and fast. Up."

They rose to their knees as one and rushed the vault door. Grunting, they gave the massive door a great shove. The heavy, stainless steel door slammed closed and then recoiled a few inches back at them. With their combined weight, they succeeded in finally pushing it flush at the frame. The blonde bank manager spun the handle and locked the door. She stood erect and then grabbed painfully at her abdomen.

Inside the vault, the terrorist waited a moment and was rewarded with the sound of the heavy door slamming closed.

Thank you, ladies.

He flipped on the vault room light switch and smiled. He slumped down against the row of highly polished cabinets and rested a minute. It was the first peaceful, satisfying moment he had since his ordeal began in Utah the day before. Pulling open the side pocket of the backpack, he popped out three more caffeine pills and swallowed them dry.

This is just too easy. They're responding slowly, methodically, and cautiously as expected. I would like to know how they found me, though. Did someone notice the missing truck from the back lot at the service station?

Thor Odin revisited the story relayed to him at the beginning of the mission. The Seattle waterfront was rebuilt in 1889 after a massive fire destroyed the better part of the skid row business district. The Seattle Underground - a popular tourist attraction - featured the old, underground, waterfront city streets, over which modern Seattle was built. In the process of rebuilding, much of the old city area was left untouched. It appeared now as it did over a hundred twenty years ago. During a recent tour, Thor Odin's keen eye spotted an interesting anomaly.

The cost of building on top of the existing foundations was a cheaper, faster alternative for the early city fathers. After considerable construction, which took decades, an abandoned underground area comprised of a dozen city blocks existed in the emptiness below modern-day Seattle. Now it was an uninhabited no-man's zone, occupied by rats and other creatures of the rodent family. Shafts of light filtered down through cracks in the street above, straining to illuminate small patches of the dark void.

The underground area ran from Cherry Street to King Street, out to the new baseball stadium and Fourth Street, and on to the waterfront. The passageways were crumbling brick walls and stone slabs. At night, the occasional street lamp threw an eerie glow on dusty archways and pillars. Miles of antiquated, rusting water pipes crisscrossed the underground area. Crawl spaces above them, with tiny openings to the street gutters, were clogged with spider webs. The place had a haunted feeling, with eerie sounds of dripping water and squeaking rats.

During the tour, Odin saw a hole in the brickwork off in the distant background. He cautiously stepped away from the back of the tour in the dark. Pulling out his key fob flashlight, he walked past the "keep out - danger" signs posted along the path.

Peering through the tiny hole in the old 1880s masonry, he spied a small room with a partially collapsed ceiling. On the far side was the foundation of Seattle's tallest skyscraper. The support pillars were obviously driven deep into the ground with modern pile-driving equipment. There, at the edge of the light, was the corner of the building. Rough concrete, musty earth, and dust-covered debris stared back at him.

He was thirty-eight feet below the current street level. An hour later, he left the bank above with a thought in mind.

That evening, Thor spoke with his father, Douglas Odin, and suggested an idea which could net hundreds of millions in assets. Douglas listened and pondered the possibilities. As he did, an opportunistic smile crawled across his unshaven face until it was a full-blown demonic grin. It was just the kind of irresistible largess that appealed to his eccentric tastes. Acquiring the liquid assets of less rich business competitors, with their overdeveloped sense of superiority, was an entertaining prospect.

Douglas ordered Thor to organize a small team to determine the plan's feasibility. Several nights later, they broke in and walked the underground trail to the chosen spot. Two of the men were prefab bank vault construction specialists. Two others were skilled electronics security systems engineers. Digging commenced the following night after they'd determined the specialized tooling required.

Enlarging the small opening, they set about creating an exterior facade so the tour couldn't see the new construction activity. Aided by the darkness, the hole was almost a hundred feet from the pathway, and well hidden. Working quietly and carefully, so as not to disturb the bank vault sensors, they cleared an eight-by-eight foot area of the outer vault wall.

The bank actually possessed two vaults. The vault for the general public was one flight up from the subbasement, on the other side of the bank. The "private client" vault room in the subbasement was where the richest clients stored their assets, liquid and illiquid alike.

Inside the spacious vault was a king's treasure, secured by the wealthiest of Seattle's elite class. One of a kind priceless artwork, cash, jewelry, and negotiable securities lined its luxuriously padded drawers. And as far as Douglas Odin was concerned, the best part of his scheme was that he would be stealing some of his own assets, adding credibility to the magnificent theft as a victim.

By the end of the week, the billionaire's entry team had the vault's interior rebar exposed, along with the remote electronic and hardwired security systems. Now they were hard at work lacing together a second security net that would tap the computerized master control console, which monitored the bank's security system. Once constructed, they would substitute it, disconnect the original system, and cut into the vault. The backup system was secured off to the side, out of the way of the exposed vault wall itself.

A four-by-five foot area of the reinforced steel vault was painstakingly cut with a wet reciprocating diamond saw two nights later. A section of metal drawers faced them after the steel casing was exposed. They disconnected the stainless steel retaining straps and pushed the heavy vertical cabinet out into the open vault space. They were in.

Climbing slowly and cautiously inside the vault, they turned their flashlights to the interior and inspected the large cavernous space. The room was forty-four feet wide and forty-six feet long. Three rows of matching, back-to-back vault drawers ran down the center of the room.

Oak rolltop desks adorned with digital calculators, gold colored pens, and bank note pads rounded out the vault's amenities. Within the hour, they managed to lift up one cabinet they'd displaced from the wall. Placing small, steel ball bearings under it made it easier to move back into place. They cleaned up the floor and pulled the cabinet back to the wall, with a man inside to confirm that the room took on its former appearance once again. With their man outside once again, he was satisfied that they had penetrated the bank without detection. They closed up and left. One of the largest bank robberies in history was on schedule. At least that was the original plan.

The weary terrorist smiled and rose to his feet with renewed vigor. Looking around he thought to himself, *I wish I could be here to see the looks on their faces when they discover an empty vault.*

36

The Black Tower Building
Wells Fargo Bank
Seattle, Washington
Friday, 1732 hours Pacific Time

Dale tiptoed down the hall, with Sullivan a few feet behind and on the opposite side of the passageway. They checked several doors as they went; all were locked. As Sullivan gripped the doorknob of the last room on the right, several female voices yelled out for help, their screams reverberating off the hallway walls. Both men moved cautiously forward, expecting to confront the trigger-happy terrorist at any moment. At the end of the hallway was another staircase leading down.

The smoke finally cleared on the bank's main floor. The ferocity of the FBI SWAT team entry was etched in their faces; their demeanor bordering on outright anger. The carefully orchestrated takedown of the terrorist had been a complete disaster. They cautiously descended the stairway, automatic weapons at the ready. Behind them, the second SWAT team was ushering in paramedics to deal with the carnage.

Slipping quietly up on the grated access door to the vault, Dale and Sullivan could see a handful of women gathered around another woman lying flat on her back on the polished marble floor.

Dale glanced over at Sullivan. He made a hand signal indicating he would crouch down and advance on the reinforced grate while Sullivan would hug the wall and ready himself in the event shots started flying. Dale inched ahead not knowing what to expect.

The women were frantic and appeared to be attending to the one who was down. Dale concluded that she was either shot or unconscious. A woman stood up and turned to yell out the vault alcove when she spotted Dale. She recoiled in momentary surprise.

Putting a finger to his lips, he whispered, "FBI. Where's the robber?"

A cacophony of squeals arose as two other women rushed the gate. "He's locked in the vault," she pointed. "He can't go anywhere. Carol is pregnant, her water just broke. The baby is coming. We need help. The grate door key is with the robber. We need an ambulance for her," she said in a rapid-fire voice. Sullivan edged forward and looked through the opening.

"I'll make contact with SWAT and get the paramedics rolling," Sullivan responded.

He turned and headed back up the hallway, announcing his presence loudly so there would be no mistake that he was coming their way.

The redheaded assistant manager pleaded, "Help us, we need to get another key from upstairs to unlock this door."

"Sullivan, hang on a second. We need to get a key from upstairs to get them out."

Sullivan stopped and waited.

"Okay, where is the key?" Dale asked.

"Top left drawer of my desk in the green plastic box."

"You get that?" Dale asked Sullivan. Sullivan nodded and turned back, once again hollering to the oncoming SWAT team. Several minutes later the women were out, and the paramedics were rolling a gurney toward the vault hallway.

The SWAT team leader took Dale aside. "Blue One is on the way over. He'll be here in a few minutes."

"Okay, thanks." Dale turned to the redhead, "How long ago did you lock the safe?"

"Oh, gosh, let me think. It was about two minutes or so before you found us." Dale and the SWAT team leader both glanced at their watches. Sullivan was interviewing one of the women further down the hallway about the robbery. They would never know that a bank robbery was not the true intention of the man who took them hostage.

"Dale, the safe has the standard one-hour timer on it. Best guess is 1733 hours to close contact with the internal vault timer. We'll have to wait it out."

Inside the anteroom of the vault, a SWAT team member was trying to talk with the trapped terrorist on the vault's intercom system. The man locked inside wasn't answering.

Within a few minutes, the entire operation - minus the SWAT team, Dale, and Sullivan - was moved back up to the bank's conference room on the main floor. The bank lobby was still occupied with police, paramedics, and crime scene personnel. Blue One was in the lobby, distracted by the activity and answering questions on his cell phone. The local media were descending like a hungry wolf pack on a warm winter kill.

The SWAT team leader conferred with one of his members for a moment. Then he stepped over to Dale.

"We've shut down the power and air conditioning to the vault. That toxic rock can't circulate its contents through the rest of the bank's ventilation. It also appears that our bad guy has yanked the closed circuit TV cable out of the camera so we can't see what he's doing inside. And since he's not talking to us, we're gonna have to wait out the hour to yank his carcass out of the vault. When the time is up, we'll flash bang him and toss in some tear gas. I've got some level three hazmat suits on the way over from the fire department."

The SWAT team leader's cell phone rang.

"Yeah, got it. I'll tell him, thanks."

"Blue One is on the way down. He's the local SAC. He's fuming mad that HQ gave you carte blanche on this stuff. Personally, I think the whole 'flying squad' approach is way overdue. Blue One has the opposite opinion. Just be aware, he's a little on the intense side under normal circumstances, so he's probably on edge right now. Next item, I have the containment team from the garage coming in to deal with the rock. I've been advised that it's really your show."

Dale looked into the man's face, confident that he was a team player, "What about the local contact who was supposed to meet him?"

"Seattle PD is filming all the crowds for later. King County S.O. and the DEA office have teams of plain clothes searching the crowds, but I think at this point that's a dead pursuit."

"I'm inclined to agree."

"You wanna stick around for the grand opening?" The SWAT boss was referring to the vault's one-hour security system time lag.

Dale turned to his partner, "Sullivan, you want to interrogate the suspect while I head back out to Friday Harbor?"

"Have you talked to Rod O'Brien since we got here?" Sullivan replied.

Dale looked pensive. "No, I need to call him and get a ride back out there. I think the Navy can pick me up at the wharf fire station. Call me when you've made some headway."

Sullivan nodded, "Mr. Canned Spam is all mine," and went back to his conversation with the bank manager.

Dale walked down the hall and passed Blue One, who looked at him and his slightly oversized, nonregulation mustache. Blue One's expression was obvious; he didn't approve of the FBI supervisor or the intrusion into his territory. Dale towered over the much shorter agent in charge of the Seattle office. He looked back at him with a blank expression and walked on.

Wait till he discovers that Sullivan's doing the interrogation. That'll add to his thinning, gray hair, he thought with a sly grin.

Inside the vault, the latex gloved terrorist was pulling on the locked drawer handle using both hands. With a deep grunt, it finally started to slide out.

Let's see, over the top of the cabinet and down through the hole. Just like Alice in Wonderland.

He hefted the backpack carefully up on the cabinet. After giving the nicely laminated drawer handle one final pull, the cabinet was out as far as it would go. He cut his finger on the edge of the cabinet's corner. He watched a second as it bled slowly.

Man, that's heavy.

He was ready for a nap. Behind him, the disembodied voice of someone, no doubt a cop was trying to get his attention on the vault speaker. He ignored that, too, and sucked the blood off his finger.

The commando's stomach growled. He hadn't eaten since dawn, back at the gas station in the woods.

He walked to the front of the vault and flipped the light off at the same time he clicked on his small LED flashlight.

Climbing up on the cabinet, he quickly wiggled his way down into the hole. Reaching behind him, he slid the backpack off the top. His body slipped through the open cement hole in the wall, where he finally stood up and brushed himself off. A minute later, he was wrestling with the two, screwed-in leather handles that the work team had secured to the back of the file drawer. With the cabinet pulled back in place, the interior of the vault was back to its original condition.

He stopped for a second with the flashlight in hand and marveled at the craftsmanship of the patchwork quilt wiring job that bypassed the bank's own alarm system. Looking around, he found the opening to the small, walled off area. After looking outside of the well-concealed room and listening for a moment, he walked off. A tired but satisfied grin spread across his face.

37

Beneath the Black Tower Building
Wells Fargo Bank, Seattle, Washington
Friday 1744 hours Pacific Time

Dale sat down in the lobby and made two phone calls, the first one to Rod O'Brien.

On the third ring, the Seattle detective picked up. "So how's the show going?" he said with a weariness in his voice. His day was long and growing longer with the workload. Hours of saltwater spray from the rescue boat had tightened his skin and he wanted a shower in the worst way.

"Takedown went sideways. Bad guy ran into one of Seattle's finer depositories for cover. The bank manager turned him into a short-term deposit by locking him in her safe."

Rod laughed uproariously. "He's stuck with a pile of money and no way to spend it?"

"You got it." Both men stifled a laughed. "You know, now that I hear it repeated, kinda makes me wonder - why he would do that?"

"What do you mean?" Rod asked.

"He left the master depository key with the manager when he entered the vault. What did he have in mind when he went in there? What he really needed was to escape."

"Well, you can ask him after SWAT peels him out of there," Rod said.

"Yeah, I suppose. By the way, I need a ride back out to Friday Harbor. I'm done here, can you help me?"

"Sure, let me make a phone call. It'll probably be by boat, may take an hour to get it for you. Why don't you grab your overnight bag from the hotel? I've got accommodations here on the island for us tonight. Meet the boat at the fire station on the wharf, let's say 1900 hours."

"Alright, I'll see you around 2100 hours. Find anything useful yet?" Dale asked.

"Yeah, but not over an unsecured phone," Rod answered.

It took a minute to wind his way around the dusty debris in the dark. The small flashlight provided just enough illumination to see a short distance. Noises echoed off the walls from a building somewhere up above. The sound of barely audible happy hour bar music was somewhere behind him. Closer in, he could hear the squeaking of mice or rats. Aside from a few cracks of dim light streaming in from an occasional passing headlight on the street above, it was eerily devoid of any illumination.

As he walked, he encountered rough-hewn, partially burnt, wooden beams he had to duck under. The heavy rock on his back almost caused him to topple over a couple of times. The charred wood was testament to the massive waterfront fire that wiped out the area in 1889.

He passed the first old building on his left, and was surprised to find intact glass in the window of an old, Chinese opium den. Several building fronts displayed faded advertisements painted across them. The last business in the row was a mercantile store with a cracked slab cement sidewalk and overturned wooden chairs lying against the closed door. Stopping a moment, he watched a large, brown rat disappear into the building. He continued on past a crumbling masonry wall and wiped cobwebs from a beam in his path. Further ahead, heavy oak planks lay in his path where they had tumbled over a hundred twenty years ago. Discarded gas lamps; rusted boilers; a few old, single-seat school desks; more faded, scorched wooden signs; and some primitive electrical wiring lay to the side of the walking path.

He stopped to read the unfolded note in his hand to get his bearings.

> Left at the pathway after the row of building fronts, and then pass the wall ahead. Take a right and follow the intersecting path. Look for the shaft of light from a crevice along the wall. Walk past the facade of the old dry goods

store, go left again, walk past the construction debris, and turn right at the sign for the "livery stable." Take a left, walk through the tunnel under the street above, and keep going until you come to an iron door. The door pins have been oiled and can be pulled up from your side. Walk up the steps and push past the boarded up doorway. Go out though the bushes into the alley, and head for the wharf straight ahead. It's a ten-minute walk. Watch out for the abandoned excavation holes along the pathway.

He looked at the flashlight. Its beam was fading. "Great, what's next?" Wasting no time, he moved on. Nine minutes later, he was lost. *I'll still be down here wandering around when they discover my bank vault exit,* he thought frustratingly. He turned around and retraced his steps, having missed the "livery" sign.

Unbeknownst to him, two of the six seals on the Lexan capsule containing the rock had separated in the truck crash. The analog humidity meter was creeping toward nine percent.

Sitting at an empty desk in a cubicle closed off from the noise and activity within the bank, Dale looked over his notes from the description the bank employees had given.

The trapped suspect was built like a military man in his early-thirties and handled himself accordingly. Quick thinking, decisive, he had a plan. He knew what he was doing when he entered the vault. Why is that bothering me?

He paused in thought. *The SWAT team will deal with him. Hmmm, no other indications of intent beyond robbing the bank, as far as the kidnapped bank employees are concerned. He definitely had the backpack, though. Sullivan can sweat him and we can compare notes in a few hours. At least we have the rock back. Now we can get the CDC to work on an antidote.*

Dale made his second call in private, and after a few minutes he finally closed up his notepad, stuffed it in his back pocket, and walked out of the cubicle.

"Agent Fox," a voice to his right called out. "We have the photos of the robbery suspect," an FBI technician said as he walked over to Dale.

Well that saves me the trouble of having to find you.

"Great, step into the cubicle and let's have a look," Dale said.

Four other agents, a second unit FBI SWAT team member, and a Seattle police captain crowded into the confined space. Dale opened the manila folder and spread eleven pictures out on the desk. Everyone looked them over. Dale was the only one to spot the anomaly.

"How soon can you make me a set of these to go?" he asked.

"Just a couple of minutes," the technician replied.

"Do it, please."

The assembled agents and local law enforcement personnel were congratulating each other and patting themselves on the back for a job well done in capturing the most wanted terrorist on U.S. soil.

I don't know how many people died here today, but there's blood all over the place. It seems to have escaped everyone in the room that a pregnant bank manager, who slammed the vault door shut, is the real hero.

Dale walked out of the bank a minute later with the pictures in hand.

Utah Valley Medical Center
Provo, Utah
Friday, 1846 hours Mountain Time

"I got your message, what do you have?" Dr. Hunack asked, looking at his colleague Dr. Keller. Hunack had hurried away from his dinner in the basement cafeteria when his pager had gone off.

"Good news, bad news," Keller replied.

"Give me the good," Hunack said.

"Brain scan on the lady paleontologist shows increased activity. She may be fighting her way back. We also know now that the first twelve hours with the virus aren't contagious."

"And the bad?"

Walt hesitated, knowing what it meant. "CDC just advised me that forty-three hospitals in six states are reporting symptoms. Everyone's going to quarantine. This afternoon the dead count went up by thirty-four. It's bad."

The Black Tower Building
Seattle, Washington
Friday, 1751 hours Pacific Time

Once outside, Dale loitered a minute to observe all the activity. The intersection was still closed. Cops, fire trucks, and ambulances were all over the place. Yellow police tape and red cones were strewn across the pedestrian square marking shell casings and other evidence. Police photographers were busy recording the aftermath of the carnage. Numerous emergency personnel went about their varied tasks.

Dale saw the crashed truck up on the building steps. Pieces of broken concrete littered the walkway.

He turned left and headed for the side street and the wharf fire station just a few minutes away. It was three blocks to the trolley stop that would take him back to the hotel. As he rounded the opposite corner of the building, he ran into a half dozen Seattle cops blocking the intersection with their vehicles. He flashed his badge and ID and proceeded under the yellow police tape. Crossing the street, he melted into the evening crowd of onlookers jamming the sidewalk.

Looking up, he scanned the sky, certain that the first raindrop would land on his face. *It's darker now than when we entered the bank. It'll probably open and drown me before I get to the hotel. Whatever happened to the sunny summer evening?* He walked on.

The city was alive with traffic, honking horns, people talking, and music from numerous restaurants pouring out onto the sidewalk cafes. He smelled beef being roasted somewhere, but couldn't decide what direction it was coming from.

As he walked, his thoughts trailed off to his weekend a month ago with Betty Jo Case, soon to be his fiancée, international research lawyer extraordinaire, and his secret information weapon. When the FBI's database and Interpol came up empty, Betty Jo frequently had resources around the world that could shed light on dark corners.

Weeks ago, they rented yellow kayaks and paddled out onto Monterey Bay, about a mile from the aquarium. Skimming across the glassy bay surface, they slid into the kelp beds, pulled next to each other, and drifted to a stop. Dale retrieved two lunch bags and they sat there peacefully talking, eating, and watching the sea otters around them provide noontime entertainment. He noted that the sky was the same blue color as Betty Jo's eyes. They had yet to settle on a wedding date. As soon as he returned from this assignment it was time to decide.

One block ahead, on the same side of the street, was a man in a hurry with a black backpack over his shoulders. He stopped for the red light and passing traffic.

Dale looked up. *Better pick up the pace before the deluge begins.*

At the end of the third block, he turned right and started across the parking lot adjacent to the railroad tracks and the Alaskan Highway. Fisherman's Wharf and Friday night tourists clogged the street as food vendors raked in the hungry. Car headlights illuminating the road cast shadows of people moving about.

That's odd, Dale said to himself slowly as his gaze focused tighter. *Where have I seen those old, black combat boots with the zippered laces before?* He stroked his mustache absentmindedly and watched.

The man ahead trotted across the street from the tracks and into the crowd. *And he's got a square backpack with side zip down pockets.*

Dale jogged across the road between cars and closed the distance on the stranger with the bulky bag over his shoulders.

Can't be him, he's locked in the bank vault.

Dale closed the gap to within sixty or seventy feet. Reaching into his jacket, he pulled out his cell phone. Taking a quick glance to autodial Sullivan, he saw the phone light wink out. The battery was dead. He'd been on the phone all day. Dale shoved it back into his pocket and looked around for a police officer on the busy walkway, but he didn't see one.

The man with the backpack turned into a side alley on the wharf and momentarily disappeared from view.

Dale reached into his jacket pocket and slipped the microtag out of its crushproof box.

Same height, same build, same boots; can't be the same guy, though. The cargo pants look like a different color, but it's the same square, bulging appearance. Dale, your imagination is working overtime. You need some sleep.

Dale trailed the man around the edge of the building and spotted him rounding the corner near the back.

There's no such thing as coincidence, Dale. Heads up.

Across the street in the parking lot, two men stood scanning the area. "There he is, across the street by the restaurant."

The second man stopped his partner as he started to move. "Hold on a second. Check out the guy in the blue jacket, it looks like he's following our contact." The two men maintained their interest for a moment and then moved out.

In the highly polished, vertical convex posts lining the walkway to his left, the commando spotted a man moving behind him. He walked around the back of the restaurant and stopped. He was supposed to meet his contact there. One thing was for certain, someone was definitely following him, someone he didn't know, and certainly not his contact.

The muscular Nordian leaned a long-handled squeegee against the edge of a stack of lettuce boxes. He didn't want the noise of a gun bringing any attention. He slipped the bulky weight off his shoulders and wrapped his hands around the straps. Leaning down, he braced himself against the back wall of the restaurant and got ready.

Dale slowly peered around the back of the building, and after a cautious second, he stepped forward. The man with the backpack was gone.

Before it registered with him, the terrorist crashed through the cardboard boxes and past the wooden crates, and swung the heavy backpack at his pursuer.

Taken by surprise, the springing attack pushed Dale backward against the dock railing, knocking the wind out of him. Regaining his feet a few seconds later, he was met with a wooden pole jammed into his chest. The terrorist had planted himself and drove hard to follow up on his initial assault. Dale reacted, throwing a vicious punch that glanced off his attacker. The terrorist grabbed the backpack off the sidewalk and swung it again, this time connecting with Dale's midsection.

Dale put up his left hand to block the backpack, but it was too late. The terrorist slammed Dale with a nasty body block. The forward momentum drove Dale up and over the low wood railing. He tumbled twenty-eight feet into the bay with a loud splash.

Sea lions sleeping on the casements below bellowed and dove into the water.

The terrorist grabbed his backpack and disappeared.

Jeez, Louise!

The cold wave of water enveloped Dale's warm, dry body. The sudden shock to his senses drove his muscles to action, and he kicked furiously for the surface. Seconds later, he shook his head and slicked his hair back to get the water out of his face. Regaining his bearings, he took a quick look around. It was apparent in the dim light that there was no ladder or boat to climb up on. He took a few measured breaths and yelled out a couple of times without hearing any reply.

Something new suddenly caught his attention: The enraged barking of the disturbed sea lions echoed all around him in the water. *They've got plenty of sharp teeth, Dale, and you don't. It's time to be gone.*

He glanced up at the railing. *Damn, he's not there anymore.*

A sleek, black body darted by just a few feet away. Dale spun around to keep it in front of him. Moments later, a rope splashed into the water to his right, startling him. He looked up to see his brother leaning over the restaurant railing.

"We got back to the fire station a few minutes ago. I was just going out to get some food when I spotted you. We yelled out, but I guess you didn't hear us. Who'd you tick off this time?"

Dale shook his head again. The barking sea lions were getting louder; one aggressively brushed by his leg. Another apparently angry sea lion swam by Dale, taunting him with a throaty bark and a show of nasty, pointed teeth.

"The natives are a little restless. Haul me outta here," Dale ordered.

The ill-mannered sea lion disappeared under the turbulent water, came up behind Dale seconds later, and intentionally bumped him.

"I tied a harness loop on the end. Put your feet in and we'll yank you up."

Sean, Barney Davis, and three illegal aliens working in the back of the restaurant all pulled together.

Dale looked back down at the water once he was near the rail and saw two sea lions staring up as if they were waiting for a tasty morsel. He clamored over the railing and dropped unceremoniously to the deck. With as much dignity as he could muster, he stood up and looked at his brother, "You say one word and I'll throw you to those obnoxious sea lions."

"How are you feeling?" Sean asked with a little brotherly concern in his voice.

"I'm thinking of throwing a rope over the beam in my living room ceiling."

After a few seconds, Dale regained his composure and reverted to his usual focused personality.

"Which way did he go?" Dale asked Sean as the water cascaded off his body.

"He went that-a-way, partner," Sean replied, pointing behind him with his thumb.

"Crap . . . Lemee have your phone."

Sean handed his cell over. *How the hell did he get out of that safe?* Dale dialed 9-1-1, and while he waited, he took note of the fact that his wet socks were down to his ankles.

"The bad guy got away. That was him who rushed me. We thought he was securely locked up in a bank vault."

Sean turned to Barney with a barely restrained laugh, "Remind me not to bank there."

Forty-seven minutes had passed since the bank manager locked the terrorist in the vault. Outside the bank's vault door, eight SWAT team members were waiting for the one-hour timed door lock to release. In the meantime, each man was slipping on a sixty-minute *"Scott"* air bottle, and an encapsulated level A hazmat suit provided by the Seattle Fire Department.

"Nine-one-one, what is your emergency?" the operator's voice inquired.

"This is FBI Supervisory Agent Dale Fox. Put me through to the Seattle FBI ASAC immediately, this is an emergency."

"Stand by, Agent Fox," The seconds crawled as he waited.

"Petrocelli. That you, Fox?"

"Tony, the suspect somehow escaped the vault. I just tangled with him out on the wharf behind a restaurant. He has the backpack with the rock. We need to flood the area with uniforms right now."

"I don't know what you're drinking out there on the wharf, Fox, but we have him corralled downstairs. The SWAT team is opening it in a few minutes."

Realizing that this was going nowhere fast, Dale got testy as the water continued dripping from his clothing onto the wood deck. "Listen, No-Knock, he's not in there. I just went face to face with him three minutes ago. The vault is empty. I need people down on the wharf right now to set up a perimeter and begin a search."

Anthony Petrocelli lowered his head so no one would see the cocky smirk on his face, "Go out to your boat, Fox. Enjoy the island. I'll talk to you later." He hit the end button and slipped the cell into his vest pocket.

"What was that?" another agent asked.

"Just some fool," Petrocelli replied with annoyance.

"Idiot." Dale said to no one in particular. He handed the phone back to Sean.

"Fubar?" Sean said with a curious look.

"Fubar," his younger brother replied in disgust. "I need to hit the hotel and grab some dry clothes."

"No problem," Barney said, "Give me a minute and I'll be back with the pickup truck." He jogged off and returned to the curb with the truck two minutes later.

"Maybe things will straighten out by the time you're cleaned up and dressed," Sean said as they hopped into the truck.

Dale's thought process went into overdrive, "Sean, I need your cell again."

On the second ring, Sullivan answered.

"Sullivan, the bad guy is gone. I ran into him behind a restaurant out on the wharf. Can you get down to the pier fire station?"

Sullivan was taken by surprise for a change. "Say what?"

"Bad guy is AWOL. I don't know how he got out, but he's not in the safe anymore. Get down to the wharf fire station as soon as you can. We need to start searching."

Sullivan had worked with Dale for the past two years and had learned to trust his partner's instincts. This was more than instinct.

"How the hell did he get out? I thought they had him locked up?"

"I don't know, but I need you five minutes ago." Dale flipped the phone shut.

Finally showered off in his hotel room, he buttoned a dry shirt. Stepping into the closet, Dale pulled out his jump bag, yanked a box out, and threw it on the bed.

"What's that?" Sean asked.

"A new, FBI encrypted satellite phone; turns out my cell phone couldn't swim."

Checking his soaked jacket pocket to make sure he had everything out before he hung it up, a thought crossed his mind. "What did I do with it? I had it in my hand," he said, thinking of the last time he held the microtag.

"My hand went inside the backpack for a moment when I blocked the second attack. If the seal broke, then the transmitter is operating."

A minute later, Dale went through the coded check-in procedure with the CTU operator and Dan Covery came on the line. He explained his run-in with the terrorist on the wharf.

"Dan, during the fight with the terrorist out on the dock, I blocked a punch and my hand went inside his backpack. I felt the plastic container. I'm pretty sure I stuck a microtag on the casing. I'm hoping I activated the transmitter. Can you check the registration number and see if NRO is picking up a signal?"

"I'll call you right back," Dan said.

A few minutes later, the three men exited the hotel and headed back to the fire station.

In the conference room at the bank, Blue One and Anthony Petrocelli took notice as Sullivan Casse broke into a trot for the nearest exit.

Blue One turned to No-Knock, "Look's like we get to do the interrogation after all. What do you want to bet the CTU won't be happy with their two china shop bulls?"

No-Knock just smiled. He wouldn't need the relentless counterterrorism agents to replenish his flagging reputation much longer.

Eight minutes passed.

Inside the lunchroom at the fire station, Barney Davis, Sullivan, Sean, and Dale looked over a detailed wharf map that showed landside access areas, ladders, recessed construction spaces, fire department connections, and other specifics.

"We need to start an immediate search. Maybe Sullivan and I will get lucky."

Barney jumped in, "If the guy came this far from inland in order to get to the docks like you said, then he's probably got transportation on the water to get out of here. Why else would he come this far?"

Dale scratched his face, "Yeah, I was thinking the same thing. Where can I commandeer a boat?"

It was Barney's turn to help the cause, now that he was aware a terrorist was on the loose in his town. Bowing his head a bit and looking past his eyebrows, he raised a finger to get their attention.

"Ahh, we occasionally check under the wharves for sleepy drunks, and others that could be in danger without realizing it. The fireboat has communications gear, radar, sonar, and safety equipment. You want to go along for a ride?"

Dale turned and smiled at Sullivan.

Two minutes later, the fireboat pulled away from the station's back dock. The big boat's crew was commanded by Barney Davis, pilot Robert Booker, engineer Terry Folsom, and deckhand Dave "Speedy Huey" Griffin. Griffin, in an ongoing battle with his voracious appetite that was always on the edge of control, seemed to be everywhere on the boat at the same time. Suffering from a hereditarily slow metabolism, he was in perpetual motion to keep the pounds off.

The *Chief Seattle* was immaculate. Clearly her crew took great pride in her. She was clean from bow to stern. The brass shined, the wood was well oiled, and the steel railing was freshly painted. In hard breaking water, she rode the lateral waves with barely an audible creak or whisper, like a willow tree that knew when to yield to heavy winds. There were no loud moans or grinding noises heard in the rougher seas further out in the sound where gale force winds sometimes drove through. She knew from plying the vast waters for years that even the mighty oak occasionally lost limbs or was uprooted. It was as if she were self-aware that her charges - from the captain to the helmsman - were integral to her very existence. She was one with the crew, both serving and protecting her human cargo.

Her draft was seven feet, so getting close into shore wasn't a welcomed prospect on some rescues. But she did carry a sixteen-foot skiff. She also sported a massive stainless-steel, water cannon on the foredeck, with a four-and-a-half-inch power tip. She could pump seawater at an amazing rate, sufficient to fill the standard built-in backyard pool in less than two minutes from bone dry. The big water gun could be operated in relative safety from the wheelhouse control panel. The flat screen Viewsonic color monitor showed the radar feed from the overhead radom.

The boat's windshield wipers slapped back and forth as a light drizzle started to come down. The promise of harder rain and choppy water followed. Black smoke belched from the twin exhaust stacks above the pilot-house as she climbed the first rolling wave headed for the wharf. Overhead, the Furuno radar dome continued to rotate.

Outside the Black Tower Building
Seattle, Washington
Friday, 1822 hours Pacific Time

A muted click hit their ears. The tinny sound reverberated in the quiet hallway.

"Go!"

As the one-ton door unlocked, two flash bang canisters bounced into the vault, followed by a tear gas grenade. The heavy vault door was momentarily pushed tight as the devices exploded.

Ten seconds passed and the eight hazmat suited FBI agents charged into the richly appointed room. As was the standard for such aggressive events, they made plenty of noise of their own, shouting "FBI" and generally overwhelming the space with their presence. It was an old tactic called swarming, designed to register shock and defeat for the suspect. They rushed the three long rows of custom mahogany cabinets with firearms at the ready, searching vainly for their target. Two minutes later, they walked back out, heads shaking, stunned that the suspect was no longer inside.

⛓—🔑

With life vests and rain suits on, the men of the *Chief Seattle* turned on several deck lights and aimed them under the docks as they slowly cruised by. Some of the recessed finger docks they passed stuck out from the wharf as much as two hundred feet. Sean and Dale stood inside the wheelhouse with binoculars to their faces, searching the light through the rain.

Sullivan was on the phone to their boss in the CTU, passing on the local SAC's lack of enthusiastic cooperation; it was now hampering their efforts to search the wharf for the terrorist and killer rock.

In the pilothouse, Dale and Sean continued scanning through the increasing downpour.

"If we find him and he's still armed, how do we take him down?" Barney asked.

"Well, last I saw of him, he was definitely armed. We can't shoot him, he has a serious hazmat problem in the backpack," Dale stated very matter-of-factly.

"Hazmat problem?" Barney echoed.

"Yup."

"What kind of hazmat problem?"

"Impregnated virus with no known cure; wouldn't be a problem if we were armed with a flame thrower."

"Maybe we should call Homeland Security," Barney suggested. "They have a fast attack, armed, rigid inflatable. They can get closer to the docks."

"Negative, the chop is getting too bad for the Zodiac's LT," Bobby said.

"Check the radar monitor, lots of red coming in." The three men looked at the color monitor on the pilot's console that foretold of worsening conditions.

"We need to get off the street level, plain clothes cops could be anywhere," the shorter man said. The commando with the bulging backpack followed his two companions down a steel-gray ladder under pier 62. The old wood planking and the support piers were green and slippery with algae and seaweed. The tide was just coming back in.

"Watch your step, it's slippery," the third man advised.

The smell of salty seawater, creosote, and rotting vegetation invaded their olfactory sense.

Somewhere under the hundred-yard-long wooden pier, seals were barking. A small octopus clinging to a barnacle-encrusted boulder slithered into the water at the intrusion. The traffic noise on the nearby Alaskan Highway fronting the wharf gave way to the sound of the lapping water.

"We couldn't get our boat into the wharf. Homeland Security units and the Coast Guard are all over the place," the shorter man said.

"How are we going to get out of here, then?"

"We've booked passage on that cruise ship you probably saw."

"Passage?"

"Yeah, you could say we're joining the longshoreman's union." The taller man grunted. The Nordian commando with the backpack wasn't sure what they had in mind, but he continued walking.

38

The Black Tower Building
Seattle, Washington
Friday, 1833 hours Pacific Time

Blue One stood at the top of the stairway on the main floor of the bank. No-Knock was standing nearby, waiting to hear that the suspect was in custody and the deadly rock secured, when his radio crackled to life.

"Vault is empty. Repeat, the vault is empty. Suspect is GOA."

Blue One grabbed the radio out of the hands of an agent standing next to him, "What the hell do you mean, he's gone? He was locked in!"

"Not anymore, the place is empty. He's history."

A moment of silence washed over the conversation.

"Petrocelli! Where the hell are your two friends?"

At that moment, Blue One's cell phone rang. Recognizing the phone number, he hit the send button. Seconds later, his angry persona went limp.

⚷

An ambulance with its electronic lights flashing pulled into the emergency driveway. It was customary to kill the siren down the block to avoid disturbing sleeping patients inside the hospital. On board, the Provo Fire Department paramedics were delivering yet another semiconscious victim of the unyielding virus that was running through the very scared community.

The local, morning newspaper indicated that area elementary schools were reporting less than thirty-five percent attendance.

On the freshly mowed lawn next to the emergency room, a cameraman and local TV reporter were preparing to do a live standup report on the medical mystery and the toll it was taking on residents.

"Our top story tonight… There appears to be a deadly, out-of-control epidemic centered in Provo, which is quickly spreading around the West. We've learned that there are at least forty hospitals in seven western states reporting symptoms of an as-yet-unnamed virus." News anchor Ben Saven peered into the camera. "Let's go live to Mara Banda."

The picture shifted to an exterior shot of the regional medical center in Provo.

"Ben, we've learned from the CDC that there are at least two hundred twelve people dead from this killer disease. We're also being told that there are some seven hundred people from all walks of life being treated in forty-three hospitals that we know of. Our sources tell us that this disease has, thus far, exhibited a one hundred percent fatality rate. A few minutes ago, we caught up with Dr. Walter Hunack, a leading research biologist, as he entered the hospital and asked him to comment."

The cameraman cut away to a conversation taped on the run.

Inside the hospital ER, a wall mounted television played out the ambush interview.

"Looks like they got you," an ER physician said to Hunack as he sipped a soft drink.

"They didn't get much. CDC is doing a full interview in the morning. Cat's finally out of the bag. Hunack wanted to shift the conversation to a subject other than himself.

"I saw the ambulance pull in. Looks like you got another patient. Is it our virus again?" the ER doc queried.

"Looks like it. It's that female pharmaceutical rep that's in here every other week."

"Who?"

"The curvy, blonde babe with the vile vocabulary. You remember her, mouth like a drunken sailor, body by Rembrandt?"

"The one with the x-rated attitude and killer smile?" He swallowed the last of his drink.

"Yup, that's her. Supposedly concludes contracts by sacking out with the purchasing department."

"I've met her. She's a twisted version of Disneyland. Wherever she goes, it's the scariest place on earth."

"That's the one. She's almost comatose, mumbled something about being kidnapped. Funny what this thing does to the mind. It's the first hallucination version we've had, probably be more. Any idea how the search for a treatment is going?"

"Isolation and one hundred percent oxygen. As soon as they have something, we'll all know immediately. I need to run, see you later." Walt Hunack walked away.

A few minutes later, Bettina Jessup slipped into a coma, from which there would be no recovery. Her body would join the growing stack of corpses in the morgue trailer in the back parking lot. The puncture mark from a needle, behind her neck and below her hairline, would never be discovered.

Climbing a wooden gangway to the busy loading dock, the three men headed for a thirty foot trailer. Looking casually around, they searched for cops; there weren't any, just lots of tourists.

Stacks of wooden boxes were piled up along the pier. A dozen dock workers were occupied with loading pallets stacked with supplies for the cruise ship. The three men climbed quickly into the long truck bed and disappeared from view. Several minutes passed and a heavy crate on a pallet moved down the side truck ramp.

On board the cruise ship, two security people watched the longshoremen as they entered and made their way to a storage area. The Rapiscan x-ray machine which normally scanned passenger luggage, sat idle off to the side. Once inside, they unloaded the heavy pallet in a corner, out of view of the security officers at the wide gangway door. One man, hidden within the hinged crate, carried a heavy backpack with an analog meter that read twelve percent.

The departing longshoremen engaged the two security officers in a few moments of conversation as a diversion.

Meanwhile, the inside hinge was unlatched on the wooden crate and the three men slipped off to the main corridor. A minute later, they found the room they were looking for at the end of a hallway. Once inside, they locked the door. Two of the men walked over to look out a porthole while the third dialed a satellite phone. Knowing that they were about to become the object of a massive manhunt, the taller man relayed their position and circumstance in code to the person on the other end of the phone. They knew that the resources of the U.S. government would be in full swing soon. They weren't about to tip off the NRO, NSA, or any other satellite eavesdroppers.

"We're aboard transport option number two. Departure should be per the published schedule. I'll leave the phone on. Call me when you have a means of retrieval."

He punched the end button.

"We need to stay out of sight until we can find a way off this ship."

The backpack-laden commando sat down on a chair, pulled out his MAC-11 submachine gun, and proceeded to reload. When he was done, he pulled out the five empty magazines and reloaded them as well. A few minutes later, his head was on the table; he was fast asleep.

The satellite phone chirped.

"*Det här är Sven* - This is Sven, *Ja, ja, okej, tack,* alright." He mashed the end button and looked at his companion. He let out a big sigh, closed his eyes, and opened them again.

"Thor wants to spread the virus throughout the cruise ship. We have to break off a small piece of the rock and place it in the coin wishing pond on the main deck. The passengers will do the rest."

"What!" The short, husky man responded. "How do we do that without getting infected?"

"I must find the galley. I need some kitchen utensils. I'll be back soon. Meanwhile, I suggest you find a hair blow-dryer."

"How do we get off the ship with the rock?"

"They're working on a way to pick us up once the ship is underway and out of port."

The tall man opened the door, checked the side hallway, and, seeing no one, walked forward.

Vibration and a low hum rumbled through the ship; they were pulling away from the dock. By the time he found the aft crew galley, the ship was moving forward and picking up speed. With such a large ship and so many new crewmembers aboard, no one paid any attention to the tall Nordian who seemed to blend in easily.

The sky above the *Chief Seattle* opened up and roared. The wind blasted the remnants of the summer evening into memory. The boat's various searchlights were barely penetrating the waves of falling water. The smell of fresh brewed coffee drifted through the passageway as the sound of thunder reverberated off the hull and shook the air. The windshield wipers on the old fireboat were working overtime trying to push away the inky wet blackness.

Sullivan appeared in the narrow, metal stairwell below.

"Dale, the CTU director just finished talking with our buddy, the Seattle SAC. Next time we see him in person, he may be leaning slightly to one side in his chair. I do believe his anterior hide was partially excavated by phone."

Dale handed his 7x50 Fuji binoculars to Sean.

"Partial excavation, I like that. Is he ready to avoid complete excavation?"

"Well, from the sound of it, the boss would like you to be judicious and not shove the man's head up his nether region. But I suspect our good friend, the SAC, would probably fetch, roll over, and play dead if we asked."

"Okay, let's flood the area and stop all surface traffic on the streets and in the water."

"I've notified the sheriff and the Seattle police chief. Every federal agency is on it, too."

"How about the Coasties and Navy?" Dale asked as he stood at the top of the stairwell.

"Navy's down, coasties are up. The Coast Guard is pulling in all their small boats and putting the bigger ones out. The storm has them shifting manpower from one to the other. They won't be out and running for another fifteen or twenty minutes. The meteorologists didn't think it would congeal, apparently. Besides, the pilot is right, weather shows dark cells strung out into the Pacific almost a thousand miles. Local police and sheriff's boats are too small for the current water conditions. Street side patrols and search teams will be on the docks in a few minutes. The on-ramps from downtown Seattle are at a standstill - nothing gets on the freeway without a hard search. NRO and NSA are queuing up to read satellite traffic, and Eagle's Claw has live ears on the software searching for key words."

"Any air assets?"

"Are you kidding, not in this weather."

Dale stared at the opposite bulkhead and reached into his jacket for the satellite phone. Half a minute later, it rang at the other end.

"Blue One. I've been expecting your call, Agent Fox. How can I help you?"

Not wanting to waste time on formalities or the awkwardness of dealing with his wounded ego, Dale got right to the point.

"Drill the boxes," Dale ordered.

Blue One paused to let the words sink in. He still didn't understand what Fox wanted. "What are you talking about, Fox?"

"Start drilling out the locks on the safe deposit boxes."

Knowing that a safe deposit requires two keys, one in the possession of the bank and one held by the box owner, Dale knew the trapped man had to have a way out of the vault. Maybe one of the safe deposit boxes held the answer. "The bank can't get into the boxes with a single key. I want to know how he got out. Tear the place apart, and please, let me know what you find, ASAP."

Dale hit the end button and looked out the window past the firefighter piloting the *Chief Seattle*. The big fireboat was rocking but hadn't thrown any coffee out of Bobby's stone mug yet.

Seeing the curiosity on the FBI agent's face, he explained, "The *Chief*

Seattle has operated in rougher conditions than this. We're one of the few small vessels that can plough through bad storms on the inner bay."

Sean heard the pilot but tugged on his life vest just the same to make certain it was snug. He put the binoculars to his face and continued searching the docks. The water was getting rougher.

The satellite phone in his jacket buzzed. "Fox."

"Dale, it's Dan. NRO has no signal on the microtag. Are you sure it got into the backpack?"

"Yeah, no question, now that I've had time to think it over in my mind. I palmed the transmitter and when I slapped the plastic cover, it came off my hand. Maybe I didn't activate it, I just don't know."

"Well, if you can think of anything else, let me know. By the way, CDC has the White House chief of staff in the loop on the virus. It's going to go epidemic. I'll call you when I have more."

⚷━

"Helm, come to one-four-one-degrees and take us down to five hundred feet," the captain ordered.

"Aye, sir." He repeated the instructions and maneuvered the stealthy submarine. The deck tilted slightly and dropped a few degrees. In a couple of minutes, the ride smoothed out.

The XO, Lieutenant Commander Sjorkon, watched the digital depth gauge slip past four hundred feet.

"Captain, moving us to the Port Angeles area puts us in the middle of the American submarine transition area."

"A little risk management, Mr. Sjorken. With them stuck on that cruise ship, our best bet is to wait it out until the ship passes by us on her way to the outer islands. I just hope that the new mission to spike the ship doesn't kill us all." Captain Ingvar Wallen noted the ship's depth at four hundred seventy feet. "Is the secondary containment box ready for our rock?"

"Yes, sir, the dry heating element has been tested and readied as well."

"Slow us to four knots and keep us on the Canadian side. Where is that cruise ship right now?"

Sjorkon checked the viewer, a twenty-inch color monitor on the bulk-head set to a twenty-five mile radius showing their primary target.

"She's coming up the strait past Edmonds, should be here in about ninety minutes. She was running at eight knots on our last check. That should be her maximum speed until she clears Port Townsend."

"Is the dive team ready?" Wallen was accustomed to delivering clipped sentences when he spoke to subordinates; it was the military brevity that he'd grown up with. His father had been a merchant seaman and eventually a ship's officer.

"Yes, sir, it's a rough surface, but they will be packed up the entire time, a diver for each of the three NCOs, and one for the rock."

"Very well, I'll be in my quarters. Run the cable out so we can maintain satellite contact with them. No one will spot it in these seas. Let me know when we hear from our men."

"Yes, sir."

Captain Wallen stood up and walked a few steps. "Mr. Sjorkon, run a test on the UV Splash. We'll paint the cruise ship when she comes by us."

"Yes, sir."

"You have the bridge, Mr. Sjorken."

Wallen continued down the companionway and out of sight. In his hand was the downloaded radar shot of the hellacious storm. Pulled off the satellite seven minutes ago, it was filled with dark-red cells.

He wasn't happy about the rest of his orders from Douglas Odin. As a career military man, he hated to see good men's lives wasted. But before this was over, he had every intention of cutting his losses and ensuring that Odin's reach into his postretirement plans would be severely constricted. He owed it to his crew.

39

Aboard the Cruise Ship Majestic Wonder
Puget Sound, Washington
Friday, 1911 hours Pacific Time

The spotless, white hull of the full-size cruise ship plowed through the building waves that seemed to increase the closer she got to the open sea. The stabilizer planes integrated into the hull below the waterline and the independent omnidirectional drive system, coupled with the gyro-driven weights, acted to provide a smooth, level ride even in ten-foot seas. To the starboard side were the lights of a coastal town, periodically obscured by the driving rain. The radar scope and the six satellites locked on the GPS kept her within a few yards of her designated track in the channel.

Party revelers filled the eight restaurants onboard, and all ten bars were running credit card receipts so fast that the scanners were ready to overheat. The ship, a relatively new design, was comprised of an all-stateroom layout, with every passenger enjoying a private balcony and deck chairs. Numerous glass elevators hauled well-dressed people to entertainment destinations and activities. The storm's only impact was to keep partygoers from strolling outside for a view of the summer sun that should have been dropping lower in the western sky.

On the bridge, the ship's command crew was occupied with maintaining their distance from a small commuter ferry that was being buffeted by the building storm and blowing headwind. The smaller vessel's progress was deteriorating by the minute.

"Captain, this just came over the fax. It's a notice from Homeland Security and the FBI," the junior officer said.

The captain of the *Majestic Wonder*, a graduate of the U.S. Naval Academy, class of 1978, took the envelope, opened it, and read the three attached pages. He did not like what he saw.

"Get the chief of security up here on the double," the captain said.

"Something wrong, sir?" the second officer asked.

"There's a high probability that we may have stowaways, correct that, dangerous stowaways."

"Stowaways?" he said, inquiring for more information.

"At least one man wanted by Homeland Security and the FBI. Here, have a look." He handed over the fax and waited for the man to finish.

The captain retrieved the fax when his fourth in command was done reading, "This man is a professional, and according to the flyer, he's probably a military operative for a foreign nation. He may be accompanied by a second person. Have the security camera operators double up. I want pictures of everyone walking the ship. Scan these into the computer system. Compare them to the bank photos attached and keep me apprised of anyone who bears even a remote resemblance. Bring on the C watch, and have the assistant captain notified. I believe he's hosting a dinner table at the steakhouse. Be discreet. "

"Yes, sir," the officer said. He turned and dispatched another crew member to relay the message to the assistant captain.

The chief of security walked onto the bridge. "You asked for me, sir?"

"Yes, have a look at this," the captain said.

The recently retired, redheaded British Army sergeant major in charge of the ship's security detail read the memo. His deep baritone voice offered its own take on the flyer. "The Americans seem, well, miffed," he commented with great understatement. "Bloody hell to pay for this one, I'd say. Nasty buggers, for sure."

He handed the memo back to the captain.

"Geoff, make copies of the notice and post it in all crew quarters and the service decks immediately."

This was the sergeant major's third tour with the captain. The two men respected and admired the skills and experiences they each brought to the job. In the last year, the sergeant major had also skunked the captain at poker on several occasions, playing in the off hours with senior staff.

"Let's begin a methodical search, starting with the critical spaces - engineering, propulsion, communications, the bank, and any other operational areas. Change the electronic door lock codes right now and notify all department managers. Check with the boarding crews and see if they recognize these faces. You know what to do, get started. I want all of your people on radio ear buds, with regular time checks. I want a heads up on anything suspicious," the captain advised. He did not like his routine disturbed by the nasty surprise that the pounding squall had provided. Now the extra workload after departing Seattle was compounded by at least one man who had shot up a bank with an automatic weapon and killed at least two innocent bystanders.

"Mr. Mayberry!" the captain called out.

The fifty-two-year-old, retired sergeant major stopped at the door to the passageway and turned to face the ship's senior officer.

"Until further notice, have your men put on their fanny packs, frangible ammunition only. Put new batteries in the tasers and pass them out."

"Yes, sir," The retired Special Forces sergeant major understood the order clearly. His security team, primarily retired British Gurkha NCOs, some of whom had worked together previously, were very familiar with the dangers of hostile personnel.

The Gurkhas were a particularly tough breed of military men. They always seemed prepared for the worst in their fellow man. The sergeant major's team had operated in fourteen different countries, protecting the ship's passengers while ashore. Thieves, bandits, and other assorted lowlife characters were bent on taking advantage of tourists who were unaware of the various dangers they presented. Within a few minutes, they would all be armed with 9mm handguns. The hunt for people they weren't sure were aboard was underway.

Onboard the twelve-car carrier *Pickle Cove*, an overheated engine bearing was about to magnify the vessel's problems. On the tiny bridge, the pilot was struggling to make headway against the raging storm.

"Well, that's it, we've reached the park," Bobby said. "Shall we turn back and take a second look?" The *Chief Seattle* had completed its initial pass along the many wharves that comprised the Seattle waterfront. The only thing they had to show for it was a call to the police when they spotted three teenagers pulling crab nets up from under a seafood restaurant.

Aboard the Ferry *Pickle Cove*
Two miles northeast of Nordland Point, Washington
Friday, 1915 hours Pacific Time

Fire!!

The crewman in the engine compartment was on the intercom. The lone pilot reached up and grabbed his microphone, "Mayday, mayday, this is *Pickle Cove* . . ."

Aboard the *Chief Seattle*

"LT, we're picking up a mayday call. It's the *Pickle Cove*. She's advising that a fire has broken out in her engine room. Here's the GPS on her. She's about eighteen miles up the channel," Bobby said.

"Does she have power and steerage?"

"I don't know. It's a four-man crew, and they're probably pretty occupied at the moment."

"Search is over, let's go," Barney ordered. He pushed the three chrome handles forward and the *Chief Seattle* heeled over, her Detroit diesel engines soaring to two thousand rpm. Behind him, he noted the time on the brass clock.

"Come to a heading of two-eight-seven, we have a big commuter inbound."

"What else is on the water?" the pilot asked Barney. He had his hands full with the blinding rain, nasty crosscurrent, and wind pummeling the boat. Barney was keeping an eye on the Standard Horizon color GPS radar screen.

"We're clear past the inbound, Bobby." Barney turned and yelled down the ladder to one of his firefighters, "You guys get your survival suits and harnesses on. Terry, I want you topside when we arrive. I need eyes on the ferry when we power up the bow water cannon. Tell Dave to notify dispatch that we're en route to a call."

There were three Motorola radios along the rear rack in the cockpit of the *Chief Seattle*. Grabbing the marine radio microphone off the radio set, Barney Davis called the *Pickle Cove* to notify them that they were en route, and to see if he could get a little more information.

The *Chief Seattle*, with a maximum speed of twenty-four knots, would need almost forty minutes to reach the distressed vessel. The only real hope for the *Pickle Cove*, at the moment, was to start unloading the automatic fire extinguishing system inside the engine room and hope it would be adequate for the task.

One of the four crew members was already scrambling to outfit the thirty-four passengers with Coast Guard approved floatation devices, formerly know as life vests, and provide survival instructions. One man, with his seven-year-old granddaughter in tow, looked out the port window at the pounding waves and hoped the vessel would stay afloat until help arrived. Since the boat wasn't at maximum capacity, he grabbed a third life preserver for extra security.

Dale, Sean, and Sullivan were now in the way. The three men bounded down the spiral, steel staircase. Barney took notice and appreciated the professionalism of his guests.

"I'm going to see if I can contact dispatch and find us a way out of here," Sullivan said to Dale.

"Maybe the Navy can pick us up."

"Captain Fox, could you come up, please?" Barney yelled below.

The sound of boots pounding up the spiral stairwell alerted Barney that Sean was almost there.

"Sean, I know you don't have much experience with fireboats, but when we get there, can I ask you to help Bobby with the radios and anything else he might need? I think most of our Ten Code is the same as yours."

"Yeah, sure," Sean replied.

"The ferry's location is outside of our primary operational area. However, we're the second biggest fireboat on the water after the *Leschi*, and capable of operating in rougher water than all of the other fire-rescue craft on the Puget Sound. Until or unless another emergency vessel, or Navy, or Coast Guard ship can reply and respond, we may be their only hope."

Turning to his pilot, Robert Booker, Barney said, "Bobby, give Sean a crash course on the water monitors and deck guns while you're at it. Alright guys, I'm going below to suit up." Davis turned and slid down the brass railing on the stairwell.

⚹━⟶

"Sir, the *Pickle Cove*, that small ferry about four hundred yards ahead to starboard is declaring an emergency. They're reporting a fire onboard in the engine room. I also picked up a reply from the *Chief Seattle,* behind us about eight or nine miles away. *Chief Seattle* is en route, but it will take her a good twenty-five minutes to arrive."

The captain was now dealing with three matters, aside from running his tourist ship during happy hour, happy hour for everyone but him.

"Mr. Humphreys," he said.

"Yes, sir."

"Detail the fire crew and stand by. We will be stopping to render assistance to the *Pickle Cove.*

Get one transport boat over the side with fire suppression equipment and a second to take passengers off the ferry."

"Yes, sir." The first officer wheeled around and headed for the stairwell below decks.

Aboard the *Pickle Cove*, two crew members were now unleashing half a dozen handheld fire extinguishers to supplement the auto fire suppression system. The engine room was dark with thick smoke, which drifted upwards into the rear stairwell, yet a faint red glow was still visible.

"Let's vent the compartment and see what it looks like," the older crewman said to his younger companion. The sound of the dual marine diesel engines could still be heard idling in the background.

Aboard the *Chief Seattle*
A mile and a half west of the Chittenden Locks
Puget Sound, Washington
Friday, 1924 hours Pacific Time

Dale Fox and Sullivan Casse sat on the long, wooden diver's bench below the main deck and near the rear of the fireboat. Both men looked like deflated pumpkins in their survival suits. The deck housed the three, thousand-horsepower diesel engines that were pounding away as fast as they could go. At the back of the engines were generators that provided electricity for the boat. Their whine was peacefully mesmerizing and blocked out some of the noise from the engines.

The rear of the deck was semi-segregated from the engine space and held lockers with rescue gear, miscellaneous marine tooling, and equipment. Dale rubbed his hands together deep in thought.

Sullivan pulled out his PDA and started reading. His cell phone rang suddenly.

"Sullivan. Yeah, yeah, yeah. Okay, I'll get back to you." He flipped the cell phone closed and leaned back with his eyes shut. The deck was vibrating and his feet tingled.

"Well, no ride out yet, the storm is walloping the bejesus out of the coast. Covery will get us out of here; he's working on it right now." Looking out the back hatch, Sullivan saw nothing but a sheet of rain, "This squall is going to go all night and into the morning before it runs out of steam. Oh, some good news, too. The technicians lifted a nice print from the vault. The guy cut himself and left a nice, bloody twelve-pointer behind."

"Really? They got a name to go with it yet?"

"There's nothing in NCIC, Homeland, state, or the CIA's computers. They've passed it on to the Interpol folks to see if they have anything."

Dale blew a breath of air through pursed lips, "Well, that's not good, but it tells us one thing - they're not domestic. Fits right into the picture, doesn't it."

Since they were temporarily stuck, Sullivan let his thoughts wander as he scanned the interior of the boat, and after a minute, something came to mind, "I did three years as a legal attache' in Great Britain. If there's a record somewhere on that print, Interpol will find it."

He reached into his back pocket, pulled out his wallet, and rummaged around for a minute.

"Hmmm, I still have it."

"Have what?" Dale asked.

"My diplomatic carnet." He passed it over to Dale, who looked at it and handed it back.

"Diplomatic immunity flag, get out of jail free card, park anywhere passport, ignore tickets and citations all in one. Only used it twice, once to park alongside the road and watch the Queen's entourage pass by, and once at a restaurant in Westminster when I couldn't find a parking spot to meet my counterpart from MI-6. I stuffed the car into a red zone and went to eat."

"Do you have the new passport with the embedded chip?" Dale asked.

"Not yet. I need new pictures. I'm not due for another six months. I wonder if the latest version will look any different. The MI-6 Brits have a burgundy passport with a gold lion, horse, and crown on it. Ours don't say much for creative flair."

Sullivan returned the carnet to his wallet and leaned back against the bulkhead.

"When the politicians find out about this Nord Island operation, how much help or hindrance do you think they will be, given that there's a megabillionaire involved?" he wondered.

"Congress," Dale said with a laugh, "In the last twenty-five years, the

Republicans have become Democrats and Democrats have become Marxist-Socialists. Are you kidding? The politically correct are reality-challenged, I'm afraid."

The two FBI counterterrorism agents sat in silence on the bench seats for a minute, listening to the old fireboat creak and groan in the building waves. The smell of diesel fuel finally overcame the aroma of freshly brewed coffee. Dale had a pent-up restlessness; he rubbed his face for the fourth time. They were out of the hunt, at least for the time being, and it grated on both men. They felt like distinguished guest hostages.

"Ever thought about being a firefighter?" Sullivan said, looking around the interior of the fireboat again.

Dale leaned forward and put his elbows on his knees, "I'm a cop with a law degree, masquerading as an FBI agent. I'm thinking my plate's probably pretty full. I like what we do, so long as I don't become so successful at it that I end up a deskbound bureaucrat. It reminds me of one of Sean's FBI-isms - 'Failure to Be Independent.'"

Sullivan laughed, not having heard that one before. "Does that mean you're refusing any further promotions?"

"I haven't thought that far ahead," Dale admitted, stretching his arms out and yawning. "My penchant for using the bureau's policies and procedures manual as a door stop to keep the anal retentive BS out will probably catch up to me one day. When I feel that my assured immortality has expired, maybe then," he laughed.

He stroked his oversized mustache with both hands.

"Besides, Sean has it covered. He's the aggressive pit bull in the family, he and Dad, same cookie cutter. Marines gave him the Silver Star for rescuing a downed fighter pilot in Vietnam. He stayed behind and picked off the officers in a company of NVA that gave chase up the mountain pass, while the rest of his squad made tracks with the wounded pilot. One eighteen-year-old corporal with a hunting rifle against a company of hardcore regulars with AK-47s. I think he's down to his last two cat lives, though."

The boat rolled unexpectedly and Dale stuck his hand out to keep himself upright. "You know, I don't mind trying to negotiate with an armed maniac. Sometimes you can reach them. But Sean runs into searing hot, smoke-filled buildings when everyone else is clawing to get the hell out. I sometimes get the impression that he's already seen hell, so a roaring fire or bloody accident doesn't bother him. I do know that he and Dad, both of them having shared similar experiences in combat, sometimes talk about things they won't speak about to anyone else."

"I take it that's a no," Sullivan said, shaking his head.

"Well, they do have more free time without being shot at. Maybe so." He straightened up to the sound of his satellite phone chirping, "Fox."

"Agent Fox, Blue One. One of my men tapped into the row of boxes where the fingerprint was found. When they pulled the drawer out, they found two screws tapped into the back of the metal casing. We jacked the cabinet away from the wall and found a hole." Blue One related the balance of details regarding their discovery.

"We're following the trail out to the walking path people use to tour the Underground. I'll get back to you when I know more." This time Blue One hung up first.

"Well that solves the 'how did he get out' mystery." Dale related the call from the Seattle SAC to Sullivan.

"Didn't do the guy any good, you still found him."

"More like he found me."

Dale sat back again. He was considering his options and what to do next. He felt like the finish line was falling further behind him in the rearview mirror.

"Bad guy's getting away and we're on the fire department's version of a self-serve cruise ship without amenities."

"Be happy they retrofitted this old tub with stabilizer planes. Otherwise we'd be leaning over five-gallon buckets," Sullivan chuckled.

Several miles and one island behind them, Seattle cops and King County deputies joined the wharf patrols en masse, showing the bank photographs to as many tourists as possible, in search of a lead into the disappearance of their terrorist suspect.

Dale stood up, grabbed the overhead rail, and walked to the rear of the boat to stretch his legs. To his right was a small desk built into the bulkhead. He stared at it for a second, turned, and ran back past Sullivan, "I'll be right back."

He charged up the steps to the pilothouse.

"Barney, you got a computer hookup on board?"

"Yeah, we have one up here and one at the engineer's station at the rear of the engine room. We use it to download fire data, shipping information, the harbor master, the VTS - Vehicle Traffic System - and Coast Guard databases. Why?"

"Does it have Internet capability?"

"Yeah."

"Can I use the one at the engineer's station?"

Barney turned to his pilot. "Bob, we got the info on the *Pickle Cove* yet?" he asked, referring to the ferry's operational data.

"Up here," Bob said, pointing to the metal clip holding half a dozen sheets of paper.

Barney turned back to Dale, "We're making good time. You've got about twelve to thirteen minutes before we may need access again. Go ahead and use it until then. I'll let you know if I need to jump on it. Oh, by the way, we just got word that a Coast Guard chopper is responding and a commercial tug is in the area transiting to another island. We'll have some help when we get there."

Dale pounded back down the stairwell and headed for the engineer's computer.

"Sullivan, guess what I found?"

Sullivan stood up and followed Dale to the back of the boat.

The computer chimed as the Internet connection popped on thirty seconds later.

"Hypothetically, if you were in a major rush to get to Nord Island and safety, would it be by land, sea, or air?" Dale said, looking at Sullivan.

"Can't fly there in this weather, can't walk out, so water is the only option. But in this storm, I don't know," Sullivan replied with a thoughtful crease in his forehead.

"What if you were hitchhiking?" Dale suggested.

"Bring up the shipping database. Let's see who sailed since," Sullivan looked at his watch, "1800 hours."

It took a minute to get to the right window inside the Harbormaster's database. "There it is. Click on departures and arrivals," Sullivan said, pointing at the small icon on the right side of the screen. "Scroll down to departures, there." He reached up and grabbed a yellow pad from the shelf above the computer desk.

"Got it," Dale said with renewed enthusiasm once again in his voice, "Five ships accounted for - the *Pickle Cove* at 1816, the *Majestic Wonder* at 1828, the ferry to Anacortes at 1830, the *Tax Deduction* at 1834. What the heck is that anyway? Oh, looks like a big yacht. Probably belongs to some hot shot CPA. Last one out is the fast hydroplane ferry to Victoria at 1856."

Dale pulled up the encrypted satellite phone's bulky antenna and waited for the signal to appear in the LED window. The encrypted algorithm provided a constantly shifting six hundred seventy megahertz frequency range every time a voice stopped talking and a momentary dead spot in conversation was detected by the software program. He dialed a number, heard a fixed pitch tone, and put in five more digits. While it was ringing, he referred to his laminated weekly code card.

The FBI counterterrorism unit, also known as the "Flying Squad," was an extremely low-profile, high-risk operations group comprised of seven field teams of highly experienced agents. As for the general public, they couldn't tell one FBI special agent from another. Dale and Sullivan were the pilot team upon which the others were built. No one outside of the CTU, the Homeland Security secretary, the DCI, the FBI director, his deputy, and the White House really knew the scope of their activities or responsibilities.

Dozens of legitimate, intercepted threats against the United States, on its own soil, since 9/11 had made the unit a necessity. The less than cooperative Seattle FBI special agent-in-charge and his deputy found out about the small details an hour earlier when they had their heads handed to them in a basket. The director of CTU called the SAC personally to inform him of their real authority. Words to the effect that he would "fully comply or find himself doing background checks on FBI academy candidates" had readjusted his level of support for Dale and Sullivan. The FBI's pecking order of agent, senior agent, supervisor, ASAC, SAC, and a variety of directorships did not apply in Dale Fox's case since his immediate superior was, in fact, the CTU director.

In the past thirty months, the list of terrorist groups penetrating the U.S. southern border had grown dramatically. Aside from Al-Qaeda, and

Hamas, nine other independent terrorist organizations operating in northern Mexico had all enjoyed some measure of success. One enterprisingly creative group, comprised of Islamic radicals, was hiding in plain sight by permanently changing their Arabic names to Hispanic surnames in Mexican courts.

None as yet had been able to penetrate the Flying Squad. Their various attempts ranged from communications intercepts and identity theft, to impersonation of FBI special agents. Unit integrity was so tight that a local traffic cop running Dale and Betty Jo's personal license plates on their cars would get a phony address that was actually a city-owned parking lot in San Jose, California. It also flagged the law enforcement agency and specific officer seeking the information for a quick follow-up counter inquiry.

After a series of pitched tones, a human voice came on the line.

"CTU, Mr. Smith. This line is secure. What is today's chase code?" the voice required, in an even but firm tone.

"We are color paisley and today's object is the Alamo," Dale replied. He waited patiently.

"Digits?"

Dale fed off the last seven numbers from the back of his gold FBI badge.

"Code is confirmed. To whom am I speaking?"

"Supervisor Fox."

"Confirmed, stand by for the watch commander."

A few seconds passed in silence and a new voice came online. "Dale, it's Dan. How are you and Sullivan doing?"

As director over the CTU, Covery's seven field teams and the forty-eight-person support team were his day-to-day priority. All of the team members were well acquainted with each other. Unlike the turf protecting, promotion-driven mentality that permeated other levels of the Bureau, this group of highly motivated and dedicated people had a front row seat to the mission. It showed in their approach to the CTU men in the field.

"We need military assistance, Dan."

"I have your last voice report up in front of me from 1748 hours today. What's your status?"

"Hot pursuit; we need to stop a high-speed ferry outbound from Seattle to Victoria, Canada."

"Copy, go ahead." Dale provided the information on the Canada bound hydrofoil and asked for Navy or Coast Guard interdiction.

"Wait one."

A minute and half later, Dan came back on line. "Dale, stand by for the captain of the Coast Guard cutter *Snowquallamie*. There was a pause, and then Dale heard a husky voice. "Lieutenant Commander Moret. How may I help you, Agent Fox?"

Dale detailed the circumstances of the FBI/Homeland flash traffic regarding the terrorist activity of the past several hours. Lieutenant Commander Moret informed Dale that he had the NTCGS – notice to all Coast Guard stations – memo.

"We have them at the edge of our radar, inside the straits. We'll hail them, and I'll have two teams transferred over. How do I get back to you?"

Dale gave the skipper of the cutter his satellite number to be routed through the CTU and ended the conversation.

A few seconds later, Covery came back on line, "Ballistics has the bullets from the Provo Airport, but no shell casings. They policed up after themselves; more than likely they had brass catchers. They've run the bullets through the computer imaging system. We can't tell how many shooters there were. We're guessing it was a small, highly specialized group, like a Navy Seal or Delta Force Team."

"How close are they?" Dale asked.

"Not close enough for court. The lab examiners say the 'shot-peening' of metal to metal contact on the bullets passing through the gun barrels are too modified. They think the team ran the edge of a coat hangar through the barrel to change the striation markings."

"What's the best guess from the lab?"

"Educated assumption is there were three or four, possibly five shooters involved. There's nothing else in the computer database that matches them up to anything beyond the bullets' diameter and powder residue."

"Any help on that end?"

"Not beyond the manufactured date from the propellant, almost two and a half years old. It was 'Blue Dot' powder; could have been bought almost anywhere. These could even be reloads."

"Alright, thanks. Let me know if anything else surfaces."

"By the way, you and Sullivan are showing a weak return on your chips right now." The "chips" were the surgically imbedded micro transponders. Dale's was implanted behind his right knee, where he had a previous scar. Sullivan's was under his left arm, also behind a prior scar resulting from a motorcycle accident in his teen years. It was part of the deal when they became CTU operatives.

"We're below decks on an aluminum hulled tub. They don't make fire-boats like this anymore. That and the storm, together, are probably playing havoc with the signal."

"One last item for you guys: The White House, specifically the president's chief of staff, wants results. The death toll from the virus is climbing fast toward five digits. He said that the president is now monitoring it on an hourly basis and considers the speed at which you and Sullivan have unraveled this thing so far is nothing short of great work. POTUS issued a P.D. - Presidential Directive - that whatever you require has a rubber stamp on it."

"Hmmm," Dale reflected a second, "I have one request at the moment, then. My brother, the fire rescue expert, is with us by a quirk of circumstance. He's also a decorated combat Marine; his background is in my personal history file. He was here to train Seattle firefighters as a dive instructor, but he's on the boat with us now. I want to federalize him without the yearlong committee review process. I may need his unique skills before this is over. Can I do that?"

"I'll take care of it immediately. Consider it done."

"Okay, then. I think we're good to go," Dale replied.

"Get back to me when you have more to report. And Dale, I don't need to impress on you the effect this is starting to have on the country. This is the headline in every major newspaper, on talk radio, and television news reports. People in Congress are privately scared, too. They're telling the president to do whatever he deems necessary. The leaders of both parties just offered him a blanket hunting license on this virus." Covery had a severity in his voice that Dale rarely heard. "I'll talk to you again soon."

Dale waited until the operator asked if he had another call.

"Negative, CTU, shut the line down." The operator at the CTU un-plugged Dale from the secure satellite connection.

Sullivan caught Dale's eye, "Okay, we've got the hydrofoil taken care of." Dale related the call with Covery and tucked the satellite phone back into his pumpkin suit. Sullivan looked pensive, "Bad news?"

"Sound's like the screws are getting tightened down harder," Dale said.

"More like the screws are getting stripped," Sullivan thought out loud.

At the computer desk, Sullivan's e-mail chime popped up.

"Looks like the local authorities managed to detour that yacht to the locks at Washington Lake," Sullivan said. "The yacht's owner will not be making the run to British Columbia tonight. I took care of the ferry to Anacortes as well. The sheriff is at the dock waiting for it to pull in."

Dale stood up, "Alright, three down, two to go. Let's see how close we are to the *Pickle Cove*."

He stopped and put his hand over his mouth. "You know, the more I think about it . . ."

Sullivan interrupted, "They're definitely trying to get out of U.S. ter-ritorial waters. Nord Island again."

"Douglas Odin is feeding big bucks into the parking meter," Dale said in deference to his instincts.

"I'm going to talk to Barney."

"I'll call Dan and see if we have any human resources on the island," Sullivan added.

Not long after, Dale went back down and grabbed the satellite phone off the computer desk as Sullivan typed away.

The phone rang twice at the mountainside condo in Saratoga, Califor-nia. "Hello," a southern, female voice answered.

"Hi there, how are the city lights?" Dale asked Betty Jo.

"Beautiful, as always," she remarked. "Nice, clear night sky, it's even warm outside. How about you?"

"It's stormy and windy, the usual for a summer's night in Washington."

Dale could imagine her long, strawberry-blonde hair blowing in the breeze on the patio that looked out over the valley. He thought she was more strawberry then blonde but never said anything.

"Well, I know you're working, so I'll get to the point," she said. "I found out from a maritime contact in South America that an old diesel sub, the U.S.S. *Triggerfish*, SS 583, which first sailed in late 1960, was lost at sea several years ago off the coast of Chile. It's one of three unaccounted for in the last twenty years. It was sold to the Swedish Navy as a training ship. They, in turn, sold it to a private firm a few years later. That took me a while to cut through. And it turns out that company was a fifth tier subsidiary of an Odin Industries firm. They claimed it was refitted as a research vessel, designed to search for natural gas pockets on the ocean floor. The maritime report shows it was lost with a skeleton crew aboard. A surface ship that was accompanying them said the captain of the sub reported that the AC generators tripped and went off line. The sub was operating at two hundred eighty feet and moving along at eleven knots. The sub's down angle increased in spite of the 'full back' on the engines and blowing ballast."

Betty Jo pushed her bangs out of her eyes and turned the note page to continue.

"Her down angle was reported as forty-two degrees when they lost contact. The ocean's depth at the sight is near a canyon that drops to almost twelve thousand feet, which makes me wonder what it was really doing there. It's much too deep for natural gas research. The other two unaccounted for subs were in the south Atlantic and belonged to governmental agencies, and like I said, this was co-owned by Odin as a shell; took me awhile to find its origin of sale. Honey, I don't think it sunk. I think the surface boat was a tender and shepherded her to Nord Island after the initial search by the Chilean Coast Guard and Navy got underway. My guess is they rebuilt her," she said, closing the blue folder, "and modernized her in the process."

Betty Jo leaned back on the couch, "The Odin Industries shell company that owns the sub has top-secret contracts with the government in experimental electronics and other high technology areas. I'm just thinking out loud here, but what if they outfitted their own boat with technology they haven't released to the U.S. government yet?"

Dale was making notes in his unique shorthand and finished a second later.

"We're paying the R and D bill without day-to-day oversight. Good point, sweetie. Baby, keep this to yourself; it's dangerous information," he advised.

A minute later, they said goodbye, but not before she told him how much she missed him. Dale looked around at the stark surrounding of the fireboat and quietly told her he loved her. The call ended.

⚬━┓

"Captain, I've been down to the starboard access door. The waves are rolling across the hatch. I recommend that we not deploy the two boats. If we do, we may need rescue ourselves," the deck officer said.

The captain of the *Majestic Wonder* mulled that over.

"Have the crew members stand by. If worse comes to worse, and the Coast Guard needs to pull those passengers off a sinking ferry, I'll maneuver the ship to the windward side of the *Pickle Cove*. The computer and GPS will keep us stationary, acting as a buffer against the incoming waves. See to it and keep me informed."

The deck officer turned and departed.

Outside the bridge window, curtains of rain were flying at an angle.

Aboard the cruise ship *Majestic Wonder*
A mile and a half northeast of Fort Flagler State Park
Puget Sound, Washington
Friday, 1956 hours Pacific Time

The crew decks on levels two and three were being plastered with the picture and watch notice of the homicidal bank robber from Seattle. Everyone from the ship's food preparation staff to the housekeeping personnel were on the lookout for the face. ID badges were displayed conspicuously on shirt pockets or hanging from shirt collars. The ship's security staff were sweeping the boat from bow to stern and opening every door onboard in their hunt. A noticeably heightened awareness ran throughout the ship's personnel.

In a storage room on deck two, a tall man with a white baseball cap that read *Majestic Wonder* across the brim opened a utility room door and stepped in. Inside, his two companions waited impatiently.

"What took you so long?" the rock-bearing commando demanded.

"Your picture from the bank is up on the crew deck walls, they're looking for us," he replied. "We need to get moving toward the back of the ship and see if there is some way off. I think we're about twenty or so miles from the sub's location."

He opened his satellite phone and called an unlisted number in Seattle. The phone, sitting in a closed drawer on an empty desk in a warehouse, never rang. It answered silently and forwarded the call back to the satellite on another frequency. Twenty seconds passed and a voice spoke up, "We have you coming out of the straits in just a few minutes. What is your situation?"

"They have the bank photo from the robbery posted in all of the service deck hallways, and I think it would be dangerous to assume there is no active search going on."

The three men were eager to get off the cruise liner. American authorities would be brutal in their search to capture them. There was a pause. "We can't wait any longer. We need to get you off the ship immediately. Listen carefully, every cruise ship has rigid inflatables onboard."

"You mean a rubber raft, like a Zodiac?"

"Yes, exactly," Ingvar Wallen said. He was standing in the sub's CIC.

"There's usually a large hold aft, where equipment is stored for cleaning the ship's hull when in port. There will be at least one or more tenders on hoists. Get to the very back of the ship; if it's not there, go down one deck. You'll find it."

"You want us to go out in this weather. We'll drown out there. The seas are tossing water all over the place."

"You are presently in an open channel running east-west, where the wind and wave action are accented. The ship will turn north shortly and pass between two long islands running north-south. The seas in that last channel, prior to the open ocean, are running at four to six feet. The Zodiac is capable of negotiating that without much difficulty. The ship will hit the channel marker for her turn in about twelve to fifteen minutes, so you must hurry. Your lives depend on it. We'll paint the ship with the UV Splash, and then you, once you're on the inflatable. Steer for the lights on the island to the west, it's their main harbor. We'll flash you from the sub. Once you reach the middle of the channel, you'll see an illuminated ball floating on the surface. We'll have divers waiting there. They'll have weight belts and pony bottles for you, so we can get you down to the sub. Any questions?"

The three men had been listening to the satellite phone speaker together. They looked at each other without comment.

"No questions. We need to get going before a search finds us in the maintenance closet," the tall man responded.

"One last thing," Wallen offered, "Be sure you put on life vests, two for whoever is carrying the rock. We don't want to lose you."

In the main corridor a hundred fifty feet away, four retired British SAS men with master keys were opening and investigating each room as they progressed toward the aft section of the ship. In a parallel corridor not far away, four retired Gurkha sergeants were doing the same.

Onboard the *Pickle Cove*, the fire was out. Smoke rapidly dissipated as the open vents flushed fresh salt air through the engine room. One of the diesel engines had quit, the other was running close to maximum temperature. The pilot was holding steerage and three knots in the twisting current. Outside, an orange and white Coast Guard helicopter was being bruised by the crosswinds and thundering downpour. They would not be able to remain on station much longer without endangering the aircrew; the storm was worsening.

A few hundred feet off the port bow of the *Pickle Cove*, a sea-going tug was about to shoot a line to the small, stricken passenger ferry. If the first shot was successful and the *Pickle Cove* crew could secure the hawser line, they would take the passenger boat in tow to a sheltered cove three miles to the east.

A few hundred yards off the port quarter of the *Pickle Cove*, the *Chief Seattle* had its five-million-candlepower Sun Beam main light illuminating the commuter boat.

"Stand by for shot, *Pickle Cove*," the captain of the tug announced over the radio.

"*Pickle Cove* is ready, go ahead," the pilot replied.

Moments later, a loud blast sounded and a rope rocketed off the deck of the tug. On the open deck of the *Pickle Cove*, the two crewmen, tied to the super structure railing on safety lines, retrieved the hawser line and wrapped it around a powered deck reel. In the rocking sea, it took four minutes to haul over the towline. Two minutes later, it was secured to the *Pickle Cove* and the slack was taken up. The tug straightened the line out and took the ferry safely under tow.

"The Coast Guard helicopter is departing for its base at Port Angeles. Looks like the fire is out and the tug has her. The straits are a little less turbulent, so she should be okay to the cove. Let's tuck in and loiter on the leeward side of the inlet," Barney said. "As soon as we know the ferry is safe, we'll head back."

The *Chief Seattle's* pilot heeled her over to starboard and cut in front of the *Majestic Wonder*, who was still a good half mile away and coming on slowly.

"Thank you for your assistance in standing by, *Majestic*. Have a safe night. *Chief Seattle*, out," Barney said over the Motorola in the center of the console.

⚷

The door to the maintenance supply receded a foot into the utility room. The tall man with the baseball cap and the commando with the backpack peered into the hallway. Two women were headed in the opposite direction, one holding a clipboard and chatting as they walked.

The wide corridor was well lit by large, overhead, fluorescent lights that accented the stark, white walls and the fresh coat of medium-blue paint on the floor. The commando had discovered an empty cardboard box against a service locker. Placing his rock-enclosed backpack inside it, he put the box on the bottom shelf of a rolling maintenance cart. His submachine gun lay on top of the cart under some red rags, ready in the event it was needed. Both men, now dressed in maintenance overalls, prepared to push the stainless steel cart ahead of them. In the hallway, their efforts would appear routine to the other crew members.

In the wide passageway, the ship's lateral ribs protruded several inches into the walkway every fifteen feet. The protrusions were painted with a red, vertical stripe. Along the walls, service phones with long cords were placed at regular intervals. The end of each section of hallway was also marked in red, with stenciled numbering indicating the deck, section, and passageway.

The third man stepped out a moment later and pulled the utility door closed behind him. Carrying a tool bag, he proceeded aft behind his two friends, trying as much as possible to look like a busy crew member.

"Who are those guys moving down three-two-seventeen? I don't see their personnel badges displayed."

"Where?"

"Look," said the uniformed crewman from "C" shift, pointing to the color monitor on his right.

The older woman next to him slid over to her left and leaned in to observe the three men wearing electrician's overalls. The tall one looked suspicious. His clothing appeared too tight and short for him. As they continued walking, they passed by a ceiling mounted, optical camera lens situated midway between the ship's spars. She glanced up at the wanted memo from the FBI that had been posted a half hour earlier.

"Call up team four and have them intercept and check their ID badges," she requested. "That second guy pushing the cart resembles the photo."

The 'C' shift crewman picked up the radio microphone and called team four's leader, who at the moment was descending the companionway into the main passageway less than a hundred feet behind the trio.

"I see them ahead," he replied a few seconds later into his radio.

The 5'7", stocky, muscular Gurkha unzipped his fanny pack partway; his partner did the same. They followed the suspects until they reached a side corridor that fed into the main laundry service area. The hallway was strewn with white, canvas pushcarts that transported dirty linen from the ship's various room service storage locations on each passenger deck. The Gurkha stepped out of the main passageway and behind one of the ship's protruding ribs for cover.

The two people monitoring the cameras in the security center watched the Gurkhas order the three men to stop.

"Gentlemen, could we please see your personnel badges?"

Having heard the footsteps following close behind, the trio knew that any further attempt at subterfuge was wasted. All three men stopped and turned to face the ship's two burly security men. While the trailing man made a convincing show of patting his shirt pocket for his ID, his move shielded the commando with the suppressed submachine gun. In a single, quick move, he dropped to the floor as the commando kicked his foot from behind. The commando let loose with a short burst from the deadly 9mm firearm.

Nine copper rounds zinged thirty-three feet down the corridor, one finding its mark in the security team leader's left forearm.

Both security men dove behind the steel bulkhead in the laundry side hall. The second Gurkha stumbled into one of the still full laundry carts and rolled off onto the deck. He pulled out his pistol and started firing from a prone position on the floor as the team leader blasted away from behind the exposed rib. The entire exchange lasted only a few seconds. The second security man spoke calmly on his radio, but quickly sought help from the other search teams.

The three commandos spread out and ran aft, throwing rounds indiscriminately behind them. The machine gun wielding commando retrieved his backpack in the seconds after the initial blast, and sprayed lead all over the corridor.

The sound of hard-soled shoes pounding down the passageway echoed off the steel bulkhead and drifted into the open doors lining the hallway. The noisy gunfire screamed off the walls.

Staff employees in the side rooms, who recognized the racket outside, hit the deck immediately, while a few others moved to poke their heads out the doorways to see what was happening. Most heeded the panicked warnings of fellow employees and resisted the natural urge of their curiosity.

"We've got gunfire in three-two-seventeen," the C team security room man called out to the bridge.

⚷━✦

On the bridge of the *Chief Seattle*, the captain stopped his conversation with another crewman as the words poured out of the bridge intercom. Barney Davis, fire engineer Robert Booker, and Sean and Dale Fox turned toward the speaker.

⚷━✦

"Mayday, mayday, mayday! This is the cruise ship *Majestic Wonder*, on VHF sixteen, a mile west of Sierra Foxtrot, GPS at 122.260 latitude and 47.3 minutes 48 seconds longitude. Ship is under attack, shots fired from automatic weapons, multiple gunmen, possible bank robbery suspect and associates from Seattle."

A few seconds passed and the Coast Guard station at Anacortes replied and verified the information. *Majestic Wonder*, we are responding a Homeland Security team from Port Angeles. ETA is twenty-five minutes due to the storm. The Cutter *Sisquay* is en route to your location. Can you provide further details?"

As the commentary on the shootout from the *Majestic Wonder* continued, Dale yelled down the spiral stairwell, "Sullivan, we got trouble!"

Moments later, heavy feet leapfrogged every other step up the steel ladder rungs to the bridge.

"Talk to me," Sullivan said as he halted just a few feet from Dale.

Dale filled him in as they continued to listen in on the mayday conversation with the Coast Guard.

Davis was the first to interrupt, "There is no way that the *Sisquay* is going to make it in twenty-five minutes. She's in open water with twelve-foot seas roaring up her skirt, and nasty crosswinds slamming her from port. She'll be lucky to make it in forty-five minutes."

"Well, it sounds like they've confined them to a lower deck, away from the passenger activity four decks up," Dale said.

"Yeah, but for how long? Clearly the ship's security detail is outgunned," Sullivan blurted out.

"They're up to something," Dale stated to no one in particular. He was looking through the bow windshield into the black abyss. "Were they forced to the back of the ship by circumstance or do they have a plan?"

Sean looked at Dale. "They were spotted walking down the corridor. Choice," he replied.

"What's at the back of a typical cruise ship on the crew deck?" he asked Barney while spinning sideways to face the group.

Barney reached out and tapped the laptop computer's keys on the counter. After a few key strokes, he brought up the *Majestic Wonder* from the registration database schematic on the monitor. He zeroed in on the lower aft section of the cruise ship and expanded the picture to fill the screen.

"Mechanicals, service areas, storage, power plant, and miscellaneous maintenance shops," he said, pointing with a grease pencil to each area. "They can stop the ship, set it on fire, maybe. I think the automated fire suppression system would defeat that, though. Ahh, they could barricade themselves past the flood crash doors at the back of the ship, but to what end?"

Dale and Sean looked at each other. "They want to get off the ship," they chimed in unison.

Team four nosed around the corner of the vertical spar. The team leader fired two rounds at the fleeing men and suddenly stopped as a head of long, brown hair poked out of a side door, curious as to what the commotion was all about.

"They're headed aft toward the maintenance area. Notify team one to descend from above in the service elevator and meet us at bulkhead three-two-twenty-one. The intruders have gone down a side corridor from there," the team leader relayed by radio. "Have team three move up the corridor on their side of the ship and block the passageway. Keep employees out of the area."

He looked at his arm, which was bleeding, but not badly. Pulling back the sleeve, he decided it was a minor wound. The two Gurkhas moved swiftly and as quietly as possible off opposite bulkheads in pursuit of the terrorists. They yelled out for service employees as they went, advising them to stay in their rooms and barricade the doors. The sound of tables and chairs being used to block doors could be heard in the main corridor a few seconds later.

"Do we know where we're going?" the short commando asked as they ran left from the side passageway.

"To the very back of the ship; we need to find the service Zodiac, get it started, and overboard."

As they ran, they came to a large steel door that spanned a ten-foot width of the corridor. The rock-carrying commando took up a defensive position behind a six-foot tall, wall-mounted locker. The tall man hit a button on the opposite wall that activated a hydraulic motor. The big access door in front of him opened. An alarm sounded and a ceiling mounted red light flashed. A few seconds later, they squeezed through to the other side. Several rounds slapped the bulkhead behind them as the two security officers finally caught up. One round hit the shortest of the three men in the back between the shoulder blades. He went down as the large door closed behind him.

"I'm hit!" he grunted between gritted teeth. The other two commandos stopped and scooped him up under the arms. The taller commando smashed the door access control box with the butt of his pistol. Sparks shot out and the control panel went dead, "That ought to slow them up." The third man regained his feet a moment later, took a deep breath, and continued walking under his own power, albeit slower than before.

Realizing that his injury was impeding their progress, he looked at his two companions, "Go ahead, I'll cover our rear. Find the boat and get started. I'll catch up by the time you have the Zodiac ready to go over the side." He stopped and bent over with his hands on his knees as if to catch his breath.

The other two men looked at the injured commando's back and saw a slowly spreading pool of blood trickling down his shirt. The bullet had penetrated far enough that the man was in serious trouble.

The tall commando looked at his bent over companion, "We're going to keep to the right until we reach the aft most area of the ship. It will be outside the confined spaces. If the Zodiac is below us on another deck, we'll retrieve you and move down one level together. Keep moving forward, kill anyone who gets in your way."

The short commando nodded and stood up ready to walk again. The other two men turned and ran ahead.

Twelve miles south of Lopez Island
San Juan Straits, Washington

"Helm, bring us around at the channel marker just southeast of Decatur off Lopez Island, and point us back toward Seattle. Notify other shipping in the straits that we are declaring an emergency," the captain of the *Majestic Wonder* ordered. "Activate the service deck flood doors and secure all elevators, I don't want them getting up to the passenger decks. Let's keep our paying customers happy and have the security teams push the robber and his friends to the rear of the ship and trap them there. Wake up the next watch and have them turn to the aft crew access areas above the third deck. Turn the music up in the aft restaurant on deck five to drown out any sound of gunfire."

"Aye, Captain," someone behind him replied.

Looking out the thick, angle-paned, command deck window into the black rain hammering the glass, the captain wished the storm would abate. A few seconds, later he strolled over to the color monitor that painted the weather cells outside. Tapping the monitor, he brought up the range adjustment, clicked the five hundred mile radius graph, and the monitor refreshed.

The deep, furrowed lines in his tanned forehead creased tighter. The dark-red cells spread across the weather monitor as far as he could see. Outside, the wind indicator danced across the fifty-five mile per hour bar. He punched up the SOLAS manual – Safety of Life at Sea - on the computer and looked over the table of contents.

It was an hour back to port, without any help from the authorities unless they intercepted the *Sisquay,* which was a remote possibility since it would be behind them once they turned in the channel. The Coast Guard's helicopters were grounded due to numerous heavy wind shear reports, and the worsening storm was isolating his ship even as the thought crossed his mind. A lot could happen in that time. He took one more glace at the barometric pressure reading on the weather computer screen; it hovered around 29.1. The helmsman was slowly turning the raised, twin, horseshoe shaped levers toward the left.

The five men on the bridge of the *Chief Seattle* scrutinized the aft portion of the ship from all angles on the computer monitor; they were deep in thought. "Look here," Sean said, pointing to deck three. "It's open to the sea."

Dale peered at the open aft section, "Barney, what do they store back here on the open deck, or adjacent to it in this aft storage area?"

"Well, it's usually maintenance materials. You know, paint, ship primer, roller brushes, ropes, rappelling gear, pressure washers, that sort of thing."

"It says 'hydraulic hoist' here. What's that?"

"That's for the maintenance launches that work around the ship while it's in port."

Sullivan and Sean said it at the same time: "They're gonna bail."

Aboard the cruise ship *Majestic Wonder*
Puget Sound, Washington
Friday, 2038 hours Pacific Time

Rounding the corner, the two armed commandos quietly moved past four maroon and bronze coffins stacked against the far wall. Behind the coffins, a commercial coroner's refrigerator was recessed into the bulkhead. People occasionally died onboard cruise ships, so the cruise line was prepared to accommodate such unpleasant events.

Across the aisleway were stacks of crates and cardboard boxes on pallets, with various dry goods supplies that could not be stored elsewhere. The two men walked slowly and quietly, listening for anyone who might be there working. Hearing no one, they passed through the storage maze to the back of the room. Beyond the one large, sliding steel door was the exposed aft deck that looked out upon the open sea.

Undogging the dual piano latch-locking mechanisms, the two men began sliding the solid steel storm door to the left. At first it barely inched its way along. After a few, tough moments, it finally gave up its stubborn resistance, as the recently lubed ball bearing track made opening it a bit easier.

Stepping out into the howling wind, both men could see intermittent lights from Fidalgo Island to the east and Lopez Island directly west. The submarine was somewhere in the immediate neighborhood. South of them, four and a half miles away in the small cove in Fort Ebey State Park on Whidbey Island, was the *Chief Seattle*.

Onboard the *Chief Seattle*

The fireboat was well out of its primary area of operation. And now it had been commandeered by the FBI under a little-known federal law that Congress had passed after 9/11; Barney's boat had just become a law enforcement vessel.

Pilot Bobby Booker stumbled sideways and bounced off Barney as the boat took a rolling rogue wave from the port side. "You okay?" he asked Barney as he put out a hand to pick him up off the floor.

"We're going to need more than life vests if this keeps up," Barney replied, standing up. "Can you see her lights yet?" he asked, referring to the big cruise ship.

"Negative. I have her beacon, though. She's about four thousand yards dead ahead. She's making seven knots and getting ready to turn at the channel marker. We'll turn outside of her and come up on the starboard side. How do the FBI guys plan to get aboard if the waves are rolling over the boarding ladder?"

"We'll shoot a line to the open access hatch to secure them as they climb. Agent Fox said he was going below to pray to God he doesn't drown. He knows he has to do it. Terry is hooking them into their rescue harnesses right now."

Sixty-two hundred yards southwest of the *Majestic Wonder*, and two hundred thirty-four feet down, the stealthy Nordian sub was closing in.

Aboard the cruise ship *Majestic Wonder*

The submachine gun toting commando stood ready at the opening of the aft hatchway as he reloaded an additional magazine. The open sea deck that housed the cruise ship's eighteen foot work skiff and the twenty foot Zodiac was just a few feet behind him.

The wind screamed and an icy-cold blast of air blew at the strings on their jacket zippers as the sea door opened. The howling noise from the storm was deafening. Several coiled ropes had unwound and were flailing across the metal deck. An unsecured footlocker against the bulkhead had dumped its contents. Paint cans rolled around the deck, slamming into stationary work objects. One can was sloshing its remaining contents of gray paint across the deck.

The tall commando dodged the debris and found the overhead manual control for the hoist. A second later, he released the safety and raised the rigid inflatable off its davits. A few moments passed and it was dangling in the air, rocking slowly with the rhythm of the ship.

He rushed to the back of the rigid pontoon boat and pulled the starter rope on the engine. After a couple of unsuccessful attempts, he spotted the choke lever and slid it all the way over. On the next pull, the engine caught and started. He immediately shut it off, spun the fuel cap, and confirmed that it was full.

The rock-carrying commando had donned the backpack again and was tightening the straps down when the third and injured commando staggered through the passage door.

"They're right behind me," he said with a gravely voice almost drowned out by the whipping torrent.

The tall commando pulled his injured companion further into the stack of crates at the back of the storage area. Several lightweight boxes skidded by in the wind.

"How far?"

"They had a hydraulic tool that they were using to force the crash door open. I waited until there was room to fire and sent a few rounds through the space to force them back."

"There's foul weather gear on the back wall. Grab one," the tall commando said.

⚊⚊⚊

"They're six hundred yards and turning in the channel, sir," the sonar operator called out.

"Helm, take us to PD," Ingvar Wallen ordered. "Mr. Sjorken, mind the planes and ballast. It looks rough up there. Keep an ear out for that Coast Guard cutter, he's somewhere behind us and coming in fast."

"Aye, sir."

It took forty seconds to ascend to within thirty feet of the boiling cauldron surface that the ocean had become.

"Leveling off at thirty-five, Captain," the helmsman called out.

"XO, power up the UV Splash and raise the trailing arm." Seconds on the bulkhead-mounted chronograph ticked by as Wallen waited for the oxygen sensor on the digital array above the ship to show two green lights.

"We're up," Sjorken said as they blinked on.

"Monitor test is in the green!" another sailor yelled out.

"Pan left," Wallen said, speaking into the boom mike around his neck. He waited patiently as the array stabilized in the stormy sea. "Stop," he ordered about ten seconds later. "Magnify three times." The view in the twenty-inch, color monitor grew bigger as the computer system adjusted the distance.

"There she is, all lit up like a Christmas tree." The laser range finder flashed in the upper right corner of the monitor."

"XO, give me forty percent power on the UV, and stand by to fire."

"UV at forty percent and free, Captain. Standing by to fire," Sjorken replied.

Several cardboard boxes behind him exploded as shots rang out. Chunks of tan paper went flying in several directions. Two very fit, retired SAS officers and six angry Gurkhas opened up, sending a fusillade of hot lead toward the back of the storage area.

The submachine gun in the commando's hands returned fire even before his mind had focused on the task. In his previous life, he'd been a Swedish antiterrorism commando. With the rock in its case strapped tightly to his back, his movement was restricted. Nevertheless, he laid down a nasty barrage that sent rounds pinging off bulkheads and forcing the ship's security personnel to the floor.

Outside on the open deck, the tall commando had the Zodiac over the edge of the ship on the leeward side. The winds and sea were manageable but dangerous.

What will this be like out in the open? the tall commando thought. *Cold and wet.*

Just then, a couple of bullets struck the crane and rigging a few feet behind him.

With the Zodiac starting to twist in the wind, it was time to depart. He pulled the crane arm in closer to the ship so the Zodiac would slide down the side to the water twenty-five feet below. The sound of gunfire from the ship's storm door was growing more intense. He spotted the rock-carrying commando hunkered down behind the paint cabinet just outside the doorway. Through the curtain of rain, he could see the man moving his aim around as he shot back at the security team. A blast from inside popped the paint cabinet door open.

⸙

"Fire!"

The XO pushed the "enter" key on the computer keyboard and the invisible beam pelted the side of the big cruise ship with a splat.

"Is the dive team ready?" Wallen demanded of the master chief at the dive chamber.

"All ready, sir."

"Very well, stand by. I'm looking for the escape boat. It should be out in a minute."

⸙

The third commando, his wounds slowing his reflexes, was hit with two rounds, one in the right leg and the other in the left shoulder. He banged off the back bulkhead and stumbled out through the open sea door.

The tall commando yelled at the commando with the rock that it was time to go. The wounded commando lost his balance and slide across the deck when a rogue wave washed through the open space and knocked him down. As he leveraged his right hand against an exposed water return pipe and stood erect, the ship tilted with the turn and the blowing wind threw him into the metal railing face first. He slammed into the top bar and flipped end over end into the raging waters below.

The tall commando reached out to catch him, but it was too late. He was gone.

The rock-laden commando slammed another thirty-round magazine into the submachine gun and saw a head pop up inside the ship. Firing a short burst, he forced the incoming rounds from the Gurkhas to cease momentarily.

Looking down at the brass casings at his feet, he spotted several five-gallon cans of paint solvent in the cabinet next to him.

He signaled the tall commando that he was going to make a dash for the railing and the Zodiac. He aimed and unleashed a long blast, and charged out from behind the paint cabinet.

The radio earbud in the team leader's left ear came alive. "Cease fire. Cease fire," the voice of the captain ordered. "They have an unstable high explosive in the backpack."

The team leader called out to his men to take up defensive positions. The adrenaline pumping through their veins and the incoming gunfire was counter to their instincts and experience, but their training and discipline won out in the few seconds they had to consider the hasty demand from the ship's captain.

"The FBI has informed us that they are in possession of a compact, high explosive device. A bullet hitting the thing could set it off. They're asking us to contain the shooters until the Navy can get a SWAT team aboard. They have a cutter inbound that should be alongside in twenty minutes. Can you do that?" the captain asked.

Geoff Mayberry keyed his radio, "Aye, sir. We'll hold them where they are."

His team could see that he was clearly not happy, yet he understood that setting off an accidental explosive of some kind could damage the ship and possibly kill them, along with passengers three decks above.

"Mr. Mayberry, the Seattle fireboat, *Chief Seattle*, is coming alongside in just a few minutes. There are two counterterrorism FBI agents onboard. They will be sent down to you directly."

"Aye, sir," the grizzled, old SAS vet said.

The captain was livid that his ship was endangered by the maniacs on her fantail. The order to stop shooting them and requesting containment only made his anger with the situation grow. The decision to get the two FBI agents involved probably wasn't going to solve the problem. His ship would be held hostage in U.S. waters, his crew and passengers detained, and the entire voyage cancelled. He reluctantly reached for the satellite phone on the wall next to him and called his company headquarters to report on their circumstances.

A quarter of a mile behind the Coast Guard cutter *Sisquay*, a Sikorsky SH-60K Spec Ops chopper was coming in to land. Ten men of MarSOC team Sierra, from the nearby Navy base, were poised to unload. The chopper was being buffeted and rocked by the increasing wind. Rain slammed the windshield sideways at sixty miles an hour. The pilot was in a constant state of maneuvering to keep the helo airborne. The first of the two choppers deployed was already on the aft landing pad of the *Sisquay* and the other six team members were offloading.

The Marine Special Ops team had been on assault tactics training with SEAL team five, which included high-risk sea boarding operations, when they were called up. They were loaded aboard their Sea Hawk choppers in response to a presidential authorization initiated by Fox and Sullivan.

8—⋆

Inside the storage room, the senior security officer saw the bank robber bolt from behind the cabinet across the open deck. He rallied his men toward the storm door. As they approached, guns ready, a fiery explosion ripped through the open hatch, blowing them all off their feet and into the supply of crates and boxes. The aft storm doors buckled, fire broke out, alarms and sirens sounded, and three men were dead.

The paint locker, loaded with flammable solvent, had been laced with 9mm bullets from the submachine gun with deadly effect.

Several Gurkhas grabbed fire extinguishers off the bulkheads and set about putting out the fire.

Their brethren took up positions to carry the attack forward to the open sea deck, orders be damned. Twenty seconds passed when the first two Gurkhas finally emerged from inside the storage room. They looked around cautiously, guns aimed, as they turned toward the last known position of the robber and his friends. They were joined by four more security officers a few seconds later.

Taking in the view of the entire deck, one of them noticed the Zodiac crane swinging freely on the port side. Motioning to the others, he slowly crossed the deck. The stinging wind and water pelted him. Reaching the other side of the deck, he discovered four empty lines dangling wildly in the wind.

43

Aboard the *Chief Seattle*
Puget Sound, Washington
Friday, 2102 hours Pacific Time

"There she is, dead ahead," Bobby called out, " . . . six degrees right."

"What the," Barney said, "look!!"

An orange-yellow ball of flame erupted from the back of the *Majestic Wonder*.

Dale looked at the rising mushroom and charged down the spiral stairs.

The *Chief Seattle* leaned with yet another good-sized wave. The ship wasn't being pounded as much as she was being constantly rolled in the fast moving waves. Sean and Sullivan were below decks helping the lone deckhand, Dave, secure all of the loose equipment and tools that had started bouncing and roaming across the floor below decks.

It was a tough job, bending over with the bulky survival gear. Given the fairly cool temperature on the boat, the warmth of the suits was an appreciated trade-off. So far, the only casualty had been Sean, when he lost his balance on one unexpected wave and banged into the diesel engine shielding. The lost skin on his knuckles was a minor inconvenience.

"Sean, you okay?" Sullivan yelled over the sound of the crashing waves. The noise was echoing around the lower deck like a racketball bouncing off the walls. Sean slid involuntarily up against the bulkhead and grabbed the leg of a machinist stand. He leaned precariously against it, waiting for another wave.

This must be what it's like inside a beer can at spring break just before the pop top is opened.

"Yeah, I'm fine," he said regaining his feet.

The ship rolled again to the opposite side; Sean hung on with his undamaged hand.

The overhead PA barked to life. "We have her in sight. Stand by to board the *Majestic Wonder.*

Four minutes to contact." Sean watched an empty, white five-gallon bucket roll by for the second time.

Sullivan headed for the spiral stairwell hanging on to anything secure as he went.

Dale grabbed the overhead railing, "Sullivan, we've got an explosion onboard the cruise ship. It's on the back of the ship near the waterline. We'll be alongside in a few minutes," Dale said. "We need to get topside now."

Barney turned as the radio behind him crackled, "*Chief Seattle*, this is the *Majestic Wonder.* Our guests have departed over the side in a Zodiac."

Barney, Bobby, Terry, and Dale all looked at each other. Dale grabbed the microphone and keyed the side, "*Majestic Wonder,* we need details - how long ago, direction of travel, how many men, how big is the Zodiac?"

"*Chief Seattle*, there were three men. They went over the side about two minutes ago, aft of the ship. The Zodiac is twenty-two feet long."

"Was the Zodiac fully fueled? Did it have any storm cover, other equipment?"

"We always load up the fuel cell. It has a partial storm tarp on the front. We have them on radar, behind us about two hundred yards, but it's getting weaker as the distance increases."

Dale looked at Barney, eyebrow raised, "Thank you, *Majestic Wonder. Chief Seattle* out."

Twenty feet long, in this weather. They'll drown within a few minutes, Dale thought. "What do you think the odds of survival are out there?" he asked Barney as he hung up the microphone.

"It's bad weather, but people have been known to make it through in worse. As long as they ride the rolling waves and don't encounter breaking water, they might be okay. The Zodiac sits low in the water. If they face the waves and control the engine well, they might make it to an island nearby."

Dale turned to face Barney, "Let's head astern of the cruise ship and see if we can find them."

Barney looked at Bobby with a what-the-hell expression. "We've been commandeered by the federal government, let's go."

Bobby heaved the fireboat to port about ten degrees and advanced the throttles to the stops. They rose over a tall, rolling wave and down the other side. Barney reached up and flipped several toggle switches to the up position. A few seconds later, the tail of the cruise ship passed astern.

Outside, intermittent beams of light stabbed out into the darkness on either side of the fireboat, searching for any sign of the escaping craft. "Sun Beam coming up," Barney announced. A five-million candlepower light switched on, bathing the stormy sea in almost daylight conditions.

"What's our status?" Sullivan asked from the stairwell.

"We have to get that backpack intact," Dale replied, taking up station on the port side light inside the cramped command cabin. He gazed intently into the darkness, seeking any reflective object bobbing around on the waters.

"For sure they didn't get into that Zodiac without life vests. If they go into the water, at least they'll float," Dale said.

In the stairwell behind Sullivan, Sean held onto the handrail, listening to the conversation as the boat rocked again in another wave trough. His left hand still hurt.

"I see lots of wave trail and foamy streaks. How do we know whether they're from an engine trail?" Sean asked, stepping up to watch a light off the stern deck. He'd never seen seas so high before. It was as if the ship was being momentarily swallowed whole between waves. He found it a little unnerving.

Barney watched the radar scope, but the waves were much too high to pick out the Zodiac in the clutter. *Dale may be right, the sea may have already claimed them.*

"Dave," Barney said, "Contact the *Sisquay* and give her our GPS coordinates, and tell her we're searching for the escaped terrorists."

The firefighter went below to use the radio desk.

Five sets of eyes patiently scanned the waters looking for the terrorists as the illumination from the party cruiser receded behind them. Several minutes passed in rapt attention of the sea.

"Lieutenant," Dave called up from below. "The *Sisquay* will be in the area in twenty minutes. She says she'll take up station between us and the leeward island," he continued, referring to the body of land to the west of them. "I get the impression that the Marines onboard her are itching to get involved. The Marine captain in charge of the team asked the *Sisquay's* skipper for a storm boat when they got into the area."

Sean and Dale perked up at what they heard.

"Speaking of the *Sisquay*, keep an eye on the scope, Terry. I don't want to get run over in the dark by our own people," Barney said.

They kept searching the waters, moving the Sun Beam around to keep their eyes from fixating.

The bridge was silent again except for radio traffic from oceangoing vessels reporting in on the VTS.

The *Chief Seattle* slid down the backside of several more large waves that seemed to loom over the boat. It was Sean who first noticed a glint of reflection just beyond his searchlight. He moved it out a little farther, but the light was diffused in the driving rain. He could see no more then eighty to ninety feet with the water spray constantly obscuring his vision. Squinting to focus better didn't seem to help him.

Several fast knocks on the side of the steel bridge housing caught his attention. The small window above him blew out. A tiny chunk of copper hit the stainless steel center post above the radio rack and fell to the floor. Dale turned around and picked it up, now aware of the wind whistling thru the narrow vent window.

He examined it briefly as all eyes on the bridge turned inward. Holding it in his hand, it took a moment for him to realize its true shape.

"It's a bullet," he said looking closely.

Just then, a pinging sound reverberated in the bridge. Several more bullets lodged in the thick wooden trim of the *Chief Seattle's* hide. Shards of oiled teak sailed past the window.

"We're under fire!" Sullivan yelled out.

"There they are. They have reflective bands on their weather gear. Mr. Sjorken, ready another shot on my command." The stealthy, high-tech foreign submarine cruised along at six knots.

Hovering over the console, the XO readied the computer for another target, "Aye, Captain, stand by." An uneasy peace took hold as the thrashing sound of the heavy sea just above echoed across the submarines hull. She was designed to glide silently along beneath the water, not ride in the waves that would toss her around violently like a rubber duck in a splashing bathtub.

"We're ready, Captain, UV is up." The XO glanced at the big flat screen monitor on the bulkhead.

"The waves are pushing them," he said impassively.

The laser range finder on the screen was moving rapidly in and out. *Or are they . . . they're maneuvering oddly.* He continued his observation of the rolling surface.

"*Next wave crest,*" Wallen said to himself. He waited and counted the seconds between wave tops.

"Stand by... *There they are* . . . Fire!"

The UV Splash reached out and invisibly painted both men and Zodiac a split second later.

"Captain, I'm picking up twin screws, very close in."

Wallen turned to the sonar operator fifteen feet away, "What? Why didn't we hear it sooner? Belay that, what is it, identify?"

The sole non-crewman on the bridge had a sudden rush of fear. His face went white, but he kept quiet so as not to disrupt the captain's concentration. He needed the man to get their package, but now their survival might be at stake. His legs suddenly went wobbly and the acid in his stomach rose to his throat.

"Is it the U.S. destroyer?" Wallen asked with a hurried demand.

"No, sir. It's smaller, much smaller." The sonar operator went quiet a moment as he hit the search function on his computer and pressed his stereo headset to his head.

"Searching the database, stand by. We may have a recording, but it's definitely not an American warship."

The guest on the bridge and the other six men waited nervously, but after relaxing a bit they realized it was not an American combat vessel. The computer monitor froze on a matching recording.

"Sir, it's the fireboat *Chief Seattle*. The original recording is two weeks old. It was made during a transition between islands, during the daytime in good weather. Not much chance of an error. She's ninety-two feet long, drafting seven feet. The only other thing I can hear is the cruise ship fading off to the east."

"Do you have anything on that American destroyer that's coming our way?"

"No, sir. We're flooded with transients from the storm. The fireboat will be on top of us in minutes though. She's heading straight at us."

"How fast is she moving?"

"About eight knots, sir. She's coming right through our pickup zone."

Wallen glanced at his guest for a second. The man's face was pale.

"Captain, we're at forty feet on the gauge, with five-to-seven-foot-waves in the channel. Our safety margin is almost nonexistent."

"Very well, helm, take us down to seventy feet. Sonar, let me know when the fireboat passes."

The stranger took two weak steps forward and put his hand on Wallen's shoulder with as strong a grip as he could muster. "Those men will drown and the package will be lost if we don't act immediately."

Wallen looked him in the face undaunted, "I know the situation."

The stranger stepped back as the sub's deck angled slightly.

"Captain, we're at seventy-five feet," the helmsman called out.

Wallen squeezed the pencil-thin microphone hanging by a cord around his neck, "Combat, prepare a blue shot computer solution for an aft target at three hundred fifty yards, set depth for five feet. Let me know when it's ready." Wallen looked back at his guest with indifference.

"Aye sir, confirm blue shot."

"Affirmative, blue shot," Wallen repeated, looking away. *We'll punch a hole right through her.*

Heading toward them with the oncoming wave was the Zodiac. One man was shooting an automatic weapon. In the spotlight, he looked like the third horseman of the Apocalypse, with a flashing light emitting from the barrel of his weapon. Unbeknownst to the *Chief Seattle,* she was riding the very spot where the sub was supposed to pick them up. Unseen seventy feet to her right was the floating, basketball-sized buoy tethered to the submarine.

"Duck!"

Bullets slapped the tough, reinforced Plexiglas windows, carving small holes in them.

Barney spun the wheel left to put them bow on to the Zodiac. "Terry, topside now, we need you!" he yelled. "Dave, call the *Sisquay.* Tell them we're under fire from the Zodiac off the *Majestic Wonder.*"

Dale's adrenaline went off the scale. The *Chief Seattle* slewed sideways down another wave. Dale held on to the spotlight's heavy brass handle and went parallel to the deck for a second. Grunting, he hung on for his life.

Terry scrambled up the stairwell and saw the bullet holes. A heavy pinging sound wafted into the bridge as more bullets struck the side of the fireboat and the heavy, teak radio mast.

Sullivan reached for his .45 and got off two shots from the wheelhouse door before it became apparent that the sound was going to deafen them all.

"I thought you said we couldn't shoot at them for some hazmat reason," Barney hollered over the noise.

"The stakes just changed," Sullivan replied. "I need to get out there where I can fire back."

"You can't go out there under these conditions, you'll get thrown overboard and drown," Barney said. He yanked the back of Sullivan's pumpkin suit in and kicked the hatch closed.

"Their bullets probably won't punch a hole in the boat's hull. I'm open to suggestions. How do we defend ourselves?" Sullivan shot back, clearly not happy with the situation.

The Zodiac driver skidded down the side of a wave toward the bigger vessel. The rigid inflatable quickly rose on another as the second man unleashed an additional volley of metal at the *Chief Seattle*. Bullets stretched from the hull to the bridge as the man's aim slid over the fireboat. Moments later, another long burst connected with the Sun Beam and the light went dark.

"The deck gun," Sean blurted out. "We can use the deck gun. The controls are right here. Let's power up and try to swamp them."

Barney turned the boat over to Bobby and hit the toggle for the hydraulic post. The water cannon rose five feet and then stopped. Soon after a stream of water started flowing, slowly at first, but increasing with every second until it was a serious blast. Dale swiveled his side spotlight around, as did Sean. They played the light over the water, searching for the Zodiac in the darkness and heavy, driving rain.

Just out of view of the searchlights, the Zodiac bobbed like a cork in the water. More bullets reached out and hit the front of the bridge. Small metal shards and wood trim bounced off the Plexiglas windshield.

⊶⊶★

"Where are they?" Wallen asked.

"We can see sporadic reflections from the UV, sir. The Zodiac appears to be about four hundred or so feet ahead. I can see that fireboat. They look like they're practically on top of each other."

Wallen moved quickly from the dive chamber, where he had been checking on the diver's preparations along with his unwelcome guest.

"Captain on the bridge," someone called out a minute later.

"Helm, take us to fifty-five feet," Wallen took over the station on the view scope.

"XO, prepare a UV shot on that fireboat."

"UV is up, Captain," he replied.

The Plasma-Luminal gas laser, known as the UV Splash, was not an ordinary laser. It was comprised of three parts: a source of energy to power it, an active medium, and an optical cavity. The submarine's power was substantial. The plasma and liquid luminal were converted to a gaseous state by inductive heat. The main ingredient was the gas. Where the device reached its zenith was in the reflective cavity, which Wallen was about to activate.

"Stand by to fire," Wallen ordered. He counted the seconds between the waves as the *Chief Seattle* rose and fell from view. "Coming up, stand by. Stand by, fire!"

The UV Splash painted the port side of the *Chief Seattle* with a spectacular return of neon ultraviolet color. "Stand by another shot for the Zodiac," he ordered. The submarine was rocking slightly from her close proximity to the surface. Again Wallen counted the seconds. "Ready, fire!"

A regular laser used a reflective surface at either end of a cavity, its limited output being restricted to a burst of about one hundred milliseconds. That basic design characteristic created a high intensity, optical environment to contain a single photon atom. The UV Splash poured energy into the tube for a-two second duration. Its potential destructive power could only be imagined.

The Zodiac and both men were bathed in an ultraviolet rainbow of color, visible only by someone with the proper UV lens.

By modifying the wavelength output of the UV Splash, close-in, it would coat its target with a searing, hot blast that burned the skin like napalm. They had seen its effect on a few past encounters that ultimately went to the bottom.

Swiveling the hydraulic water monitor around, Barney searched for the target. A hard, steady stream of solid water reached out about ninety feet. It would have been further, but the screaming winds were pushing back.

"Where is it?" Barney called out.

"They're off to the right. We went right by them a second ago," Dale said. As the words left his mouth, several shots hit the bridge housing below the windshield. Barney could see the burst of light from the barrel of the machine gun that was firing at them.

"LT, our radio mast just went down!" Bob yelled.

Barney cussed out loud.

More rounds impacted the fireboat, one of them finding its mark. Robert Booker fell back and slumped to the metal deck.

"Terry, Bob's down, help him. Barney grabbed the boat's wheel as Sean and Terry looked Bob over. An instant later, they were half-dragging, half-carrying him to the stairwell.

"Dave, on the double, we need help!" Terry hollered over the wailing sound of the wind pouring into the small bridge area. The three of them managed to get the unconscious man down to the lower deck and onto one of the four, seven-foot-long fiberglass survival bunks, where they strapped him in. Sean, Terry, and Speedy Huey attached the hooks to their survival suits and tied off to the overhead railing. All three men were highly experienced paramedics. Sean grabbed a medical jump kit from the wall and laid it on Bob's legs.

The unresponsive firefighter was bleeding profusely from his upper left chest.

⚷━➤

"Sir, the fireboat is passing overhead again," the sonar man said.

The sound of the twin screws driven by the *Chief Seattle*'s diesel engines could be heard by every man onboard the submarine. The fireboat was less than sixty feet above them, making a very unstealthy racket.

"Combat, she's going by. Prepare to lock her up once she's clear of our track," Wallen ordered.

"Aye, sir, standing by."

"Ops, pop the ball again and turn on the strobe so the Zodiac can see us," Wallen commanded.

A couple of seconds passed and the location buoy cleared the surface again. A strobe light immediately began flashing from inside.

"Dive master," the captain called out on the intercom, "flood the chamber."

⚷━➤

"Coming around, watch the waves," Barney warned.

With the sound of the diesels cranking away behind them, the three paramedics worked feverishly in orchestrated unison, trying to stop the bleeding. Bob's shirt was off, and the problem presented by the ragged hole in his chest was compounded by a collapsed lung underneath.

Another twelve-foot wave crashed over the bow as the *Chief Seattle* twisted in place and reversed course. The wind caught the exposed hull, wrenching the big boat sideways and down the backside of the sloping wave. A wall of water tumbled over the boat, rocking her halfway to horizontal. In an almost ungainly rebound, she slowly rose back up before the next wave smashed into her. Water poured in through the numerous bullet holes in the bridge.

"Hang on, we're gonna get hit again!" Barney said.

The *Chief Seattle* creaked loudly as she was slammed broadside.

"Hang in there, old girl. We'll make it," Barney mumbled as he spun the wheel again to line up with the wind. When he looked down at the console mounted water monitor controls, he noticed the red light flashing.

"We've lost the hydraulics on the deck gun! I have to shut it down before it swings back on us!" he yelled over the noise.

Dale looked at Sullivan knowing full well they were losing the battle to the Zodiac. *This will be over before the Sisquay can help us,* he thought. He looked at his pumpkin suit and realized he was still warm and dry despite the sea's repeated attempts to drown them inside the bridge.

At least the controls and gauges are waterproof, Dale said to himself. "Can it be operated manually from outside?" he asked Barney.

"Yeah, we do it all the time in calm water. We just strap into the two long arms on either side of it and aim. But you can't go out there. One good toss from a wave and you're a dead man." The starboard door banged open and snapped back a moment later as Dale grabbed the outside rail and forced his way against the wind. Barney was stunned and pulled the wheel around to the right to ride the boat parallel to the trough between the waves.

The *Chief Seattle* steadied up and Dale rushed forward, grabbing the big, hydraulic water cannon, which was now down and recessed on its casing. Dale hadn't anticipated its weight as it swung free; it was heavier than it looked. In a few seconds, he was attached by his harness safety lines to both sides of the handles on the water cannon. He seized the World War II style mechanical spade grips and leaned in.

On the bridge, Sullivan was turning the smaller, two million-candle-power beam above his head trying to relocate the Zodiac.

Dale pushed down on the articulated foot pedal and the water from the deck cannon shot out into the dark, stormy void. The salt spray that had been washing over him suddenly ceased as the massive water volume created by the cannon's seventy-five-hundred-gallon vortice seemed to suck air forward from behind him. Regaining his bearings, he looked around, following the light that Sullivan was manipulating.

He had to let go for a second to tighten the straps on the goggles that the wind was trying to rip off his face. Reacquiring the handgrips, he saw a reflection off to the right. It wasn't the Zodiac, but rather a round, flashing object. He wrote it off as some kind of channel marker buoy.

As the *Chief Seattle* rode up another wave, this one a long roller, the beam of light caught the small Zodiac again. Barney turned the wheel, the whole time cussing to himself that the FBI agent was going to drown and his fire career would be over.

While struggling to stay upright and turn the boat, Sullivan's eyes wandered from Dale to the Zodiac and Barney's maneuvering. He caught the fire lieutenant's sudden, uneasy mood.

"Barney, Dale has survived far more dangerous things. I think God likes him. He keeps him out of trouble with his own personal entourage of guardian angels. They're out there with him now."

Barney looked at Sullivan a second to say something but saw that the agent's face was calm and concentrating on the battle. *If he survives, I'll kill him myself.*

Outside, the Zodiac disappeared from view again.

Sean trudged up the stairwell, arms wrapped around the top rail in the swaying motion. Sullivan saw his orange suited arm reach out and pull his body up to the bridge rung. Barney heard him step into the cockpit a moment later.

"How's Bob?" Barney asked, looking through the Plexiglas windshield at Dale.

Sean suddenly spotted his brother outside in the rainsquall.

"Holding his own on one lung," he said, focusing on Dale. "We need to get out of this rough water. We can't get to the bullet with all this rocking. Can you help us? He's in bad shape!" Sean replied over the noise of the tossing vessel. "He needs blood. Dave is the same type, so we're gonna tap him for a pint. But we can't do it while we're bouncing all over the place."

"No IV?" Barney asked.

"Can't stick him with the waves slapping us like this," Sean responded. "His BP is sufficient, but that's about it."

Sullivan and Barney saw the blood splotches streaking the front of Sean's orange jumpsuit. Sean retreated below deck again.

Aboard the *Chief Seattle*
Puget Sound, Washington
Friday, 2122 hours Pacific Time

Sullivan shifted his attention off Dale when the edge of the light caught his eye. There, right in front of them, was the tough, little Zodiac with two men clearly outlined in the light.

Shots rang out and bullets ricocheted off the *Chief Seattle's* hull and in front of the water cannon. What was left of the wooden nameplate splintered and disappeared into the screaming wind.

Dale swiveled to the right, struggling with the bulky weight of the water monitor. *I'm gettin' real tired of these guys. Maybe drowning them wouldn't be that bad an idea.* His hands were getting cold.

He shoved his foot down on the operator's pedal and the water stream gushed forth. At seventy-five hundred gallons per minute, the water cannon could fill an Olympic pool in minutes. At first, the water went right over the top of the Zodiac. Dale realized they were too close. Pinging and whizzing noises surrounded him. As each second ticked by, the two vessels pulled further apart until finally he was able to bring the massive deck gun to bear.

The high-volume wave of water struck the small inflatable runabout and snapped it viciously sideways.

Shake that off, dirt bag! That'll teach you to screw with an FBI agent with a big-ass squirt gun.

A wave rolled by, raising the Zodiac out of his line of fire and back into the darkness. A few seconds passed as he searched for it.

Pulling down on the water cannon, he raised the stream and kept aiming at the last spot where he'd seen them. Suddenly he noticed that his orange suit was ripped open and an onslaught of cold was rushing in. A constant wash of icy water and whipping wind poured through over the next thirty seconds. His feet were soaked and the leather belt holding up his pants constricted. His body heat quickly disappeared as the bitter chill enveloped him. Spinning the water cannon around several times, he searched the dark trying to work up some warmth.

Arrhhh, think s-s-s-skiing Dale, b-b-b-beautiful, white powder skiing in the mountains, and steaming, hot c-c-c-chocolate.

The Zodiac appeared directly in front of him again. With a newfound death grip on the hand-sized hydraulic swivel, he blinked hard once and twisted the deck gun left while easing off the foot pedal. The powerful water stream dropped right over the edge and onto the Zodiac. The little runabout disappeared next to the fireboat.

Dale was shivering uncontrollably, but refused to give up the battle. *Just a f-f-f-few more minutes, that's all I need, a few m-m-m-more minutes.* He had a sudden thought and started laughing out loud. *That g-g-g-guy's gonna run out of bullets sooner or l-l-l-later,* he grinned again as his teeth chattered. *I have an inexhaustible s-s-s-supply of seawater to s-s-s-shoot back.* He shook his head stiffly from side to side in an effort to clear the salt spray from his goggles.

Inside the bridge, Barney turned the wheel right to spin the *Chief* around the Zodiac and give Dale another shot. He was enraged that his friend and fellow firefighter might be dying below decks. He would give Dale all the maneuvering room he could to drown these animals.

Sullivan and Sean each manned a spotlight, looking for the little rubber boat to reappear.

Another large wave rolled in, and as it did, the Zodiac rose up level to the *Chief Seattle's* bridge deck, directly abreast of the cockpit. The man on the bow of the inflatable pulled the trigger on his machine gun and unleashed a long burst that blew out what was left of the side windows of the bridge. Sharp pieces of Plexiglas and lead flew around the cockpit. A heavy volume of solid water flashed by the bridge a split second later and slammed the Zodiac before the wave dropped away. Dale threw his weight down on the pedal again and the artificial torrent exploded forward, catching the weather cover on the articulated raft.

From inside the bridge, a startling "whoosh" noise erupted over the storm. Out of sheer frustration, Sullivan fired a blazing red signal flare at the motorized, ribbed craft, hoping to do some damage. The flare zipped by a few feet from the man steering it and disappeared into a wave. Sullivan hurried to reload, but the Zodiac had disappeared.

"Jeez! You guys, okay?" Sean hollered as he reappeared at the top of the stairwell.

Pieces of Plexiglas and cabin debris washed around the floor as the *Chief Seattle* was thrown again by the rolling sea. Sullivan stood up hanging onto the console. He had a long, jagged piece of Plexiglas clearly imbedded in his left shoulder. Barney was lying wounded on the deck. Sean lunged forward, grabbed the wheel, and steered straight for the oncoming wave. Barney put his hand out to push away from the back wall of the bridge, but passed out. His head rolled back and forth as the waves continued pounding the fireboat.

The sound of boots running up from below captured Sean's attention. Terry and Speedy Huey had come up and were viewing the carnage. Seeing Sean at the wheel, Terry rushed in and took over.

With Sean's help, Speedy Huey managed to get Barney below and into another wall mounted survival cot, where the two men began treating him.

The door to the bridge burst open and Dale bounced off the back console. Sullivan reached out and pushed it back to its latch, but not before a heavy torrent of seawater sloshed in.

Dale slid to the floor with his eyes wide open and looked up at Sullivan, "Remember what I t-t-t-told you about being a fire f-f-f-fighter earlier, Sullivan? I've been t-t-t-thinking that over. I'd r-r-r-rather be shot at instead. It's much s-s-s-safer."

Dale took a couple of deep breaths and slowly hoisted himself up off the deck. He noticed the piece of bloody Plexiglas sticking out of Sullivan's shoulder. Staring at his partner's upper arm a moment, he wiped his face free of wet hair. He reached out to Sullivan, and in one quick motion with his gloved right hand, pulled the big sliver out. Dale held it up to his face studying it, his hand still shaking from the frigid temperature.

"Damn, that hurt!" Sullivan yelled in recoil.

"Keep t-t-t-this. Think of it as a s-s-s-souvenir of our day on the water," Dale said, holding out the prize.

It was then that Sullivan saw the bullet holes and torn material in Dale's survival suit, and a red spot on his left leg where the suit flapped open.

"You cold?" Sullivan asked, concentrating on Dale's facial response.

"Not a-a-a-anymore, numb more that anything. Ww-w-w-why do you ask?" he said, shivering uncontrollably.

Sullivan hustled Dale below deck, leaving Terry alone on the bridge. The fight was over. Terry spun the wheel in between waves and headed for the nearest shore.

⚷

"There it is!" the tall man yelled out over the howling sea. "just ahead of us."

The backpack had taken its toll on the commando. His shoulders were in agony, he was battered and bruised, and he was out of ammunition. With any luck, they'd driven the fireboat away. He could see the strobe light ball in the water a few seconds away. He looked around again; the fireboat was out of sight. The Zodiac surged ahead.

⚷

"Stand by to release the divers," Wallen ordered. "Where's the fire-boat?"

"Astern of us, Captain, four hundred-plus yards."

"Combat, do you have a firing solution on target designated number one?"

"Aye, sir, she's locked up."

"Fire!"

The third officer hit the red button on his console. The Mylar-encased, neutered torpedo slipped out of its deck-mounted housing and shot forward, heading for the *Chief Seattle*.

"Chamber, release the divers," Wallen ordered.

The dive chamber at the back of the sub filled quickly. After a few seconds, the four divers ascended up the cabled line toward the raging storm above.

"Grab the ball and hang on. They know we're here!" the tall man yelled. But it wasn't necessary since the flashing, basketball-sized buoy washed into the Zodiac as it drifted by.

"How soon?" the backpack laden commando yelled over the wind, holding firmly onto the ball.

"Within sixty seconds, just hang on."

The two men, who were draped in storm gear and life preservers they had found on the fantail of the cruise ship, kept looking behind the Zodiac, watching for the next set of breaking waves like hawks hunting for field mice.

A moment later, one hooded head, then another, appeared on the line.

"Where's your third man?" a diver asked.

"He didn't make it."

The first diver held out the octopus regulator from his scuba tank and showed the commando how to breathe through it. Seconds later, the taller man went over the side doing the same with a second diver. The third diver took the backpack and disappeared below the waves with the fourth diver.

Sixty feet down, the ghostly, gray image of the submarine came into view below them.

The salt water stung the commando's eyes as he suddenly lost the spare oxygen tether and reacted instinctively to the lack of oxygen. The tall man also found he was suddenly without his air line. The four divers released the air from their buoyancy compensators and drifted lower and out of reach of the two men. The commando lunged for the surface, kicking furiously as the last vestige of oxygen burned off in his lungs. Fifteen feet from the surface, his body fell slowly back to the depths. By the time the four

Nordian divers had cleared the dive chamber inside the submarine, both lifeless bodies were well below the sub.

"Status," the voice on the intercom demanded.

"Sir, the divers are in and the package is secured and contained in the sealed tub; the heater is on.

My handler was in a hazmat suit as you ordered," the dive master reported.

"What about the three men we retrieved it from?"

There was a moment's hesitation on the part of the master chief at the dive chamber. "Two men, sir. Apparently one drowned somewhere along the way. The other two did not make it, sir," he said with barely concealed disgust. He knew clear well that their "guest" was responsible for the "accidental drowning." The extra pay for hazardous duty was a small consolation when he considered that the "guest" viewed everyone aboard the submarine as disposable.

"Very well, chief," Wallen sighed heavily. "thank you."

The captain looked at his "guest."

Thor Odin just smiled. "*Vad är det för* problem, *lugna dig* – relax, Captain, we got what we came for."

The men on the sub's bridge fell silent as the "guest" walked off to the captain's quarters, where he had taken over the master's bunk and room. There was no disguising the ill will of the men aboard.

Perhaps you might pay us a visit later when this is over, Wallen thought silently. *We'll show you the inner workings of the forward torpedo tube, Jäkel*

"Captain," the sonar operator called out, "I just picked up the sound of that Coast Guard cutter. She's driving straight in on us. Sir, I think she heard us when we brought the divers aboard and flooded the chamber."

"Combat, give me a new firing solution on target designated number two with the safeties on. Power up two CHINOs; combat spread at twenty-five feet. Set detonation at fifteen feet below the keel."

"Captain, they're heading straight for us. Evasive maneuvers?"

"Helm, emergency dive, take us down to four hundred feet. Turn to one-nine-five. Combat, where's my firing solution?"

"Still calculating, sir."

As the deck angled down steeply, the sonar man grabbed hold of his computer desk to keep from sliding away. Several pencils and a calculator fell to the deck as the overhead lights throughout the sub switched to red. The declination gauge registered sixteen degrees.

"Captain, we have a solution," the chief called out.

"Where is she?"

⚷

Onboard the *Chief Seattle*, Terry was fighting a tail wave that was trying to slew the boat around. He had the throttle stops all the way up but the water under the keel still seemed to be going by quicker than he was. Another fast moving wall of water lifted him twelve feet as it passed beneath the boat.

To his right in the spotlight that was still on, a huge splash caught his attention. What looked like a small, gray fluke submerged in the passing illumination.

Strange time for a whale to breach, he thought. He returned his attention to reaching the cove and safety, two and a half miles away. Patchy fog was drifting in and out now with the changing temperature, and Terry didn't want to waste any time.

⚷

"She's six hundred yards, sir."

"Fire!"

Two torpedoes silently departed the deck of the sub for their target and quickly gained speed.

The *Sisquay* sliced through the water, chasing the last known position of the subsurface contact.

Her ASW suite was up and running.

Rounding the shallow water edge at the north side of the cove, the fireboat steadied as the water calmed to less than three-foot swells. Terry cut the throttles once he was certain that they were out of the main approach to the cove and engaged the GPS computer. Three hundreds yards in, he turned the fireboat into the wind and hit the autopilot. The *Chief Seattle* held her place, unattended spotlight and all. Terry dashed down the stairwell to check on the status of things.

"How are we doing topside?" Dale asked.

"We're fine, I have the GPS on. We're on the sheltered side of the inlet." They could hear the engines surging to hold the GPS heading.

He looked over at the warm survival bunk and saw Barney lying motionless. His breathing seemed faint. A few feet further down the wall he saw Bob Booker with his feet and legs propped up, also unconscious.

Dale huddled with Sullivan and Sean in the corner.

"Those two guys that were out there in the Zodiac shooting at us may have been picked up by a clandestine submarine from Nord Island. They were shooting at us because we were probably bobbing around on top of their ride out. I talked to Betty Jo earlier, and with all that was happening, I forgot to tell you. She tracked a couple of lost subs and is certain that Nord has some kind of advanced submersible setup." Dale flipped his notepad over.

"She also found out that Odin Pharmaceutical has since moved all of its primary research operations offshore to Nord within the last week. I got confirmation from the FDA when I called in after the bank robbery. Betty Jo was the first to figure it out. If they can create a huge epidemic, then the profits from an antidote could be worth billions. As soon as we set down, we'll notify the Navy. If they can't find the sub and put it down, or get it to surrender, we may be going to Nord to retrieve the rock by force. Needless to say, with Nord Island's owner spreading the disease as fast as he can, we've got a huge problem."

"So everywhere they went with the rock then, they've been spreading contamination," Sean thought out loud, sitting back with his eyes down and focused. He wiped his face slowly as he continued thinking.

"We need to call the CTU again when we land and have that cruise ship quarantined and the bank searched again. We'll have to backtrack the guy's entire route with hazmat teams - from the stores he stopped at to fuel up, to the private airstrips he landed at and the Provo Airport." Dale made another note on the paper in his hand.

Sean looked at Dale as he scribbled. "By the way, whatever possessed you to rush out into a raging storm to throw more water at those guys? I figured they'd drown anyway," Sullivan asked.

"I'm a committed masochist," Dale replied, still writing.

Dave was sitting at the engineer's station. Sean was preparing to put a large bore needle into Dave's arm to siphon off a pint of blood for Bob. Speedy Huey smiled, hoping the makeshift line and bottle Sean rigged up would do the trick.

Sean looked up at the engineer. "Could you check his vitals, Terry?"

A minute later, he announced Bob's blood pressure and respiration, and slipped the oxygen cannula back on Booker's face. "What about Barney?" he asked. "Is he sleeping or unconscious?"

"Unconscious," Speedy Huey replied. "He'll be okay. Eyes aren't dilated, pupils are equal and responsive, BP is good, and respiration is normal but shallow. We took a bagful of Plexiglas shards out of his survival suit and his hide though. I'm all out of small bandages."

"The concussion from the fall put him out," Sean surmised. "Hopefully, all he'll have is a whopper of a headache. We'll need to keep an eye on the swelling, vitals, and check his pupil response frequently."

"I tried the radio," Terry said. "We can't get out to anyone."

"What about the computer?" Dale asked.

"Same mast as the radio," Terry replied.

"Anybody try a cell phone?" Sullivan asked.

Every head took a moment to see if they were getting any signal. No one came up positive.

Dale looked around at the faces. "Hey, Sullivan, better break out the playing cards. We're gonna be here awhile."

"What about your satellite phone?" Terry asked.

"Dead battery," Sullivan replied, holding it up, " . . . and no charger."

Outside, the wind was howling.

"XO, hit the music. Battle stations," the captain ordered.

With a determined look on his face, the balding, thirty-two-year-old executive officer brought the ship to its battle ready standard. The captain passed him the faxed sheet from fleet HQ as the ship went dark.

Grabbing the handset, he pushed the intercom button to the shipwide address setting.

"Battle stations, battle stations, all hands turn to." He passed the word about the rogue submarine to the ship's crew - that and the fact that they were hunting in conjunction with several other regular Navy surface ships that were inbound to join the search.

Men scrambled to their assigned stations, watertight hatches were dogged, loose equipment secured, weapons loaded, and another sonar operator took his seat at the sonar console. Every man aboard knew it was not a drill; their ship had been attacked well within U.S. territorial waters. Their tension now had a release.

On the bridge of the Coast Guard cutter, the damage control party was reporting to the ship's skipper that they had the unexploded torpedo. It was lodged in the starboard side aft supply room, disarmed. The master chief, who was standing over the torpedo, had come aboard the *Sisquay* two weeks earlier, having transferred in from the EOD school as an instructor in exchange for coastal patrol duty.

"Skipper, the body of the torpedo is made of a case-hardened, spun fiberglass design, covered in a Mylar skin. It's not like anything I've ever seen before."

"Can you get it off my ship, Chief?"

"Sir, I've rendered it inert already. We can pull it into the ship a lot easier and dolly it to engineering. I suggest we keep this and turn it over to fleet."

"Tell me why, Chief?" the captain asked.

"The fish's internals are kind of like a high performance, automotive, screw type supercharger. The arming mechanism is similar to our MK 48 torpedoes, but there are some serious differences in the guidance and pro-pulsion systems. I'd like permission to detail the chief engineer to the aft engineering bay where we can open it up further, take pictures, and make a schematic. It's using PBXN explosive, but a lot more than ours. The war-head is about twice the size of a standard MK 48."

"Alright, Chief. Are the extra pumps on and running?"

"Yes, sir."

"Thank you, Chief. Advise me when it's out and the hole is patched."

"Yes, sir."

The sound of high-pitched whistling air and gurgling water ceased with the chief's voice. Turning to the watch officer, the *Sisquay's* captain asked, "Any word on the whereabouts of that fireboat with the FBI agents aboard?"

"Nothing, sir. She's off the air and no one has seen her in the chan-nel."

The captain grimaced and shook his head, "Helm, keep us at eight knots until we have things patched up below."

"Yes, sir." Standing before the automated control panel, the helmsman watched as the ship's speed slowed to ten knots. A barely perceptible tilt to port caused him to shift his footing.

One deck down, the officer in charge of the Special Forces Marines had his team assembled on the captain's orders.

"Something's up," the senior Marine said as he started his briefing. "The *Sisquay's* skipper informed me that the loud bang we heard earlier was a dud torpedo that slammed the hull."

The team's eyes went wide and every ear perked up.

"He thinks there's a foreign nation running a clandestine submarine in U.S. territorial waters. At least that's the word he just gave to fleet. When we dock, we're heading back to Whidbey Island. NMCC may be issuing orders soon and we'll need to prep the mission container," he said, referring to their predeployed cargo containers with mission specific gear.

He held up the e-mail message that had come off the computer four minutes before. It was from his boss, a Marine colonel in Florida.

On the bridge ten minutes later, a second call from Coast Guard fleet HQ came through.

"Captain, you have a secure call from fleet," the watch officer said warily. The captain walked over to the end of the bridge console and picked up the receiver.

Grabbing the intercom mike off its cradle a minute later, he keyed the side button, "Chief, what's the status of the unexploded torpedo?" His tone had switched to no-nonsense and the senior NCO picked up on it immediately.

"She's out and being run into the aft work bay, sir. The, jack, cap, and boards are up and I've got the welder putting on the patch as we speak. It won't be pretty, but it'll be secure."

"Very well, Chief. We're heading out to sea, so make sure it's a *very* secure patch. I don't like the idea of not heading in immediately for repairs, but we've been ordered out so long as we're seaworthy. Oversee it yourself and report back to me when it's done. I'm sending down a work party to move out the supplies and other materials from the space. When it's done, clear the room and make it water tight."

"Yes, sir."

The captain of the *Sisquay* rubbed his eyes and looked out at the nasty storm.

⚷

"The kid is awake and the female paleontologist is stirring!" the micro-virologist exclaimed loudly as he entered the secured lab. All heads turned his way.

"I have the neutrophil traps in the white blood cell count here; they're beating the pathogen." He walked over to the table a few feet away.

"The NETs are on the slide," he said, sitting down at the microscope and putting the sample under the node. "Look, the lemon-green color is encapsulating the red-celled organism. It's killing the viral enzyme," he announced with a flourish.

The three lab physicians in the room took turns looking at the blood sample. The oldest one, from the Fort Detrick military research facility and wearing the uniform of a lieutenant colonel, leaned back, "Now we just need to know why and how the microbes are affected. No one else is exhibiting anything similar to this on their blood workups in this hospital. Last time I checked the transmittals from the collection point, there wasn't anything like this at any other hospital either."

Dr. Hunack looked at his colleagues, "We need to go back to the basics again. We've obviously missed something, some form of ingestion, perhaps? That's the only thing I can think of, the only commonality."

"What?" another doctor asked, trying to understand the issue on the periphery of his technical knowledge.

"How long have those two been in isolation? What was the last thing they ate? What was the chemical composition of the food? What was the interaction between chemical compositions? What is the acidic breakdown release on the chemical compound in the stomach? How about the IV food we're feeding them? Time to take another look," he reiterated.

⸻

The submarine was pushing seventeen knots, knowing that any surface warship would find it hard to pick up their signature on sonar. The first torpedo launched at the cutter had failed to explode. The second missed as the cutter rode the top of a wave trough; it had simply shot by underneath the ship. The captain of the submarine had no idea what had happened to the torpedo dispatched to take out the fireboat, given all the noise they were hearing from the heavy chop in the seas. That torpedo would be discovered two days later, exploded against a cliff on an island just a few miles from the running gun battle between the Zodiac and the *Chief Seattle*.

"Helm, where are we?"

"We're adjacent to the headlands, sir, coming up on deep water. We should clear the straits in a few minutes."

"What's under us?" Wallen asked.

Knowing exactly what the captain was looking for, he scanned the screen to his right. "We're at four fifty-five with six hundred under the keel. It will drop off to fourteen hundred in just a few minutes, sir. New course?"

"Let's turn north to two-eight-five after we exit the straits. Take us down to six hundred-fifty feet and cut us back to twelve knots. Let's see if there's a thermal cline. We should be safe lost in the clutter."

"Mr. Sjorken, you have the bridge."

Wallen walked aft to inspect the sealed tub holding the alien rock that was causing so much work.

⚷

"Captain, we have something in the water just ahead," the watch officer said.

"What's it look like?" the captain asked from his cabin intercom.

"Looks like an empty raft, sir. It may have been lost in the storm off another vessel, or maybe from a shore location."

"Ignore it and keep us on track."

A few seconds later, the *Sisquay* plowed through the water and past the empty Zodiac from the *Majestic Wonder*.

⚷

"We're at sixteen hundred; drop the sonobuoys," the copilot ordered. The P-3 Orion aircraft, now running on all four engines due to the weather, flew straight and level in spite of the nasty buffeting it was experiencing. Through the marked tubes on the floor in the back of the plane, six sonobuoys were slowly jettisoned at designated waypoints. Eight seconds later, the first one splashed into the raging sea and began searching the waters below. Five minutes later, the computer onboard the P-3 Orion showed all six active and pinging away in the pattern.

"DIFAR and MAD are up and looking," the senior chief petty officer said, referring to the magnetic anomaly detector and frequency ranging sensors onboard the sonobuoys.

The eleven-man crew stayed glued to their respective scopes and responsibilities. In the modern nuclear submarine business, a submerged sub could shoot back at aircraft from beneath the waves. The fact that it was a deadly business where the hunter could become the hunted was not lost on the crew.

The P-3 banked left and came back around in an extended sweep.

"Drop two ready?" the copilot asked.

"Yes, sir, just give me the word," the Lieutenant. J.G. replied.

"Torpedoes?"

"Fish are up and running; ready to swim," he responded.

"Okay, stand by for GPS slave to the computer," he said. "Anything on Pulse?" The EP-2060 Pulse Analyzer was searching electromagnetic signals that might be emitted from the submarine they were hunting.

"No joy, still looking."

Seven hundred feet under the cold, north Pacific waters a calm crew felt a chill run down their spines. The overhead speaker on the bridge made every man shiver.

"Captain, we have active sonobuoys in the water," a rushed voice declared over the sub's intercom.

Wallen bolted from the bench in the engine room where he had been talking with his senior chief and dashed forward. Several crewmen pulled back as he jumped over the evenly spaced risers on the deck and raced ahead. Sweat was beading up on his forehead. Everyone onboard could hear the incessant staccato pinging on the hull.

Four miles to the east of the submarine in the channel, the *Sisquay* was pounding away with her sonar. Working in conjunction with the P-3 Orion, she was trying to drive the unknown intruder out to the open sea and into the waiting arms of the U.S. Navy. The *U.S.S. Gary*, a guided missile frigate, was nineteen miles southwest of the channel. The *U.S.S. Pinckney*, a destroyer, was northwest of the channel at about sixteen miles.

Aboard the *Chief Seattle*
Puget Sound, Washington
Friday, 2142 hours Pacific Time

"It doesn't look too bad," Dale yelled to Terry over the screeching winds. "Maybe we can rig another antenna. I saw several below stored on the back wall." Both men stared up to where the long departed antenna post used to be.

"We can sure give it a try. Think you can do it with that bandaged up arm?" Terry yelled over the noise. The inlet was providing relief from the unrelenting storm in the channel. At worst, the *Chief Seattle* was still rocking, but not violently as it had been.

Dale turned away from the rain that was coming down sideways and slapping his face. "It doesn't need to go up high, just needs to be the right kind of antenna. Dave is the only other one onboard uninjured. Let's see if we can have him attach it with some of those heavy plastic tie downs we found in the toolbox."

Both men stepped carefully back down the steel ladder behind the cockpit to the enclosed cabin. The boat swayed a good six feet to the left. In the past half hour, they'd made repairs to the bullet holes with fiberglass patches and industrial sealing caulk. The makeshift fixes were holding up to the wind, so far.

The deck beneath the wood slats on the bridge was dry, the wing windows were boarded up, and the bilge pumps had pumped out the gushing water that had pooled below. Behind them, the engines could be heard occasionally surging to hold their GPS position.

Dale and Terry stepped off the stairwell to hear several voices speaking at once.

Barney was awake with a migraine-sized headache. He tried to sit up but it hurt too much. His almost naked body looked like a patchwork quilt of bandages and gauze strips. He lay back and listened as they discussed the storm and their predicament. All seven men were cooped up below deck, waiting out the storm with no communications to alert anyone to their situation. For all they knew, a search party was out looking for them, or worse, someone may have already assumed they'd gone down in the channel.

"Hey, good to see you awake," Dale said with a ready smile.

Terry leaned in and inspected the bandage on Barney's cheek. He decided it needed changing.

"We're going to try rigging another antenna and see if we can get anyone on the VTS," Terry said.

Lying on the floor on a dry piece of carpeting, Sean opened his eyes, "Hey Dale," he called out, "know what FBI stands for?"

Dale let out a breath and stood motionless. Sullivan nudged Speedy Huey, who looked confused. "Wait for it," he whispered.

"Finally, a Brilliant Idea," he said with feigned sarcasm.

Barney chuckled between the aches.

"Well, that oughtta to do it." Sean said. "Wish we had some saline left for backup, though." He closed his eyes again and tried to sleep.

Terry wrapped the BP cuff around Bob's arm and announced an increase in blood pressure.

"Where did you learn to do that little transfusion routine?" Speedy Huey asked, referring to the unorthodox procedure he had just taken part in. He had been a paramedic for the past thirty-six months and had never seen anything like it.

With his eyes still closed, Sean answered his question, "Old battlefield tactic I pickup up from a Navy corpsman. The platoon I was supporting with my rifle got trapped on a hilltop during a monsoon downpour. The platoon sergeant got blown out of his boots when we got mortared. We ran for cover in the darkness to an old French fort a thousand meters or so away. A Special Forces 'arty camp' shelled the NVA into the ground and things settled down. The rain was so bad, though, that they couldn't put a dust-off in the air for the sergant. So the corpsman crossed his fingers and tapped two guys with matching blood. Thank goodness for dog tags."

Dale and Sullivan threw a handful of radio antennas of varying lengths on the floor and started sorting through them.

"We still had the same problem then that we have right now, though," Sean said. "We need to get Bob to a hospital quick. By the way, little brother, how's the leg?"

Dale patted his calf. "That patch did the job; it was just a small wound," he said, referring to the 9mm bullet that had nicked him.

Sullivan stood up suddenly. "This one should to do it. We can splice it in and tie it off," he declared, holding up a six-foot whip antenna.

Terry grabbed a handful of tools and stuffed them in his pants pockets. He, Dale, and Speedy Huey went topside.

"There's a naval air station on Whidbey Island," Speedy Huey said. "We might be able to raise some help there." Moments later, the trio was out in the pummeling wind hoping for a small miracle.

Utah Valley Regional Medical Center
Secured research lab floor
Provo, Utah, 2158 hours Mountain Time

Sitting down on the new, plush carpeting in the hospital's second floor alcove, Dr. Hunack crossed his legs and leaned back against the open railing. No one would be bothering him since the area was now off limits to the public. He scanned the report that had grown from three pages just a few days ago to eleven pages fresh off the latest, restricted e-mail. Mixed in with the good news that the little boy was alive and complaining about the IV in his arm was the data that showed four hundred twenty-two hospitals in nineteen states with over three thousand dead and a probable infected figure of slightly over sixty-seven thousand.

Schools were now closed in many affected areas, along with public transit and a host of government services that were working by phone, fax, and e-mail only. Commercial businesses were restricting their activities and fast food operators were working the drive-thru windows only. Commerce and banking were being hit hard.

Hunack was trying to comprehend the statistical estimate that said hundreds of thousands would die if the virus wasn't checked quickly. The military actuary he had heard from was right; the exponential explosion of infected patients was killing the country's transportation, finances, services sector, and almost everything else he could imagine.

The little boy's blood workup was being analyzed alongside the twenty-three-year-old female paleontologist. He put the report down, bowed his head, and did something he had not done in awhile. He prayed.

Walking through the hospital foyer at the same time was BYU's dinosaur celebrity, Dalton Jordan, Ph.D. He had come to talk to the doctors treating Tori Evans. He'd made the trip twice a day ever since she was hospitalized.

After first admitting to himself that she was indeed beautiful, inside and out, he finally examined whether there was any substance to the attraction beyond that and the natural sympathy for her condition. It took him a day to realize he had real feelings for her. He had subsequently become more morose and depressed as a result.

On the second day, he met her parents. He did the best he could to comfort them in her absence. They quickly formed a mutual bond.

The physicians treating Tori seemed to have a never-ending stream of new questions every time Jordan was present. After intense questioning about her activities leading up the moment of her collapse in the helicopter, they finally told him that she was semiconscious and stable. As of yet, she wasn't aware of her surroundings, but that seemed just a matter of hours away. He wondered how much of that was just wishful thinking.

Dalton had really arrived that evening with two missions in mind. The second one was to identify the remains of his cousin, Sally, who had died early that afternoon from the virus. The authorities suspected she had contracted the disease at her pharmacy from another infected person. Jordan felt a great deal of grief since it was his university crew that had unleashed the dug-up virus that was killing people.

Standing idly in front of a painting hanging in the main hallway, he could see his reflection in the glass, and it was downright gloomy. After a moment, he moved on.

The normally cheerful, outgoing Jordan was looking forward to his upcoming trip by private jet to Seattle for the grand opening of a new, ultramodern, Dane-Cutter interactive museum collection of Cretaceous period creatures. He and the museum's primary sponsor would be cutting the ribbon together. He had never met the museum's reticent benefactor, but he had seen his picture on many occasions and knew all about him. The man's presence was a well-kept secret that would only be revealed to patrons at the opening ceremony on Sunday at noon.

Jordan stopped at the water cooler and took a drink. He looked down at his size twelve shoes and decided they needed polishing.

I wonder what Douglas Odin is really like behind all the public relations hype? Probably a regular guy with an incredibly large bank account, he thought.

"Take us down to eight hundred and level off," Wallen ordered. "Sonar, I'm looking for another thermal. Call it out for me when you have it. Helm, when we hit the next thermal, I want you to come around to one-nine-five and slow us to eight knots. Combat, I want four CHINOs up and ready to counter any ordinance they may send down. Mr. Sjorken, condition red, and pass the word 'no noise.' Secure everything onboard immediately."

The men on duty were feeding off adrenaline. The sonar operator was listening intently for a helo or aircraft launched torpedo being dropped into the water.

"Mr. Sjorken, secure all nonessential electrical usage on the boat, minimal life support. I want the tiles boosted to one hundred ten percent as long as you can hold it; everyone to their bunks if they're not on duty."

⚷—★

"The only thing so far is a pod of killer whales, lieutenant," the Lieutenant J.G. replied into his headset.

"Alright, we're going to run out a little further and drop a few more and extend the grid," the pilot said. The big P-3 Orion banked right and headed west. In four minutes the aircraft would take up a new heading, drop down from its current altitude of forty-three hundred feet, and feed out another six sonobuoys.

⚷—★

"This is *Chief Seattle* at 'Boon's Cove.' any Coast Guard station copy?"

A few seconds went by without anything but static.

"*Chief Seattle,* this is Whidbey N.A.S. Good to hear from you, sir. We thought we'd lost you in the storm," the radio operator said. "What is your status?"

"We have two injured on board, including one in serious condition," Terry replied. He gave them their GPS position.

"*Chief Seattle,* Boon's Cove has an unmarked, small ship dock about a half mile from your position. There is a channel running east-west from the cove entrance. If you approach it on a direct ninety degree heading, you can tie up to it. We'll have a medevac in the air in five minutes for the clearing at the end of the dock."

"Whidbey N.A.S., we will head for the dock. See you in a few minutes," Terry responded.

Twenty minutes later, the Sea Hawk rescue chopper lifted off with Barney and Bob being attended to by Navy corpsmen. A second, unexpected helo settled to the ground right behind it. Racing up the steel dock was a Navy ensign. He was soaked to the skin by the time he opened the door to the fireboat's bridge.

"Agent Fox! Agent Casse!" he yelled out, not seeing anyone.

"Someone's here. Did you order pizza?" Sullivan said to Dale.

"Down below, watch the stairwell," Dale hollered back.

Sean slowly opened his eyes and sat up. "Hawaiian pizza, I hope he brought Hawaiian."

Agent Fox, I'm Ensign Poole," the harried, young naval officer said. "We have a helicopter outside. We have to leave immediately, sir."

"Can we stop for pizza on the way?" Sean asked.

"What's up, Ensign?" Dale said ignoring his brother's hunger pangs.

"Sir, Mr. Covery at the CTU has a tasking order from NMCC - National Military Command Center." He handed a sealed envelope to Dale, who ripped it open.

Sullivan was now standing next to Dale, looking at the single piece of paper.

"NMCC my ass," Sullivan remarked. "That's got bigger fingerprints on it," he whispered to Dale.

"Yeah, I agree." Dale folded it up and put it in his pocket.

"Okay, Ensign, let's go." Thinking for a moment, he looked at his brother, "Sean you can't stay here waiting out the storm. Better go with us. Oh, I forgot to tell you, I had you federally deputized by presidential decree a little while ago. Congratulations, Special Agent Sean Fox."

"The White House called your fire chief and he said we could have you. They sent him a bushel of apples for the deal and a new recruit to be named later," he chuckled. "Take that, fire twit."

Sean stood up, twisted his neck around and got the sleep out of his bones. "Hmmm, I'll have to give that some thought. But if I'm going to get wet again, I want a hot pizza. Can the Navy handle that, Ensign?" he said with mock indignation.

The ensign looked bewildered.

The four men plodded up the stairwell and said goodbye to Terry and Speedy Huey, who were now stuck until the storm subsided and they could get the boat back to Seattle.

"Sullivan, you got the satellite phone?" Dale asked.

Sullivan handed it over to his partner.

Turning to the copilot, Dale tapped his elbow, "You have a universal connector for a satellite phone?"

"Yeah, hold on. Here you go, it's plugged in."

Dale slipped the receiving end into the phone and it lit up immediately.

Ninety seconds later, he was talking with Dan Covery at the CTU and updating their progress.

Once in the air, Sean noticed they were heading out to sea. "We're not going to the base, Ensign?"

"No, sir, we're on our way out to the *U.S.S. Pinckney*."

"You don't have to call me, sir, Ensign. I'm a firefighter."

"I'm the lowest ranking commissioned officer in the U.S. military. I call everyone sir," he replied, not knowing the full scope of what he was into.

"My orders come from fleet headquarters through a full bird captain. I was told to give you any assistance you asked for, with the understanding that everyone I meet greatly outranks me." He tactfully retreated to the far side of the helicopter.

Sean looked at his brother, "Am I really a federal agent or were you yanking my chain?"

"Yeah, I really did it, and blessed by the powers that be."

"Why?"

"We may need a creative rescue expert before this is over, and you're the closest thing I know of to a human Swiss knife."

Letting that sink in, Sean sat back in his mesh net seat, singing Johnny Rivers' "Secret Agent Man" to himself.

"I'll take care of the back track if you can find out what's in front of us as soon as we land," Sullivan said. He turned to address the ensign, "What kind of ship is the *Pinckney*?"

"It's a destroyer, sir."

"Good," Sean thought out loud. "They'll have hot pizza."

The helicopter roared into the storm, bouncing as it hit air pockets and wind shear.

Aboard the *U.S.S. Pinckney*
Twenty-two miles off the Washington coast
Friday, 2340 hours Pacific Time

As the helicopter descended in the wind and fog, the ship's aft landing deck lights came into view. Off to the port side of the ship, Sullivan spotted another chopper moving downwind.

"What's with the other chopper?" he asked the copilot.

"Two choppers, actually; MarSOC guys off the *Sisquay*."

"The temperature on the stove just went up," Sullivan said to Dale.

Dale dug into his backpack. "Sean put this on." He threw his brother his yellow windbreaker with the bold lettering on the back that read FBI. "Now you're official."

Sean zipped it up and smiled momentarily at the smaller FBI lettering on the front pocket.

Four minutes later, they were on the bridge of the *Pinckney*, talking with her commander.

"We have her boxed in," he said to Dale and Sullivan, referring to the foreign sub. "It's just a matter of time. We're operating on the assumption that it's probably North Korean, though they haven't really been open sea mariners in submarines before. Could be Red Chinese or Russian, but that's a long shot."

"Captain, we believe this submarine is from Nord Island," Dale said.

"What? That's a recreational paradise for the rich. What the hell would

Nord be doing with a submarine? Where did you get that information?" he asked with surprise.

"What do you know about our mission, Captain?"

"Just that we took you aboard in relation to a foreign submarine bearing some kind of toxic geode. I assumed you were involved as technical experts in high-risk, low profile hazmat security. That and arrest the crew if we can force her to the surface. Where did I go wrong?" he said with a commanding stance.

"It's a stealthy submarine or it wouldn't have gotten into the straits undetected. Douglas Odin owns it."

"The billionaire?" he replied, loosening up.

"Odin is the wizard behind the curtain. As for us, we are not technicians. I am the senior field supervisor with the FBI's counterterrorism unit. I want to recover that rock intact and get it back to Fort Detrick to reverse engineer an antidote because that virus is killing our citizenry."

"Yeah, we've seen the TV reports. Where did you obtain this information?" he said, not ready to concede his position.

Dale stood his ground and took a breath, "Confidential sources developed during our investigation. It's solid. If you would like, I'll be happy to have the White House call you." He pulled a faxed memo out of his pocket and handed it to the captain. He handed it back after reading it twice.

The commander of the *Pinckney* thought about it a briefly. "Son, I believe you. It's just on the other side of the realm of consideration. Okay, we'll proceed on that basis."

The skipper of the destroyer laid out the search plan and promised to notify the three FBI agents the moment anything happened.

"By the way, the admiral tells me your father is an MOH. Says you two guys are a chip off the old block, former Marines yourselves. But I thought you were a firefighter," he said, pointing to Sean, who was decked out in his new FBI jacket.

"He was, until an hour ago when he was federalized. He's a full-fledged and sanctioned FBI agent now. Skipper, any chance we can get him armed up? He's going to need it," Dale asked.

"Master-at-arms to the bridge," the quartermaster called out behind them.

"We'll get you escorted to your quarters to settle in. If you have a few minutes, say hello to your brethren that just came aboard," he replied, referring to the MarSOC team that had landed behind them. "They're getting settled in with their own gear below. From the sound of it, you guys may be working together before this is over."

The master-at-arms entered the bridge.

"Chief," the XO said, "Take this FBI agent below to the weapons locker and let him pick out a firearm and supply. He lost his in the storm through no fault of his own. Then show them all to their quarters."

"Aye, sir. Gentlemen, if you'll follow me."

"Captain, one last thing," Sullivan asked. "We need to use the comm room for a few minutes."

"Fine. Whenever you're ready, I'll have the XO show you where it is and get you set up. Joe, can you see to that?"

"Yes, sir. This way, gentlemen."

Dale's second secure call was to the CTU, where Dan Covery informed him of a further presidential finding that dealt with Nord Island, and additional clarification from the presidential directive. The gloves were off. A congressman from Utah and two state senators from Idaho were infected. The death toll had gone over four thousand.

"The president has asked me to pass on his praise for the work you and Sullivan have done so far. You found the sunken cabin cruiser, reacquired the terrorist on the wharf, and called the bank vault escape right. You commandeered the only seaworthy vessel in the area and gave pursuit, and shot it out with armed terrorists on the water in a raging storm. He called that damn amazing, using the fireboat's water cannon to fight back. Nice job of figuring out that that unaccounted-for Black Hawk was Nordian. We still don't know where they requisitioned it, but twenty-eight countries have them now. Given the crisis status of this situation, his only bright moment was when I told him you guys were doing all of this while you were supposed to be on vacation. He says we're going to make that up to you with interest. Oh, by the way, how's that gunshot wound?"

"Minor item, I'm fine."

"How about Sullivan's shoulder?"

"He's hard as nails. He's alright."

"I'll amend the last report," Covery said.

"Thanks, I've got one more round peg to insert here," Dale continued. "I may have found the origin of this submarine we're searching for." Dale took three minutes to brief Covery on the information he'd picked up.

"Ah, one last thing, Dale," Covery interjected, "the president has instructed the U.S. ambassador to the U.N. to sign on as a signatory to the 'Nord Island Independence Treaty' first thing in the morning. That'll make them a recognized, belligerent, foreign power for all intents and purposes."

"I like it," Dale replied.

Dale returned to his cabin, where Sullivan was busy with the new, in-room comm uplink. Sean was sitting on the lower bunk eating pizza.

"Sullivan, do you know when we change time zones going west?"

"Funny you should ask. Straight down from Alaska; Nord Island is the next zone over."

"Anything on the database?" Dale asked

"Sentinel Phase II is up and running. I love this database, beats the hell out of ACS. Now we're out of the dark ages and catching up with the rest of the world."

"What's ACS?" Sean asked.

"The FBI's version of an abacus," Dale replied sarcastically. "Now we can query all kinds of bureau info unless it's on hold or a current pending investigation. As a supervisory level employee in CTU, I can bypass some of the lockouts to get data on current activity. Anything else we need, Covery can download to us."

"I got something here," Sullivan announced, "It's the latest report from ground zero on the virus, ahh, bad news."

Sean sat up and put down his pizza.

"Local Centers for Disease Control officer says the death toll was about forty-two hundred at 1100 hours local time. Estimated infection is now almost seventy thousand in twenty-eight states. Europe is considering a ban on U.S. travelers. In the small miracle department, a little kid and the twenty-three-year-old female paleontologist who found the rock in a dinosaur quarry in eastern Utah are both awake. Now if the medical wizards can just figure out why, maybe we'll be closer to a solution."

"My fire department's at the other end of the valley. I wonder how they're doing?" Sean said.

"Give 'em a call in the morning. Meanwhile we need to get some sleep. We'll be running hard tomorrow, we're going to Nord," Sullivan said.

"Good idea," he replied, pulling off his shoes and socks. "Dibs on the first shower in the morning."

Aboard the Nordian submarine
Twenty-nine miles off the Washington coast
Friday, 2344 hours Pacific Time

Nine hundred sixty feet down no one was resting. The pinging noise from the *Sisquay* and the sonobuoy's was keeping the stealthy submarine's crew on edge. They were at their operational maximum depth.

"Captain, we're through the second thermal cline and the tiles are running at one hundred three percent. I don't think they're going to detect us, sir, we're pretty well cloaked," the XO said.

"We'll see, Mr. Sjorken. In the meantime, get some sleep. I'll stand the watch for the next three hours."

The XO walked off the bridge and headed aft. He was now bunking with the chief of the boat since the captain had been displaced by Thor Odin.

"Helm, slow us to five knots, and let's see if we can squeeze through this gap here," he said, pointing to a map reference on the color monitor. "Reel out the sonar drape three hundred yards astern, and let's put a pod of killer whales on the line. That ought to overload their sonar."

"Aye, Captain."

The constant incessant pinging was taking its toll on the crew, especially the sonar operator whose nerves were frayed.

Aboard the *U.S.S. Pinckney*
One hundred twelve miles west of Washington state
Saturday, 0600 hours Pacific Time

Reveille came in the form of a hard door knock at 0600. A petty officer informed the three men that the mess was open and serving. The stormy, dark morning sea was still causing havoc outside as Sean observed from the seat of his pants.

"Always full of good news," Dale said, rolling out of his bunk and searching for his shoes that had migrated across the room during the night's storm.

"How big is this ship, anyway?" Sullivan asked, not knowing if Dale or Sean knew.

"Five hundred twenty feet or so, and about nine thousand tons," Sean offered, "not quite a cruise ship." He looked around for his shoes, too.

True to his word, Dale was in the shower first.

On the bridge of the *Pinckney,* the end of the red weather cells could be seen at the far end of the meteorologist's weather scope. But they had the rest of the day and into the early night before it would subside. Sheets of rain and the dark sky still stared at the crew through the bridge windshield.

"Why don't you guys get some chow. I'm going to talk to someone on the bridge and check our status. I'll catch up to you shortly," Dale said ten minutes later. He opened the door and turned right, walking purposefully down the passageway with his gold shield FBI badge clearly evident on his jacket.

In the ship's mess hall, Sean and Sullivan got in line, loaded up a tray of food, and found a seat. They quickly became the topic of discussion among the sailors sitting around them. They ate quietly and looked around the interior of the room, taking in the occasional stares without responding.

"Wonder where we'll be sleeping tonight." Sullivan commented.

"A warm fire station would be nice," Sean replied. "We'll know in a minute. Here comes Dale with a Marine officer in tow."

"Captain, this is Agent Casse and Agent Fox, my older brother by chance."

The all business, muscular Marine officer held out his hand, "Israel George," he said, "pleasure to meet you."

"I gotta ask, Captain, which one is your first name?" Sullivan said.

"I guess I could ask you the same thing, sir."

"Touché, Captain, it's Sullivan."

"Mine's Israel," he replied with a firm handshake. "I'm the C.O. of Marine Special Forces Team Sierra."

"Grab some food and let's talk," Sullivan said.

The sailors around them took immediate note of the hard-edged Special Forces Marine officer, something they rarely encountered on a destroyer. The buzz was all over the ship, a big nasty op was coming.

"No contact or luck with the Nordian submarine," Dale said quietly so no one else could hear. "Looks like it slipped away in the storm. A couple of P-3s dropped sonobouys all night long with no success."

He took a bite of food as Sean refilled his cup with cold milk.

"Got a message from O'Brien on e-mail. He found a bill of lading on the cabin cruiser for a big bunker oil shipment that doesn't show up on any manifest from Nord Island's accounts payable financial complex. Somebody squealed and the cabin cruiser was attacked. Best guess is they were trying to hide the submarine's existence and somebody sent the bill to the wrong department, all on Odin Industries letterhead. We have our smoking gun," Sullivan said.

They all became silent, stopping a moment to consider the implications of that find.

Dale rubbed his nose and started to talk. "I'll call Dan at the CTU and pass it on, decision time by noon. Meanwhile, we tune up our game for the inevitable. When we're done here, let's check e-mail, take care of any calls, and then join Captain George back here for a field ops session."

The Marine captain leaned in, "Our orders are coming from MarSOC HQ at Camp Pendleton. They get theirs from MarSOC, who get theirs from NMCC, which in turn gets it from the White House, which I understand is information you guys are supplying them. Do I have that right?"

"That's what they tell us. We're the point of the spear, you might say," Sullivan said between bites of sausage patty.

"I understand your dad is a Marine Medal of Honor recipient," the officer said to Dale and Sean. "The *Pinckney's* skipper told me last night."

Sean looked at Dale and lowered his head back down to his fork.

"Yeah," Dale responded.

"We had dinner with a retired Marine MOH in Montana a few months back. He served the best cornfed steaks I've ever had. It was a once in a lifetime treat to spend time with someone of his caliber. That man mentioned he had a legacy with two sons. You wouldn't be them by chance?" George asked.

"If you met Dad, then you completed the 'Punch and Pulverize' course," Sean said quietly. "That lake you spent time on is our home and favorite childhood fishing hole. I hope you didn't disturb the fish. I'm going back there next month for a few days with my best fishing pole."

A camaraderie and Marine Corps bond with Sean was instantly created. Captain Israel George came to like the father and now the sons.

"You're the shooter?" he asked.

"I'm the shooter," Sean replied quietly.

"Your father says you still compete," he stated, fishing for a response.

"Oh, now and then, for fun," Sean said humbly.

Israel took a little time to explain to them how the new Special Forces Marines were structured and how they operated.

"So other than the uniform, you're just like the Navy SEALs, Green Berets, or Parajumpers," Sullivan replied.

"We like to think that the new training, equipment, and tactics are a build-on to what's been done previously. All of the Special Forces community crosstrain and support each other. The uniforms may be slightly different, but we all bleed the same American blood. Even when we were Force

Recon Marines, we worked in conjunction with the SEALs for decades. Marine Special Forces first appeared in WWII as Marine Raiders. Force Recon Marines surfaced in Vietnam. In 2006, MarSOC stood up," he said, pushing his empty plate out of the way.

"Unlike the Navy SEALs or Green Berets, MarSOC Marines do not wear any special uniform insignia. It makes it easier to maintain a low profile and sustain the Corps' cohesive nature."

A few minutes of conversation later, they finished eating, shook hands, and disappeared in different directions, with an agreement to meet up at 0930 hours in the Marine's assigned hangar bay to look at options for assaulting Nord Island. The deadly geode was getting closer.

Aboard the Nordian submarine
One hundred forty-nine miles off shore
Saturday, 0608 hours Pacific Time

"Captain, the destroyer is falling behind us. We're eight thousand yards out from her search pattern," the sonar operator said.

"Are the seas still running high?" he asked, yawning. He had rolled out of his bunk two minutes before and came to the bridge.

"They're about fifteen to eighteen feet, sir. The end of the heavy storm cells came up an hour ago at the edge of the weather scope. The storm will start to dissipate around dusk."

"How far is Nord?"

"It's about one hundred eighty nautical miles, sir."

"What's on the radar scope?"

"We have five cargo containers south of us, inbound toward Washington or Canada. I show three combat vessels, probably all U.S. origin, and an oil tanker, outbound north of us about twenty miles."

"That's it, pretty light because of the storm, then. We'll be home by dark." He looked up at the bulkhead gauge and saw that they were running at eight knots and seven hundred forty feet.

"Has our guest been up to visit yet?"

"No, sir, he's in his, I mean, your stateroom."

Good, he thought to himself. *The sooner we get home, the sooner I can get rid of him.*

Fog and whipping rain still lashed the sea above.

"Mr. Sjorken," Wallen said quietly, leaning into his second in command, " . . . when this mission is complete, I want the ship restocked with full provisions immediately. I believe that our usefulness to Mr. Odin may be at an end. We will wait until Odin senior departs for the mainland. Retrieve the balance of our crew from the island and make ready to depart."

Wallen was referring to the CHINO torpedoes, which were worth a million and a half dollars each. He had made arrangements to sell the fifteen in the deck-mounted enclosure for a little over thirteen million to Malaysian pirates. Wallen had used his commando team to capture five cargo vessels, whereupon he stole their payroll and useable valuables before sinking them. One of the ships had almost two million U.S. dollars onboard in its safe. He set the sailors adrift and opened the seacocks to send their ships to the bottom. So far, the crew had amassed a small fortune they would each share in, much like the pirates of the 17th century.

Unlike those pirates, this crew had a warship that rivaled anything plying the ocean. Now if Wallen could just make good on his plans to deliver the rock and depart unnoticed from Nord.

At 0928, Dale, Sullivan, and Sean walked down the long corridor to the helo bay together. According to a notice on the hangar bay door, the area was restricted. Out of respect for the Marines, he knocked. A moment later, a crew cut Marine staff sergeant opened the door.

"Gentlemen, you must be the FBI CTU guys we've heard about. Come on in. The door opened wider and closed quickly behind them. If you'll follow me, sirs, Captain George is out by the fantail door."

Two dozen hardcore Marine Special Operators were walking through a drill about seventy feet back. The three FBI agents waited and watched until they were finished.

Israel George trotted over. "I got my package download about twenty minutes ago. How did you do at your end?"

"My intel source provided me the schematics to their security net," Dale responded. He didn't let on that it was his fiancée. "Last update was four months ago, but it's an expensive and extensive network system. I doubt it's seen much modification, if any. Let's find a room with a conference table and look at what we have."

At 1155 hours, they broke for lunch. As the thirty-two Marines, with Dale, Sullivan, and Sean bringing up the rear, marched through the mess hall doors, the *Pinckney's* sailors looked on with a bit of awe. After lunch, Israel George, his XO, a first lieutenant, and two of his senior NCOs retreated back to the conference room, where several overlay schematics of the island were laid out on the table and tacked up on the walls.

Aboard the Nordian submarine
Eighty-four miles from Nord Island
Saturday, 1611 hours Pacific Time

"Captain on the bridge," a sailor called out. Behind him was their casually dressed guest, Thor Odin.

"Where are we, Mr. Sjorken?" Wallen asked.

Sjorken's composure changed with Odin on the bridge. Sjorken viewed the man as the devil's offspring. He had considered spiking the man's food with a small sliver of the virus embedded rock. If not for the technical difficulty, he would have already done so.

With monitor control in hand, Wallen punched the zoom button and waited a few seconds as the picture enlarged.

"We're estimating our position here, sir, about ninety-seven miles directly east of Nord. We won't know our exact position until we can access a satellite."

Wallen looked at the screen and noted their speed and depth. They were running at seven hundred fifty feet.

"Let's confirm our position," Odin stated, with the understanding that he expected it done immediately. "I want to know how soon we'll be back."

"With all due respect, Mr. Odin, that could be a dangerous thing to do. Sonar, what's above us?"

"The storm has been tapering off, sir. We have seas running at ten to fourteen feet. There are two container ships south of us, about thirty-one and thirty-seven miles respectively, heading southwest on a heading of two-one-five degrees. We had a big 'drifter' – commercial fishing trawler - of unknown origin directly behind us two hours ago, but they went over the horizon heading due east. And a cruise ship passed by about two hours ago southbound, but they're off the scope now as well. There's no way right now to determine what air assets are above us."

"Helm, take us up to two hundred feet, slow bubble up, and let's see if there's anything in the air."

"Aye, Captain." The submarine inclined slightly.

Odin stood off to the side with his arms crossed and a blank look on his face. No one in the room knew what he was thinking due to his impassive stare. His previously broken nose and the noticeable scar on his jaw made him look like an unsavory character when he hadn't shaved for a few days.

As the two-hundred-sixty-three-foot-long sub rose slowly, the sonar operator closed his eyes and listened carefully for the sound of any surface activity. Not hearing anything, he opened his eyes and looked at the color screen in front of him. There were no electrical oscillations present. He slid the primary wavelength bar from far right to its stop on the low frequency scale on the left. He nudged the secondary lever hesitantly back in the other direction, carefully searching for any electrical transient.

He leaned back and keyed his intercom, "Clear so far, sir."

Helm, slow us to four knots, then take us up to seventy-five feet," Wallen ordered.

Odin stood mute and waited.

"Seventy-five feet, sir."

"Sonar, anything?"

Another minute passed. "Nothing, sir."

"Raise the mast," Wallen said into the microphone around his neck. He waited until the two green lights came up, indicating the mast had detected mass oxygen.

"Pan left," he said softly into the boom mike around his neck. The mast spun as the ship made minimal headway. After a full turn he reversed direction.

Lots of long waves, he thought to himself.

"Pan vertical," he said into the boom mike. He couldn't see any aircraft due to the low scud that wafted over the waves like a dirty blanket.

Suddenly the light in the camera array went dark, and a moment later the mast jutted out of the water. The entire length of the submarine slapped the surface.

"We're porpoising! Emergency dive, three hundred feet. What happened?"

The ship settled down hard at a steep angle.

"Sir, it looks like we ran through a rogue wave trough and got air," the helmsman said. The declination gauge showed fourteen degrees down angle.

"Did we pick off a satellite?" he said angrily, hoping for the best.

"Yes, sir. Calculating GPS, stand by."

Odin held fast to the ship's rib and waited.

"We're eight-four nautical at two-eight-zero to the airport beacon," he said, reading off the reverse angle to the New Borgholm City Airport on Nord Island.

"Helm, take us back down to nine hundred and inform me when we hit a thermal."

"Aye, sir, nine hundred with a thermal."

Wallen looked at Odin, who suddenly appeared satisfied. He walked off the bridge and disappeared aft.

Wallen enjoyed the challenge of submarine operations, but he was filled with conflict, not the least of which occurred the day he took the job and Odin's seven-digit check. It wasn't until a week later that he came to realize that his family, three nieces, and two nephews would always be in danger if he didn't perform as directed by his vicious boss. It was a conversation he had with the head of Odin's security team, who had delivered the news that lack of compliance to even the slightest demand from Odin might create a problem back in Sweden for his relatives. Wallen understood immediately that he wasn't in this alone. His unhappiness had turned to disgust, and finally a latent hatred for the man. Killing his arrogant son would not bother him in the least.

Onboard the U.S.S. Pinckney

At 1623 hours, the wall phone in the hangar ready room went off.

"Gunny Corbett." The conversation was short and pointed. He hung the phone back up seconds later.

"Captain needs you on the bridge, double time," he said looking at Dale. "Something's up."

Dale trotted out of the room and through the restricted door to the passageway outside where he picked up the pace. The door to the bridge swung open as he got close. A chief petty officer closed it behind Dale.

The captain was holding out a phone in his hand, "It's for you, Agent Fox."

"Fox."

"Dale, it's Dan Covery. Somebody activated that transmitter you slapped on the Lexan casing. Copy this GPS coordinate down."

Dale grabbed his pen from his pocket, "I need a piece of paper."

The quartermaster handed him a yellow pad.

"Go ahead, Dan."

"The signal matches the registry number on the transmitter you thought you hit the box with. About seven minutes ago, we picked up a weak transient that went on for about fifteen seconds and then disappeared again." Covery gave him the GPS figures.

"Captain, where is this on the map?" Dale asked, turning toward the *Pinckney*'s skipper.

After checking the coordinates, he pointed to a spot on the electronic map in the ocean west of them.

"It's aboard that Nordian submarine," Dale said to Covery as the bridge crew overheard his end of the conversation. All ears perked up. Sullivan and Sean entered the bridge.

"Looks like she got away," the captain complained. "She's about eighty-five miles east of Nord Island. She's a long way from us."

"Dan, there's no way to catch up to her. But it does confirm that the rock's case is on the sub. She probably surfaced for a few seconds to have a look around."

"Dale, the president has pushed everything else off his calendar. I spoke with him and the Joint Chiefs less than an hour ago. The death toll is over fifty-five hundred now. I have to call him back immediately. Get ready, we're going in."

The line to the CTU went dead.

"Time to go see Israel George and have a chat," Dale said to Sullivan. The three men strolled from the bridge.

49

Aboard the *U.S.S. Pinckney*
One hundred six miles southwest of Nord Island
Saturday, 1634 hours Pacific Time

"We'll see blue sky tomorrow morning, Captain," the Navy lieutenant-meteorologist said. "It will taper off over the next few hours. Winds are crossing over us at thirty-three knots from two-five-zero."

"Get this down to Captain George and those FBI agents. God help them all."

The commercial jet touched down in Seattle. Smoke curled off the back of the tires as the thrust reversers engaged. After picking up his luggage and grabbing a cab, Dr. Dalton Jordan made his way to his harborside hotel less than a mile from the new museum.

"Do you know where the new dinosaur museum is down by the wharf?"

"Yes. It's scheduled to open in the next few days," the driver said.

"Do you think we could drive by it on the way to the hotel?"

"Sure, no problem."

Jordan sat back and thought about the dignitaries invited to attend, including several other notable paleontologists from around the country. The trip was made a little better with the knowledge that Tori was recovering. His self-realization that she was more than a simple personal interest was digging under his skin. He wondered for a moment if the ten-year age difference between them was insurmountable. His stomach growled and he suddenly aware that he had yet to eat anything since rising that morning.

⚷

Dr. Walter Hunack walked into the lab for the third time during his shift. Four other research scientists were busy running another test on Tori Evans' blood sample, trying to find some common thread with the sample obtained from the orphaned boy who had also survived. As yet, their efforts had proven frustrating.

"Good news. We have another survivor," Hunack announced.

One by one they disengaged from their project and looked at Hunack.

"We have a thirty-two-year-old, white male adult from Salt Lake who came down ill four days ago. He's a delivery driver for a grocery chain. He woke up." Hunack looked at his watch, "…eleven minutes ago. I'm on my way up there now. I'll be back in an hour with the blood samples."

"It's a longer drive than that," one of the scientists said.

"They're warming up a chopper in the parking lot," Hunack replied. "Hopefully, a third sample will get us somewhere." Hunack exited the door and trotted down the hallway for the elevator.

⚷

The sleek, blue helicopter slowed and circled the mountainside mansion southwest of Portland, Oregon. The retractable wheels were lowered and the pilot aimed for the circular landing pad off to the side of the forty-four-acre compound. The mansion's owner was in Europe on vacation for a month. He was a longtime business associate of Douglas Odin. Odin had cultivated the man more than two decades earlier for his exceptional management talent, and in the process, made him very wealthy in his own right. Indebted to Odin, the mansion's owner had made a standing offer to his mentor; Odin could use the place anytime he wished.

The staff came running out with umbrellas as the carbon fiber blades of the helicopter quickly spun down. Odin and his son, Thor, stepped out with two security people after the overhead blades stopped rotating. Nine other Odin security men were already on the property. He could see four of them as he headed up the walkway steps bordered by the recently trimmed hedge.

Down the hill was a seven-acre, man-made lake with a small dock the owner spent time on when his young grandkids visited.

"It's an honor to have you visit us again, your highness," the chief butler said, greeting Odin by his preferred princely title. "The full staff is in attendance and ready to serve you as you require." The man backed away and waited for Odin to acknowledge him. Odin smiled, thanked him, and walked inside.

The two burly security people from the helicopter followed closely behind.

Aboard the U.S.S. Pinckney
Twenty-two miles southwest of Nord Island
Sunday, 0318 hours Pacific Time

In the aft hangar bay that had been turned over to the MarSOC Marines, the Special Forces Operators were all dressed in their new, digital camo-pattern RAGS assault gear. The Radar Absorbent Gear Suits were newly issued to the Special Forces community. Constructed of Kevlar, Nomex, and synthetic honeycomb systo-poly fibers, they trapped and dissipated radar waves. Parachuting in at three thousand feet, they looked to be about the size of a seagull on a radar return. Any metal equipment, such as firearms, radios, and other hardware they carried, were double bagged in RAGS sling bags and afforded the same protection. The only downside was that the gear was a little warm to wear on a sunny day.

Captain Israel George slid a waterproof, low altitude orientation map across the table. The ship's data center had just printed it off from a satellite.

"We have an AWACs wheels up in about fifteen minutes from Kitsap. They'll take over the airport radar system when we're a couple of minutes from the horizon. SEAL teams two and three will HALO in the new gear to the west side of the island and take over the airport and the power station master grid. The radar will remain up but the operators will not be controlling or reporting what they see. We need it open for the commercial traffic beacon for north-south international sea traffic. Team three will cut power to the south side of the island. When the power goes out, the backup power systems will kick in at the various Odin secure facilities. When that happens, Watt One will drop down from its standoff track and will overload burst their transmitters."

"What is Watt One?" Sullivan asked.

"It's something new from G.E. Electric that the 22nd Special Tactics Squadron out at McChord Air Force Base has. It's a stealthy upgrade C-130P that directs a frequency specific energy beam in a burst that can overload any electronics or electrical grid so long as they can get in range. They work in tandem with the AWACs or E2-C Hawkeye. Kind of like a giant bug zapper, it seeks out the matching frequency of missiles, multiphase radar, Pulse Doppler, or anything else it can find and then overloads it and blows it out. It'll even take out shielded equipment if it can get in close. By the time the bad guys can reset their computers off of a backup supply source, it'll be over anyway."

Israel George stopped to take a drink of water from the glass he had on the table. Sean wrote several notes and waited for him to continue.

"MarSOC Echo - call sign 'Snoopy' - will come in from the west off the submarine *U.S.S. Day,* which they rendezvoused with a little while ago."

Israel George leaned into the table and continued. "We had an AWACs from McChord A.F.B. make a couple of passes a short time ago in the commercial lanes. They picked up broad-spectrum UHF and VHF emissions, along with two burst communications at fifteen-minute intervals. They came from this." He laid out four satellite photos of what appeared to be a ranch house on the west side of the island.

"It doesn't look like anything other than a typical ranch type facility for the grazing acreage on the coast. We found another facility, which is the actual operation for the cattle and sheep herding. It operates out of a warehouse type facility about a mile and a quarter away. At altitude you can see the animal trails around the warehouse, but not around the ranch house.

This fence here is almost impossible to see, but it keeps the cows from the ranch house grounds. The ranch equipment is a sham for display only. We couldn't figure out why until the AWACs picked up a constant, shifting frequency. They have imbedded sensors in the ground around the facility. We will frequency burst them on their own wavelength and overload their sensors just before Snoopy hits the beach. So this is where their command center is located. Snoopy will access the site from the north of the command center. This road to the south of the ranch house is their driveway to the facility. Snoopy will be moving out from the *U.S.S. Day* in an SDV – Seal Delivery Vehicle - up this subterranean wall." He pointed to a spot on the map.

"The island construction crews used this area as a dumping ground when they built out the shoreline. It's full of clutter, and the Nordian wave current anomaly detection equipment has a problem with that corridor. The folks at Langley analyzed the approaches from a Keyhole II satellite with thermal imaging equipment and found the currents went in every direction. That will eliminate the second radar system on the west side."

"What about air cover?" a sergeant asked.

"The president has detailed four F-35s Lightning's from the new Ghost Squadron. They haven't even stood up to full operation yet and they're already in business. They will be our air strike component on three-two-two-point-eight. Guard channel will be on three-one-seven, and operations will be three-zero-nine-point-six. Your bailout alternate will be UHF Hi on six-eight-zero."

The team wrote down the radio frequencies.

"Our intrepid little group - call sign 'Pig Pen' - will be coming in here to Mr. Odin's mansion." Everybody leaned in to have a closer look.

"We don't know where he is presently, but he shouldn't be hard to find. He has his own version of a presidential security detail and they're on comm gear all the time, so we'll find him. All we can do is isolate him so he can't cause trouble by issuing orders to his people. We can't arrest him yet due to international law, but we're sure as hell going to detain and isolate him. There's some kind of problem with officially recognizing his crappy, little island kingdom as a sovereign nation over at the U.N. So we're going to protect him from harm because we're sure his people are running a rogue operation behind his back and we don't want the prince harmed. At least that's the story the media will get unless we obtain hard intel that he's running the whole thing, which he is. If you find any of his three sons - Thor, Magnus, or Tobias - secure them as well, since they're part of this little viper's nest. Heads up on Thor, he has a bad attitude and will fight. They have a variety of weapons available, so stay sharp."

George grabbed a small stack of laminated maps and handed them out. "The island map is on one side and the target zone area on the reverse."

Pulling out another set of color 8x10 photos, George dropped them on the table.

"These satellite photos show that they have at least three choppers that are set up like ours in a combat configuration. These rear panels along the sides have internal gun bays. We don't know the caliber but these are definitely gunships. They also have some Hueys, Sea Knights, and a few Bell Jet Rangers," he said, spreading them across the tabletop. He reached into the folder at his elbow and pulled out several additional pictures.

"This set of photos is from last summer, when our Coast Guard participated in mutual aid exercises. One of the coasty pilots snapped a few pictures from the cockpit that caught this in a secure area behind their furthest hangar. You are looking at Chinese Youdong missile loaders. Those helos may be a problem if they are missile capable. The Youdong is a short-range, air-to-air and air-to-ground attack missile. Those choppers will be targeted by the Raptors. The president wants proof of their arms capability so he can shove it down the U.N.'s throat. Those loaders will be seized by the SEALs. "

He gathered up the photos again.

"Once the SEALs secure this place, they'll split into two components. The second component will depart for the main police station, down the road about five miles near the visitor and recreational center."

Dale took another drink of cold, chocolate milk from the quart container at his feet. He refused to eat before deployment to a possible gunfight.

"Alright, let's look at our own specifics. We will come in on OASIS – Over the horizon Airborne Sensor Info System - once we get word that the airport radar at New Borgholm station is down. You will be parachuting in from twelve thousand feet to take out the suspected military compound with the submarine and Black Hawk helicopters. Your target LZ is behind this small hill, three quarters of a mile from Odin's mansion. The suspected sub base and several combat choppers are here. Langley and NRO have satellite photos of several Black Hawks operating out of this camouflaged facility not far from Odin's mansion. These photos are side shots from a geo-synchronous satellite sitting south of Hawaii. You can see a bloom near the surface in several photos. Those are pictures of a sub just below the surface, sliding into the warehouse below the water. It surfaces out of the overhead satellite photo from inside that hill on the south side of the island. This will be a hardened facility. Secure it quickly, or the fighting may be heavy, since this target is a secret asset we're not supposed to know about."

He went through the details of the team's responsibilities and rules of engagement.

"For you FBI agents, the Kevlar vests you're wearing have comm gear in the right zippered pocket. Gunny Corbett will go over it with you when we're done here."

"Any questions so far?"

No one raised a hand.

"Agent Fox, you had a few things to add," Israel George said, standing fully erect.

"This entire mission is about the stolen toxic rock - that's our priority. Once the initial target is secure, Captain George, Gunny Corbett, and a few Marines will be going with us. The second element can catch up after they're finished with the sub and choppers. The casing that holds the rock has a microtag that's been giving off a continuous signal. That signal is coming from this building about two miles from Odin's compound." Dale pointed to a spot on the map.

"How did it get tagged? Do they know about it?" a sergeant asked.

"I tagged it in a fight with the terrorist on the wharf in Seattle a day ago. I don't think they're aware of it, it's tiny and blends in with the clear plastic of the case the rock was in," Dale replied. "We expect it to be well guarded. Odin will not allow it to be seized, so expect a fight."

Dale stepped back, reached down, and drained the last of his milk.

"Any questions?" Israel George asked. "Okay, gear check in five. We'll be departing in our new rides in ten."

Seven miles aft of the *Pinckney*, two VJ-22 Harpy Eagle jet engine versions of the twin turboprop V-22 Osprey lined up with the destroyer. There were eight of these unique, clandestine special ops birds in the inventory of SOCOM. In the dark, their swivel engines began to reconfigure to vertical flight as they slowed from one hundred thirty-five knots. The aircraft was designed to carry eighteen men and their gear. With a top speed of three hundred fifty knots, they could get to their target much faster than the older Sea Hawk choppers. Owl Two carried the parachute team, while Owl One would land after they were in place to take the sub pen and Nordian Black Hawks.

"*Pinckney*, Owl One inbound at . . ."

Three minutes passed, and out of the murky, black darkness Owl One descended to the aft deck of the destroyer. Two minutes later, Owl Two also landed, and the balance of Pig Pen's men and equipment departed for Nord Island.

Sean sat back on the mesh seat, looking across at Dale. Next to him, Sullivan seemed to be in a trance. The hum of the jet engines had lulled him to sleep.

"You ready?" Dale asked his brother.

"Yeah, ready for the landing. After that it's up in the air. In Vietnam, no plan survived beyond initial contact. Even a well thought out ambush can go in the toilet real fast. I just hope the bad guys will stick to the script."

⚬━🔑

"Captain, we're picking up transients in the air about two miles behind us," the radar operator reported.

"Can you identify them?" Wallen asked. His submarine had departed Nord for the last time, after replenishment and the early departure of Douglas and Thor Odin. They were now two hundred feet down and moving along at five knots, with the trailing drape antenna strung out behind them.

"There is a slow moving airborne craft inbound toward Nord. There's burst radio traffic, too, but it's scrambled."

"How slow?"

"About seventy knots, sir."

"A helicopter . . . is it Nordian?"

"I don't think so, sir. We're forty miles out, and all of the inbound traffic comes from the east. This bird is inbound on a heading of two-six-six. He's flying in from the south-southwest," the sonar man replied.

Wallen thought about that for a few seconds. *If I notify Nord, they might wonder why we're at sea already. On the other hand, Odin is in Oregon. They would go on alert looking for whatever was inbound, which might be beneficial to us. Whoever it is, they haven't dropped dipping sonar in the water, and there isn't a torpedo splash yet; better to slip away unnoticed.*

"Helm, take us down to nine hundred fifty feet quietly."

⚷—

The Marine VJ-22 Harpy Eagle continued on its way, unaware of its over flight of the submarine. Inside the cockpit, the radio crackled to life.

"Owl One, Snoopy is feet dry."

The pilot pushed the throttles forward and gained speed while dropping to within fifty feet of the ocean's surface. The pilot's NVGs lit up the ocean's surface in a green tint. He could see Owl Two a mile to starboard, gaining altitude.

50

Pacific Ocean
Thirty-two miles south of Nord Island
Sunday, 0358 hours Alaska Time

The VJ-22 roared along at two hundred sixty-five knots.

"Gentlemen, we're about to hit the horizon," the pilot announced. "We'll be feet dry in six minutes."

Sean yawned, still trying to get the sleep out of his system.

"Dale, what are we going to do for transportation on the ground?"

"Simple, we'll commandeer wheels from Odin and company, snatch the rock, and head over to the casino for some blackjack and margaritas. Why, what did you have in mind?"

Sean twisted his neck around and stretched his arms out.

"Nice plan. Hey, Dale, know what FBI stands for?"

Sullivan woke all the way up. He secretly enjoyed this form of mental torture, even if it was aimed at his partner. A couple of Marines wondered where this exchange was going.

"Federal Bureau of Insanity," Sean roared, shaking his head. "Or perhaps, Forgot to Bring Instructions, or maybe, Federal Blunder Incoming. No wait . . . Flying Blind with Inspiration, ahh . . . Far-Fetched Battle Intellect."

There were snickers and constrained laughter among the Special Forces operators. The old Marine sniper turned fire boss, turned ad-hoc FBI agent, was never at a loss to describe something with a jaundiced appeal.

Dale looked at Sean, "How about First Be Innovative."

"Nah," Sean replied, "Firefighter Believes in gathering Intelligence."

Outright humor at Sean's outbursts could no longer be contained. The Marines filled the back of the VJ-22 with raucous laughter.

Up front the radio crackled to life.

"Owl One, Phantom One. We have a Sea Knight off the ground at your target. Give us two minutes to let it exit the area and swat it," the lead pilot of the Raptor flight announced.

"Copy," the pilot of Owl One announced.

"Hang on in back, we're making a holding turn!" the Harpy copilot yelled to those behind him. The plane banked around hard to the left and held its altitude. The communications computer screen in the upper center console came alive with a message from the AWACs high overhead to the north. The airport radar was being jammed and the SEALs were on the ground heading into the control tower unopposed.

"Finally, good news," the copilot said.

"How's the OASIS?" the pilot asked.

"I have the AWACs, Owl Two, two Sea Hawks, radar emissions from the airport, and transients from the west side of the island. Snoopy should be close to taking out the west side comm station. I don't show anything aggressive or IFF negative, aside from that Nordian Sea Knight."

Two minutes passed as Owl One made a wide, left-hand turn.

"The Sea Knight just disappeared off the scope," the copilot stated.

"Any moment then," the pilot responded.

Five seconds later, "Owl One, Phantom One. Splash one whirlybird. Went down wet, a mile out and four miles downrange from target. No smoke, no flame."

Another double click went out over the radio.

A quick, sharp bank and a moment later the VJ-22 straightened out and once again accelerated toward the island.

"Six minutes," the copilot announced.

"O.K. Corral time, gentlemen," Israel George said. Each man did a final, quick equipment check and called out when they were done. Sean patted himself down and counted the ten, fifteen-round magazines he was wearing in a harness under his vest.

"Think you got enough ammo there, cowboy?" Sullivan asked, watching Sean's gyration.

Dale carried the same number of loaded magazines but managed to tuck them into the vest pockets under his Pendleton shirt.

"How much ammo you carrying, Sullivan?"

"Four mags and one in the gun, for a total of seventy-five rounds. I figure these guys will handle the heavy lifting," Sullivan said, looking at the Marine Spec Ops folks. "I'm going to put on some sandals, a tank top, and snooze in a chaise lounge on Odin's back deck. With any luck, his staff will know how to make a mean mint julep."

"Target in sight," the copilot said. "Two minutes to feet dry."

Silence fell over the men in the cabin.

A minute out, the engine nacelles rotated to vertical lift. It was pitch-black outside. The air was moist and cool. Each man, including the three FBI agents, turned on their NVGs as the aft red floor lights went out. Two minutes later, the Marine Special Forces team and their law enforcement escorts were prone against the small hillside about eight hundred yards to the west of Odin's mansion.

"Looks like Watt One did its job," Israel George said, scanning the ground before them. There were small pockmarks on the landscape where the sound and vibration sensors had been electronically overloaded and destroyed. Looking closer around the house, George spotted several cameras.

"Cameras under the awnings - I count six, seven, eight of them. George slipped off his NVGs and looked through the night scope on his M-4 rifle. "They're not turning, let's give it a moment."

A minute later, the Marines split into two elements. The Marine sergeant with the second element, who was Israel George's number four man, disappeared into the darkness with five Marines behind him.

They moved off toward the shoreline to join up with Owl Two's detachment.

"We'll give em' seven minutes to get into place." Israel George looked through the scope again and noticed the cameras were still in the same position. "I think the motors are burned out. We'll need to scoot down the hill a hundred feet to stay out of view of that one camera on the northwest corner of the building."

Switching to his thermal imaging device, he scanned the large mansion.

"I count six bodies - two vertical, four horizontal. The four are upstairs and appear to be sleeping. The two are downstairs sitting in chairs."

Three minutes later, they were off.

8—

"A technician is on the way over; he'll be here in fifteen minutes. We better go outside and walk around the building just to make sure Mr. Odin doesn't find out we're sitting on our hands. It could be an operational test of the security team," the tall, burly commando said. The two men, who were monitoring the cameras and other security devices planted around the grounds, walked out of the monitoring room unaware that their ground sensors were permanently inoperable.

"Hold it, we got armed company," George said. "Looks like they have Swedish autos."

Two men walked across the back porch of the mansion.

The three Marines and FBI agents went prone again.

"Gunny, take the one on the left, I'll take the other." Two Colt, short-barreled, night vision equipped M-4 rifles with Gemtech snap-on suppressors came up. The range finder in the corner of the scope read seventy-seven yards.

"In five seconds," Gunny Corbett whispered.

Both men let out a breath and waited. Each rifle spit out a round with a single report between them. The seventy-decibel sound instantly dissipated in the foliage. Both Nordian commandos dropped to the colorful, acid washed, concrete patio deck.

"Two down and a bushel to go," Corbett commented quietly. "Kevin, you're with me. Let's go."

Gunny and the Marine sergeant moved quietly and quickly - like experienced ninjas - across the open ground while Israel George continued scanning the mansion for any signs of movement.

Sean looked around behind them, hearing a rustling noise. It was the wind off the beach nearby, blowing through the weeds and wildflowers.

In Israel George's headset, a voice announced that Owl Two was on the ground and en route to the beach rendezvous with the rest of their men. The Nordian military compound was just around the other side of the jetty.

Gunny Corbett signaled for George and the FBI agents to move up.

Six minutes later, the four sleeping occupants, all staff to Douglas Odin, were bound and unconscious, having ingested a nasal spray know as Sandman Mist. They would be out for six hours.

"Odin is not here," Sullivan said. "His recessed helicopter pad near the rose garden is empty. We missed him."

"Damn," Dale responded. "He got away."

Sullivan pulled out the satellite phone and called the CTU. After the security handshake, Dan Covery came on the line.

"Dan, we're in the mansion. Odin is not here. Can you contact the FAA and see if they can identify any inbound aircraft crossing the ADIZ in the last forty-eight hours?"

"Hold the phone a moment, Sullivan," Covery said.

Two full minutes passed and Dan Covery's voice came back on line. "Odin's encrypted satellite phone algorithm can be unwound. The Odin Industries communication satellite he's bouncing off of has a separate computer that we installed at the launch facility. They don't know about the added hardware. It records the redigitization on a special software program monitored by NSA. When the client's own encryption software is engaged and the random sequencing begins, it seizes the inputs for storage before the retransmission can occur. The numbers are trapped and stored in a data matrix that we can reverse and read."

Sullivan could hear Covery talking to someone in the background.

"The last time he used the satellite phone was out on the island at 0228 hours. His whereabouts are unknown. We have a trap on his satellite phone number and the numbers of his three kids. As soon as we see any of those numbers appear, I'll call you immediately."

"Thanks, Dan. What about the ADIZ?"

"We have the FAA on the phone right now. If they have any info, I'll get back to you or Dale right away. By the way, the airport radar, the west side comm center, police and power operations are in our hands. Good luck with your operation."

Sullivan looked at Dale and Sean, "Dan will get back to us as soon as he has anything solid."

"No point in standing around here," Sean said, "let's find something productive to do."

☗—⚐

The sound of automatic weapons fire could be heard coming from the military compound over the hilly rise a half mile away. Within a few seconds, it was apparent that a full-on firefight was underway. Captain Israel George, Dale, Sean, and Sullivan ran toward the distant rise in the dark, dodging lawn chairs, bushes, and manicured foliage along the way. Several seagulls flew by low to the ground, screeching as they disappeared behind them. Captain George was talking to one of his operators as he hustled by a hedge.

On the small hill five hundred feet away, one of the MarSOC Marines cradled his highly accurized M-14 sniper rifle. The rifle's primary function was sniper work, but in the event heavier resistance was encountered, the main battle rifle could be switched via a manual selector to full auto. One by one, five Nordian commandos went down before the sniper was pinpointed.

A forty millimeter grenade roared out of one of the side entrances of the compound toward the hilltop perch and exploded.

The sound of small automatic arms and a heavy machine gun could be heard up ahead. Israel George ran across the base of the hill with Dale and Sullivan on his tail, unaware of the detonation in front of his sniper. The Marine captain was heading for the front side of the compound where the heaviest fighting was underway. The element of surprise was obviously gone and the game had changed, just as Sean had predicted.

Sean felt rather than saw the explosive concussion behind him. He stopped and hit the ground. Through the NVGs he saw the remnants of the explosion and a body that looked like a Marine at the top of the rise about a football field's length away. Clearly the man was injured. Sean turned and cautiously made his way across the hill, his Colt .45 at the ready.

Staying below the top of the hill so as not to silhouette himself, he felt for a pulse in the Marine sniper's neck. The man had a good pulse and was breathing, but he was unconscious. Sean looked him over with the red pen light from his vest and found blood. Taking the small med kit from the Marine's backpack, he opened the Quick Clot handiwipe and applied it to the downed Marine once he had the man's gear off. The facial and chest bleeding stopped almost immediately.

Suddenly a series of bullets raked the grassy hilltop to Sean's left and he instinctively ducked. Peeking over the top past a flowering plant, he saw two armed, black-clad commandos coming his way.

Seizing the highly accurized M-14, he pushed the release button with his right thumb and saw that he had a handful of rounds. He shoved the magazine back in and heard the distinctive click as it seated. Running the barrel right through the flower bed, he took aim quickly as one man was rushing the bottom of the shallow hill. The rifle bucked in his hands. The charging commando lost his feet and tumbled backward as his AK-74 bounced unceremoniously on the greenery. A second shot blasted away almost immediately and the other commando was thrown off his feet as well. Sean grabbed two more full magazines from the downed Marine and retreated below the crest of the hill to a new shooting position.

"Sean, where the hell did you go?" Dale suddenly barked in his headset.

"George's sniper went down from a blast concussion. I got people trying to squirt out a tunnel access for a counterattack along the east side of the jetty. I'm a little busy right now. I'll call you when I'm done," Sean replied.

Dropping to the ground, Sean edged up the hillside again. *Light breeze from his right . . . seems dialed in, though, from that last shot. Who's next?*

He could hear another explosion. This time the MarSOC Marines were hitting back with heavier weapons. He crept into a wiry dune bush and looked over the top of the rifle's night scope. He could see bodies rushing by a few hundred feet down the hill. Settling in, he knew he would only get a few quick shots off before he had to move again.

Zeroing in on one particular man, he could see others taking direction from him. *Next.*

The rifle recoiled and the man in charge went down. The rest of the men around him hit the deck and crawled into the bushes to conceal themselves.

Sean looked around for a second and spotted a pair of boots sticking out in the open. Seconds later, he put a bullet into the bush. *Two down.*

A big commando ran between the tunnel exit and a vehicle with a mounted, heavy machine gun. Seconds behind him another man followed. Sean lay on his back and checked the two magazines he carried. The second one had black-tip ammo. He switched out the magazine for the new one and scooted twenty feet to the right. He relocated the Humvee and saw, two men with NVGs of their own searching the bushes to his left. The .50 caliber Ma Deuce opened up and dug chunks out of the plant life where he had been moments before. He took a shallow breath, took aim, and slowly pulled the trigger between heartbeats, as he had done in Vietnam years ago. The bullet screamed down the barrel with an imparted spin. The new suppressor on the end of the barrel cut the noise in half.

The 7.62 mm armor-piercing round hit the one-eighth-inch armor plating on the front of the .50 caliber machine gun and drilled right through it. The shooting ceased as the man who was operating it fell back and over the side of the vehicle and onto the concrete driveway. The second man grabbed the handle and pulled the trigger, not learning the lesson his friend had just paid for. Sean's follow-up shot blew him right over the back of the Humvee to the concrete as well.

Behind him, Sean felt a sudden rush of wind. A chill ran down to his feet. He could just make out the heavy barrel of a chain gun aimed in his direction. The Apache helicopter opened up with its hyperspeed electric Gatling gun. The entire field below him erupted with lead and flame. The sound of rotor blades replaced the shooting a few seconds later as the Apache banked left and disappeared into the darkness. Rising to his knees, he looked over the hilltop, scanning quickly in both directions. He could see lethal carnage and destruction; nothing moved. He waited two minutes and watched to be certain.

"Sean, you okay?" Dale called out.

Clearing his head, he took a breath, "Bad guys are history. Almost thought I was, too, for a second. Who called the cavalry?"

"We did."

"I don't hear any more shooting. What's going on at your end?"

"The Apache crew unloaded on the bad guys. The Marines are in the compound now, looks like all the Tangos are horizontal. The sub is gone, but it was definitely here a few hours ago."

A thought hit Sean. He broke into a run, heading back to the Marine he'd left on the hillside not far away. "Dale, I need a corpsman for the downed shooter. Can you get me some help?"

"I'm on it, should be to you in a few minutes."

"Call you back in a few, then," Sean said as he slid in the grass next to the injured Marine sniper and felt for a pulse. True to his word, a MarSOC medic appeared out of nowhere shortly thereafter. Ten minutes later Dale, Sullivan, and Sean stood at the entrance to the Nordian military compound. Inside, the Marine Spec Ops team was already through the building and out the tunnel on the other side. They had two angry, slightly damaged survivors in custody.

"Agent Fox," Israel George called out, "the sub is gone, as are the three Black Hawk choppers."

Dale's eyebrows went up and he keyed his transmitter. "Everyone, heads up, the Nordian combat choppers are missing, too. If you hear what sounds like an incoming helicopter, take cover, it may not be one of ours."

Israel George changed tactical frequencies.

"Phantom One, Owl One. We're in the compound, but the helos and the sub are not. Suspect they may be on the loose."

"Copy that, Owl One. We're looking."

As the words left his mouth, a streak of flame crossed the sky from the sea south of them. All the men in the compound watched it rip across the black sky. An explosion a mile down the beach caused the early morning darkness to disappear for a moment. The Apache that had just flown off erupted in an orange ball of fire and plummeted to the sandy beach below. From the compound, it looked like a huge summer bonfire.

8—ᴛ

"Tiles still at one hundred percent?" the pilot asked.

"Yes," his copilot answered, "and I have the Sea Hawk lined up, looking for a lock." The warble tone in his headset was replaced by a steady hum.

"Got him!" Another Youdong missile leapt off its rail and sped toward its new target.

In the cockpit of the Navy Sea Hawk, the missile warning tone screamed at the pilot. He had seen the explosion of the Apache two miles away. He shoved the collective over and spun downward toward the ground less than six hundred feet away. The missile impacted the rear rotor as he dove for cover. The tail sheared off of the helicopter and it crashed into the water forty yards from the shore.

"Who else do we have?" the pilot asked.

"Just the three of us on the radar," the copilot replied, referring to the other two airborne Nordian choppers.

Elsewhere on the island, another stealthy Black Hawk was attacking the airport control tower, aware now that it was in the hands of someone other than Nordian air traffic controllers.

⚷

"Whoa, what was that?" Phantom One said. "Two, did you see anything on the threat scope?"

"Negative."

"Phantom Three, Four, we have air-to-air flying and no launch platform showing. Heads up!"

"We copy your transmission, One. Four, go to combat spread," Phantom Three called out.

The two stealthy Lightning jets spread apart and changed altitude.

"What the . . ." Phantom Two looked at his Pulse Doppler on the heads-up display and saw a sudden, strong return thirty-seven hundred feet directly beneath him. Then, just as quickly, it faded away.

"Phantom One, I just got a hard return that disappeared after a few seconds."

The flight leader was nine hundred feet above and five hundred yards to his right.

"I picked it up for a second, too."

⚷

The well-balanced, carbon fiber helicopter blades angled over as the almost invisible helicopter maneuvered in the darkness.

"There it is again!" Phantom One called out. "Two, switch to NVGs, we've got something airborne that the Doppler isn't painting." Within a few seconds, both pilots were staring at the island and seascape below with a green tint.

"See anything, Four?"

"Negative. I'm looking, no joy," the Navy lieutenant in the almost invisible fighter replied.

The stealthy Black Hawk descended toward the pine tree laden beach on the southeast side of the island. The chopper settled on the knurled skid plates in the sand and the weight sensitive steel track retracted into the heavy foliage, carrying the aircraft along with it.

"We'll rearm at the supply hut and start looking for new targets," the pilot said.

Pacific Ocean
Thirty-two miles south of Nord Island
Sunday, 0454 hours Alaska Time

"Wanna toss to see who stays behind?" Sullivan asked his partner as he flipped a quarter in the air.

"Heads," Dale called.

The coin hit the pavement, rolled a few feet, and fell over.

"Tails it is," Sullivan announced.

"Good," Dale said, "I hope someone from the Odin family is at the research lab."

"That seems a little personal, partner."

"I'm not really opinionated; I just have some inconclusive convictions I need to clear up."

"Something tells me you're getting the better deal," Sullivan said with a lack of enthusiasm.

Dale dropped his harness and vest, undid his belt and tucked his shirt back in. He slipped the harness back over his vest and tightened it up. The big FBI agent put the three empty magazines from his .45 in the back pocket of his vest.

Turning to his brother, he patted the .45 dubiously. "I'd rather have a big rifle, but I guess our Marine brethren will handle the heavy fireworks. What are we going to drive? Everything in the compound is shot to hell, thanks to the Apache," he wondered aloud.

Sean smiled a knowing look. "I have an idea. We passed his car museum back there. Why don't we go have a look and see what's available for rent."

"I'm thinking seizure. You need to expand your imagination now that you're an FBI agent," Dale replied with dry humor as they walked.

Two minutes later, both men, along with ten MarSOC Marines, popped the locked door to Douglas Odin's collection of rare and expensive vehicles. Dale found the light switch to the overheads and flipped the toggle.

"Wow, nice collection!" one Marine blurted out as the fluorescent light slowly illuminated the warehouse decorated to look like an Indy workshop and old-fashioned restaurant stop.

"I don't see any rolling armor," Sean said somewhat disappointed.

"Yeah, but he's got some great restored muscle cars over here!" Dale yelled out, "and the keys are in them! Sean, look at this! It's a '39 Lincoln Zephyr Roadster."

"I see it. Check this out! There's a Noble M400, a '65 AC Cobra, a McLaren F-1, and a '59 Rolls Silver Cloud Estate Wagon over here."

"Sunrise in an hour forty minutes," Israel George interrupted as the engine on a Lamborghini Diablo came to life. "Let's go, gentlemen."

The Diablo, with George at the wheel, stopped next to Sean. "Thanks for what you did for my shooter back there. Look's like you haven't lost your touch with the M-14, either."

Sean gave him a quick thumbs up and hopped into the passenger side of the Shelby Mustang.

After a weapons check, one of the Marines opened the tall roll door at the end of the building. The motorized caravan headed for the pharmaceutical building, with Dale and Sean in the lead in a '68 Shelby GT500 Mustang. Behind them, a parade of muscle cars from Lamborghini, Ferrari, and Aston Martin shot by. A Swedish Koenigsegg CCX sports car glaring under the warehouse show lights roared out into the early morning sunshine kicking dust up in its wake.

⚷━

Inside the pharmaceutical research facility, sixteen men armed to the teeth were waiting for the inevitable.

"We'll contact you when we see them coming," the man on the fiber-optic handset said.

He put the phone down, "You two go outside on the roof with the night vision gear and start looking for anyone headed toward the building from the main road. Four more of you take the hill behind the building and stick to the trees. They have limited resources, keep that in mind."

$\quad$ ⚷

"All secure?" the pilot asked.

"All set, everything's in the green," the copilot replied, "and full fuel."

"Let's go hunting."

Below the trees, the blades of the Black Hawk started turning as the pilot tightened the strap on his helmet.

$\quad$ ⚷

On the tactical radio net, Captain Israel George could hear the SEALs at the airport calling for air cover. A counterattack had been organized and a Nordian helicopter was throwing heavy ordinance at their position. *Our Sunday afternoon walk in the park has become a workout,* he thought silently. *Wonder if we're in for any surprises?*

The stealth Black Hawk lifted off slowly and kept low to the trees.

"FLIR on?"

"Copy."

$\quad$ ⚷

Dale was astonished by the undulating topography and the wooded beauty. "I thought this island creation was an almost flat, featureless creation," he said to Sean as they drove along slowly in the dark.

"The guy's got rolling hills and a pine forest. I saw what looked like a stand of California redwoods back there, too." From the visor of the Mustang, Sean pulled out a color flyer on the island's features.

"The brochure details the two golf courses, recreational facilities, fishing, and so on. Ah, here it is.

The island has four different kinds of trees in the forested area. Over a half million trees have been planted, including thirty thousand redwoods. Too bad an insane maniac owns it all."

Sean looked out the window through the NVGs and could make out the tree line along the road. "They look to be about thirty-five feet tall, reminds me of southern Germany, around the Bavarian area."

Behind the Mustang, six other cars kept pace. Automatic weapons bristled out the rolled down windows.

"Let's stop below this hilly rise here," Dale said, looking over the topographical map he was given on the ship, "and look out across the open terrain. Maybe we can make out the pharmaceutical facility."

A quarter mile down the road, the caravan pulled to the side in the dark.

"Okay Captain, it's your show until it's secure. How do you want to do it?" Dale asked.

Reviewing the topographical map himself, Israel George had already figured out their approach. He leaned in to show Dale and Sean.

"The road splits here for the west side of the island," he said, pointing at the map. "You two take this road up behind the building. One of my guys will go with you. You'll be able to observe from there and keep an eye out for our flank. The rest of us will drive this dirt road through the woods. We'll hoof it to the south side of the facility along the edge of the meadow and enter through these doors here. Remember, gentlemen, soft targets only, no explosives, the rock is our mission."

Dale and Sean watched as the other vehicles made their way down the graded, dirt road until they disappeared.

"What?" Sean said as he looked at his brother.

"I hated smashing out the tail lights on that Lamborghini Diablo," Dale replied.

"Yeah, I wonder how hard it will be to replace the ones on the vintage Shelby?" Sean said, looking at the broken plastic covers on the back end of the Mustang with the snake emblem on its gas cap.

The Marine corporal hopped in the back of the car and the three of them started over the rise, one more hill and a mile to go.

8—⚡

"We have a target, switching to guns."

"Copy," the copilot added.

The helo nosed over and dove for the road ahead.

8—⚡

"You two put the rock in its case and hustle over to the communications facility. I'll let them know that you're coming. Hurry!" the senior Nordian NCO ordered.

The men headed for the rear of the research building.

Unbeknownst to the two, the communication farm was now in the hands of the Navy SEALs.

8—⚡

Twenty millimeter shells exploded in the road behind and to the right of them, pelting the Mustang with soft dirt and bits of asphalt.

"Holy sh . . !" The words were cut off as a second volley ripped the road-bed ahead of them. Dale swerved around the damage, shoved the pedal to the floor, and the Shelby roared ahead, gaining speed quickly as it burned rubber. In the back seat, the corporal was on the radio to Israel George.

"Coming around," the pilot said.

"We gotta get out of this car and into the woods!" Sean yelled over the noise of the Shelby's powerful engine.

"Hard left coming up!" Dale hollered back. He took the corner wide, tires screeching as the Mustang slid sideways, and he hit the gas again. "We'll dump it at the edge of the trees and take cover."

Four hundred feet up and behind the Shelby, the matte-gray helicopter veered left and opened up again. Several rounds impacted the trunk and the car flipped over, skidding on its top to the side of the two-lane boulevard.

"You okay, corporal?" Sean asked as he unbuckled his seatbelt. He fell a few inches to the interior ceiling of the car and looked back.

The young warrior was dead, blood dripping off the top of his head to the tan, cloth ceiling.

"Damn."

"Let's get the hell out of here!" Dale shouted. "That chopper's coming around again."

Dale reached back as Sean rolled out the window and picked up the corporal's M-4 rifle and several loaded magazines.

"I have two running for the woods." the copilot said. "No point wasting a missile, let's spray 'em."

Hearing the chopper behind them, Sean elected to veer off the paved road to the right and take cover behind an electronic sign that displayed weather, road conditions, time, and temperature. Dale darted to the left and into the tree line across the road. He spotted his brother ducking behind the digital sign next to the wounded Shelby.

Seconds later, another two-second blast erupted as the pilot focused in on the ghostly-white return on the side of the little highway. The stream of heavy shells tore the sign, its support posts, and the power box to pieces, sending metal debris flying in every direction. When the dust settled a few moments later, there was nothing left but a hole at the side of the road.

Dale went skidding down the shallow embankment, but kept a death grip on the M-4. As the chopper zipped by, he stood up and looked back across the road.

"Sean!" Dale yelled at the top of his lungs. Nothing moved, the sign was destroyed, and a cloud of dust and reflective particles hung in the air. The ground behind it was shredded, as if a tractor had just finished plowing. "Noooo!"

His brother was dead.

The sound of the helicopter turbines whining caught his attention. With the NVGs on his head, he looked around carefully while the menacing helicopter banked again to search for him.

Dale put the trunk of a large tree between him and the chopper; it would block his image to the FLIR he knew the pilot was using to locate targets. He rolled on his back, ejected the magazine, and discovered that it was full. As the helicopter passed overhead, he stood up and took aim. The small 5.56 millimeter bullets bounced off the exterior of the big combat chopper. Dale unleashed a full clip.

"He's shooting back at us. Very brave and very stupid. Now we know where you are," the pilot said.

Dale jammed another magazine into the rifle and let the slide slam forward. As the helicopter banked left to come around for another shot, he ran back across the roadway and into the woods, two hundred feet from the overturned Mustang. Again he sought cover behind the trees. As the helicopter came in for another run, Dale peeked out and took aim.

The chopper blasted the trees where it had last seen the man. Large chunks of pine were split into kindling and exploded in every direction. As the aircraft went by, Dale pulled the trigger and emptied the second magazine. He realized it was having no effect.

The trees branches are absorbing the bullets, he thought.

In his NVGs, he spotted a couple of boulders off to his right out in the open. He made a mad dash before the chopper could turn back and reacquire him. Hugging the ground, he slammed the last full magazine into the rifle and readied himself. The anger inside of him at Sean's horrific death raised bile in his throat. He vomited.

Hearing the twin, turbofan engines returning, he pushed the barrel of the rifle between the rocks and waited. This time the helicopter slowed and appeared to look around. Dale leaned in and pulled the trigger again. Twenty of the thirty rounds hit their mark and ricocheted off the skin of the Black Hawk.

"It's bulletproof to small arms, sh . . ."

The chopper heeled over and opened up on the heavy grouping of boulders, carving thousands of small shrapnellike bits out of them. Dale put his face in the dirt and squeezed his body under the biggest of the boulders. His vest was peppered with hundreds of tiny rock chips.

The chopper came around the backside of the small outcropping and saw the ghostly-white return running for the opposite side of the rocks.

Stubborn target. "Coming around again. Let's get this over with," the copilot said on the helo's intercom.

The helicopter slowly circled the rock.

Dale was on his knees. *Think Dale, everything has an Achilles' heel; what is the helicopter's?*

He crawled around the last of the boulders again, trying to stay ahead of the helicopter as it circled him from behind.

I'm all out of, no, I'm not. He has a weak spot.

As the deadly helicopter passed the last of the boulders, Dale popped up and took careful aim with his M-4.

"There he is, at the end of the rock pile," the copilot said.

The helo was less than a hundred twenty feet away and presenting its profile. Dale fired the M-4. Suddenly, the big airborne craft pitched up and sideways as the engine whine increased. The Black Hawk flew straight up several hundred feet, rolled over on its back, and dove straight into the ground, exploding as it impacted the sloping field only a few hundred feet below him.

Dale's seventy-grain rounds had hit the exposed tail rotor, breaking a blade, and the chopper lost lateral stability.

A few, satisfying seconds later, he realized someone was leaving the back of the pharmaceutical research building in a darkened car and heading across the field in his direction. In the NVGs he could see three men. The man in the rear passenger seat was holding a clear plastic container that reflected the light from the nearby building. Suspended inside was a dark mass.

It's the rock. They're trying to get away.

Dusting himself off, Dale saw where two well-worn pea gravel tracks crossed the meadow. If he hurried, he could get close. He hunkered down low and ran as fast as he could.

The car's headlights finally came on and illuminated the track. The men inside saw the blazing helicopter crash, unaware it was one of their own. They assumed it was a U.S. chopper and were glad it was down. Now they could escape with their charge.

Dale quickly closed the gap on the dirt and rock pathway. At the edge of the tall grass he waited, knowing the car would be upon him in a matter of seconds. He slipped the magazine out of his .45 and checked that it was full. As the car came up over the last, small rise, Dale stepped just out of the headlight's glare, and without warning, fired at the driver's side of the windshield. The third round smashed through the laminated glass and into the driver's neck, punching a hole in the man's windpipe. The vehicle veered left into the sloping meadow as the man grabbed for his throat with both hands. The passenger holding the clear plastic container reached for the wheel and overcorrected. The car spun and rolled twice.

Dale was up and charging down the grass-covered hill. He was surprised to be met with gunfire moments later from the broken passenger window.

I'm not taking prisoners in this field, especially after you guys killed my brother.

As the passenger from the front seat crawled out the side door and into the moist, green grass, he fired off two more rounds in Dale's direction, not knowing exactly where his attacker was.

The two bullets zinged past Dale, a dozen feet to the left, while he went flat in the wild meadow grasses. The man in the car stood up, outlined by the burning helicopter behind him. Dale took aim and another seventy-grain, hollow-point bullet found its mark. The front seat passenger went down.

The remaining Nordian shooter however, wasn't done. He crawled to his right, toward the building he'd just left, dragging the case with the rock behind him and bleeding as he went.

Dale moved left toward the research facility. He knew where the man would instinctively head. He did not want to get shot by a Nordian sniper with a night scope from the building, so he kept low. Backtracking to the dirt and gravel path, forty feet later he reentered the tall grass.

The Nordian stayed motionless a moment, hoping his attacker would give himself away. Unbeknownst to both men, they were low crawling on an intersecting course.

Dale crept past a small rock outcropping. As he exited from behind it, he saw the Nordians right leg. Dale came up with a five-inch, black bladed knife, only to find himself staring down the barrel of the Nordian's gun.

Click.

The empty gun fell on a dead chamber when the revolver rotated into a previously fired shell casing.

Dale rushed the man. The Nordian's reflexes were slow due to the bullet hole in his hip and the blood soaking his pant leg. Dale tackled him, knife first, and twisted the carbon steel blade hard into his upper chest. In seconds, the man was dead.

Dale rolled off onto his back and breathed deeply, wiping the sweat from his forehead with his hand. It was only then that he noticed the lump he was resting on. To his horror, it was the lethal geode. Turning around to move away, his sweaty palm brushed the rock.

Shattered pieces of Lexan decorated the ground.

The case is broken, he thought, looking at the torn-up ground. *Oh no, did I touch the surface of the rock? Am I gonna be infected?* He looked again at his hand. His sweaty skin had clearly scraped the rock.

He had several deep scratches and a red, streaking welt.

He tore off his vest, shirt, and gloves and stepped back, falling into the rock outcropping. He lay there for a minute thinking about the ramifications of coming in contact with it.

An explosion and gunfire raked the quiet darkness at the research facility less than a thousand feet away. He grabbed his radio and called Israel George.

"I have the rock."

"Where are you?"

"Better not say, I'm alone. The corporal is dead . . . and so is Sean." The words were hard to express.

Israel George detected a wavering response in Dale's voice. He wasn't certain of the agent's state of mind, given the circumstances. But it was clear to the Marine captain that the lone FBI agent was a sitting duck for a counterattack from the Nordian commandos, wherever he was.

"Are you near the building?"

"Negative."

"Sit tight and stay hidden, then. This will be over in a few minutes. We'll be right there," Israel George ordered.

Two minutes of small arms fire suddenly receded.

"Fox, are you there?"

Dale grabbed the lapel mike and keyed it, "Yeah."

"Take cover."

Dale scurried away to the far side of the rock outcropping and dropped down.

The early morning was shattered by a loud explosion. A few seconds later, a second blast erupted and lit up the large meadow. The shock wave rolled past Dale. He peeked over the rocks a few moments later, and by the fading light of the helicopter fire saw a mist where the pharmaceutical building had been. The Marines had apparently called in an air strike from the F-35 Lightnings.

Dale slumped back down alone with his thoughts.

Sean's gone. I shoulda never brought him along. And now I'm infected, hmmm . . . some justice, eh' Dale.

He thought of Betty Jo Case and sunk down into the tall grass to await the Marines. He wiped the sweat from his forehead and closed his eyes. The crackling fire from the helicopter was a lonely reminder of his personal failure and impending finality.

Nord Island
Sunday, 0525 hours Alaska Time

Blood dripped into Dale's eyes from a seeping head wound. He closed them tight again, shook his head, and rubbed his face with his long tee-shirt sleeve. He could hear birds chirping in the trees around him as dawn broke. The moisture from wisps of broken fog cooled his skin. Looking over at the virus impregnated rock, he cursed under his breath.

"Agent Fox!" A loud voice called out.

It took a moment to realize that it was his radio.

"Fox, are you there?"

"Yeah, I'm here," Dale said keying the radio.

"We're secure," the voice of Captain Israel George announced.

"Yeah, okay, I'm adjacent to the access road in the tall grass near the tree line."

"I have two of my guys heading your way. We have a couple of helos coming in with more Marines to help secure the island. They'll be overhead in a few minutes . . . You alright?"

Dale thought a second, "I'm fine. Gonna need a hazmat team for the rock ASAP."

"Got it covered. The second chopper in has a couple of military engineers in suits and another container for the specimen. They'll be landing in the meadow."

"Sounds good."

Dale stood and walked toward the road where the Shelby sat upside down on its roof.

The dew on the morning grass wet his boots with each step. The fire from the crashed Nordian helicopter was now a pile of burning embers. To the east, the distant sky was showing telltale signs of lightening up. Off in the distance, the sound of approaching rotors could be heard coming closer.

The size-twelve boots stepped on black asphalt. Dale stopped and looked around, uncertain if any enemy combatants were still on the loose and suddenly aware that it might not be over. He kneeled down and ejected the clip from the .45. He pushed a fresh magazine into the well of the gun and put the partially loaded clip in his pocket. The slide slammed closed with a round in the chamber.

Standing up, he slowly turned and made his way toward the spot where the decimated information sign once stood. He saw two figures coming his way from the intersection. *Marines,* he thought.

The thought of digging out his brother's body just drained him. A flood of tears clouded his vision. He leaned against the Mustang, and a minute later the two Marines reached the car.

"You okay?" one asked with genuine concern.

Dale just stared at the side of the road.

The second man didn't wait for an answer, opting to look inside the steel-gray coupe. He stood up with a sad look on his face.

"Carl is dead."

For a few seconds, it seemed none of the men were breathing.

A CH-46 helicopter flared for a landing and a dozen combat equipped Marines raced out taking up defensive positions.

Dale finally walked over to where the electronic road sign had been and looked at the shredded hole in the ground.

A hand gripped his shoulder. "We're sorry about your brother," the beefy Marine said sympathetically.

Without responding to the comment, Dale looked up glassy-eyed and nodded, "Let's see if we can move some of the junk away."

Dale reached into his vest and pulled on a set of waterproof, pigskin gloves. A minute passed as he stood taking in the carnage. He sighed, leaned over, and grabbed a piece of metal that looked like a support beam. Grunting, he yanked it from the pile of rubble and tossed it onto the asphalt.

A loud engine screamed around the corner behind the three men. The brakes locked up, and before the car stopped, Sullivan was out and running over.

"I got here as quickly as I could."

"Put on some gloves and give us a hand, will you, Sullivan," Dale asked without any conviction behind the words. His big, broad shoulders drooped.

Nearby, the Marines from the helicopter fanned out and approached the damaged pharmaceutical facility at the ready.

The four men pulled debris into the road for a few minutes, when suddenly, an open hand appeared.

"Help . . . outta here," the weak voice declared.

"Sean!" Dale yelled.

He dug in, flinging bits and pieces of metal and plastic away from the hole. To his left, Sullivan and the Marines went into overdrive.

Two minutes later, a badly bruised and battered Sean Fox emerged from the beneath the rubble. Dale jumped down into the hole and grabbed Sean under the arms. The Marines reached down and pulled up the half-dead man.

"Did we win?" Sean asked weakly.

Dale applied a moist cloth to Sean's forehead, handed down by one of the Marines.

"We won, cowboy," Deal responded with enthusiasm. "Cowboy" was Dale's nickname for Sean. "We won. How did you ever survive the missile blast?"

Sean coughed a few times as he lay on the blacktop holding his left side. Dale knelt down to hear his brother's whisper.

"I fell into the open ditch behind the sign and dropped about seven feet a split second before the explosion." Sean coughed again and groaned. "Everything caved in. That's the last I remember."

The two corpsmen checked for broken bones and attended to Sean cuts and lacerations.

A second Marine helicopter landed in the field, throwing grass and plant matter in the air. The sky was turning light over the treetops. Several civilians stepped out of the chopper with gear bags in hand. A few minutes later, they were dressed in hazmat suits and approached the exposed rock, which was marked by a red bandanna. Ten minutes later, the virus-laden rock and its escorts flew off for the main Nordian airfield.

"Can you stand?" the corpsman asked.

With help, Sean stood slowly and wobbled. Moments later, he steadied up on his feet. "Left side hurts, might be a rib." They laid him back down on an emergency air cushion they'd inflated from a carbon dioxide pellet. His hands had some minor burns from shielding his face during the explosion.

Up the road came two vehicles with headlights glaring. Captain George and two of his men hopped out and hurried over.

Looking down at Sean, George shook his head. "Agent Fox, you look like hell. I guess this means you used up another of your nine lives."

"He's running out of 'em for sure," Dale said.

"Well, we have another chopper at the airport to take you off to the ship for medical care," George said. "Can you sit in the front of the Lamborghini?"

"Not a lot of leg room in there. Can we roll the Shelby over?"

A few minutes later, the Shelby, now on its wheels, fired right up. Sean, Dale, and Sullivan climbed in and followed one of the Marines the three miles to the airport.

The sun slipped over the horizon and splashed against the control tower, making the brick facade glow. Sean walked on his own, aided by Sullivan, to the side door of the medevac chopper. Three wounded Marines on stretchers were already onboard.

All three agents looked up in the sky toward the sound of jet engines approaching.

Dale turned to one of the Marines, "What do we have going on here?"

"They're bringing in an F-35 Lightning, sir. President wants the rock back at Fort Detrick as fast as it can be delivered. The epidemic has over eight thousand dead. They need a cure, and fast."

"It'll take five or six hours crossing the country."

Dale was already wondering how long he had before the virus showed symptoms.

"No, sir, the FAA has waived the rules; it's going supersonic all the way. It should be there in two hours, Mach two plus all the way."

The roar of the stealthy, twin-engine fighter jet grew closer as it lined up for landing.

"He'll burn up the engines and suck down fuel like there's no tomorrow," Dale commented, not thinking about the words.

"They'll refuel him along the way. President doesn't care about the engines. They'll just put new ones in later. The CDC guys and some military engineer types are parked over there," he said, pointing to the far side of the airport near the quay.

"It'll be here just long enough to load it in the back and he'll be gone."

Sean's helicopter spun up behind Dale and Sullivan. Dale turned around and waved to Sean as the side door slammed shut.

"Time to find Odin," Sullivan said. "We need to call the CTU."

Pacific Ocean
198 Miles southwest of Nord Island
Wednesday, 0711 hours Pacific Time

Four hundred fifty-five feet down, the submarine cruised along at seven knots.

"Captain, we're at the two hundred mile mark," the helmsman called out.

"Anything on the scope?"

"Negative, we're clear, sir."

"Very well, take us up to twelve knots, and down to five hundred feet. But stay alert, I don't want to be surprised by another subsurface vessel."

Wallen walked off the command deck and headed aft.

Three days to Malaysia and a fourth to complete the sale. Dump the submarine and get home to the islands. I miss Stockholm and the long summer days. Va skönt.

Wallen settled into the bench seat and dug into the fresh kabobs the cook had just made up for him. He was almost home free. His hatred for

Odin was evident now to the crew, who shared their master's dislike for their former employer.

Sullivan lay the stubby antenna down on the satellite phone, "Covery says that Odin's helicopter was seen dropping in at a friend's home near Portland yesterday. The Portland PD has overflown the mountaintop mansion and reports it's still on the ground, our call on it."

"We're done here. I'm just glad the AWACs and the Raptors found the helos as fast as they did. Everything was stealthy on them except the helicopter blades. I wonder if they ever considered that little oversight?"

"Yeah, and who knew we'd end up with almost two hundred prisoners," Sullivan said.

Dale suddenly had a faraway look on his face.

"Sullivan, there's something you need to know."

Sullivan looked at Dale quizzically and leaned back against the car.

"I was sweating when I touched the rock in the field. It broke out of its case after I stuck that commando who tried to shoot me. I ended up lying on top of it."

Dale looked his partner in the eye. "I'm pretty sure that I'm infected. In fact, I don't have any doubt about it, Sullivan. Before I die, I want to take Odin with me. When the time comes, you'll know what to do."

Sullivan's mouth dropped wide open. He understood what Dale was asking: look the other way when the time came. After what seemed like an eternity standing on the tarmac, an immobile Sullivan finally put his hand on Dale's shoulder.

"Let's go find Odin, partner," Sullivan said.

Nord Island Airport
Sunday, 0716 hours Alaska Time

The matte-grey F-35 screamed down the runway with afterburners lit. Near the end of the runway, the stealthy jet gracefully lifted straight up and streaked into the early morning sun. A fog of condensation formed on the top of the wings for a few seconds. The sound of the F-35 Lightning's powerful engines reverberated off the warming cement below. Within thirty seconds, it was out of sight and accelerating eastward.

A breeze, blew across the open airport grounds. Trees along the rocky waters edge nearby swayed in the breeze. Seagulls raised a racket as a Navy helicopter swung in toward the tarmac in front of the long hangar building just behind the two FBI agents. Sullivan buttoned up his parka and walked back over to Dale, who had just finished talking to a Marine sergeant.

"Let's hope for a miracle, Dale. The rock will be in a lab in less than four hours," Sullivan said, having nothing else to offer. Dale looked at his partner without saying anything. They walked toward the Black Hawk helicopter designated Wolf 71, which they had commandeered on presidential authority. Their next stop was a mountaintop mansion in Portland.

Near Portland, Oregon
Sunday, 0818 hours Pacific Time

"Your helicopter is ready," the security officer in Odin's protective detail said to Thor Odin.

"Thank you. My two brothers will be staying behind for a few days of relaxation," Thor replied. Magnus and Tobias had flown in the day before and were more interested in a few days of female company that was bought and paid for in advance. The mansion grounds were large, well manicured, and secluded, with several out buildings that included two riverside cottages.

"We'll be out in fifteen minutes," Thor advised.

Utah Valley Medical Center
Sunday, 0820 hours Mountain Time

"We have two more patients coming around," Dr. Walter Hunack said excitedly. "How are the tests coming?"

Dr. Hunack was in the newly erected federal lab on the hospital's back grounds. The street immediately behind the massive hospital complex had been shut down and taken over by the federal government. It was lined with mobile buildings that comprised an extensive research facility. Heavy, black power cables snaked their way around the white structures.

"We've narrowed it down to less than two hundred specific enzymes, so we're making progress."

"It doesn't sound like it's moving very fast," Hunack replied.

"Each enzyme has eleven specific tests. It takes time to get results from everything but the stain and acid tests. Fortunately, we have the rock now, and it's being flown in from the Pacific. Fort Detrick will have the thing in a few hours. Once they can break down the chemical composition and conduct the standard reaction tests, we may be able to eliminate some of our experimentation," the senior lab manager responded.

Dr. Hunack was hopeful, and it showed in his face when he walked out the door and back to his hospital lab.

Aboard the F-35 Lightning
Andrews Air Force Base
Sunday, 1247 hours Eastern Time

The twin-engine combat jet had flown the distance from the West Coast to the Eastern Seaboard of the United States in record time. Broken dishes and cracked plaster littered its wake from the fifteen hundred mile per hour dash. Coming to a stop on the tarmac, ground crews chalked the wheels, and a large contingent of air police surrounded the aircraft. Hazmat engineers retrieved the rock casing from the back seat of the fighter a few minutes later.

Fifty yards away, a helicopter revved its engines and took off for the Fort Detrick Army Base and the lab that awaited its mortal acquisition.

Aboard Wolf 71
Over the Pacific Ocean
Fifty-two miles northwest of Portland, Oregon
Sunday, 0951 hours Pacific Time

"What do you have to drink?" Dale asked the crew chief of the U.S. Navy Black Hawk.

The crew chief opened the little 1.7-cubic-foot refrigerator tucked in the back of the helicopter. It was nonstandard equipment requisitioned by the pilot for the benefit of those onboard. Lately, he'd flown as many non-military types around as he had combat troops on exercises. Keeping thirsty people happy seemed to make them more agreeable flying guests.

"We have a variety of soft drinks, bottled water, and a couple cartons of cold milk," the crew chief said.

"I'll have a Coke," Sullivan said, eyeing the contents of the fridge.

"How about that orange drink?" Dale asked. "No wait, on second thought, my stomach might prefer the chocolate milk right now. It's been bothering me for the past hour, and I haven't had anything to eat in awhile."

The crew chief passed the two drinks forward.

Dale stood up, drink in hand, secured in a flight harness, and looked out the sliding door window at the sea forty-seven hundred feet below. The morning sun warmed his face as he drank. Sullivan was on the satellite phone to the CTU, updating their situation.

"Tell them we would appreciate their help. And Dan, let them know we're inbound in a Navy Black Hawk. Have their SWAT team contact us on . . . Lieutenant, I need a frequency in the low range for the county sheriff to talk to us!" Sullivan yelled forward.

"Have them contact us on 154.6, sir," the copilot replied.

"Okay, give them 154.6, Dan, and we'll monitor that," Sullivan said.

A minute later, he folded the stubby antenna back and passed the satellite phone to the crew chief, who plugged it back into the universal charger.

In the mountains southwest of Portland, Oregon
Sunday, 0951 hours Pacific Time

The two-tone, dark-blue Agusta Grand executive helicopter shone in the dull morning light. It's three-layer, high gloss paint job, with the Odin Industries logo on the side, was as sleek looking as the five million dollar helicopter's aerodynamic lines.

The Pratt & Whitney engines came on line and the pilot pushed both buttons to spool up power to the rotors. He was in a hurry. A few moments later, Thor Odin and his father climbed aboard the fast, luxury aircraft, followed by three security members of his protective detail. Shortly after, it lifted off and headed north.

Heavy fog, like the remnants from a major forest fire that was burning out, had descended on the mountainous terrain. The sound was muffed and visibility reduced. The helicopter moved along slowly, picking its way below the mountain ridges as it went.

"What's our arrival time?" Odin asked the pilot.

"We'll be there at eleven on the nose, sir," he responded.

"Good, a half hour for the board and a little time to look around before the ceremony. How many people on the detail in Seattle?" he asked his head of security.

"Sixteen people total, sir, two at the helicopter, four outside, five on the outer ring, and five in close."

"Very well, autographs and pictures for the celebrities and politicians only. Keep everyone else away from me."

Odin was not yet aware that his island had been taken over. The U.S. military had seized all communications and killed the power to the sea cable, radio, and satellite system. Circling over the island, the AWACs was still on station, crippling anyone with a transmitter from making contact with the mainland and Douglas Odin.

Odin's next semidaily update wasn't due until noon Nordian time, one o'clock in the afternoon local. He knew that constant checking would only slow the development of an antidote, so he left his lab research team to their work. They were the best that money could buy and he didn't want to disrupt that flow.

Two miles behind the mansion, in the heavy wilderness area, the helicopter banked left into the long, tree-lined canyon that paralleled the mountain range between the woods and the coastline. The aircraft was well below any coastal radar coverage and would only appear when it crossed the river into Washington State. At that point, it would appear to be a helicopter airborne from a local ranch.

Coming up the street below the mansion was an unmarked sheriff's van with magnetic signs on either side that advertised an electrical contractor. The county sheriff was moving quickly with a SWAT team to support a federal request for assistance in apprehending several fugitives under the RICO act. The sheriff did not know who the actual suspects were, but did know that the FBI's counterterrorism unit was on the way by chopper. That made it a big deal and the sheriff was mustering as many men as possible.

Aboard Wolf 71
Over the Pacific Ocean
Forty-seven miles northwest of Portland, Oregon
Sunday, 0955 hours Pacific Time

"Are the SWAT teams in place and ready to enter?" Dale asked.

"Only the local sheriff's unit is here. The FBI team hasn't arrived yet, sir.

According to their dispatcher, the Feds are about thirty minutes out. We're ten minutes away at this point. What do you want to do?"

"Do you have them on the headset?"

"Yes, sir."

Dale slipped the stereo headset over his hair and adjusted the boom mike.

"This is Wolf 71. I'm in a Black Hawk Navy chopper about ten minutes out. We're inbound from the west. When you see our chopper, go ahead and deploy the entry teams. Confirm the street is shut down, the power company has pulled the plug, and the land line phone company has them off-line?"

"That's affirmative, Wolf 71, the tactical commander replied.

"Are the local cell towers shut down as well?"

"Affirmative to that, also."

"Make sure everybody is up to speed. Let's get the ball rolling according to the briefing."

"Copy Wolf 71. Team leaders are advised and both teams are in position. Due to the terrain and heavy fog, we cannot confirm the presence of the suspect's helicopter anymore. There is a disguised hangar just below the garden area and it may be parked inside."

"Alright, Wolf 71 standing by." Dale handed the headset back to the copilot and looked at Sullivan.

"They'll breach the mansion's security by the time we land. Hopefully, they'll have control of it quickly."

"If the old man is there, his security detail probably won't be all that cooperative," Sullivan said, checking his .45 to see that he had a round in the chamber.

"Yeah, I agree," Dale said, pulling his .45 out. "This is the first time I've hotfooted it in on a carte blanch presidential free-for-all. The travel amenities are nice. I feel like I'm bringing down the wrath of God here."

The noise from the helicopter's blades caused both men to have to almost yell to be heard. Dale could see the coastline getting closer. Two of his oversized Band-Aids needed changing; they were bloody.

Wonder if I'm contagious? Dale thought.

54

Aboard Wolf 71
Eleven miles southwest of Portland, Oregon
Sunday, 1012 hours Pacific Time

"Overwatch Blue, any movement?" a voice over the radio asked.

"Negative," the blue team sniper replied. "This rolling muck is blanking out some pretty good-sized areas of the target. Observation of target grounds and structures are patchy at best."

"Copy, do your best. The clock is ticking down, you know what we need."

Two clicks of the radio followed.

"They're looking for Dad," Tobias said as he shifted the 10x35 binoculars slightly left. The horizontal, wooden slats above the third floor loft vent hid his gaze from the SWAT teams outside.

Seven minutes had passed since the first German shepherd guard dog patrolling the grounds near the twelve foot tall, north rock wall had alerted them to someone's presence. The fourteen hundred forty foot long wall bordered the grounds all the way back to the beginning of the privately owned designated wilderness area. The owner of that wooded land was the mansion's master, and it was posted as private property.

The articulated grounds behind the twenty seven thousand square foot mansion were dotted with guest buildings, a pool, hot tub, grotto, a slow flowing river, waterfalls, out garages with sporting goods equipment, horse corrals, and other appendages. In addition, there were several natural meadows frequented by deer, moose, elk, and an occasional wolf.

"My cell is dead, I can't get a signal," Magnus said.

"Check the satellite phone," his brother replied.

A moment later, he looked at the LED face. "Nothing, no signal."

"They've cut off communications! They're getting ready to attack!" Tobias said angrily. "We're at war, brother!"

The camouflaged cameras in the overhanging pine trees allowed them to count two unmarked police cars and several hard-looking men they assumed could only be cops.

"We have no way to warn Dad," Magnus said in disgust.

"Get downstairs and gather the security team. Lock up the house staff so they're out of the way. We'll hit them when they come over the walls and onto the property. We need to buy Dad some time to get out of the country and back to Nord. We'll have to leave the area to get away from the communications block they've set up. Take both phones and head out the back to the subgarage with the dirt bikes. I'll meet you there in a few minutes. We'll ride down the mountain until we get a signal for one of the phones. Go quickly, and be careful."

Magnus, the younger twin by six minutes, disappeared down the narrow corridor off the tiny loft.

"Overwatch Blue," the radio crackled.

"Go ahead, Overwatch Blue," the sheriff's lieutenant in the van responded.

"I hear a chopper somewhere behind me."

The sniper's perch was designed to look like a seventy foot tall pine tree to match the landscape. It was occupied by two men - the blue team sniper and his spotter. They were a little over three hundred fifty feet from the mansion gate and well hidden among the living trees that surrounded them.

"All units, stand by. Blue and red teams to execute," the senior officer said into the radio.

Another nine seconds passed until the sound of the military helicopter was clearly evident.

"Go!"

The forty-four-acre grounds were more than the thirty-eight SWAT team officers could effectively cover. It was all the sheriff could muster on such short notice.

The two big German shepherds let out a low snarl. They had been trained to stalk and attack quietly to keep intruders oblivious to their presence. As seven men clad in black came through the rear, side gate a couple of hundred feet from the main garage, one man called out, "Dogs," on his headset.

It was too late. Both attack dogs were on the nearest two men almost immediately. Shots rang out and surprise was lost. Twenty seconds later, both dogs lay dead from knife wounds, but three officers were out of the fight.

Gunfire erupted from various locations in and around the mansion as the Odin security team had gone on the offensive. Several more SWAT officers were down, but not dead, thanks to their bulletproof vests. The tide of the fight was no longer an overwhelming advantage for the sheriff's deputies. The treebound sniper of the blue team couldn't get a shot off due to the rolling fog, yet he pulled the trigger to lay suppressive fire down to aid one officer caught out in the open.

Above and behind him, the Black Hawk roared by, shaking trees in its wake. A few seconds passed and it flared to a fast landing on the backyard lawn, east of the mansion and as far away from the house as it could get.

"Got a plan yet?" Sullivan asked while they dove to the ground. Bullets tore into the soil close by.

"I'm working on one that should get me a Nobel Prize for creative thinking," Dale said as they checked for action both left and right.

"Wanna tell me what it is?"

"When I think of one, I'll let you know."

They jumped up and sprinted for cover.

"Wolf 71 and 72 are on the ground at the rear of the mansion about a hundred yards back," Dale barked into his lapel mike from behind a brick facade.

The sheriff's lieutenant made note of it as the fight continued to deteriorate. He was on the phone to the county dispatch center, putting out a call for mutual aid. It was tough enough to operate one SWAT team, but two took tremendous concentration on everyone's part because assaults were famous for their unpredictable fluidity. This entry attempt was dead in its tracks and the FBI SWAT team was still fifteen minutes away by car.

With a variety of weapons brought to bear by both sides, a red team SWAT officer with a 37mm grenade launcher fired a tear gas grenade at the big picture window on the corner of the mansion. He was stunned to see it bounce off into the foliage seconds later. The three-layer bulletproof armored windows resisted the assault.

The mansion's staff of eight was now huddled together in the dumb-waiter turned pantry, one floor below the main kitchen. They could hear the gunfight and voices in the house yelling directions. Their guests had been none too kind.

From a number of points around the mansion, the automatic weapons fire intensified and the two SWAT teams found themselves retreating to sheltered positions.

Six deputies lay wounded behind the hedgerows near the front of the property, one of them bleeding profusely from a severed artery. The remaining nine-man, personal security team for Douglas Odin had successfully repelled the sheriff's SWAT teams. They were now on the defensive.

Seventeen hundred feet up and clear of the waning fog bank, the Black Hawk crew was busy reconfiguring the chopper for battle. The crew chief and his assistant had pulled the two 7.62 automatic rifles from their carriage in the back. They were attaching them to the pintels on either side of the helicopter and slaving them to the pilot's helmet controls.

The U.S. military was barred by statute from such airborne tactical operations inside the United States. However, the presidential finding, along with a congressional waiver and the support of the U.S. Attorney General, FBI, and Homeland Security, all agreed to the authorized emergency powers if the need arose.

The on-site incident commander, FBI Supervising Agent Dale Fox, was now calling the shots for a domestic soil attack on terrorists - using American military assets - for the first time in U.S. history.

While en route to the coast, Dale and Sullivan had been apprised that the deadly geode specimen was missing a small piece, apparently broken off by the lab staff. They were now operating on the assumption that it was in the possession of Douglas Odin. They were hoping it would be located at the Oregon mansion, along with Douglas Odin himself.

Dale's thoughts briefly turned inward. *There's a high probability you're dying from the contracted virus, so if this turns to shit later, prosecution will be meaningless since you'll already be dead. For once in your life, you're free to act.*

Dale and Sullivan bolted for cover.

The Black Hawk circled the stately grounds overhead awaiting Dale's call and watching the fog continue to dissipate with the rising morning temperature.

"Sullivan," Dale said into his lapel mike, "let's see if we can work our way around to the south side and enter by the gardens."

Two clicks on the radio told Dale his partner was ready.

The two men moved into cover along the hedgerow and finally to the end of the colorful, blooming rose garden.

"So far, so good," Sullivan said into his lapel mike. He slid to a stop on his belly behind a brick facade at the end of the rosebush line.

"Be right there," Dale replied. Moments later, they were lying prone together next to the last stand of mature roses.

"We're exposed to the second-floor balcony," Sullivan observed.

Raging gunfire could still be heard on the opposite side of the mansion and to their right a couple hundred feet away. As they lay there breathing heavily from the crouched run, Dale saw a man low crawl between them and the subgarage beyond them.

"We got movement over here," Dale said, pointing for Sullivan.

"I'd hate to think we're being flanked," Sullivan replied. "Maybe we oughtta back up until more help arrives."

"I was just thinking along the same lines. Besides, we don't want to get caught in a crossfire from blue and red."

Paralleling the stranger from the house, they followed as he made his way to the subgarage.

They watched as the stranger stopped, turned, and motioned another person from the house. The first man came up with an Uzi submachine gun to cover the second man's advance.

"Bad guys," Dale whispered to Sullivan. They were less than eighty feet from the garage now. Both agents watched as the second person moved up carefully; he was also armed with a submachine gun.

"Bad guys," Sullivan nodded.

The smell of cordite wafted through the air as the fighting continued around the mansion. A stray bullet zinged by and hit a metal pole near the hot tub behind them.

Inside the subgarage, the sound of one, then two motorcycles became apparent. A side door burst open and a 250 Suzuki dirt bike sped away from the building. Sullivan was up and running to cut off the bike rider, who had to turn past the pool to make it to the open meadow beyond.

Hearing the second bike grow louder, Dale sprang from cover and raced for the open double doors. Several rounds pelted the decorative stone wall to his right as someone from the mansion had discovered what they assumed could only be SWAT team members.

The sound of the engine burst from the enclosed building as Dale lept.

Nearby, Sullivan tumbled over a heavy, padded pool chair and missed the rider by a few feet. The man on the dirt bike was surprised to see he was being chased by someone on foot. He gunned the engine and rode up over the small rise in the lawn and down the other side.

Sullivan jumped up on the large, brick fireplace to see over the small rise. He took aim and pulled the trigger.

A round whizzed by the rider and lodged in a Chinese Elm. A second round fared no better. The big .45 was no long-distance firearm; it was meant for heavy hitting, close-in work.

"Farmer," Sullivan called out on his lapel mike to the armed Black Hawk, "Wolf 72. The chicken has escaped the coop. He's in the meadow to the east of the mansion, take him down."

"Copy, Wolf 72. Farmer has chicken in view and is engaging," the co-pilot replied.

The pilot twisted the combat chopper left and nose dived for the large meadow.

"Light him up," the pilot said to the copilot. The copilot squeezed the trigger seconds later and a steady stream of 7.62 mm shells zipped out of the thousand-round ammo boxes toward the fleeing rider.

Tracer rounds ripped up ground cover in the meadow, sending clumps of dirt and wild grasses flying in every direction. The rider darted to the left, seeing the debris out of his peripheral vision. It was only a few hundred yards to the heavily wooded area around the end of the small lake.

The chopper overshot, and then with amazing agility pulled straight up and spun around its own axis, pointing once again toward the fleeing rider. The two pilots grunted as the crew chief and his assistant got airborne inside the closed door helo. The two crewmen were attached by their harnesses to the overhead rail and found their footing again quickly. Out the right window of the door, the crew chief saw the rounds impacting the ground, even while his ears reported the blast of the weapons.

At five hundred seventy-five feet, the chopper closed in on the rider as he hit the end of the meadow and crossed into the tree line. The automatic weapons sliced through the smaller, outer pines and raked the rider. The dirt bike exploded in a ball of fire as several bullets passed through the man's body and into the gas tank.

Nearly a thousand yards away, Sullivan saw the explosion. He turned and ran for the last place he'd seen Dale. As he did, bullets found the brick fireplace and gouged chunks out of the poolside barbecue. Sullivan hunkered down and sprinted to the cover of the decorative wall near the hot tub. Bullets traced his footsteps as he ran for his life.

With a thumping heart, Sullivan listened for more gunfire being directed his way.

"Wolf 72," his radio suddenly interrupted, "we've got crispy chicken on greens."

Sullivan clicked the mike, "Copy that, Farmer. Do you see Wolf 71? He's not where I left him."

The Black Hawk slowed to a hover eight hundred feet above. "Wolf 72, I see two men on the ground fighting behind a small outbuilding about two hundred feet just ahead of your position. Also be advised, the FBI SWAT team has just arrived out front. I see what looks like a string of red and blue lights winding their way up the mountain. Looks like the reinforcements have arrived."

Sullivan didn't stop to acknowledge the Black Hawk; he was up and running again.

The Mansion
Southwest of Portland, Oregon
Sunday, 1042 hours Pacific Time

The razor-sharp, five-inch blade slid down the camouflage colored vest and ripped through two straps. Dale was on his side with both feet trapped beneath the wheel spokes; the rider's weight on the overturned motorcycle had him pinned. The knife came down a second time as Dale raised his own six-inch KA-BAR to defend himself. Steel caught steel when Dale turned his knife upward and slashed down with lightning speed into the man's leather shoe.

The rider fell forward and rolled out of his reach, screaming from the gaping wound in his foot.

Dale got one leg free just as the man regained his feet and reached for the .45 laying only a couple of steps away.

Turning around, the rider saw his attacker was out from under the motorcycle and starting to rise. Pulling back on the parkerized hammer, he slipped his index finger into the trigger well.

"Bam!!"

Everything went into slow motion as the rider seemed to topple over just in front of Dale, gun first. Dale was momentarily stunned and surprised that the pain hadn't hit him outright. He dove for the ground, assuming the rider had lost his balance, and hoping a second bullet from the man would miss. But the rider never fired.

Sullivan was shooting from seventy feet away in a crouched position. "Bam!!"

A second bullet found its mark and the rider fell dead.

"Dale, you okay?" Sullivan yelled. Getting no answer, he knelt down by Dale's side and shook him. "You okay?"

"I dunno. Where did he hit me?"

"He didn't, he never got off a shot. I hit him twice. How do you feel?"

Dale looked at the stainless steel hunting knife the rider had tried to impale him with. It was sticking out of the ground a few inches from his head.

He blinked, "Hit me in the chest, Sullivan. I need to restart my heart."

Rolling over and kneeling by the dead man, both men realized the face belonged to Tobias Odin.

"The other guy who almost got away looked just like him," Sullivan said.

"Twins," Dale replied. "It must have been Magnus."

At the front and sides of the mansion, the regrouped sheriff and FBI SWAT teams were turning the battle. Dale could finally hear the Black Hawk overhead as the ringing in his ears cleared up.

"This isn't over. Where's my gun?" Dale said, now angry again.

Both men made their way to the side of the subgarage a minute later while the gunfire from the house intensified.

Just when it looked like the shootout was about to start throwing lead in their direction, a bullhorn could be heard calling for a cease-fire. The SWAT teams took cover and stopped firing at the mansion. The sheriff's hostage negotiation team leader was trying to convince the Odin security detail to stop shooting since they were now vastly outnumbered.

Realizing they were in a losing situation, Odin security finally surrendered. The SWAT teams took each man out one by one and secured them on the street. After a thorough search of the mansion, the eight staff employees were rescued from the locked pantry. Douglas Odin was nowhere to be found.

"Farmer, Wolf 71. Put it down on the landing pad behind the house, we're secure."

"Let's talk to the staff and see what they know," Dale said to Sullivan.

Ten minutes later, both men bolted out of the back of the mansion for the Black Hawk.

"How fast will this thing go?" Sullivan asked the copilot while jumping in.

"About three hundred kph."

"In miles per hour," Sullivan restated.

"About a hundred eighty-five. Why?"

Dale hopped in behind Sullivan, still favoring his sore left leg. "Downtown Seattle, how far?"

"Ah, a hundred thirty-five, maybe a hundred forty miles. Why?"

"What's the flying time from here to there?"

The copilot was on his knee map and flipped the page over. "Providing we don't hit any snags, I'd say fifty minutes, possibly a little more." He gave up asking why, knowing the answer was bound to come.

Dale looked at his watch. It was 11:17 a.m. "Let's go, don't spare the whip," he said.

The copilot looked at the fuel gauge and brought it to the attention of the pilot.

"Sir, a fast flight to Seattle will put us on the edge of, or into our fuel reserve. We should stop and take on some fuel."

"Can you make it on the reserve?" Dale asked, making it clear he was not in the mood for an argument.

"Yes, I'm pretty sure we can," he said reluctantly.

"Odin is in Seattle as a special unannounced guest of the city, about to dedicate a museum. He may be looking to spread the virus among the dignitaries before he disappears. We can't allow him to escape. He's responsible for the disease that's killed thousands in the last week or so. You with me?"

The pilot thought for a moment of all the dead he had seen on the news, wondering only when it would hit someone in his own family. The engines roared and the chopper rose rapidly into the now clear sky above the mansion. The big chopper spun around, nosed over, and gained speed quickly, like a greyhound pursuing a jack rabbit.

Aboard the *U.S.S. Pinckney*, FBI special agent Sean Fox was finally throwing his status around in the ship's medical ward. His frustration with his less than serious injuries was keeping him out of the hunt for Odin. He threw on a shirt and covered the numerous bandages and the stitches he could see in the mirror. Marching down the hall, he went straight to the comm room and walked in unannounced.

"Can we help you, sir?" the ensign inquired.

"Yeah, where is Wolf 71?" he asked, his FBI jacket plainly visible to the junior naval officer.

Not long after, Sean rose to his full six-foot-four frame and headed for the bridge.

Ten minutes later and a hundred sixty-two miles from downtown Seattle, the LAMPs helicopter lifted off the fantail and pointed itself toward the port city. Inside, Sean Fox was seething. Dale couldn't hide the fact that he had been infected by the virus, at least not from Sean. The satellite phone conversation between Sean and Dale had been a private event, as Dale's Blackhawk sped on toward Seattle.

⚷

Dalton Jordan arrived at the visiting dignitary entrance at the side of the museum. The sound of cars and people along the wharf filled the background. Stepping from the cab, he elected not to wait for his change. He immediately spotted an old colleague from Colorado State University and headed in his direction. The man walked down the wide threshold steps and shook hands with Dalton Jordan. After chatting and eyeing the new building, they made their way inside and out of the late morning sun.

⚷

Tori Evans stood up and put both hands on the bed rail. Her head was swimming from the cocktail of drugs and one hundred percent oxygen she'd been subjected to. The catheter attached to her abdomen hung freely at her side. She felt naked and abused, seeing herself inside the quarantine room, separated by the wall of heavy plastic and dressed in a hospital gown with the back open to the elements. She could only guess at her appearance. Looking around, she took note of the fact that there were no personal grooming devices, like a simple hairbrush or toothpaste tube.

"Hey," she called out to the nurse whose back was turned to her. "Hey, you, where am I?"

The nurse spun around in shock. The two doctors who routinely attended to the patient had had only a few drug induced conversations with her that were more stuporus then cogent.

Pushing the intercom button, someone in the CDC trailer in the back lot finally answered.

"Yes, what is it?"

"The female paleontologist is up," she blurted out.

"Yes, we've talked to her several times in the last thirty-six hours," a voice replied.

"No, I mean she's up and staring at me asking questions," she replied.

"She's vertical and coherent?"

"Vertical, coherent, and not at all happy from the look on her face."

Aboard Wolf 71
Six miles south of Seattle, Washington
Sunday, 1214 hours Pacific time

"Look's like the roof is open. Put us down in the ballpark. An agency car is waiting for us," Dale said to the pilot. "Then gas up and orbit just off the south harbor area. It's possible we may need you again."

The pilot acknowledged the directions and headed for the Coast Guard station just twenty miles up the coast.

Building 362, Lab B
Fort Detrick, Maryland
Sunday, 1515 hours Eastern Time

"Do we have all of the data?" the CDC microbiologist asked. The open communications line and the forty-two-inch, plasma flat screen allowed the parties at both ends real-time interaction.

"Yes, we are synced up, doctor," Dr. Walter Hunack responded from Provo, Utah.

The sound of the positive pressure ventilation system humming in the background was almost soothing.

"Let's begin."

The Cutter-Dane Museum
Main display hall
Seattle, Washington
Sunday, 1216 hours Pacific Time

The magnificent Great Hall was adorned with some of the best skeletal remains of the Cretaceous, Triassic, and Jurassic periods of Earth's distant past. For contrast, tiny Eohippus, the "dawn horse," was displayed prominently in front of a fully erect adult Tyrannosaurus Rex. Most of the public were not aware that many of the more valuable pieces in the museum's collection were actually casts of the original bones with the missing portions added in.

The T-Rex, on the other hand, was better than seventy percent original, the real thing. It dominated the main hall entry area, its open jaws almost five feet apart in a threatening pose. The eleven-inch teeth were a testament to its prowess as the most feared killer of its day.

Douglas Odin looked out over the well-heeled crowd of several hundred patrons of the arts from the white and green tablecloth draped stand. Most of them were multimillionaires. His presence was unique since multibillionaires were a far more rare commodity. He was keenly aware of his rockstar status as the second richest man on the planet, something that privately grated on him.

His speech would last for only a few minutes, after which he would head for the roof and his helicopter. Stepping to the podium, he began his remarks.

Safeco Field
Seattle, Washington
Sunday, 1218 hours Pacific Time

The Navy chopper tapped the grass beyond second base and settled to the ground. Two men in suits stood in the portal. One was detective Rod O'Brien of the Seattle PD. The other was Anthony Petrocelli. Dale and

Sullivan bailed out the side door of the helicopter and hurried across the outfield toward the arched walkway.

Behind them, the helo quickly took to the air and headed out over the bay for refueling.

"My agency has a plainclothes team at the museum, four men keeping an eye on Odin and company. I just checked with them as you were landing. He's on the stand giving a little talk about the value of the new museum to the local economy and science in general. We count at least a dozen men in his security detail."

As a foreign head of state and royalty," Rod O'Brien said with some loathing, "his men are armed with automatic weapons. Needless to say, we don't need a bloodbath with some of our leading citizens as the diversion."

Not wanting to waste much time with the FBI ASAC, Dale turned to him and looked down his nose at the smaller man in the impeccable, three-thousand-dollar suit.

"I just got off the satellite with Dan Covery, the attorney general, the president, and a few of his closest friends," Dale revealed. "Wanna know what they said?"

Not waiting for No-Knock to respond, he leaned slightly forward and spoke quietly, "You've been transferred to me until I don't need you anymore." Dale handed him a note from FBI headquarters.

A lump in his throat made Petrocelli's Adam's apple rise suddenly. "I'm thinking of using you as cannon fodder," Dale said very pointedly. Accepting his new, limited mortality, unexpectedly freed Dale up from a lifetime of political diplomacy.

Rod O'Brien, who was not impressed with No-Knock's reputation, turned his head and stifled a smile. He found Dale's candor surprisingly refreshing, like an ice-cold soft drink overloaded with caffeine.

"How are your men deployed?" Dale asked, directing his question to No-Knock.

"We have eight men: two are on the roofs of the buildings across from the front and rear of the museum; I have six on the ground, two out back and four inside the Great Hall."

"Alright, Sullivan and I are using Wolf 71 and 72 as our call sign. Get the word out on the net. I'm the IC. Let's go."

Once in the car, Dale and Sullivan got an update on Odin's speech. He was still at the podium talking between moments of applause.

Building 362, Lab B
Fort Detrick, Maryland
Sunday, 1520 hours Eastern Time

"All the baselines are in. Start the recorders," the microbiologist said.

A graph with multiple colored lines and bars appeared, along with the corresponding test data that had been previously run.

"Let's eliminate the obvious dead ends and move on to the inconclusive results," he said.

Thirty-two people in three locations watched as the chemical brew was applied to the wafer-thin slice of the fatal geode. As the vapors rose from the rock sample, the sensors began recording the composition results.

The Cutter-Dane Museum
Main display hall
Seattle, Washington
Sunday, 1222 hours Pacific Time

"Move a team into the stairwells between the Great Hall and his helicopter on the roof. I want another team on the side of the museum where the three Odin SUVs are parked. Do we know which way he's leaving?" Dale asked.

"We don't know his plans," Rod O'Brien responded.

Sullivan murmured something under his breath and looked out the window stone-faced.

"Sullivan, why don't you take Rod and cut off their access to the roof. I'll take No-Knock here and we'll head for the back of the museum behind the presentation area and see what develops. He should be done talking in a few minutes. One of us will get lucky and take him into custody," Dale said.

"I'm not so sure his security detail is going to be cooperative," Sullivan thought out loud, still looking through the window. Turning back, he looked at O'Brien, "Can we get a few more men to seal off the roof? Maybe that helicopter, in case we need air cover?"

O'Brien was immediately on his cell phone to his dispatch center, pulling in more assets.

"We're almost a block from the museum," the rookie FBI agent driving the car said. "Do you want to drive right up or slip in the back way?"

"Park it over there," Dale said, pointing to a red zone, "and we'll walk in."

Ninety seconds later, the five men stepped through the side door of the museum, flashing their identification cards for the museum security staff.

Building 362, Lab B
Fort Detrick, Maryland
Sunday, 1527 hours Eastern Time

"Do we have the ELISA ready?" the scientist conducting the test asked.

"All set," the CDC microbiologist replied, "let's see what it does."

Aboard the Navy helicopter
West of Seattle, Washington
Sunday, 1228 hours Pacific Time

"How much longer, son?" Sean asked the pilot of the LAMPs helicopter.

"About five minutes, sir. That's Bainbridge Island up ahead. Where do you want to land?"

"Huh, hadn't thought about that. Ah, let's circle the museum and look for a spot to set it down. I'll walk it from there."

Sean looked at the bleeding bandage on his left forearm and then back out the chopper's canopy to the Seattle skyline in the distance. His body was still sore, but the endorphins had pumped up his anger.

The Cutter-Dane Museum
Main display hall
Seattle, Washington
Sunday, 1229 hours Pacific Time

"We need to go, sir. There are law enforcement personnel milling about that we didn't ask for. I think something's up," the chief of Odin's detail said discreetly. He didn't like the look of intensity focused on Douglas Odin. He smelled trouble.

Douglas Odin kept on talking, but made it apparent he was about to wrap up his comments. The security chief called his man on the roof and ordered the Agusta helicopter engines brought on line for a quick departure.

Two seats over, another dignitary, the famous paleontologist, Dr. Dalton Jordan, was preparing to rise and step to the podium. He'd found Odin charming and interesting.

The cell phone in his pocket vibrated without the usual ringtone. Dale looked at the LED and saw that it was his brother. Standing in the corner, he watched Sullivan and Rod O'Brien make their way up the back steps toward the rooftop elevator.

"How are you feeling?" Dale asked, answering the phone.

"Better by the minute," Sean replied. "How are you feeling? Any symptoms?"

"Nothing yet, maybe my good genetics will pull me through."

Both men knew that wasn't going to happen; they needed a miracle.

"Let's hope. I'm inbound on the *Pinckney*'s LAMPs helo. I used my new status to commandeer the ride. Don't give me any grief over it either. I'm not in the mood. CTU says you headed to Seattle, so here I am. I'll be there in a few minutes. Where can I set down?"

Dale was taken aback for a moment by his older sibling's outright charge into probable trouble. Then it occurred to him that it was normal operating procedure for Sean.

"Well, we passed a corner park about an acre in size just south of the museum. It's across the street from us. I guess you can put it down there."

"Good, see you a few minutes."

Dale closed the phone and looked at Douglas Odin again. On the helicopter ride in from Portland, he had time to think about the virus. Odin's billions might keep him out of a courtroom for a good, long time. Dale was not going to let justice be denied because of money. His pursuit of Odin had boiled down to catching his own killer.

The crowd stood and applauded the normally reticent billionaire. He paused a moment to absorb the assembly and bowed his head in appreciation. Dr. Dalton Jordan took a few steps forward and shook the industrial giant's hand. Odin looked past Jordan to his chief of security, who was keeping a watchful eye on the law enforcement personnel.

Behind the elevated stage area, several Odin men had cleared a path to the steps that led to the elevator, which they were holding open. As Odin and his cadre reached the elevator, a few men in business suits raised gold badges and announced they were FBI agents.

Dale stepped forward, only to find himself being bumped hard by two of Odin's security people while Odin was hustled inside.

Okay, boys, we can play this game, Dale thought.

Grabbing the closest man's arm, Dale clamped on and twisted left, forcing the man forward. He stuck out his foot, which caught the man's ankle. Odin's security agent went sprawling across the polished rock floor. No-Knock was on him, with his foot pressed to the guy's neck and attempting to apply plasticuffs to his wrists. The man resisted and the fight was on.

The elevator closed before Dale could get to it. The second security officer reacted by throwing a punch at Dale to buy his employer time to escape. Dale ducked, the fist and arm scraping over his back. Then Dale charged ahead, crashing into the man's midsection and knocking the wind out of him. One smashing right blow caught the security officer on the left temple; he crumpled to the ground.

Dale grabbed Petrocelli's radio off the floor while No-Knock continued to wrestle with the suspect. "They're on the way up," he said, his adrenaline pumping.

With a quick elbow, he smashed the first security officer in the face as he stood up to flee. The big security man recoiled but stayed on his feet. Dale jabbed his foot into the man's knee and heard it crack. The man dropped to the ground in a gut wrenching groan yet reached into his jacket for his gun. Having no choice, Dale pulled his .45 when the man raised his own firearm.

Petrocelli saw the escalated exchange and rolled clear of Dale's shot.

Dale pumped two rounds in double tap fashion into the security officer's upper torso. A pool of bright-crimson blood began to spread across the tan-colored floor surface.

The sound of gunfire startled the audience on the other side of the curtain. The clatter of falling chairs and shoes rushing out of the room could be heard. Dalton Jordan climbed off the podium and pulled back the curtain in curiosity, never once giving thought to the possibility of danger. It was instantly clear that several law enforcement types were involved in subduing a couple of men with weapons.

"He's all yours, No-Knock," Dale said, charging headlong for the stairs.

Above him, he could make out the sound of gunfire, somewhere near the roof six floors above. It instantly elevated to many weapons going off at once. Over the din of shooting, Dale could clearly hear the big, luxury helicopter's twin jet engines winding up. Looking over his shoulder, he saw No-Knock cuffing the live suspect.

Odin was going to get away and Dale's helicopter had yet to return. *Damn.* As he headed for the wall stairs, he abruptly stopped and pulled out his phone. Hitting speed dial, he pressed his ear to the speaker.

"Sean Fox."

"It's Dale. You still in the air?"

"Yeah, we're just descending into the park."

"Don't. I need you to stop Odin's chopper from taking off from the museum's roof. Can you do that?"

In the background, he could hear his brother talking to the LAMPs' pilot. The pilot seemed reluctant until Sean pulled out his copy of the presidential authorization and stuck it under the pilot's nose to show him the signature of the President of the United States. Sean's name appeared prominently in the text, along with the words "international terrorist," "Douglas Odin," and "any action deemed necessary by the aforementioned FBI personnel."

"For real?" the pilot asked. The airborne tactical officer in the right seat finally nodded as well.

"We'll be right there," Sean said to Dale as he closed his phone.

The twin-engine SH-60B LAMPs configured Sea Hawk attack helicopter, still bristling with antisubmarine warfare weapons on the pylons, shot skyward. Seconds later, the powerful copter cleared the top of the museum roofline.

Odin was just coming up the last few steps to the roof from the elevator. Several men from his security detail heard another loud noise suddenly echoing off the rooftop. Stunned by what they saw, they hustled their employer back into the building.

Inside the Agusta executive helicopter, the copilot went white as a sheet. There, staring straight at him through the windshield was a heavily armed, U.S. Navy attack helicopter. He immediately took note of the fact that the thing was armed with a pair of Mark II Penguin missiles slung beneath the extended wing pylons. He was definitely on the wrong end of this encounter.

Staring at the anonymous helmeted men in the attack chopper, the copilot saw one man slide his open hand across his throat in a cutting motion. His pants were suddenly wet.

Odin's men in the rooftop stairwell made a beeline for the Great Hall grand staircase.

Off in a side room from the stairway, taking cover, Sullivan and Rod O'Brien were engaged in a gun battle that they were sure to lose as soon as they ran out of ammunition. Screaming sirens could be heard outside the building, with police cars arriving to take up defensive positions on the front street.

"We get some of our men to the SUV and have them take off through the park grounds behind the museum. Everyone will think you're in the vehicle," the security chief told Odin. "I have three chase cars that can run interference for them. We'll draw off that Navy helicopter to follow them and return and escape in our helo."

The eight security men and their boss went down two more flights of stairs, shooting as they went.

The detective's hand was bleeding slowly from a round that grazed him and lodged in his bulletproof vest. He found that he couldn't squeeze his fingers together anymore. Looking under the vest, he could see the large, purple welt on his torso. It was painful.

"I'm almost out of ammo," O'Brien said.

Not hearing any response from Sullivan, he looked over to see the FBI agent holding a wad of white tablecloth from the room's conference table against his abdomen. He was still aiming his .45 toward the door, but the glassy-eyed look told O'Brien the man was in serious trouble. Sullivan had taken one round in the side and was bleeding badly.

O'Brien grabbed his radio from his suit pocket, "Delta 22 has an officer down on the museum fourth floor. Armed suspects are descending the building toward the ground floor."

He hoped the dispatcher could make out the call, considering all the noise from the gunfire outside the room. He kicked the heavy, solid core door closed, spun the lock, and raced over to Sullivan, who was slumped over the highly polished, twelve foot long, mahogany table.

No-Knock hustled his handcuffed suspect out the side door and crossed the street to a police car.

Dale and the rookie FBI agent took up defensive positions on the second floors ante area. Seconds after getting into place, two advance men from the security detail came running into the passageway.

"FBI, drop your weapons!" he shouted.

Dale knew they would never do it. They were highly paid, well trained, seasoned professionals whose options did not include surrender. As soon as the first one turned to engage him and the rookie, Dale fired.

Bullets crisscrossed the long room from both ends until finally Dale's third round and the rookie's fourth made contact. The first security officer went down but kept firing from behind a large porcelain floor display.

His partner, a few feet behind, stepped into the path of an errant projectile from the rookie, who was off target and firing rapidly, more for suppression than anything else. The stray slug slammed into the bridge of the unlucky gunman's nose. He hit the floor and died as the deadly clash continued.

A glass display case shattered. The stainless steel drinking faucet against the wall sprayed water on the floor. A bullet had severed the copper water line inside the thin, outer casing.

Four men sidestepped the shooting gallery in the passageway by running through an adjoining exhibit room. They made their way down the hall to the main floor, where they joined up with another Odin security agent. The group of men bulldozed their way, firing automatic weapons as they ran. Outside, Seattle police officers were armed with pistols, shotguns, and a few semiauto rifles. The police and sheriff's SWAT teams were just pulling up.

"Okay, we wait while they drive off and go back up. The Navy chopper should be gone in a minute." He keyed his wrist microphone, "Ahlstrom, is the Navy helicopter still on the roof?"

The pilot of Odin's copter pushed the button on the yoke, "Yes Einar, he is flying all around us. We cannot move. They have ordered us to shut down our engines."

"Can you take off if we return?"

"I don't think so."

Fan, det hållet, Odin swore out loud.

"We'll still get out of here, Father. It'll just take a bit longer," Thor said. The second security officer, standing in front of Thor, scanned the hallway.

The security chief looked around, "We should get to the main floor and climb into the blacked out rafters near the ceiling. If we can conceal ourselves among the heavy curtains there until dark, we may be able to slip out later."

"How about taking a hostage and getting out that way?" Thor asked, thumbing his Uzi submachine gun.

"Taking hostages only focuses attention on you, and you'll be greatly outnumbered by the authorities," the security chief said. "No, it's better to hide and wait until dark. We're on the wharf, so we may be able to disappear into the crowds later. We need to go quickly, before they're better organized, and let them think we've escaped."

The four men quietly slipped out the side door to the exhibit room and started down the empty hall for the main gallery.

"Swing around so I can get to the roof," Sean demanded.

"Sir?"

"I need to get out," Sean yelled over the noise.

The SH-60 chopper swung its tail around, the side door slid open, and Sean dropped seven feet to the roof. The helicopter backed up a few dozen yards as Sean charged the Agusta. The pilot and tactical officer of the LAMPs watched as Sean dragged the two pilots from the executive helicopter. He handcuffed them to the outer door of their aircraft and went into the Agusta to kill the power.

Emerging from the Agusta, Sean indicated that he wanted the LAMPs pilot to hold station. Two minutes later, he materialized at the rooftop access door with a uniformed deputy sheriff in tow.

Sean stood talking to the deputy briefly before waving the LAMPs chopper in closer.

He watched as the deputy climbed aboard the Navy helo, which turned it into an airborne law enforcement vehicle. Only then did he become aware that his FBI parka was flapping wildly in the artificial wind. Running back to the rooftop access door, he started buttoning up.

Several floors below Sean, the wounded Odin security agent took cover behind a large rock in the wide, arched hallway next to the Triceratops nesting exhibit.

"Pin him down with a few rounds while I move around that tall exhibit floor sign. I'll get behind him and we'll have him," Dale instructed the rookie.

57

Building 362, Lab B
Fort Detrick, Maryland
Sunday, 1542 hours Eastern Time

"It's working!" the CDC scientist exclaimed. "It's working. Look at it go!"

The colored graph slowly charted an increasingly dissipating gas factor on the ELISA software program. As if willing the test results to reach the end of the box graph above the nominal base line, everyone in the room held their breath until finally the graph peaked. Clapping and cheers broke out in all three secured facilities logged into the secretive military research test facility.

"Everyone settle down. Before we get carried away, we need to replicate the results. Feed another wafer into the chamber," the scientist insisted. "Reset the ELISA and let's go again."

The lab went silent.

The Cutter-Dane Museum
Main display hall
Seattle, Washington
Sunday, 1242 hours Pacific Time

"Come on, you can make it. We're almost out," O'Brien said with confidence. The soothing tone of the elevator bell chimed as the ground floor doors opened up. Rod O'Brien quickly glanced around the massive exhibition hall. With one arm around Sullivan and another on his gun, the two men half walked, half dragged their wounded bodies out into the Great Hall.

A man in a cowboy hat, wearing a BYU parka, held his hands up upon seeing the two men emerge from the elevator. He had been crouching behind a large, commercial popcorn machine. Seeing the police badge on the man's belt, he stood up.

O'Brien recognized him as the visiting paleontologist from Utah, celebrated for his discovery of the Utah Raptor.

"What the hell are you doing here?" Rod O'Brien demanded in a low voice.

"Trapped by my curiosity, I'm afraid. I came back to see what all the commotion was about and found myself huddled down here for safety. The cops are all outside, I guess, waiting for the SWAT team. They have the building practically surrounded. A group of men ran through here a minute ago and went out the side door," he said, pointing behind him. "I'm Dr. Dalton Jordan, by the way."

"Grab him under the arm, Dalton, and let's head for a side door."

The three men kept close to the back wall, using the various displays as cover until they reached a fire door. O'Brien put his gun in its holster and keyed his radio, "Delta 22 coming out with a wounded officer and dignitary on the north side."

He grabbed his gold badge off his belt and held it out. Kicking the door open, they emerged into the sunlight . . . and a dozen Seattle police officers pointing weapons their way.

Two minutes later, an ambulance with FBI agent Sullivan Casse and detective Rod O'Brien inside took off for the hospital.

⚷

Slipping in behind the Odin security officer, Dale could see the man slumped over. He had succumbed to his wounds.

"He's dead," Dale said in a low voice. "Let's see if we can find those guys who gave us the slip a few minutes ago in the side hall."

Both FBI agents advanced slowly in the exhibit hall. After a few seconds, it was apparent their quarry had gone out the door which was standing open on the opposite side of the room.

Outside the museum grounds, the Seattle Police Department had shut down all the surrounding roads and had the streets vacated in a containment move. They knew they had several local officers and an unknown quantity of federal agents still inside the building. They had no way of knowing how many suspects were still at large, or how heavily armed they were.

"They're gone. Let's head for the catwalk," Odin's security chief said. The four men moved forward, with Thor bringing up the rear.

"Freeze, FBI!" the rookie called out.

Dale was twenty feet away, next to a black interior skywalk door, which he had opened for cover. He was operating in the dark shadows of the elevated catwalk system.

The security man pushed Odin forward, pulling the trigger on his Uzi at the same time. Bullets flew across the Great Hall, impacting guy wires, walls, conduit, cooling vents, pipes, and miscellaneous integrated support structures.

The FBI rookie dropped on his stomach and returned fire. The catwalk complex was dark and the bullet flash at the end of the gun's muzzle caused his pupils to constrict, reducing his visibility.

The rounds from the Odin security agent's Uzi inadvertently shredded the heavy, forty foot long drape ties above the Great Hall. Thor Odin was quickly ensnared in the unwinding crushed velvet cabling from above. The rookie agent moved in, gun first, to take control of the suspect.

Dale moved cautiously out on the catwalk to pursue the other three men, leaving the rookie behind.

"Keep moving. We'll go around the corner and get behind another drape," the security man said as he prodded the elder Odin to move. Odin cursed in Swedish beneath his breath.

Dale spotted the two men with their backs to him. He crouched down, watching them turn right at the corner of the catwalk. Spotting a weighted rope just in front of him, he reached out and swung across the twenty-five-foot span to the other side.

The two men walked past Dale, who was lurking in the darkness on an adjoining ledge, and continued along the narrow, railed walkway.

In the last few hours, Dale's stomach had begun to hurt. His abdominal muscles were grinding as if he were incredibly hungry. His eyesight wasn't as sharp or focused; it felt like the eyestrain brought on by lack of sleep. He was sick and he knew it. The man responsible for his impending death was right in front of him.

"Hold it right there!" he yelled at the top of his lungs, hoping the sudden shock would momentarily disorient them. "Drop the weapon and put your hands on . . ."

The Uzi spit out several rounds and went empty.

Dale was already zeroed in on the big security agent. Instinct and adrenaline took over as two quick rounds from the .45 rocketed down the barrel. The security agent was still moving on the floor after being hit, so Dale double-tapped a third and fourth bullet from the fifteen-round semi-auto pistol to ensure he stayed down.

The tall, athletic security chief fell back against the black tubular railing. The first bullet from Dale's gun penetrated his groin, and as the recoil raised the .45, the second full metal jacketed bullet punched through his stomach and exited his kidney. He teetered for a moment and finally toppled over the railing, falling the forty-two feet to the highly polished rock floor in front of the podium.

Looking around, Dale couldn't find Douglas Odin or the remaining security officer. During the shooting, they had escaped down the long, dark catwalk system.

The rookie agent dragged the handcuffed Thor Odin, who was a full four inches taller than him, off the wide catwalk staging area and out into the big, arched hallway.

Thor, though, wasn't going to be so easily subdued. As the agent dropped him on the floor face down, Odin slid his legs out behind him, catching the young agent by surprise and sweeping him off his feet.

The agent hit the floor hard and cracked his skull. His head started to spin and he began to lose consciousness.

Odin rolled up on his back and slipped his cuffed hands in front. He grabbed the agent's gun off the floor and kicked him viciously in the head once. Regaining his feet, he looked down at the rookie agent and pulled the hammer on the 9mm. "Bye-bye."

The sound of gunfire from the catwalk caught the younger Odin's attention. He needed to go to the aid of his father. Turning back to the semiconscious agent, he swung the gun around.

The recoil of the pistol reverberated off the walls. Another round followed.

Thor Odin fell backward. The gun in his hand dropped to the ground and bounced with a clank. The rookie had retrieved his backup .380 auto from the hip pocket in his suit. The hole in Thor's lung wouldn't have killed him outright, but the second bullet hit him in the neck, severing an artery and blocking his airway. In a few moments, his lifeless body relaxed on the floor.

The rookie agent passed out.

The sound of heavy, pounding feet came to a stop in the hallway off the catwalk area. The remaining Odin security agent, sent by the old man, was there to retrieve Douglas Odin's son. Looking at the two men lying prone, he stepped over to check for a pulse on Thor. It was obvious before reaching the billionaire's son that he was probably dead. Stepping over to the downed FBI agent, he discovered the man was still breathing. Holding out his firearm, he leaned over to finish the job Thor had started.

Two shots rang out and the security officer staggered back a few feet. He slumped to the floor next to Odin's body and attempted to raise his gun. A third shot went off and he fell dead, a pool of blood staining the travertine tile floor.

Sean Fox approached slowly. Seeing the area was clear, he checked the downed FBI agent. The man's pulse was strong but his facial injuries were serious. Holstering his .45, he raised the agent up in a fireman's carry, got him over his shoulder, and moved out. Shortly thereafter, Sean made it outside and to an ambulance.

The sound of shooting down the hallway reached Dale. He hoped that it wasn't bad news. His attention was temporarily drawn away, but when he heard a different noise up ahead, he refocused on his pursuit of Douglas Odin.

Odin walked toward the dead end of the long catwalk overlooking the south side of the Great Hall.

Reaching the blacked out wall, he turned to hurriedly retreat to the next intersecting walkway. Looking down, he could see exhibits of various sizes below.

Dale stopped and listened, hoping to hear the billionaire moving around. After a few seconds, the footfalls he was expecting could be heard. He crouched low to reduce his silhouette against the lighting from below and moved forward.

"You can't get out Odin, you're trapped," Dale called out. "The building is surrounded, and your status as a foreign head of state has been negated by an international arrest warrant. Give up and you can stay alive, at least for awhile."

Two rounds whizzed by just as Dale tried moving forward again. *Damn, that was close. Okay, pal, let's try it the hard way.* Dale backed up a few feet and slid down on his stomach.

"Odin, you have the right to remain hidden. If you give up the right to hide, then it's just you and me, and I will beat your sorry ass to a pulp. You have a right to the presence of a paramedic. If you cannot afford a paramedic, don't worry, I've got a hefty cinch sack bag to drag your carcass out to a dumpster." Dale went silent and waited. The angry outburst made him feel better.

Realizing that the FBI agent was close behind, Odin stepped off the catwalk. The narrow service steps led down to the skull of the forty-foot-long T-Rex. Holding onto the guy wires, he chose his footing carefully. Might he be able to climb down and get away yet? After several steps, he saw the shadowy outline of the relentless FBI agent above him.

The jaws, they're big enough for me to stoop behind, Odin thought. *I can wait for him to get closer and finish it.* He climbed down slowly and crouched behind the massive, six foot cranium filled with ancient, petrified teeth. Kneeling behind the foot-long canines, he stuck his gun out and waited.

From his peripheral vision, Dale noticed a high-strength steel wire moving to his right. He stopped and let his eyes follow it down to the T-Rex skeleton just ahead.

There, inside the skeleton. He's there.

Shots rang out from the T-Rex. Odin was premature in his desire for revenge and his bullets went wide, crashing into the high ceiling beyond the FBI agent.

Dale dropped prone on the catwalk again and took cover.

Odin's vision was partially blocked by the big, ancient jaws, so he stood up. His heart was pounding and his hands were sweating. The wire overhead was straining with the extra weight.

Dale was caught out in the open less than forty feet away, while Odin was protected by the thick oral cavity of the sixty-five-million-year-old dinosaur. Dale saw Odin's gun come forward, but from his flat position on the floor of the sturdy catwalk, he was unable to get his .45 over the grate and tubing.

Odin leaned out, preparing to shoot the hapless agent.

Realizing his position was untenable, Dale jumped up to run and saw the support line shake again. He scanned the catwalk quickly, placed the muzzle of his .45 against the thin, steel cable, and pulled the trigger. A loud whipping noise, like a high-speed blender, filled the air. The main guy wire holding the skeleton's head open gave way.

Inside the T-Rex skull, gravity slammed the long-dead creature's heavy head down on its lower jawbone with a nasty crunch. The pistol the ruthless billionaire was holding out dropped to the floor below and cartwheeled into the coin fountain.

Like a macabre scene from an old horror flick, the dinosaur's massive teeth had cut Douglas Odin nearly in half.

Building 362, Lab B
Fort Detrick, Maryland
Sunday, 1610 hours Eastern Time

All eyes focused on the sealed chamber. "It's working! The stain and acid test is working. The virus is dying. Ladies and gentlemen, we have an antidote!"

Cheers went up in all three facilities. Within a few minutes, the president and his advisors were brought on line.

"Mr. President, we have a resolution to the viral infection," the senior military scientist advised.

"We managed to isolate several contributing factors and came up with an enzyme that not only counters the effect of the anomalous characteristics of the infection, but defeats its replication."

The president - a college history teacher and former Marine helicopter pilot - understood the necessity of hearing the man's explanation within his own unique, scientific language. He knew the microbiologist would eventually reduce it to laymen's terms he would understand. He leaned back in his large, overstuffed executive chair in the oval office, which was mostly a ceremonial gathering place, while his advisors listened in silently.

"What did you find, doctor?" he finally inquired, moving the lengthy explanation along.

"We ran several conclusive tests and performed an additional examination in an attempt to produce matching results. We found a protein, which, if subflash pasteurized at one hundred forty-four degrees for thirty-two seconds, produces a pathogen with a light-brown sludge. The soluble molecular weight and solids composition decreased the pantothenic acids in the sludge by a factor of two. The result is that the amino acid byproduct modifies the target enzyme in the virus that we haven't been able to defeat. The radioimmunoassay produces a very narrow linear range - between point-zero-one and three-point-two. The enzyme based ELISA test shows monoclonal antibodies in the antigen enzyme. The P55N enzyme we isolated and used against it is killing the replicated function of the enzyme in the virus. We have a cure, Mr. President."

The president looked at one of his advisors and then back at the high-definition digital screen. "Congratulations, doctor, and all of you at the lab." Smiles and backslaps followed the president's statement. "Now, doctor, what do we need to do to mass produce it for the public?"

"Our antidotal enzyme is readily available, Mr. President," the doctor said, almost wondering why the man hadn't followed his explanation.

"It is?" The president sounded a little surprised, and leaned forward in his chair.

"Yes, sir, let me put it this way. If Guernsey cows had been around during the Cretaceous Period, we might still have dinosaurs roaming the woods today."

"What?!"

"It's a whole milk enzyme, Mr. President. The antidote is in the molecular composition of whole milk. A quart of whole milk contains enough antigens and enzymes to kill the virus in about five hours. That's how our infected viral survivors managed to stay alive - they all consumed whole milk before contracting the disease. The milk retarded the viral enzyme and stunted the progression of the illness's replication."

The president sat back a moment, then rose from his leather chair.

Speaking to his secretaries of health and interior, he started issuing orders. "And Sam, call the Agriculture Department, U.S. Dairy Association, and the Milk Board. We're going to need their help, too."

Pacific Ocean
Eighty-four miles east of Klang, Malaysia
Thursday, 2320 hours Malaysian Time

Four days after escaping the U.S. Navy, the stealthy submarine surfaced low in the water. It was a moonless night.

The one hundred thirty-eight foot coastal lumber carrier nearby was the primary pirate support ship for the Terengganu-Musa Islamic terrorist group that raided shipping along the poorly patrolled Malaysian coast.

Ingvar Wallen's larger warship glided to a stop three hundred feet parallel to the pirate vessel. The main hatch opened and Wallen and his second mate stepped out on the deck in the sweltering, South Pacific heat.

A twenty-six foot tender from the converted coastal lumber hauler slid alongside a few minutes later. The first five of eighteen CHINO torpedoes were released from the deck mounted enclosures and transferred to the tender. The smaller boat could only carry five torpedoes at a time, so the transfer took almost an hour to complete.

On the third trip, the pirates were delighted to see the torpedo enclosure totally empty. With the exchange of money and weapons finally finished, the two ships parted company.

Wallen received fifteen-and-a-half million dollars for the sale of the torpedoes, and almost three million from previous seizures at sea. With his surviving crew of twenty-five men, each man's share was close to one million dollars. Along with half of their wages which were banked with a financial firm on the island of Vanuatu, each man had well over one-point-two million to his name.

As the ships drifted apart, the sub sank beneath the calm, sultry sea. Wallen ordered the helmsman to emergency dive to six hundred feet and brought the antisonar tiles to full power. As expected, the pirate ship turned back, with its sonar blasting away a few minutes later. The ship dropped several post-Vietnam War era Chinese torpedoes in the water in an attempt to kill the submarine.

Wallen ordered minimal speed. The sub glided along at four knots while the old communist torpedoes searched in vain until they ran out of fuel and dropped to the ocean floor. Wallen took the liberty of blowing a couple of countermeasure noisemakers once the torpedoes from the pirate ship were no longer a threat.

Aboard the pirate ship, the Malaysian sailors were certain they had sunk the submarine. The pirate ship turned and headed due west, her crew celebrating with flowing alcohol.

Seven miles away from the transfer site, Wallen ordered the sub's dormant forward torpedo doors opened. The two CHINO torpedoes that graced the torpedo room for emergencies were quickly fired and the doors closed again.

Two minutes passed in silence aboard the submersed warship until a reverberating sound washed over the submarine. The pirates and their newly acquired lethal torpedoes were headed to the bottom, eleven thousand feet down.

Wallen's remorse for his actions of the past few years was only partly salved. The pirates were miscreants that no one would really miss. He had, perhaps, paid back some misfortunate victims of their predation upon the seas.

Retiring to his cabin, Wallen's thoughts were filled with regret for his recent past spent in the employ of Douglas Odin. How much havoc and grief had he visited upon otherwise good people? His demons had caught up with him. His only wish was to find a way to repent of his misdeeds.

A knock on the cabin door broke his train of thought. "Enter."

"Captain, we are heading due south toward our rendezvous," his XO said.

"Thank you, Mr. Sjorken."

Looking at the captain, Sjorken offered his own thoughts. "Our deeds as rogue seamen are over, sir, and none too late for me."

Wallen looked up at his executive officer. "Are you reading my thoughts, Hans?"

"No more so, sir, than you can read mine. I wish we could rededicate our ship to a more positive service. Perhaps hunting down more pirates and clearing up some shipping channels along the Malaca Straits might be good penance."

Wallen mustered a slight smile and nodded his head. "How much penance would it take to salve our souls, eh, Hans? No, this ship must not fall into the wrong hands. We must carry through with our plans and find another way to beg forgiveness from our nightmares."

Hans Sjorken, lost in his own thoughts, finally bid the captain goodnight, then turned and left.

Wallen decided that his share of the treasure would be donated to the International Lost Sailors Fund operating out of Norway.

In a few days, Wallen would put all but four of his men off the submarine on an island in the Marianas chain, where further transportation would disperse them and return them home. He intended to scuttle the submarine and motor back in the sub's underwater delivery vehicle.

The millions would be transferred to a retail bank on Vanuatu Island. His men would eventually draw on their money as legal income, based on a contract shipping job they had worked off the last two years in the Pacific. That company, for legitimate purposes, was now out of business.

Wallen would return home to Sweden to be with nephews, nieces, and his Navy pension. His demons might never forgive him for trying to relive his glory days as a submarine skipper playing cat and mouse with the old Soviet Navy in the Baltic Sea. That work, he felt, was best left to younger men whose loyalty had not drifted over the years.

Utah Valley Medical Center
Provo, Utah
Saturday, 1012 hours Mountain Time

Tori Evans finally left the hospital after exhaustive testing. Her immune system was back on track and her organs showed no sign of deterioration.

Walking out with her parents into the sunshine, she found news cameras and reporters clogging the medical facility driveway. Her parents informed her on the way out that Dr. Dalton Jordan had visited or called twice a day, every day, while she was hospitalized. It was apparent that they were appreciative of his kind and caring nature. Tori was enamored of the famous paleontologist and confided to her mother that she had more than a schoolgirl crush on the man.

Standing next to the stretch, white limo, Dalton Jordan saw them exit the building. He held the door open while they got in. As he was about to close it and watch them drive away, Tori grabbed his hand and pulled him in.

The personal residence of the commanding admiral
Near Everett, Washington
Saturday, 1205 hours Pacific Time

Sullivan Casse was the first to arrive. He cruised down the driveway in his temporary wheelchair to the freshly mowed backyard overlooking

Puget Sound. Seagulls wheeled around like acrobats in the sunny sky above. The warm temperature and typical breeze made the catered barbecue that much more pleasant. Sullivan's nose detected steak in the air and he wheeled ahead a little faster.

Dale and Sean pulled up in a cab. Dale's fiancée, Betty Jo Case, and Sean's wife, Kelly, emerged from the opposite side of the taxi and walked to the back: A small knot of people were already there, including the firefighters from the *Chief Seattle*, Marine Captain Israel George, Detective Rod O'Brien and Sean and Dale's parents.

"Well, how's it feel to be a firefighter again?" his dad asked, seeing him for the first time in months.

"I'm happy to be relieved of my temporary status as an FBI agent. Much safer, no one ever shoots at a firefighter. Besides, the perks aren't all that great, given the risk factors."

He gave both of his sons bear hugs. Behind the senior Fox was his wife, wearing a broad smile. She hugged her sons so hard she almost popped their bandages off.

"I understand the FBI is making some changes to the local office?" the admiral inquired, stepping out onto the patio with a cold beer in hand.

"Yes, sir. No-Knock, I mean ASAC Petrocelli, has been asked to retire at the end of the year, along with his boss," Dale replied. The admiral nodded stoic approval.

The admiral casually tilted his head, indicating to Dale he should go into the house. Dale excused himself and went inside with the admiral to the second floor study.

"I have been asked to pass something on to you privately that will eventually filter down through the chain of command." The admiral looked out the picture window to the bay, then turned and faced Dale.

"You talked to your father on the phone sometime in the past few days. Did you know the president was once a junior officer on your dad's staff in the Marine Corps?"

Dale cocked his ear. "I knew the president was a combat vet in Vietnam, but you say he worked for my dad?"

"He did, indeed. Your dad had a conversation with him a few days ago.

You noticed the FBI removed the local ASAC from your path rather quickly, and all other impediments disappeared?"

"Yeah, I saw that. Surprised me a little, given the ASAC's political clout and my own low level rank in the system."

"We have two dead congressmen, a dead senator, and a score of other political figures who died during this outbreak. Things like that cut a lot of red tape. The short of it is that the man with the MOH went to bat when the country needed its A team unhindered and tightly focused on the job. You're not supposed to know that your old man made a call to one of his junior officers now sitting in the Oval Office. But he didn't make me promise not to tell either – I think it was an oversight on his part. Anyway, you and Sullivan are going to get additional staff inside the CTU from here on out to support you and each independent field team with an active antiterrorism case. The CTU director's additional duties will include running interference and making logistical assets quickly available from any source you deem necessary. The FBI is also creating a new position for you that will let you chase any counterterrorism case you choose, anywhere in the world. Your GS rating just jumped another grade. Congratulations . . . don't tell anyone, including Sullivan, just yet."

Dale stared at the admiral without blinking, deep in thought, and a thousand miles away.

The admiral walked out of the room, leaving Dale to himself. After a few moments, Dale snapped out of his trance and caught up to the admiral at the bottom of the stairs. Both men walked outside together, greeted by the sounds of hearty conversation.

"Thankfully, no one on the cruise ship came down ill," Sean said.

Dale smiled, "That rookie agent is recovering from his injuries. He's being assigned to regular duties in the Seattle office when he returns. He did a great job for a guy in his first week in the field."

"You know what's weird," Sean offered, "who would have thought that whole milk would be a cure for a deadly disease?"

"It bothers me, though, that the Nordian sub and her crew managed to get away," the admiral interjected. "She had technology we would like to see firsthand, although we're looking inside of Odin's Silicon Valley holdings for the technical data. It's the only place it could have come from."

The smell of steaks sizzling on the grill wafted over the small gathering. A neatly pressed Navy steward walked around serving snacks.

"Gentlemen," the admiral said loudly, "the Nord Island caretaker government sent over something to the president. Since he couldn't give it to you, he awarded it to your dad as a contract bonus for the cattle ranch."

Dale's father held out a set of keys. "It's around the other side of the house in the garage," he said.

The entire group moved to the open garage and looked inside. There, sitting on four new, Michelin Tiger Paw tires was a highly polished, full-restored, 1968 Shelby GT500.

"It's the one we crashed out on the island," Sean said, looking closer. "They repaired the bullet holes and everything."

"By the way," the elder Fox said, "We also have a Mercedes SL600 Turbo for Sullivan, and a Hennessy Venom Coupe for Sean. They're yours when you get out to the ranch, courtesy of the Nord Island folks who appreciate all you did for them."

"Hey, Dale. Know what FBI stands for?"

"Oh man, what?" his brother replied, with some misgiving.

"Finally, a Better Incentive," he said with a wry grin, running his hand over the glossy hood of the rare, collectible Mustang. "I'm ready to be an FBI agent again."

After the laughter died down, the admiral motioned everyone back to the patio. The stewards were putting a white linen tablecloth over the large dining table under an outsized green parasol.

"You asked me earlier what would become of the island," the admiral said to Dale. "It will remain a sovereign nation, thanks to the UN. Turns out Odin had a distant cousin in Sweden, probably never even met the guy. He assumes the title of prince, ownership of the island, and forty billion-plus dollars, minus reparation costs already agreed to."

"Wow, how would you like to be that guy?" Kelly said.

"Yeah, megabucks that would make a lottery winner jealous. Anybody know who he is?" Sean asked.

The admiral scanned the report from the State Department he had in his back pocket and found the information. "After an exhaustive search of genealogical records in Stockholm, they turned up a retired Swedish Navy captain by the name of Ingvar Wallen."

Tom can be e-mailed at "Tomforest2002@aol.com"

Or go to:

"Tomforest.com"

For a preview of Tom's next book, turn the page.

COLD HARD KNOCK

Tom Forest

The nuclear physicist slowly, methodically, and carefully lowered the angled grip cutter down the side of the narrow, recessed hole. Touching the stainless steel siding could short the electrical process and trigger the nuclear bomb. He had no way of knowing what fail-safes had been built in to defeat someone trying to diffuse the device.

It took three precious minutes, minutes they really didn't have to spare, to reach the blue wire beneath the coil. Stripping away a small amount of sheathing, he gently pulled the slack, exposed wire and twisted it onto the bottom of the pigtail. He gave it a little tug and felt relieved to see it hold. The connective loop was complete.

With the hands of a skilled cardiovascular surgeon, he raised the grip cutter tool slowly up the shaft. Carefully squeezing the pigtail with a firm grip, the wire snapped a few seconds later. Watching with the eyes of a hawk zeroing in on a ground squirrel, he meticulously retrieved the wire. It took a moment to pull the coil boosted, radio communication remote detonator from the narrow hole. He dropped it into the leather pouch on the sled with a nervous reprieve. Laying the tool down, the scientist wiped his brow.

"Nasty," he said out loud to no one in particular, "just nasty." He sat on the edge of the sled and took a deep breath.

The device was about twice the size of a case of paper, but heavier.

The seven men standing about let out a collective sigh of relief, almost disbelieving that the well machined contraption could be so deadly.

Dr. Stephen Nash was one of the senior nuclear troubleshooters for NEST – the Nuclear Emergency Search Team response unit out of Las Vegas.

"It appears to be in the neighborhood of fifteen to eighteen kilotons, from the measured readings it was throwing off. My calibration is limited here, but when we get it back to the lab, we'll know more about it. The yield, if detonated at three thousand feet above the ground, would be a little more than the Hiroshima device. The shielding and construction are excellent, an almost classic laboratory design, with a few shortcuts thrown in to save time. This device was built by someone with serious resources and expertise. Whoever made or assembled it is indeed a very talented person. It's the best I've ever seen outside of our own controlled manufacturing process."

Looking it over more closely, however, Dr. Nash added, "Made in America with foreign parts, though. Not good, not good."

A Secret Service agent held up the coiled receiver from the pouch and looked at it. "It doesn't look all that deadly."

"As a component, perhaps not, but I assure you that if someone had pressed the remote detonator from a few miles away, we would already be a vaporized mist. And not even that, because the vapor would cease to exist as well."

Dr. Nash closed the cover plate and put the tool back in his kit. "Unfortunately, that won't kill the device. I can't reach the internal mechanism or the clock. I've honestly never seen anyone strip-weld over the countersinks before. It's brilliant, really. Whoever built this knows we do not carry a weld breaker in the emergency kit.

"Gentleman, it appears that our antagonists have reneged on their end of the agreement," Nash stated matter-of-factly. "It's time to switch to disposal mode. What other options do you suppose we have available to us?" He looked around at the assembled men.

The flashing digital clock face rolled down to twenty-nine minutes. Above them, the heavy snow continued to fall.

The Marine staff sergeant spoke up. "Maybe we could minimize the explosive damage by moving it to another location. There's a recessed valley about five miles to the west of us. The nuclear detonation would be partially contained within the natural landscape. And the heavy snow will keep the radiation fallout down to a minimum."

The sergeant reached into the sleeve pocket on his jacket and pulled out a laminated topographical map of the wilderness area. Spreading the map out on the oak plank, they all looked it over. The sergeant came up with a grease pen and marked the target valley.

"How long will it take to get there?" the Secret Service agent asked. The Marine NCO thought for a moment before answering.

"Given the terrain and obstacles, I'd say about twenty minutes to the bottom. We're down to twenty-eight minutes now. I don't think we can get a helicopter in here anymore even if we had time to bring one up, which we don't. The snow flurries are right on top of us."

"We'll have to take it in on a snowmobile," the agent replied.

"Excuse me," Dr. Nash interrupted. "In case it has not occurred to any of you, I'm afraid that the person delivering that thing into the valley will probably not be returning." He pointed to the close terrain lines on the map. "There won't be time to climb back out on the snowmobile and escape the blast."

The eight men looked at the topography represented by the map markings in silence. They were considering the merits of fleeing for their lives and deciding which unlikely hero should carry the explosive to his doom. "The alternative is thousands dead and an uninhabitable Park City," the scientist observed.

FBI agent Dale Fox paced back and forth in the packed snow around the group of men, racking his brain for another solution.

"Negative!" Dale blurted out. The big FBI agent pushed the Secret Service man aside. "I've spent some time in these mountains hunting deer with my brother."

Dale grabbed the map.

"I've hiked all over this area. The Echols mineshaft is over fifty-one hundred feet straight down. It's just over that ridgeline above us and a mile to the south." He pointed to it on the map. "We dump it in there and let the mountain eat the explosion. The last hundred feet of the shaft is underwater. That should help contain it."

"Doctor, do you think that will be enough to minimize the blast?" the Marine NCO asked.

"How do we safely lower it down the shaft?" Dr. Nash asked Dale.

"The mine has a fifty-two-hundred-foot cable on a big commercial, electric reel. There's no power to the mine anymore, but we can unlock the mechanical brake and reel it out on the emergency hand lever. We only have one problem. Last summer the Forest Service sealed the shaft for safety reasons."

The Marine sergeant jumped in. "I'll get us in. Don't worry about the opening."

"We can transport it on the Marine supply sled," Dale suggested, rubbing his ungloved hands for warmth.

"Can you find the mineshaft with all of this deep snowpack on the ground?" the Secret Service agent wondered.

"The opening sits under a wide, granite face cliff almost a mile long, it'll be easy to find."

The digital clock face flashed twenty-six minutes.

"Is it safe to move it, doctor?" Dale asked.

"Let us hope so!" he replied.

As the clock hit twenty-four minutes, the group of men had securely bundled the three-foot-long nuclear explosive to the Marine sled. The seven snowmobiles started up the mountain.

Dale pulled out in the lead, followed by the Marine with the ticking nuke. Two Secret Service agents took up positions on either side of the bomb, and the other Marines with the heavy weapons followed in trail.

They rode through the eerie looking, ice-covered, windblown trees and past snowcapped boulders, avoiding obvious depressions in the snow as they went. Turning around a group of frozen, twisted, tall pines put them in front of a granite cliff that towered over five hundred feet. The tree line came to an end with the eleven-thousand-foot altitude. Above them was a mountain of heavy, deep, packed snow.

Two Marines dismounted and looked over the mine entrance. The place was sealed up tight with brick and natural rock.

"How far in does it go before it drops off?" the Marine NCO asked Dale.

"It's horizontal for about eighty feet. There's a step down of about three feet, then horizontal for another fifteen feet or so, with a built-in work deck, and then it drops straight off into oblivion," he answered.

The two Marines stood before the sealed up cave entrance and talked for a moment.

"Everyone, back down the hillside behind the stand of trees. We're going to blow a small entrance hole and hope it'll be sufficient."

The Marines removed a rocket-propelled grenade from an aluminum case on the weapons sled. The younger Marine knelt down in the snow behind a thick tree trunk and took aim. The Marine NCO tapped him on the helmet and the kneeling Marine pulled the trigger. The artificial wall to the entrance disappeared in a snowy vapor.

The explosive roar bounced all over the wooded area, reverberating several times before it finally went silent. The smoke cleared quickly in the wind. Now, back on their snowmobiles, they drove up the hillside once again to the newly opened mineshaft. Each man dismounted and walked through the freshly blown hole. It was pitch black inside.

A Secret Service agent stepped back onto his mount and restarted his snowmobile engine. He drove the vehicle slowly into the mine opening and turned on the headlight.

"Guys, I hate to rush you, but we only have about fifteen minutes left before this thing wreaks havoc," Dale urged.

The realization that time was against them suddenly motivated the entire group back to action. Two more snowmobiles were driven into the hole, their lights adding illumination in the tunnel. The Marines, along with Dr. Nash, removed the nuclear weapon from the towed sled. The Secret Service agents found the massive electric Hannay reel off to the side of the cave's unpowered electrical junction station and managed to uncouple the locking brake.

Dale and another Secret Service agent stepped down to the lower platform area and looked around. A minute later, they were able to hook up the cable end from the crane rigging arm that hung suspended over the center of the tunnel to the loop cable on the explosives netting. Dale pulled the crane cable back as the reel gave up some slack.

"We're all set on the cable line. How's the cradle sling for the bomb coming?" Dale inquired.

"Almost done," the younger Marine responded.

The two Marines had the bomb securely fastened into a cargo net. A second net was added to the first, then hooked into the loop cable. They moved the entire thing to the platform area and tied it securely. Then they backed away.

Satisfied that the series of knots would hold, Dale let the bomb swing out into the center of the tunnel. As he did, he noticed the red LED bomb timer hit nine minutes.

Dale yelled to the Secret Service agents to lower away.

The bomb dropped into the void and out of sight. The reel began to spin out slowly, the brake set for minimal resistance. Dale would have to add increasing back pressure every thirty seconds or so as the bomb was lowered to counter the effect of the added cable weight in the shaft.

Dr. Nash was busy at work with his HP handheld scientific calculator near the tunnel entrance.

"Gentlemen," he said loudly, "the reel is approximately eight feet in circumference. Since each rotation will take approximately one second on the reel, it will take a little more than ten minutes for the explosive to reach the very bottom."

"Ten minutes?" Dale said as he looked at the scientist in amazement, remembering the nine minute digit he'd just seen as the bomb dropped away. Whatever hope he had about a last second clean getaway was gone.

"I'm afraid so." The two men briefly stared at each other silently. Dale ground his teeth together back and forth.

"Someone has to remain behind to monitor the reel and brake. If that reel slips into a free fall with no one to reapply the brake, the bomb could hit the mineshaft wall and detonate before it's safely lowered. The blast may only be partially contained within the mountain. And if the top of this shaft entrance blows off, a fireball will breech the tunnel opening, spewing radiation all over the place. There is no question in my mind it will trigger an earthquake and avalanches all around us if that should happen."

Dale wiped his gloved hands over his hood.

"A premature detonation on this slope could very well create a rupture zone that would fracture a sizeable section of the mountainside, similar to the results we saw on Mount St. Helens in Washington back in the 1980s," the scientist explained. "It could still bury the town indirectly, killing thousands."

"That's just great. What else can go wrong today?" Dale groaned to himself.

A few seconds of silence cloaked the tunnel, except for the sound of the big reel unwinding. No one wanted to be the first to speak.

Slowly, as if he were being led to the slaughter, yet resigned to his inevitable fate, Dale looked up. "If someone has to remain behind . . ." his voice trailed off in a reluctant but reconciled tone as he scanned the other faces in the dim light. "When it hits seven and a half minutes, I'll cinch down on the back pressure bar and see if I can make it out the entrance and away from the snowbank above."

Each man stared at Dale, half in appreciation, half in relief. They shook his hand on the way out of the tunnel, wishing him godspeed but knowing full well that his decision was a death sentence.

"Good luck, son," the old physicist said, walking away. He followed behind the others with obvious frustration at the miserable situation.

"Hey!" Dale called out. "Leave me a snowmobile in here so I have some light, will ya."

A lone vehicle remained to illuminate the tunnel. The rumble of the snowmobile engines quickly trailed off to silence as they roared away as fast as they could.

"Well, that's the dumbest thing I've ever done."

As an afterthought, Dale took the gas cap off the snowmobile fuel tank and peered inside, "At least I've got plenty of juice. I hope this beast is fast."

He walked over and applied some more back pressure to the brake bar to slow down the rotation. The unwound cable was adding a lot of free weight to the reel support. As Dale watched the reel play out, he had so many thoughts he couldn't organize them all at once. He remembered the only time his girlfriend, Betty Jo, had seen him in action, rescuing a woman with a broken leg who'd fallen fifty feet off the face of a mountain ledge. He'd rappelled over a sheer cliff face and . . . "That gives me an idea," he suddenly said to himself.

Dale looked at the snowmobile. Talking to himself to fortify his thought process, he rushed to the cave entrance. "What did they do with all that rope they took off of the sled? There it is, thank goodness they left it behind."

Dale grabbed the bundled ropes and ran back into the cave.

"Six minutes and counting," he said as he unbundled the five, hundred-foot, dynamic rope lines.

"If the cable weighs about one pound per foot, times forty-five hundred pounds, that's two and a quarter tons." He ran back outside with his hand-held Motorola radio and twisted the knob to the ON position.

Scanning the laminated map the team had left with the gear, he found his grid coordinate.

"Utah National Guard Apache helicopter, this is FBI agent Dale Fox on guard at GZ-17. Do you copy me?" He waited a moment. "Utah National Guard Apache helicopter, this is FBI agent Dale Fox on guard at GZ-17. I have an emergency. Can you hear me?"

"Fox at GZ-17, this is Buzzard one-four. Who the hell are you?" the pilot asked.

Dale explained his circumstances and the idea he had. The pilot agreed to his hasty plan, diverted from his search pattern, and immediately raced toward the map coordinate.

Dale hustled back inside and checked the reel. Pushing down again he applied more back pressure. He played the rope out on the cavern floor and checked his watch. Four minutes to nuclear hell.

Attaching the long rope to the steel bar on the back of the snowmobile with his best redundant double knot, he started the engine and drove to the cave entrance. Meanwhile, the huge drum reel continued to unwind and lower the thermonuclear explosive.

Putting the snowmobile in gear, he allowed it to creep out of the cave entrance and down the hill, straight out from the large opening. Running back inside, he put more pressure on the massive Hannay reel with the brake.

Dale connected the other end of the rope to the big reel so the rope would wind around the drum as the cable unwound. He tied it off and checked his watch. Three minutes before the mushroom cloud kicked off.

Hustling back outside, he checked the progress of the snowmobile. The rope was pulling along behind the heavy, riderless mechanical mount. Dale grabbed the rope in his gloved hands and slowed the snowmobile as it neared the end of the rescue rope's length.

Several hundred yards away, the Apache helicopter edged slowly into view through the snowy fog crawling its way toward the opening in front of the cave entrance. An artificial snowstorm of fresh powder bracketed it on either side as it moved in closer.

Dale cinched up the chest safety harness he found in the equipment the Marines had left behind. It was twenty-seven-degrees outside, but Dale was sweating like it was summer in Death Valley.

"I'm just up the hillside from you, a few hundred yards," he barked into the radio.

The pilot spotted him and moved the sinister looking attack chopper in closer. "Two minutes," he recited to himself.

Rushing back inside the cavern and down the now darkened tunnel to the Hannay reel, he kicked the brake with his foot, releasing it.

And then he ran for his life.

He leaped through the cave entrance and made straight for the helo. As he ran downhill, the six-hundred-forty-pound snowmobile was being pulled into the cavern by the weight of the reel. The fifty two hundred feet of cable that was dangling down the vertical mineshaft had overcome the dead weight of the attached recreational vehicle.

The snowmobile was just heavy enough to counter a free fall.

"One minute twenty-nine seconds, twenty-eight seconds, twenty-seven . . . !"

The copter hovered five feet off the ground just a few dozen yards from the mineshaft entrance. The rotor wash blew a storm of snowflakes everywhere. Dale was half blind as he reached up and found the helicopter's exposed snow skid in the ministorm of white, swirling snow.

With one hand over his face to shield his eyes and the other extended, he slapped two steel carabiners from his harness over the helicopter's left landing skid. He let go of the carabiners and yelled into his dangling radio microphone, "Go, go, go!"

The Apache rose in the sky, turning toward the town of Park City.

Dale hung precariously on the safety harness as the speed of the helicopter increased. He was counting to himself as the freezing wind buffeted him in the rushing, open air.

"Forty-six, forty-five." He looked back as the snowmobile approached the entrance to the cave.

"Forty, thirty-nine, thirty-eight . . ." The snowmobile disappeared inside. The helicopter rose to clear a treetop that Dale's legs managed to miss by only a few feet.

The cold cut through his heavy jacket and gloves as the Apache's speed passed eighty-five miles an hour. Dale searched through the snow flurries that were falling. The fog on the mountainside was dissipating. He hoped they were far enough away from the blast to avoid being knocked out of the sky by a pressure wave.

Dale noticed a third carabineer on the harness was waving free in the breeze, bouncing off the chopper's skid. He fumbled for it and slipped it over the tubing.

"Fifteen, fourteen . . ." He opened his eyes and saw that they were nearing the edge of the ski resort property. The mountaintop restaurant was at the very edge of his vision. It was still more than two and a half miles from the ski resort base. He glanced over his shoulder a moment later, hoping he wouldn't be vaporized in the next few seconds by a nuclear fireball.

Deep down in the mineshaft, six miles from town, an ugly, guttural, rumbling sound came to life. The trees on the mountainside began shaking themselves free of their white dusting. Snow cascaded off the hillsides all around him as avalanches began moving across the mountain. Tourists and locals alike felt the earthquake shake the city far below.

Dale turned back toward the mountain from his high altitude view and saw the cave entrance beyond the ridgeline belch a massive, breathtaking, orange-red flash. It looked like the long, wide tongue of the devil was reaching out for him. For just a second, Dale thought the radiant colors against the backdrop of the pristine, white snow were beautiful.

The irregular opening to the cavern finally disappeared as the helo nosed over the ridgeline below the restaurant. The mountainside cave was sealed forever by the tremendous collapse of millions of tons of age-old red granite.

Once again, Dale Fox had cheated death.

In a parking lot sixteen miles away, two men sat patiently in a white non-descript van, watching the data meters on the nuclear weapon the federal agents had found.

"They've detonated the first one in a secured area away from the venue, now they'll relax. They're not going to find the second one so easy to deal with," the rogue CIA agent said with satisfaction. The driver took his eyes off the metering device and started the vehicle. He checked the rearview mirror and pulled out from the parking space along the side street. He drove south to leave the blast area. Two blocks away in the basement of an empty elementary school, a twenty-kiloton nuclear device awoke.

The rogue CIA agent dialed 911 on his prepaid cell phone and set the mayhem in motion. In less than an hour, Park City would be a memory.

TOM FOREST

Tom Forest has never been a spectator in life. He is a former United States Marine. He's raced cars, motorcycles, flown airplanes, hunted big game, been an exhibition gun fighter and dived the world's oceans. He retired from a northern Utah Fire Agency as the Supervisor of Rescue Operations. Over the years he's rescued people from caves, high angle entrapments, swift water accidents, train collisions, and diving mishaps. He was certified in downed aircraft rescue and taught Vehicle Extrication and Rescue tactics at the Utah State Fire and Rescue Academy. He's owned several successful businesses, wrote a financial advice column for his local newspaper, and two novels: *The T-Rex Virus* and the forthcoming *Cold Hard Knock*. His 3rd novel *Flash Burn* is in the works.